UNCIVILIZED

Catherine Williams

ISBN: 0994966601
ISBN 13: 9780994966605

For my husband, Matthew Benjamin

Now I am terrified at the Earth!
it is that calm and patient,
It grows such sweet things out of such corruptions

—Walt Whitman, "This Compost"

CONTENTS

A MOMENT OF GRACE

A baked potato with dollops of tangy sour cream, thick strips of bacon sizzling in a pan, a homemade pie heating gently in the oven: these were just a few of the ghosts that haunted Simone's brain and her empty, shrinking stomach. Staring out into the lonesome landscape, she felt like screaming in frustration, but her mouth was dry, and making too much noise was dangerous. She wasn't the only one starving around here.

The wind tore at her face as she settled back against the hillside and watched the nimbus clouds pass overhead. She didn't need to see the sun to know it was setting; she could feel the coming night in the air. Yet here she was, so far from Elwood's and empty handed once again. Gazing across the horizon of stoic rock and pine, she lifted her binoculars once more to scan the last patches of snow that languished on the valley floor. Seeing nothing of interest, she decided to head for home. It was getting colder by the minute, and a strange wind was rising, sobbing out of the east. She had to get back to Perla.

Simone stood. Brushing the refuse off her long leather jacket, she stretched her arms to the sky. Slipping her shotgun sling over her head, she whistled for her horse, Alfred, who plodded amiably into sight. With numb fingers, she struggled to secure the saddle-bags, watching the way Alfred tilted his head, craning his ears as she worked.

"You hear something, boy?" she asked, patting his neck fondly. She tightened the straps on her bag. "Does it sound edible?"

A bloodcurdling scream answered her from the valley below.

Startled, Simone dropped to the ground and crawled to the edge of the hillside, ripping open her last pair of jeans at the knee. Holding her breath, she listened, watching the clearing with mounting dread, waiting for the cry to come again. But the land had grown silent once more. The forest would give nothing away.

Suddenly a flash of motion drew her eye, and Simone watched a woman emerge from the trees, a tiny figure in the vast and un-feeling wilderness. She was running, glancing over her shoulder as she fled, pumping her arms and lunging forward with evident fatigue and desperation. The woman was such a compelling sight that Simone didn't notice the men chasing her until they were right at her heels. And even then, they hardly looked like living men at all, bearing more than a passing resemblance to two wizened corpses, plucked from the depths of a sweat-soaked nightmare and set loose upon the lonely vale.

Simone felt the adrenalin surge through her veins, banishing all thoughts of starvation and jogging her limbs into action. Her first instinct was to rush down there, but she fought the temptation and clenched her fists instead, holding herself steady. *Just wait*, she thought. *Keep cool and wait. It could be a trap.* Because things were never what they seemed in the valley; knowing that much had got-ten her here.

Below, the woman ran across a melting patch of snow. Her boots broke through the surface, and the slushy white underbelly dragged her down, slowing her pace. One of her pursuers charged forward, grabbing for her coat, but she shook him off and kept running. Doggedly, she ran a few paces more before wheeling around to face the men, calling out to them in the fading light. Her boldness seemed to surprise them, but not for long. The closest figure hesitated only for a moment before rushing towards her, his spindly legs arcing across the frozen ground, his arms outstretched, reaching, reaching for her.

But the woman reached him first. Wrapping her hands around her attacker's arm she pulled him forward, using his momentum to send him hurtling past her and landing, face first, in another patch of snow.

Like a great bear, the second man attacked, seizing the woman by the shoulders. She fought back with equal resolve, and they jostled together, fighting and pulling each other across the valley floor. In their starved and feral state, both parties tired quickly, and it wasn't long before the larger figure managed to catch the woman's arms, subduing her.

By this time, the first man had pulled himself out of the snow and was wiping his face with angry, jerking movements. Hunching his narrow shoulders, he marched across the clearing and struck the woman in the stomach with his fist. Winded, she fell to the ground as the larger man moved aside so his partner could continue his attack. Crouching over her, the bony figure grabbed the woman by the throat, throttling her until she reared up without warning, head-butting him in the nose. Screeching in pain, the man scrambled away from her, clutching at his face as the snow below him became spattered with blood. Outraged, he began kicking at the woman with heavy, forceful blows.

On the bluff above their heads, Simone leaped on Alfred's back. She had seen enough.

She rode quickly, taking the less direct path down the hillside to conceal her approach. At the bottom, she skirted the woods before dismounting, leaving Alfred to mind himself as she entered the brush, wading through scrub and bushes still bound by winter's spell. Branches slashed at her face and snagged her jacket as she fought her way to the edge of the thicket and crouched behind a rotten old stump. Removing her shotgun from its sling, she peered past the crumbling wood. Both men were standing beside the woman now, obscuring her view. She caught a glimpse of the woman's feet moving and breathed a sigh of relief; she was still alive.

"Dumb bitch," the first man snarled, his hands still cupping his bloody nose. He shoved his boot in her face and laughed, a rusty, scraping noise that got louder and louder before trailing away like a broken car. Simone couldn't see the man's face from her vantage point, but he looked small and scrawny, wearing a trapper's cap to cover his thin wisps of hair. The second man with him was taller and thicker boned by comparison. *The mouthpiece and the mountain,* she thought.

On the ground, the injured woman made a muttering noise that didn't sound polite.

"What was that? What'd you just say?" the mouthpiece barked. The woman tried lunging at him again, but his partner cuffed her across the cheek and pushed her back to the ground.

"I'll kill you!" the woman screamed, kicking her feet. "I'll kill you both!"

"Yeah, that seems likely," the mouthpiece replied, looking smug.

"I'll shut her up," the mountain said. "You hold her down." He began unbuttoning his pants; the smaller man grabbed the woman by the wrists.

That was the moment Simone strode out from her hiding place, her shotgun pressed firmly against her shoulder. "Let her go," she said in a steady voice. "That woman's coming with me."

Both men turned and stared at Simone in complete bewilderment as she sized them up. They were thin and desperate looking like everyone else these days, clothes badly worn and threadbare. The smaller man had a bandana wrapped across one eye that was filthy and crusted with blood. His bigger-boned companion had a face like an anvil with greasy hair and a tight, frowning mouth.

"Who are you?" the mountain asked; he narrowed his eyes.

"I didn't come here for a goddamn chitchat," Simone answered. "Now you let her go, before I make you let her go."

"This ain't your business." The mouthpiece sneered. "We've been chasing her. We caught her. That means we got rights to her." He took a tentative step forward.

Simone clicked the safety off and the man froze in his tracks. "Hand her over," she said.

"Now hold on a minute," the mouthpiece said. "How do we know that gun is even loaded? Last time I checked, shotgun shells weren't easy to come by." He gave Simone a cunning smile, and a handful of dirty brown teeth hung in his mouth like bats sleeping in a cave. "You gotta prove that thing's loaded."

"I don't gotta prove shit, babe," she said. Her eyes flicked over to the man's partner and she suppressed a low groan. Somehow, the bastard had closed the gap between himself and the battered woman on the ground and was now holding a knife against her throat. A deranged smile spilled across his meaty face as he yanked on her hair, tilting her head back and leaving her neck exposed. The woman made no movement to speak of; she remained completely still, her gaze fixed on Simone.

"You're out of shells," the mouthpiece jeered, working his pointy, whiskered jaw. He cocked his head to his shoulder, looking at his partner behind him. "Slit that bitch's throat, Knox. We got ourselves a new one now."

But the mountain didn't have time to slit anything before Simone shot him through the eyes, sending a mist of blood, bone, and brain spraying into the air. The shotgun blast ricocheted across the valley, sending birds flying from the trees as the man's dripping, headless body dropped the knife and slumped heavily across his intended victim's torso.

Frozen to the spot, the smaller man stared at the remains of his friend as they oozed and gurgled their way across the valley floor. He licked his lips furtively and turned his good eye back to Simone. "Now…you've got to understand," he squeaked, his voice quivering. "I was just following orders. We had to catch the girl, or he would've killed us—or worse. I didn't want to hurt her, I swear!"

The man burst into tears as Simone watched the girl in question rise slowly to her feet behind him, covered from head to toe in his partner's blood. She wielded the knife now; the blade glittered in her hands as it caught the final snatches of day, sending defiant sparks of light into the dark, wild woods. She planted her feet and moved both arms until they were pointing toward the man and then brought her right arm back. With a fast swing, she stepped forward, releasing the knife.

The man's hands were in the air when the blade ripped into his back with a wet slapping sound. Warm, tin-scented blood speckled Simone's face as he fell to his side, struggling to breathe. Writhing in agony, he seemed to reach up for her before falling back again with a low moan. Blood had begun trickling from his mouth; his one good eye rolled back in his head. The ground around him was crimson and steaming.

When Simone looked up again, she saw the injured woman limping across the clearing toward them. She moved gingerly but with a purpose, her eyes set upon the dying man. When she finally reached him, she stood over him, watching dispassionately as he sputtered and choked on his final few breaths of air. Leaning down, she knocked his hat off with her fist. The filthy bandana came loose as well, revealing the hollow socket that had once housed an eye. She grabbed the man by the hair and looked down into his face; his Adam's apple bobbed, once, twice—then it stopped. Satisfied, she released her hold and his body fell back to the ground.

There was a long, electrified silence.

Then the woman looked at Simone. "Ever have one of those days when you wish you never got out of bed?" she asked, in a high, youthful voice. She made an odd face, then erupted into a series of loud braying sounds that Simone realized was laughter. The woman laughed hysterically, doubled over where she stood, until the sound turned into a long howl. Drawing her eyebrows together, Simone watched the woman carefully, wondering what to make of her. She was skilled with a knife—that much was certain. Simone had never seen such an accurate throw before, except for back in the days of television and movies, but that had been make-believe. This was the straight goods right here. That kind of skill could be useful to them—tremendously useful. But it could also be dangerous.

Finally, the woman quieted and began wiping at the tears in her eyes, her breath coming fast in squeaks and exclamation marks. Simone moved closer and looked into her face. She didn't look much older than a teenager, although it was hard to tell with her face so streaked with grime and gore. Even her hair was coated in it, matted into thick dreadlocks that hung heavily around her shoulders.

"I'm Simone," she offered. "That's some arm you got there."

"I'm Grace," the woman replied, taking her extended hand. She immediately let out a high-pitched shriek and Simone stepped back in surprise.

"Sorry," Grace said, rubbing at her hand. "I think my finger's broken."

Simone sighed. She had the feeling it was going to be a long night.

ON RECYCLING

The women regarded one another in the falling twilight as the trees around them swayed and rattled like bones. Grace hugged her arms to her chest. She was sticky and wet with blood. The pungent, animal warmth that had enveloped her was cooling; her clothes were stiffening. She wanted nothing more than to wipe her hands, but she had nothing to wipe them on—except snow. God, she was sick of snow.

She raised her eyes, meeting a pair of frank brown ones. *Simone.* The woman was tall and pointy looking, like you could skin a knee on her. But Grace liked her face: serious but not unpleasant, with a narrow nose and nostrils that flared out over a thin mouth. A faded cowboy hat sat snug on her head; she wore the brim low over her eyes.

"How tall are you?" Grace asked impulsively.

"I didn't think *that* would be your first question," Simone replied.

Grace suddenly felt embarrassed and tired and couldn't think of much else to say. Both women fell silent again, and the wind whistled between them like it had nothing better to do.

"Do you have somewhere to go?" Simone asked in a softer tone.

"No. Not really, I guess."

"Not really?"

"No, I have nowhere. I have nowhere to go. It's just—well, it's the first time I've ever said that." Grace's eyes filled with tears.

Simone moved closer, placing a hand on her shoulder. "What happened to you out there? Why were those men chasing you?"

"I don't know." Grace wept. "I've never even seen them before. I was just out fetching water, and when I got home, there was a wagon in front of our house. I thought it was our neighbor, but everything was so quiet, so still. It felt like something was wrong, so I peeked in the window." She covered her eyes with shaking hands. "I could see my dad and my sister, Lora, in the living room, tied up. There were strange men everywhere—too many for me to handle on my own. They both looked so scared. Lora saw me at the window; I could tell she wanted me to run. So I ran to the neighbor's house for help nearly a mile away, but when I got there, it was already on fire. Then I knew what the men were going to do…I knew." She paused, swallowing hard. "When I made it home again, it was too late. Everything was gone. My house…my family…everything was up in flames. These two bastards were all that was left." She gestured to the corpses behind them. "They'd been left behind to deal with me."

Simone's thoughts turned to Elwood's Compound. To Perla. "Where did this happen, Grace, and when?"

"Colborne County. Two days ago."

Simone's eyebrows arched in disbelief. "They tracked you all the way from Colborne? That's quite a ways from here."

"It feels like quite a ways from here," Grace replied.

"Listen, you better come with me," Simone said. "It's a bit of a ride back to the compound, but we'll be safe there."

Grace nodded; she was shivering.

"But first let's strip these guys. Maybe we can get you something dry to wear." Simone moved toward the smaller corpse and casually assessed the damage. His clothes might have fit Grace better, but the knife wound to the torso had soaked them through.

She rolled the second body over.

His clothes were bigger—blood stained, but somewhat drier than what Grace was wearing. It would have to do. Simone propped the man's body into an upright position and began to tug the sweater over his stump of a neck until the fabric caught and twisted on his exposed spinal cord. As she leaned over him, trying to work the clothing free, she noticed a crude tattoo. That was odd; she had noticed the same tattoo on the other man's neck as well: a sinister eye, dripping blood and underlined by a long curl. Simone shook her head at the unsettling symbol, yanked the sweater free from the man's body and handed it over to Grace.

Moving on to stripping the man's pants, Simone was pleasantly surprised to discover he hadn't soiled himself when he died, as people often do. He probably hadn't eaten in a few days. Whatever the reason, it would make for a more civilized trip back to the compound. She handed over the pants. When Grace pulled them on, she was swimming in them.

"My horse is just on the other side of the woods," Simone said, pointing to the thicket behind them. "I've got some twine in my pack to keep those pants up. Then we should get back to the compound."

Grace looked at her shyly. Then she asked the question people in the valley always ask: "Do you have any food?"

Simone looked evasive. "Well, we've got rice rations back at the compound."

"I'm talking protein here," Grace insisted. "I need protein. I'm starving."

"I know," Simone replied, trying to conceal her frustration. She tugged at her hat. "We are too. That's why I was out hunting today, but I came up empty handed."

Grace eyed the bodies of the two men, still sprawled across the valley floor.

"Doesn't look that way to me," she said.

A DILEMMA

Alfred bore them through the darkness. The gray twilight had unfolded into a deep and unyielding night, hiding the moon and stars in the sky and making it difficult for Simone to find her way. But she stuck to the main trail, easing her horse along the familiar track of earth, past the twisted wraiths of trees and the stern and spidery pine.

Behind her, Grace had fallen silent long ago. Exhausted but still awake, she kept one hand circling Simone's waist and the other clutching a large tin that still radiated some warmth. Her head nodded in time with the gait of the horse.

Two men down, Grace thought, shifting the tin in her hands. *Eight more to go.* For she had counted ten men in the living room when she last saw her father and her sister alive—ten sneering, stony-eyed men of murderous intent. Those men had wrenched her family from her and subjected them to a horrific death. Those men had destroyed her home. Callously, those men had crushed everything her family had built together, and unsatisfied with that, they left two guards behind to murder her. Those men. *Those men.*

Grace struggled to contain the rage that cooked and bubbled in her brain. She had escaped those men, but they would not escape her.

"It's great you had this tin, Simone," she said, a bit too brightly, breaking the silence between them. "You sure are prepared."

"Can I ask you something?" Simone inquired, tossing the compliment aside. "Have you ever eaten human organs before?"

"Is that what you're brooding about? The organ thing?"

"I'm not brooding. I'm just considering the reaction of the other residents when we come back to the compound with them."

"Oh, please." Grace scoffed. "Didn't you say you were all starving? I thought a woman like you would appreciate the transportable and nutritious quality of human organs."

"I appreciate a natural revulsion toward cannibalism."

"Come on." Grace laughed. "Have you given up or something? Face it; those bastards weren't using 'em anymore. You say you got some hungry mouths to feed; I say let's feed them. It's us or the coyotes, right? Besides, if it were up to me, we would've taken their bodies too. That big one had some good eatin' on him." She grinned, but Simone slunk deeper into the saddle. Elwood would be furious with her for bringing a stranger home in the first place. The organ dinner would simply be the coup de grace.

"They'll exile me for this," she grumbled. "They really will."

"So lie about it," Grace said. "Don't tell them what it is. They'll probably be enjoying it too much to talk anyways."

Simone meditated on that thought for several paces. "It's hard to say what's worse," she said, "bringing human organs home for dinner or lying about it."

"Starving to death—that's worse. You forgot about that option."

"Rice rations are not exactly death."

"They're as close to death as a meal can be," Grace said heatedly. "Rice just wakes your stomach up; it doesn't satisfy you. Simone, you know how this works by now. If we don't get protein, we weaken. If we weaken, we die. Listen to your survival instincts, for God's sake!"

Survival instincts. Simone turned the words over in her head. Before the storms, she thought that meant the fight-or-flight response. Now she understood it was something much more complex than that, something ruthless and ancient, more mob boss than reflex: brash, pitiless, unethical.

Survival instincts. They were not something that could be reasoned with any more than your own breath. Once summoned, they did whatever it took to keep you alive, even if that included things you never thought you would do—never would agree with—under normal circumstances. Because good people can do terrible things to survive; Simone had come to learn that, ever since that fateful day, which began so unremarkably and changed her life forever.

THE STORMS

Simone had gone to work the day it happened, patrolling the long, lonely stretches of Assumption Valley National Park as a young wildlife enforcement officer. It was a job she had loved, and as everyone does with a first love, she had taken it very seriously. That afternoon she'd been tracking a poacher when the trail had gone cold. Frustrated, she had searched the area and retraced her steps, but darkness forced her investigation to a halt; her quarry had eluded her for the day. On the way home, she remembered grinding her teeth in anger as she maneuvered her jeep down the blackened country roads that led her back to Valkyrie House.

"Simone, is that you?" her mother called through the screen door, hearing her footsteps on the porch. "When you come in, turn up the television, will you! I heard something about a storm!"

Her mother's enthusiasm had made Simone smile as she kicked off her boots in the foyer. Classic Mom. She loved nothing better than a good storm—except perhaps painting it, which was fortunate because she had built a career on doing just that. A Perla Hardy "Stormscape" had cost a pretty penny in the galleries those days. The critics had been wild for the sense of "movement" and "apprehension" displayed in the thrashing trees, ruffled grasses, and big battlefield skies she captured in her work.

But even the famous Perla Hardy couldn't capture this storm.

"Will be experiencing an X-class solar-flare eruption that's headed for earth," the news anchor had reported on the television. "The solar storm will mark what experts say is the beginning of an eleven-year solar cycle, predicted to include higher levels of solar activity…"

Two hours later, the power went out, plunging Valkyrie House into darkness, although the sky outside swirled with an incredible display of northern lights. Simone and her mother went out to the porch to watch the tumbling sea foam waves breaking across the stars, sharing a bag of chocolate chip cookies for dinner. She remembered how girlish her mother had looked then, sitting next to her on the porch with the neon colors reflecting off her face. They had both laughed in amazement, gasped at the astonishing pinwheel of colors that shimmied across the galaxy. It had seemed so beautiful then, like a miracle. Instead, it had been a warning.

When Simone awoke the next day, the power was still off, and her cell phone was dead. She was unsure if she should go into work, but her ancient jeep started just fine, and she was soon navigating her way along the backcountry roads like it was any other day. She stopped and chatted with a few coworkers at the office about the power outage, and they had been just as confused as she was about it. No one seemed to know what was happening, but everyone was certain someone was fixing it—whatever "it" was. In town, she saw a few maintenance crews at work, looking puzzled, but the phones remained silent, and the Internet stayed down. The blackout was complete.

A few days later, Simone was one of the few officers still reporting to work and was recruited by the remnants of the local police force to assist with crowd control in town, where the looting had gotten out of hand. After that, her jeep ran out of gas, and for the first time in her life, there just wasn't any more.

Unsure of when the power would return, unsettled by the lack of answers, and unable to contact friends and family living elsewhere, the isolation of valley life was complete. No glinting airplanes appeared in the sky. No army tanks rolled through town. There was only silence, punctuated by the rising and setting of the sun. There were rumors about families that had left the valley and hadn't returned, but no one knew what that meant. Simone and her mother considered leaving themselves. They even siphoned gas from the riding lawnmower to make the long journey east to Trafalgar City, but they didn't have enough to make the trip. They were stuck fast in Assumption.

With no other option in sight, the women kept close to Valkyrie House, expanding the kitchen garden and canning to pass the time. "Just in case the power never comes back," her mother had said and winked, which reminded Simone that it had been a joke at the time.

Their nearest neighbor, Zeff Davis, lived more than two miles away, but he visited every day on horseback, bringing the women beer from his dwindling supply. Then they'd sit together on the porch, catching the breeze as they sucked on the lukewarm cans, reminding each other not to think too much.

Valkyrie House had other visitors too: a hodgepodge of concerned Assumption Valley community members who claimed to be "checking in" on the women and would come huffing up their drive, bringing salacious gossip about missing livestock, missing pets, missing families—then request a little food for their trouble. Simone and her mother were relieved when those visits stopped.

Then, visits of another sort began.

Simone had been out in the garden pulling weeds the day she had spotted a small, bedraggled group at the front gate. Drawing closer, she could see it was a family of six, huddled together, watching her through the wrought-iron bars. A tall, raw-boned man waved a huge paw in her direction and gave her a smile like an animal cringing in pain.

"Excuse me," the man said. "Very sorry to disturb. My name is Jan Nowak. My family has traveled far, and we are very thirsty. Do you have spare water to share for them?"

When Simone had learned the family fled their home in Rockdale after the local militia had become an angry mob, her heart welled with sympathy for the tired family. In a matter of minutes, Jan; his wife, Irina; and their four young children were seated at the kitchen table, slurping down well water and eating a tin of beans. The family had been fatigued and malnourished after traveling for days with only the clothes on their back, hoping things would get better, and terrified they might get worse.

But things were better at Valkyrie House where the pleasant, hardworking Nowaks were a welcome addition to the household. There were more mouths to feed, but there were also more hands to work. Jan could capably perform any chore that needed to be done around the house, and Simone had started looking forward to working with Irina in the garden, enjoying the way the petite blond woman would sigh with pleasure over every seedling and sniff at the summer air like it was an expensive wine. She was a woman who took nothing for granted.

The Nowak brood of children was decidedly less helpful with the chores, but they were a pleasure to have around, filling the house with a wild, untamed energy. The children were timid at first, and Simone would only catch glimpses of them peeking out from behind half-open doors or sneaking around furniture legs like little woodland elves. But as the youngsters grew more comfortable with their surroundings, the house became a sea of bobbing curls and squeals that only ceased when her mother took them outside to tend to the chickens at the chicken coop. Simone would watch this exciting event from the window; her mother, with her bucket of kitchen trimmings, whispering secrets that made the children laugh. Her mother would smile then, a gentle, contented smile Simone hadn't seen since Emerson had died.

It wasn't long before the others came: displaced people and families from nearby towns and cities, coming in search of water and food and safety from roaming militias. Many joined the tent city that formed at the mouth of Finch Creek, a sort of refugee camp where families lived in gasless cars or under windblown tents and tarp covers. Others begged at local acreages. When they started coming to Valkyrie House, Simone gave them what she could until their supplies dwindled, and she began to panic. After that, the beggars were sent away with nothing at all.

It had to be done, she would think as she watched them go, but she never really believed that. She still remembered their faces, the unspoken accusation shining in their eyes: *This could have been you. There, but for the grace of God, this could have been you.* And they were right.

Later, the tent-city residents began their raids, first on people traveling alone, then on acreages, fighting for food and well water, for shelter, for blankets. And though many of the attackers were weak with starvation and disease, desperation drove them on, equipping them with supernatural strength and a terrifying absence of fear. They had nothing left to lose, and they knew it.

Before the raids in the valley became commonplace, Simone and her mother had gone foraging one day, determined to locate a wild-strawberry patch in a forest they used to visit. They'd searched all morning and found it when the sun was highest in the sky. By the time they had loaded their baskets with the juicy cargo and returned home, it had become a late, long-shadowed afternoon.

Simone would never forget how desolate Valkyrie House looked when they returned home that day. The front window had been shattered, the screen door ripped from its hinges. Entering the house had felt like falling into a nightmare. The cozy cream-colored foyer had been spattered with blood. The walls were covered in a frenzy of small, crimson-colored handprints. And there had been that long, ghastly silence.

Simone found Jan first, dead in the hallway upstairs, his hands still clenched in enormous fists. They found Irina's body next, sheltering the bodies of her four bludgeoned children. The next day, Simone and her mother buried the family together in a field of wildflowers behind the house. It had been grueling work, but once she had shoveled the last bit of earth over their graves, she gazed around the blossoming meadow, smudgy with petals in the fading light, and knew Irina would have approved of this resting place. It was the last thing they could ever give her.

They never found out who murdered the Nowak family or why the assailants hadn't taken Valkyrie House, although they'd certainly emptied the place. Simone and her mother lost their food, their bedding, their clothes, and their tools. The garden had been left alone but the chickens were gone. And although the women cleaned the house as best as they could, the memory of the grisly murders left a stain that no amount of scrubbing could ever wash away. Haunted by grief, it wasn't long before they abandoned the house and moved into the root cellar below the shed, joined by their faithful neighbor Zeff, who'd lost his ranch in a fire.

The three worked closely as a team then, devising a twenty-four-hour watch schedule to keep an eye out for attacks and ambushes, of which there were many, and Zeff built a fake worktable in the shed to disguise the entrance to the root cellar. It was a lawless time, marked by a strong fear of the coming winter, yet somehow they continued to survive. Between them, they had four guns and a healthy stock of ammunition, giving them the upper hand over many raiding parties who were armed with bats and lead pipes. Simone soon found that a well-aimed shotgun blast was enough to deter even the most desperate raiding party, sending them in search of easier prey.

As autumn waned and the days shortened into night, the former Valkyrie House residents spent most of their time in the root cellar. Sometimes allowing themselves the luxury of a single, sputtering candle, they practiced the art of conversation to pass the time, led primarily by Perla, who was the chattiest of the three. Simone found Zeff could be drawn into conversation if it featured crop rotation or something relatively bland and uncontroversial—not that she minded. But she had known Zeff for years and actually knew little about him. He was simply a quiet fellow, although he was pleasant and polite company to be around, with the tidy manners of a gentleman. In addition to that, he had an excellent eye for trouble and could see it coming a mile away. Simone thought the man was completely unsurprisable; he could detect the whiff of a storm on a sunny day. He could hear a raid coming when all she could hear was the birds singing in the trees.

Zeff Davis was uncanny. He was reliable. And he could stay silent for hours and hours and hours. This made Simone feel Emerson's absence even more keenly as she considered how he would have filled his time in the root cellar—probably telling jokes or stories. Her older brother used to come up with all sorts of games and little entertainments on the car rides to their mother's art shows. He was always so funny, teasing their mother about the eccentric patrons who attended her events. "Perrrla Haaardy?" he'd say, locking his jaw and moving his mouth like a nutcracker. "The painting is daaarling, wouldn't you say, daaarling? Daaarling? Daaarling!"

Emerson would tease their mother so relentlessly that she seemed to forget her troubles for a while. That was the effect he had on people. Emerson amused you. He drew you in. He got you excited about life. Simone hadn't realized what a rare gift that was until he was taken from them.

As winter blew its hoary breath through the valley, Simone noticed her mother's mind beginning to slip. She seemed to be getting confused easily, misplacing things, hiding things, asking the same questions over and over again. She spoke of chattering, endless chattering in her brain. Once Simone found her wandering aimlessly around the property when she was supposed to be on watch, her tidy bun loose and askew. The dementia escalated quickly, ravaging her mother's brain until she was gone for good, though someone else lived on in her body. That someone was Perla, and Simone became her caregiver.

Although the raids became less frequent in the winter, their food was low, and Perla's wandering was increasing. Too nervous to leave her alone, Simone stayed close to the root cellar, boiling snow with Perla tethered to her side while Zeff rode off into the wilderness to check the snares or trade with the families who were still left in the valley. Gold and silver were still accepted in barter then; that was the time when Zeff brought Alfred home one day, the intelligent mustang with the steady eyes and a white star on his forehead. "So you can get out once in a while," Zeff said with a smile as he handed Simone the reins. "Every cowgirl needs some space to roam."

It was then she had noticed his gold watch was gone, the first and last luxury item the rancher had ever allowed himself. Simone had flushed deeply with gratitude, lost for words, yet Zeff understood her completely.

She thought that they could stay there, that they could survive the long winter, the raiders, and the clammy root cellar. Then one night, Perla smashed a jar of preserves over Simone's head as she slept, and in a moment of throbbing clarity, she realized they needed help.

The next morning, they packed Perla up and left Valkyrie House for good, destined for the acreage of Elwood Hubble, a retired professor who lived a day's ride to the north. The residents had begun producing half-decent candles there and were doing swift business in trade. As a happy result, Elwood's Compound had a surplus of food, and Zeff hoped his reputation as an honest tradesman would pay off if they were to show up and beg for help.

And it did.

They had been living at Elwood's Compound for two winters now, but it might as well have been a hundred.

LADY KILLER

Feeling Alfred's ears prick up, Simone forced her way back to the present. The horse gave an apprehensive nicker and slowed his gait. Something was coming.

"What's going on?" Grace asked, stirring behind her.

"There's something ahead," Simone replied. "I can't tell you more than that." She urged Alfred off the trail and hid at the edge of the forest. There, the darkness was as thick as muslin, and they would be impossible to detect. Perhaps whatever it was would pass them by...

"Are we going to ambush them?" Grace whispered in her ear. "I'm ready. I've got that guy's knife."

"Yeah, I know," Simone whispered back. "You carved him like a goddamn turkey with it." Faint with hunger and fatigue, she threw herself off Alfred's back and drew her shotgun from its sling. She could make out a dark mass in the distance, drawing toward them. There was a musical clanging noise, followed by the muttering of crunching snow. Faintly, a wheel whined in protest. A caravan was approaching.

"Is that a wagon?" Grace asked.

"I think it's a trade-route caravan," she said.

"Do you know them?"

A tuneless whistle wobbled through the air.

Simone smiled. "I might." Sheathing her shotgun again, she jumped on Alfred's back. "Stay here," she said as the horse broke into a run.

"Wait! You're coming back, right?" Grace quietly called after her. "Right?"

Simone nudged Alfred onto a small game trail, and they skirted the trees in the darkness, looping back until the caravan was in front of them. She licked her lips and tried to slow her pulse, almost laughing under her breath. Suddenly she was feeling energized; she was going to get him good this time.

At full gallop, Simone approached the wagon from behind, enjoying the feel of the wind on her face as they whizzed across the field toward her target. She noticed the wagon was slowing, but it was too late. A bright light was thrust into her night-accustomed eyes, blinding her and sending Alfred stumbling back in surprise. She ground her thighs into her stallion's side, cursing and covering her face as she clung to him.

"Well! If it isn't the lovely Mademoiselle Simone!" Hazen Briggs crowed from the back of his caravan, lowering his torch. He whistled his horse team to a stop. "Sorry for startling you, darlin', but you startled me. How'd you sneak up on me so good?"

"I could hear that shitty whistling of yours a mile away." Simone grinned at the former Camp & Supply storeowner, and he grinned back, his eyes twinkling with merriment above a thick brown beard. Wearing a collared shirt beneath a snug-fitting sweater and a matching bandana to rein in his glorious hair, he looked like a model, preparing for his close-up in *Rugged Prepster Magazine: The Special Apocalypse Edition.*

"You're looking pretty good these days—for a man who lives in a wagon," she said.

"Mona, baby, I look good because I live in a wagon. This wagon. My beautiful Esmerrrrrrrralda." Hazen rolled the *r*'s with relish.

"What are you doing out here? I thought you were stopping at Elwood's today."

"I'm out here looking for you, girl," Hazen replied, readjusting his bandana. "I was at Elwood's. When you didn't come home, Zeff got pretty worried about you." He waggled his eyebrows obnoxiously. "Probably because the old grump's completely in love with you."

"Oh, come on, Hazen."

"He wanted to come himself, you know, to find you. Be a hero. But Barbara wouldn't have it. She's got him doing hard time at the woodpile, poor bastard."

"Well, I'm sure you weren't about to chop any wood."

"Damn right I wasn't," Hazen said, holding up a pair of supple, well-manicured hands. "These hands were made for shaking, not chopping." He cast a critical eye over Simone's calloused fingers and lingered with disgust over her overgrown cuticles and extensive display of hangnails. "I don't even want to know what you've been doing with those claws of yours."

Simone's thoughts sped back to the contents of the tin; she grimaced.

"Shoot, I didn't mean that," Hazen said in a velvety tone of voice, mistaking her revulsion for offense. "Come on up here, and ride back to Elwood's with me. We can hitch Alfred up front with the girls."

The offer sounded so sweet, Simone forgot about Grace.

Almost, anyway.

ESMERRRALDA

The inside of the caravan was warm, and the steady gait of the horses threatened to lull Simone to sleep. The air was sharp with the smell of mint and wood smoke as she gradually became aware of the unpleasant ripeness that clung to her own skin. *Hazen.* She shook her head and smiled. The man was so fastidious he could make you feel like shit just by existing.

She studied her surroundings, bathed in the light of a mason-jar candle that bumped and jostled with the movement of the wagon. Though Hazen loathed roughing up his hands, he was a skilled carpenter and handyman who used to run a thriving camp-supply store in town. After the storms, his expertise had manifested into Esmeralda, the most popular mobile trading post in Assumption Valley, and his beloved home.

The wagon cover was a colorful patchwork of windbreakers that had been sewn together. Thick carpets, comforters, and quilts lined the floors and walls, making the caravan feel like a travelling den. Animal furs and sleeping bags were laid out in a heap at the front of the caravan where Simone was nested. At her foot, a wicker basket held an assortment of jars and bottles filled with seeds and mysterious powders. A small stove squatted in the far right corner; beside it, an ornamental birdcage was filled with the homemade elixirs and tonics that comprised the tradesman's extensive skincare regimen.

Finally Simone turned her attention toward Grace, who was sitting beside her, swaddled in a weathered old bear fur Hazen had given her after they'd picked her up. She knew Hazen had been disgusted by Grace's bloodied appearance, but he knew a thing or two about women and had the sense to keep his feelings to himself. So he'd smiled and flattered Grace when they were first introduced, keeping up the charade until she had disappeared into the back of the wagon. Then the tradesman had wheeled on Simone. "That better be *dried* blood," he'd whispered angrily. "That's my best fur."

It's not that life was cheap; it's just that bear furs had gotten really expensive.

"How are you feeling?" Simone asked.

Grace turned her battered face toward her, and a smile wavered across her swollen lips. "It feels good to be warm again," she said, closing her eyes and burying herself deeper in the fur.

"Sorry about the candle, ladies," Hazen called from the driver's seat up front. "I know it's flashing like a damn strobe light back there, but it's my last one. Barb wouldn't give me any new ones until I picked you up. There's trust for you."

"We should probably ride in the dark anyway." Simone licked her fingers and extinguished the tortured flame.

"Why? Were you being followed?" Hazen asked; he sounded nervous.

"I don't think so," Simone answered.

"We might be," Grace replied at the same time.

The tradesman fell silent.

"Hey, have you heard about any more raids in the valley?" Simone asked. With all the traveling Hazen did in trade, he knew the valley intimately and had an unabashed love of gossip. If trouble was starting up again, he'd be the first one to know about it.

In the driver's seat, the question hit Hazen like a lightning bolt to the brain, and he suddenly found it difficult to breathe. His thoughts returned to yesterday, to the Darby Compound, a tidy little property inhabited by a tidy little family that was always gracious trade partners and hosts. But yesterday, for the first time ever in their partnership, the Darby family was not at home when Hazen came to trade. In fact, their compound was barely recognizable, savaged and ransacked as it was with broken windows and glass spiking the path to the front door—or at least, to where the front door had been. Inside, there had been no sign of the Darby family anywhere, only a blood-soaked kitchen whining with flies.

"Raids?" Hazen heard himself answer. "Nope. Haven't heard of any raids."

But why did he lie? His mind fumbled around for an answer and grabbed the first one that floated to the surface: *Because it wasn't a lie. Anything could have happened to the Darbys. Anything.*

Except it wasn't just anything, and he knew it. Five compounds on his trade route had been lost on his last rotation. He'd found each one empty and abandoned, each one bearing signs of a struggle. He didn't understand it. These families had been tough. They had survived many raids on their homes. So what had happened to them?

Grace moved closer to the driver's seat, and Hazen inhaled sharply, worried she might touch him with her filthy hands.

"My home was raided," she said. "In Colborne. Now you've heard of that one."

"Colborne?" Hazen's blood ran cold. "What happened?" he asked.

"They burned our house down…with my family inside." Grace's voice thickened with tears.

"I'm so sorry," he replied. He was horrified at the news, but in some way, he felt relieved. "None of the compounds I found were burned down."

"Compounds you *found?*" Simone pressed.

Shit. Hazen felt her gaze boring into the back of his head. His hands began to sweat. "Compounds I *visited.* That's what I meant to say," he corrected himself in a droll tone of voice. "Good Lordy, Simone, is this a conversation or a Mensa exam? Now, peanut." He turned his attention back to Grace, who had suddenly become the more appealing conversation partner. "You're a Colborne girl, are you? I should have guessed. Colborne girls are known for their remarkable beauty."

Grace rolled her eyes at this remark. "Oh, cut the crap, bud. I'm filthy, I'm covered in two different guys' blood, and I completely gross you out right now. Am I right, or am I right?"

Hazen hooted with laughter. "Boy, tough crowd," he said, pretending to mop his brow with an invisible handkerchief. He turned his head to the left and watched Grace with his peripheral vision, though he could barely see her in the dark. *Face doesn't look too bad under all that blood. Got a nice little pair of titties on her. Clean this one up, and she might be a real sparkplug.* The thought chased some of the chill from Hazen's bones, and he relaxed enough to slouch back against the driver's seat. He pursed his lips against the rushing darkness, but he didn't whistle this time.

ELWOOD'S COMPOUND

By the time they had reached the compound that night, a strange sexual tension had developed between Grace and Hazen that resulted in Simone driving the caravan while they sat in the back together with the flap down. Apparently the Casanova of Assumption Valley had lost some of his disdain for Grace's rough appearance—or was giving a damn fine impression of having lost it. From the driver's seat, Simone could hear them talking softly to one another. Every now and then she heard a muffled giggle. But she knew Hazen well enough to know he wouldn't lay a finger on Grace, not in that state. Besides, the girl could use something to take her mind off her family.

So Simone never complained. She clapped her eyes north and drove the team home, humming something she couldn't remember the words to.

"We're here!" she called over her shoulder when the jagged top of the stockade came into view, tearing into the night sky.

The wagon flap opened, and Hazen poked his head out, grinning from ear to ear.

"Great, thanks, Mona. You did a hell of a job driving her. I knew you would." He winked and turned his handsome face to Grace. "Your castle awaits."

Simone had to admit, from this angle, Elwood's compound did look like a castle, intimidating and utilitarian, resting like some great beast at the forest's edge, marking what had once been the perimeter of Assumption Valley National Park. A stockade of sharpened logs had been erected around the property to ward off raiders. In the distance, a guardhouse peered out over the spikes. Simone wondered if Zeff was in there right now, waiting for them to get home.

Grace peered out the front of the wagon, squinting in the dark. "Damn!" she exclaimed. "We had a fence too, but it was nothing like this. This one's ferocious!"

"If you're impressed with the fence, just wait until you get inside," Hazen replied. "Elwood's compound has a resident inventor. You should see some of his contraptions."

As the caravan approached the formidable front gate, Hazen stuck two fingers in his mouth and whistled, but it wasn't necessary; the gates of the stockade had already begun to open, emitting a low groan as they always did when their pulleys strained with effort. Simone drove the caravan through, and the gates closed behind them with a bang. Drawing to a stop just past the guardhouse, she could see Elwood and Barbara Hubble's sprawling farmhouse ahead, illuminated by the torches that lined the sloping drive. Candles sputtered in several of the windows, giving the house a welcoming, festive appearance against the chilled black night.

"Look at all those candles," Hazen said, staring at the house. "It's like she's taunting me." He turned his head. "Oh, hello there!" he called to some unseen person on the ground. "Look who I found!"

Ashamed by her soiled appearance, Grace ducked back into the wagon without a sound. But Simone didn't notice; she had turned eagerly in her seat, expecting to see Zeff looking up at her from the ground below, a half smile playing across his weather-worn face. But her eyes fell upon Lewis instead, said compound inventor and self-proclaimed Renaissance man. He was dressed in his usual safari hat and ragged tweed blazer, tugging on a hairy moustache that consumed his entire upper lip and a significant proportion of his cheeks.

"Oh! I am glad you're back, Simone," Lewis said, and the moustache jumped and twitched with delight. "Should be a nice day tomorrow! Zeff says things are warming up. Maybe we can finally complete that pit trap."

"What pit trap?" she asked, her heart sinking. Lewis had that tone in his voice, that rich baritone that suggested he had a project in mind. And his projects were a lot of work, particularly for her. Like a Pavlovian dog, her back started to ache.

"Now, my dear, I know what you're thinking," he continued. "Is a large pit suitable to catch a raider, or should we line the pit with spikes to increase the killing capacity? Never fear; I will think the matter over and run a few numbers, and I shall have an answer for you by tomorrow." Lewis wiggled a hooked finger at her. "You are a fierce taskmaster, Simone, but I respect you for it." And he turned on his heel and sailed off toward the house, his wellington boots squeaking with every step.

The compound yard grew quiet again as Simone unhitched Alfred and led him to the small stable he shared with Zeff's horse, Peaches. By the time she had returned to Hazen's caravan, she was startled to see the tradesman taking Grace by the blood-smeared hand and helping her down from the wagon without flinching once. Simone smiled; may wonders never cease.

"So, the fearless hunter has returned," a voice snidely remarked at her back. "Returned from the so-called overhunted valley. And what delights have you brought us tonight, Simone? A few mice? A rotten wolf carcass? Or the usual—nothing at all?"

She turned warily on the spot, coming face to face with Elwood and Barbara's adult son, Monty. Almost a foot shorter, he smirked up at her, revealing a row of pointed yellow teeth that glinted in the torchlight.

"You'll have to wait and see," she replied. "I'd hate to ruin the surprise."

A furious expression crossed Monty's face before vanishing completely. "I visited your mother today," he said coyly. "I didn't think she could get much worse, but apparently she can."

Simone looked at Monty, longing to wipe the sneer off his little rat face, but she remained expressionless as she leaned over him. "Listen to me," she said. "You stay away from my mother. You got that? Never, ever go near her." She leaned in further until their noses were almost touching. "Because if I think you've hurt her or harmed her in anyway—any way at all—I'm going to kill you and make it look like a cougar attack. A really, *really* bad cougar attack."

Suddenly Grace appeared at her side, holding the tin in her hands.

"Who the fuck are you?" Monty cried.

"This is Grace," Simone answered.

"Who the fuck are you?" Grace asked.

"This is Monty."

"Why the hell are you wearing a business suit?" Grace smirked at him. "You think your office is going to open tomorrow or something?"

"I am wearing this suit because I have a full-time job here," Monty replied, his voice swelling with self-importance. "I am the senior resource manager of this compound."

"That's just a fancy way of saying he doesn't do anything," Hazen said, strolling casually into the conversation and fixing Monty with a charming smile. "Ain't that right, Tee?"

"I am responsible for the mental heavy lifting around here," Monty said in a clipped tone. "The goal of any senior resource manager is to make it look easy. That's the point. If you had a master's degree in resource management from Mount Lion as I do, you would recognize the complexity of my craft."

"Oh, now, Monty, don't be upset," Hazen replied, placing a hand across the man's sharp little shoulder blades. "Everyone knows you're full of craft."

Grace emitted a strangled-sounding chuckle as the color vanished from Monty's face and a peculiar heat began radiating from his body. Simone could see the Monty barometer was falling; a storm was sure to follow.

"We should be off," she said briskly, wrapping her fingers around Grace's arm. "We need to get ready for dinner. Thanks for the ride, Hazen. We'll see you later!" Simone called over her shoulder, pulling Grace in the direction of the house.

"Wait! Stop!" Monty screamed after them. "As the senior resource manager, I have not authorized that woman's presence in this compound! Do you hear me? She is *trespassing* on *private property*!"

"Who is that guy?" Grace asked, casting a frown over her shoulder.

"That's Elwood and Barbara's son," Simone answered. "And if you liked that little display, just wait till you get a load of Elwood."

BARBARA

Simone and Grace went through the side door and into the kitchen. A wave of heat from the woodstove hit their faces as they hurried in from the chilly night. A ribbon-lined bulletin board hung on the wall nearby, displaying a complex chore list divided by season. Candles flickered in jam jars on the table, their inviting glow illuminating the monument to order and efficiency that was Barbara's kitchen, the motor that drove the compound through the darkness of the years.

Barbara herself was bent over at the stove, coaxing the fire back to life as her curvaceous rump strained against a pair of sensible woolen trousers. She had lost weight since the solar storms—they all had—but she had put on the pounds during Elwood's retirement years and had a lot of weight to lose. As the seasons passed and the other men and women at the compound hardened into sinewy string beans, Barbara managed to keep her voluptuous, womanly appearance. She was sixty-five years old, and she was blossoming.

Barbara watched the fire come back to life, emerging from its hiding place under the embers. She had laid a bed of tamarack; once that burned down, she had learned that if she placed poplar branches over the hot coals and closed the stove for the night, it would burn until morning. She sang cheerfully under her breath.

She would never openly admit it, but Barbara was happy these days—happier than she'd felt in all the years that had come before when she was simply "Professor Hubble's wife." Lord! The dinners, the soirees, the never-ending string of faculty lunches she'd dutifully attended with a smile frozen across her face, never offering an opinion unless she was asked, never being asked. Her relationship with her husband and son had been much the same. At home, she found herself at their beck and call, sometimes the target of their insults. To them, the words "mother" and "wife" were synonymous with slave, drudge, or at best, a friendly foot servant. Over time, she felt resentment build and harden in her chest. She didn't know how she'd fallen into this life, and she certainly didn't know how to get out of it. She was stuck.

The situation only got worse when Elwood retired and Monty moved home again. They bought the country estate in Assumption Valley, a beautiful place she longed to explore. Instead, Barbara found herself working around the clock to please two unpleasant men who had nowhere to go and nothing to do except complain. She wondered if she'd ever loved them, either one of them. Often, she worried that she might hate them, and the thought was horrifying to her. Sure, a wife could hate her husband—she knew lots who did—but could a mother hate her own son?

When her husband's colleague Professor Lewis Hutchinson came to stay with them for a few weeks, he was a welcome diversion from Barbara's private guilt and loneliness. In fact, he was still visiting when the solar storms hit, and she found herself relying on him rather than on her own family for survival. It was Lewis who first went bartering at other acreages when their supplies got low. It was Lewis who picked the fruit in the orchard. It was Lewis who organized the household candle-making business. And after the raids began, it was Lewis who directed the construction of the stockade while Elwood skulked around the house, grubbing about for alcohol or anything he could find to drink himself into oblivion.

For Barbara, a mighty spruce had fallen in the forest. It was time for the sapling to feel the sun.

With Barbara and Lewis at the helm, the compound population swelled to a maximum of twenty-three occupants as more and more neighbors ended up at their doorstep, seeking refuge. Barbara admitted them all and put them to work around the compound, but four were lost to a mysterious sickness, two were killed in tree-felling accidents, two more died in raids, and one died in childbirth, leaving the final headcount at fourteen. It had been two seasons since there had been a death at the compound, and Barbara was grateful for that. She had all kinds of things to be grateful for these days.

The kitchen door banged shut behind her, startling her from her thoughts. Barbara cried out in fright and turned from the stove. She was overcome with relief when she saw Simone's long, lean figure slouching in the gloom.

"Jesus wept!" she shouted, holding her hand against her magnificent breast. "Simone, do you always have to be so stealthy? It's an unhealthy habit, darling."

Simone moved toward her, the shadows playing over her high cheekbones and slightly cleft chin.

Barbara thought she looked uneasy. "You have something on your mind," she said. There was a flicker of movement in the shadows, and Barbara let out another shriek as a blood-soaked young woman with matted hair and swollen eyes crept into the candlelight.

"This is Grace," Simone said. "Her family's been killed. I found her in the valley being attacked by two men."

Barbara's round face filled with sympathy as she swooped forward, grabbing the soiled young woman and hugging her to her bosom. Though she was sore, Grace rather enjoyed the sensation; it was nice to feel a bosom again.

"Oh, my poor, sweet girl!" Barbara cried. "And here I am, shouting the house down! Never mind, my pet—we'll clean you up and give you some new clothes. And those wounds will need tending, I suppose. I've been heating some snow on the stove. It should be warm water by now. Yes, it feels lovely. And we have a bit of whiskey left; I'll give you a dram. You'd be surprised what a bit of warm water and whiskey can do for a woman's spirit."

She pulled out a chair by the kitchen table, and Grace gently lowered herself onto the thin seersucker cushion, her battered face turned upward, her eyelashes spiky and wet. Barbara dampened a clean cloth and leaned over her, dabbing at the wounds on her face.

"Thank you," Grace said, her voice breaking.

Simone found a stool to perch on and rest her weary bones. Using the last bit of her energy, she removed her weaponry, pulling off her heavy shotgun sling and chest holster and removing the knife sheaths from her boot, both arms, and waistband. She sighed gustily as she felt the weight drop from her body, throwing her hat on top of the pile.

"Have any luck in the valley today?" Barbara asked Simone.

"Depends on what you mean by luck," she replied.

"We've got organs," Grace said. "There." She pointed to the tin she'd left on the kitchen table.

Barbara's face brightened. "Well, that is excellent news, girls! Organ meat is such a good form of protein. Good for tilling and planting season."

"They're human organs," Simone added darkly.

Barbara looked startled and then composed herself. "From the men who were attacking you?" she asked Grace.

Grace nodded, and Barbara returned to cleaning her face.

There was a silence.

"So what do you think of the organ meat now?" Simone asked.

The compound matriarch paused for a moment. Then she briskly wiped her hands on her apron and said: "I think it's a good form of protein. Good for tilling and planting season."

DINNERTIME

Dinner was late in coming, but at least there was a dinner to be had, so the residents of Elwood's Compound merrily assembled themselves around the formal table in the dining room. After nearly a week of rice rations, bad potatoes, and bits of stingy, tasteless lard, word had gotten around they were having *something else* for supper. That made the evening an event, and one that generated much excitement among the residents as they dressed themselves in their finest clothing and took their seats around the table far too early, suffusing the darkened room with the buzz of anticipation like a theater before a show. As the smell of cooking meat wafted in from the kitchen, the residents sniffed at it eagerly, determined that nothing, not even the smell, would be wasted.

Simone was one of the last to arrive, leading Perla by the arm as her mother shuffled along with difficulty, her eyes shifting about the room like a frightened animal. Simone looked for Grace but could see no sign of her at the table. She nodded hello to Bob and Felicity Walker as they took their seats, their unsmiling faces set in their usual dour expressions. Across from the Walkers sat Doug Parson and his five boys, still grieving the death of his wife, Louisa, who died in childbirth last summer. Doug and his three eldest sat with their arms crossed; the two youngest slapped at each other gleefully until the smaller one started to cry.

Elwood was seated in his usual position at the head of the table, gulping greedily from a flask, his pendulous jowls shaking and shuddering with every swallow he took. In the glory of his professorhood, Elwood had been an obese man whose office perpetually smelled of popcorn, butter and oyster shells, but the new way of living had slimmed him down, leaving a gaunter fellow in his place who lived in a suit of excess skin. His ego, however, suffered no equivalent moderation and remained as bloated as ever, having gorged itself for decades on the manna of fawning university students. So when Elwood was sober enough to socialize, he listened rarely, interrupted often, and condescended always. In fact, at this very minute, Elwood was choosing to ignore his friend, Lewis, who was speaking to him with great enthusiasm, choosing instead to glower at his son, Monty, who was seated next to him and cleaning his fingernails with a dinner knife.

Simone was relieved to spot her old friend Zeff at the table, who had been watching her since she'd come in. He had taken off his cattleman cowboy hat and hung it on the chair behind him, exposing a tanned face with a tidy beard and a sharp set of features that looked as if they'd been carved out of wood. He motioned her over to two free chairs beside him and stood up to help her with Perla.

"You were late today," he said, by way of greeting. "You run into some trouble in the hills?" His manner was abrupt; Simone could tell he'd been worrying.

"I ran into two men out there," she replied. "They weren't trouble. They just seemed like it at first."

"They hurt you?" A muscle twitched along Zeff's jawline.

"Of course not," she scoffed. Beside her, Perla started to weep, brushing at her face with crooked, shaking fingers.

"Oh, Mom, it's OK, it's OK," Simone said, turning to her mother and rubbing her back consolingly. She looked at Zeff. "Look, you know I've got my hands full with Perla here. I can't spend my time worrying about you worrying about me."

"You better wake up, Mona," Zeff said quietly. "There's something happening in the valley. And from the looks of it, we've all got something to worry about."

Simone stopped rubbing her mother's back. "What are you talking about?"

"I'm talking about Peter Hislop's compound," he leaned forward in his chair. "I visited them today, and the place was empty, completely empty. The house was deserted."

"Deserted? Could they have moved?"

Zeff looked at Simone, and the fear in his face left her breathless. "The tracks in the front garden looked like someone had been dragged out of there. There were wagon tracks too. Four—maybe five different wagons must have been there."

"Are you two telling ghost stories?" Hazen interrupted, sidling up to the table with a grin. "Mind if I join in?"

"Seems like you already did," Zeff replied.

Simone regarded Hazen in the candlelight. He had removed his bandana and slicked his hair back. His face was cleanly shaven, although his knife had left a few nicks behind; one by his ear was still oozing blood. He had changed into a handsome cable-knit sweater that hugged his broad shoulders and smelled faintly of dried lavender. He had cleaned himself up, and Simone was pretty sure she knew why.

"You been to the Hislops lately?" Zeff asked him.

"Yeah, I've been to the Hislops." Hazen gazed at his feet. "Place was empty when I got there. Looks like they moved or something."

"You never told me about that," Simone said in surprise.

43

"I didn't think it was relevant," he answered.

"You didn't think it was relevant that a major trade family disappeared? Where do you think they went? On a goddamn vacation?" Zeff said. "Something happened to them, Hazen, and you know it."

"Keep your voice down," Simone hissed. "You'll upset the children."

"You're hiding from the truth—as usual," Zeff continued in a heated whisper.

"Are we still talking about the Hislops?" Hazen asked wearily. "Or have we moved on to Emerson again?"

"OK, guys, that's enough," Simone interjected. She knew where the conversation was going, and she didn't want to discuss her brother's murder again—not today. She put her head in her hands and rubbed her forehead. "Can't you two have a polite conversation for once?"

The tips of Zeff's ears reddened with embarrassment, but Hazen smiled broadly, anxious to change the subject. "You're right, Mona. We oughta be more polite. After all, we are breaking bread together." He looked at Zeff. "You know, Mona's had a hard day. And I bet you were too busy telling her the sky was falling to even ask her about it." His eyes regained their mischievous light. "Here, Simone, let me buy you a drink. God knows you could probably use one." He handed her his flask. "Drink it down, honeybunch, and park your troubles for now. They're not going anywhere."

Simone took his flask gratefully and sipped at the amber liquid, feeling the slow burn running down her throat and dripping into her belly. She closed her eyes, enjoying the sweet sensation, letting the noise of the compound residents flow over and around her until the sound stopped abruptly.

Simone opened her eyes in time to watch Barbara lead a freshly scrubbed Grace into the room. Aside from a violent black eye that was starting to blossom across her face, the young woman looked beautiful, like Venus who had emerged, battered and bruised, from the depths of a turbulent sea. Her long, golden tresses had been cleaned and combed and were still damp, rolling down her back in delicate waves. She was wearing a pair of wool leggings, a long sweater jacket, and a toque that had belonged to the late Louisa Parson. At the table, Doug's eyes moistened with tears at the sight of it.

"Now, Doug, don't you start," Barbara scolded before the man could even open his mouth. "The girl needs the clothing, and let's face it, your poor Louisa don't."

He hung his head like a chastened dog.

"All right, Miss Grace," Barbara said, just slightly out of breath as she carried a chair over to the table. "Let's get you seated."

"Over here!" Hazen called, making room at the table for Grace without taking his eyes off her. "We've got plenty of space."

"Hazen, making friends already." Barbara pursed her lips as Grace settled beside him, casting a nervous smile at no one in particular. "Be sweet to her," she ordered the tradesman.

"She's staying, Mother?" Monty cried from the other end of the table, his knife clenched defiantly in his dainty hand. "Did you forget the policy I recently drafted for you regarding the requirement to consult the senior resource officer before any such decisions are made?"

Barbara stared at her son, the creature that had made her life a misery since her first wave of morning sickness. She mustered up her best motherly smile. "Of course, my darling," she said, before exiting the room.

It was Elwood who broke the silence first. "I'm not sure who you are," he said, addressing Grace in a faint slur. "Frankly, it's not important. What is important is that you are staying here. I won't bother with unnecessary, time-wasting introductions—Simone, you can see to that." His bloodhound face peered balefully around the room, squinting at each resident with suspicion. "You will make this person feel comfortable!" he shouted, slamming his fist down on the table.

Barbara hurried in with the rice then, before returning once more from the kitchen with a steaming tureen as a respectful hush fell across the room. She set the dish down on the table. "Ladies and gentlemen," she said solemnly, "I present to you...sautéed offal stew, flavored with wizened berries and served over a bed of rice." She lifted the lid of the tureen with a dramatic flourish of her hand.

"Ahhhh!" the residents sighed in unison.

"What's 'awful'?" a child was heard to ask.

As Barbara began dishing out the meal, Lewis wafted the scent toward his nostrils with his hand, snuffling loudly through his moustache.

"Earthy," he pronounced. "With a hint of barnyard sweetness. My dear Simone, where did you get it?"

Barbara and Simone exchanged nervous glances.

"Bush pig," Grace interjected, much to the surprise of the dinner party, and, it seemed, herself. "Yup. It was bush pig all right—they were slaughtered by a mountain lion or something. We got there just in time to save this."

The residents stopped eating and looked down at their plates.

"Bush pig? How extraordinary," Lewis replied, arching a bristling brow. "I didn't know the little devils could survive so far north."

"Well, these pigs were tough," Grace replied. "Couple of real pricks, actually."

The Parson children tittered.

"In that case, I shall be delighted to take this portion of bush pig off your hands," Lewis said, tucking into his meal and snorting softly as he chewed.

Simone examined the meal in front of her and tried a bite. Shocked by how delicious it tasted, she glanced furtively around the table; the other residents were gobbling down their portions like wolves. She gave Perla a small spoonful.

"Little bites! Take your time!" Barbara reminded the residents in her motherly way. "Otherwise you'll make yourselves sick."

Once Perla had eaten, Simone cleaned her plate. And, as a matter of fact, she did make herself a little sick.

LOVE AND BLINDNESS

After dinner was over, the residents thudded around the dining room like drunken toddlers, clearing away plates that were so clean they shone in the flickering folds of the room. Only Elwood remained motionless at the table, slumbering upright in his chair, his earthworm lips smacking together as he dreamed. Bustling back to the kitchen, Barbara stopped and inspected her husband, who let out a deep exhale, and boozy cider fumes permeated the air around him. Gently, she removed the flask from his grasp. She would have it refilled and returned to him by morning.

Sleep on, dear husband, she thought. *I don't care if you ever wake up.*

"Why, Barbara, you are the picture of a devoted wife," Hazen said, smiling at her from across the room.

"A picture…that's a good word for it," Barbara said, before disappearing back into the kitchen.

Simone retrieved a lantern and began her efforts to herd Perla up the drafty old staircase, through the narrow corridor, and into the bedroom they shared. Getting her mother into her nightgown was no easier than the rest of her day had been, and it reminded her of when she was young and tried to dress barn cats in baby clothes. Once Perla was dressed, Simone sat on the edge of the bed and caught her breath. Her hands were trembling, and she didn't know if it was exhaustion or the surge of food in her system.

A few more days like this one, and someone will have to dress me for bed, she thought, watching her mother look out the window. From the back, she looked just like her old self, her mother as she remembered her—maybe a little more gray and stooped, but it was the unmistakable frame of the woman who had loved and protected her for her entire life. When Perla turned around again, Simone noticed the look in her eye: something wild and reckless had taken the place of her after-dinner fatigue. With quick hands, she caught the empty bedpan Perla hurled at her, placing it under the bed and out of her mother's reach. Then she strapped her mother into bed and kissed her forehead before turning to go.

"Good night, Mum," Simone said from the doorway, holding her lantern high to light the darkened room. "I miss you."

The candles were guttering low by the time she returned to the dining room, casting creepy shadows on the walls. Despite Simone's heavy heart, she was somewhat pleased to find Barbara trying to rouse Elwood, who had begun snoring like a buffalo from his high-backed chair as Grace looked on in open amusement.

"Oh, God, Simone!" Grace whispered, her eyes sparkling with laughter. "I'm so glad you're here to see this. Poor Barbara's been trying to wake him for ages. I've never seen anything like it—it's like he's in some kind of freaky coma."

"A coma would be a blessing!" Barbara said as she continued to shake her husband, jiggling his wattle of skin. "Oh, really, Elwood!" she cried, giving his body a frustrated shove. The snoring stopped abruptly as the man opened one eye.

"Elwood, please! I'm exhausted, and I want to go to bed," Barbara said, bending over to look into his face, seeing her only opportunity to rouse him.

"There's no need to get so excited," he grunted, straightening himself in his chair and wiping his jowls delicately along the hem of his sweater. "I'm getting up. I was merely having a moment of inward reflection."

Barbara rolled her eyes as she helped her husband out of his chair and got him to his feet. He steadied himself by placing a hand on her shapely buttocks and burped.

"Good night, you two," Barbara said, slapping Elwood's hand away. "Grace, I'm looking forward to getting to know you better. I've made a bedroom for you beside Simone's room so you'll have a friend nearby. Simone, you can take her there, can't you?"

"Isn't that Lewis's room?" Simone asked.

"No. The room right next to yours—the bathroom," Barbara replied. "We're pretty much at max capacity in this house, as you know. But I made a wonderful little padded bed for Grace in the bathtub. It's actually quite roomy." She gave Grace a warm smile. "You'll love it, dear; the tub's a beautiful claw foot—it used to be absolutely perfect for long soaks." Barbara looked wistful and then seemed to wave the thought off with a small flutter of the hand. "Might as well find another use for it."

After Barbara and Elwood had gone, Simone yawned and rubbed her eyes. "I guess we should probably head to bed ourselves," she said. "This has been one hell of a day."

"Actually," Grace started; her voice was timid. "Could we take a little walk first? I'm feeling sick from all the food. I could use some fresh air."

Hazen and his Cheshire smile suddenly appeared in the doorway. "Grace, I wouldn't mind a walk myself," he offered casually, hanging his thumbs through the belt loops of his pants. "I have yet to find a more pleasant experience than taking an evening stroll." He gave her a devouring grin.

"I'll come too," Simone said, ignoring the obvious disappointment on the tradesman's face. "I wouldn't mind dropping by the guardhouse to see Zeff."

They left through the side door, feeling the clammy kiss of the evening on their faces. The night sky had cleared; far above their heads, the stars blazed coldly. An owl flapped by, ruffling the air as they strolled around the property together, safe within the confines of the stockade.

"Well, I can tell you," Hazen said to Grace, taking her arm in his, "as far as compounds go, you've found yourself a good one. Elwood's Compound is the best in the valley, in my opinion. And I see all kinds of them on my trade route."

"Really?" Grace said, eager to hear more from such a charming tour guide.

"Really," Hazen replied in a confidential tone. "It's got everything. A solid defense from raiders." He pointed to the stockade. "And a well-constructed and reasonably hygienic outhouse." He motioned to the sturdy wooden structure at the back of the property and grinned. "You know, Monty actually climbed down there once to retrieve a cufflink he dropped."

"He did?" Simone asked, over gales of Grace's laughter.

"He did—last summer," Hazen answered. "You didn't hear about that?"

Simone shook her head.

"I don't think he found it either, poor bastard. Ah, yes, and coming up on your right, Grace, is the compound orchard. Here, let's walk through it."

The trio turned and entered the modest grove, where limbs of leafless trees pierced the night sky and held the moon captive in their arms. The conversation fell away as Grace flitted from tree to tree in the dark, running her hands tenderly over trunks and inspecting outstretched boughs.

"You've got some nice plum and cherry trees here," she said, once she'd completed her assessment. "A couple good-looking crabs too."

"You know your stuff." Hazen was impressed. "You should ask Barbara to work here in the summer. Usually Bob and Felicity Walker run the orchard, but they were caught smuggling fruit out of the compound last year."

"The Walkers were smuggling fruit?" Simone asked; the tradesman's gossip had surprised her once again.

"You didn't hear about that either?" Hazen laughed. "Mona, you oughta be more nosy. They were almost exiled."

"Exiled?"

"Key-rect. But Barbara said there were mitigating circumstances, so she let them stay."

"What kind of mitigating circumstances?" Grace asked.

"They were taking the fruit for their daughter." The amused twinkle left the tradesman's eye. "She was in Trafalgar City when the storms hit. Hasn't been heard from since. They keep checking their old house and leaving food out for her, just in case she comes back."

"Oh," Grace said and looked down at her feet. Hazen's gossip had hit too close to home, and she felt overwhelmed with sadness. She would give anything to believe that her family was still alive... that she might see them again.

"Let's keep moving, OK?" Hazen said kindly. He looked over his shoulder at Simone. "Please tell me you heard about Monty's hemorrhoids."

She grinned. "Everybody heard about Monty's hemorrhoids."

They ambled on together, past the smokehouse and its neatly stacked woodpile, past the grain-grinding bicycle and soap-making shed, then on to the large kitchen garden, still barren from the cold spring. As they walked on, Lewis's latest invention loomed out of the shadows, catching Grace's eye. "My God, what is that thing?" she wondered aloud, staring up at the massive contraption.

"That's a catapult that Lewis has been working on—Lewis and Simone, that is." Hazen was quick to correct himself. "He's the inventor, and Simone's the workhorse. It's a beautiful relationship."

"Depends on who you ask," Simone groused as she trailed along after them.

"How is the old catapult coming along, anyway?" Hazen asked.

"Last time we tested it, it threw a rock clean through the stockade. We had to replace six logs. Lewis says he's done some tweaking, but I've heard that before."

"You'll get it working eventually." Hazen wrapped an arm around Grace's shoulder. "Then you'll have a catapult to protect you from harm."

They entered the old stone garage, now dirt floored and strewn with hay. A few goats had lived there last summer, but none of the animals had made it past the long, hungry winter alive. Simone could still smell the reassuring muskiness of the animals in the air, but the garage was used only for storage now. It made her think of Valkyrie House, abandoned and alone. Maybe when Perla was having one of her better days, they could go and visit it again.

Exiting the garage, they passed the empty chicken coop and moved toward the guardhouse, positioned near the front gate to provide the best view of the valley beyond. It was an eccentric looking structure that somewhat resembled a large doghouse on stilts.

"Hello?" Zeff called, poking his head out of one of the windows.

"Don't get too excited, old fella," Hazen shouted up to him, emboldened by the presence of Grace on his arm. "We're just passing through. But Simone's coming up for a visit."

"Thank you for escorting her." Zeff gave Simone one of his long, slow smiles. He looked friendlier than he had at dinnertime. The solitude of the guardhouse must have done him some good.

"Good night, Grace," Simone said in parting. "I hope you get some sleep. You look tired. Hazen can show you where your bedroom is."

"Thank you. Thank you for everything." Grace threw her arms around Simone, hugging her so hard she couldn't breathe. "You won't regret saving my life."

"I'm sure I won't," Simone squeaked. Then, after she had detached herself from Grace's hearty embrace, she pulled Hazen aside.

"Do not, and I mean *do not* make a move on her tonight," she hissed at the tradesman. "That includes any form of kissing, touching and/or asking her to sleep in your caravan." Hazen gave her a wounded look, which further inflamed her. "I mean it. She's in a vulnerable state right now. Her family's been killed. She's been hiding in the woods for days. Today, she was beaten and almost raped, and on top of that, I'm not even sure how old she is."

Hazen hooked his thumbs through his belt loops and smiled. "Why, Simone, if you'd ever exhibited any hot-blooded feelings for a man before, I'd assume you were jealous."

Simone slapped him on the forehead with the palm of her hand. "I mean it, Hazen. Save it for later OK—when the timing is more appropriate." She turned and began climbing the ladder to the guardhouse where Zeff was waiting for her.

"What if there is no later?" Hazen asked in a stage whisper. "We could die anytime, you know."

Simone turned and gave him a withering look.

He looked away. "OK. Jesus," he muttered, shoving his hands into his pockets.

When Simone reached the top of the ladder, Zeff helped her inside and then lit a candle with his flint rock for her. He hated candlelight when he was on watch, especially now. But he knew she would enjoy the luxury for a little while, and that was what mattered. Zeff placed the candle on the little built-in table in the center of the room before wrapping a scratchy woolen blanket around Simone's shoulders. She hadn't even realized it, but she was freezing. The rough warmth of the wool chafed at her skin, but it felt wonderful. The blanket smelled like leather and perspiration. It smelled like Zeff.

Zeff pulled out the only chair in the room, and Simone sank into it with a grateful sigh.

"You've been gone awhile," she said as he leaned against the doorframe, peering out the window. "I thought you might take up trading full time, like Hazen."

Zeff directed his gaze toward the sound of her voice. After a lifetime of perfect health, it was astonishing to him how fast his eyesight was fading. He'd spent nearly three weeks in trade, trying to find a decent pair of glasses before giving up on the idea. His condition was progressing too rapidly, too hungrily. He'd finally resigned himself to the fact that something other than age was driving his vision loss—something he wasn't prepared for.

The old rancher squinted at Simone, the only woman in the world he had ever loved. He could still make out her familiar form in the room but just barely. He lived in fear of the day he wouldn't be able to make it out at all. Or the day she discovered his secret, and he'd be demoted from friend to burden.

"It's nothing like that," Zeff replied. "I just needed some time away."

"Well, now that you're back, I hope you'll stay awhile," she said with a wide yawn.

"I'll be here," he said. "If you want me to be."

Simone wasn't sure when she fell asleep; she only remembered Zeff's low voice urging her off to bed. She climbed back down the ladder and walked across the yard, cradling the lone candle from the guardhouse to light the way. With his fading eyesight, Zeff followed the light, quivering like a penny at the bottom of a well. It disappeared and then reappeared in Simone's window as she made her way to bed. Zeff stared at that window long after the light had gone and the room was veiled in darkness.

PIT TRAPPED

The next morning Simone was awakened by a loud banging on her door and the smell of something delicious in the air. She roused herself from her bedding on the floor and rubbed at a kink in her neck. She noticed, wryly, that she was still dressed in her clothes from yesterday; even her boots and jacket were still on. She got to her feet and checked on Perla, still asleep in bed, her gossamer eyelids fluttering as she slept.

The banging started on the door again.

"Simone? Simone! You are wanted in the hallway!" a voice boomed. Anxious to let Perla sleep, she scrambled for the door and was greeted by the sight of Lewis in the hallway, gripping two shovels and a pickaxe. Instantly, she felt wracked with misery. The pit trap idea had come home to roost.

"Lewis," she said, forcing a smile. "Is it pit-trap day today?"

"The woman is as observant as she is lovely," he replied with an elaborate little bow.

"Any chance you might consider asking Monty to help you?" Simone asked, starting to feel desperate. "How about Doug? Maybe Hazen would—"

"No chance at all," Lewis replied, grinning. "I wouldn't want you to miss out on creating a legacy. Something we can really be proud of."

"We built the stockade together—and the catapult. Aren't we proud of those things?" Simone put her hat on her head and then pushed it down in frustration. "You know, speaking of the catapult, Lewis, it still needs to be fixed. We should probably start working on that right away."

"Oh, Simone." Lewis shook his head and wrinkled his face as if he'd tasted something unpleasant. "The weather is far more suited for digging today. I think that should be obvious to you. The snow is almost gone. The sun is warm. The ground is soft—well, *softer.* It will hardly take any time at all." The inventor leaned in and lowered his eyebrows. "Zeff tells me trouble is afoot in the valley again. We need to get ahead of it." He straightened back up before handing both shovels to Simone. "And Barbara gave us breakfast," he added excitedly. Another project was about to begin; Lewis was overjoyed.

The two residents were soon outside the security of the stockade, but only one of them found herself pickaxing a hole. Every muscle in Simone's body screamed with fatigue as she brought down the axe, time and time again, breaking into the cold, hard earth. When the hole was big enough, she started using one of the shovels, but it wasn't much easier, and her muscles jarred and teeth rattled with every thrust of the cutting edge. She tried to distract herself from the pain by worrying about Perla; she had been left in Barbara's care today, and Simone hoped that did not mean Monty's care, the little toad. She hastened her pace.

A short distance away, Lewis sat on a blanket against a tree with his safari hat tipped back on his head, sharpening a pile of branches with a knife. Every so often his hand would snake into an old Tupperware container at his side, pop a morsel of meat into his mouth, then return to its whittling. And as his hands worked, his mind was free to wonder and muse upon the briskness of the breeze and the latent warmth of the sun, only just now trickling into his bones. He raised his face as he supposed a flower would, stretching its petals to the sky. *Rather like a tulip,* he thought. That seemed a sensible flower. Or perhaps a more fragrant blossom would suit his personality, something a little more...eccentric.

Lewis heard the complaining of the pulleys at the stockade gate and had soon spotted the newest compound resident, Grace, limping around the corner and setting her course in his direction. The wind threw her hair around her face as she made her way toward him, and he thought that from a distance she looked very beguiling indeed, although perhaps a bit too wounded for his liking.

"Over he-ere!" he called to her. Hastily, he cleared some of the woodchips away as Grace reached the blanket and plunked down next to him. He handed her a small piece of meat, which she snatched from his hand and gobbled down in an instant.

"Easy does it," Lewis cautioned.

"Where's Simone?" she asked, grabbing for another piece.

Simone's head emerged from a hole in the ground like a giant prairie dog. "Morning, Grace," she called, wiping at her forehead with her arm.

Grace got back to her feet and approached the hole with another piece of meat between her fingers. The bruises on her face had spread overnight, flinging electric blues and purples across her delicate features. But she was smiling, and she looked well rested. She looked happy to be alive.

"Have you eaten anything today?" she asked.

Simone nodded, trying to catch her breath.

"Well, you could use more. You're as skinny as a toothpick," Grace said with a friendly smile. "Open your mouth." Simone opened it, and Grace dropped the meat morsel squarely inside.

"Hanks," Simone grunted as she chewed. She squinted against the sun. "Sleep well?"

"Like a log. The tub is pretty cozy with all the blankets in there. I felt like I was in a cocoon."

"Hazen didn't give you any trouble?"

"Well, he made a move on me, if that's what you mean. But I told him to beat it. Literally." Grace rolled her eyes dramatically as Simone burst out laughing.

"Good for you," she said, and looked at the young woman approvingly. "That man needs to get rejected every now and then. Keeps him tolerable."

"Yeah," Grace said after a long pause, rubbing at a welt on her cheek. "I suppose. But I might have been a little mean about it."

Simone gave her a long look of disbelief. "After the day you had yesterday? He should have known better."

Grace still looked worried. She rubbed the welt harder.

"I'm sure he's fine. You can always talk to him about it, if it's bothering you."

"He's already gone, so it's too late for that." Grace's abused face collapsed with disappointment. "But who cares, anyway? I've got other problems," she said, more to herself than Simone. "So what's with walrus-man over there?" she said, pointing at Lewis, who quite fit the description this morning, having greased his moustache into two respectable tusks that went well past his chin. Still basking on his blanket in the sun, he was chortling about something and shaking his head.

"What do you mean?" Simone asked. "Is he crazy?"

"I mean, why are you doing all the digging? Aren't there two shovels? And a pickaxe? He isn't dirty, so I know he hasn't gotten in there yet."

"Ah, I don't know." Simone shrugged her shoulders and winced as a sudden bolt of pain traveled down her neck before settling in her lower back. "That's just the way it is around here."

Grace scowled at her. "And you thought *I* was the one who needed rescuing?" She grabbed a shovel and marched off, heading in the direction of the picnicking walrus. Once she reached him, she tossed the tool down on the blanket. "Yo, man, it's your turn to shovel," she said.

Lewis blinked up at her in surprise and then opened his mouth as if he might say something before thinking better of it and closing it again. "I suppose visionaries must get their hands dirty every now and then," he said finally, before getting to his feet. With several majestic flourishes of the hand, he brushed the woodchips off his body, although several still clung to the tips of his moustache. Then he began a series of stretching and breathing exercises that were almost frightening to behold.

Not wishing to encourage him any further in these pursuits, Grace turned away from the inventor and limped back to the pit. She held her hand out to Simone. "I can shovel for a bit," she offered.

Simone looked up at her in a daze. "Aren't you hurt?"

"Hell, no," Grace answered. "I'm ready to work. It'll keep my mind occupied."

Overcome with relief, Simone handed the shovel and work gloves to her newfound savior and hoisted herself out of the hole, biting back the grunts and shrieks that threatened to come tumbling out. Back on high land, she smiled at Grace bashfully, almost embarrassed by her own gratitude. "Thank you," she said sincerely, rubbing at her lower back. "I could use a break." She rolled her shoulders and they cracked and popped like a couple of cheap fireworks.

"Yeah, apparently you could," Grace said with a laugh. "So what is this hole?" she asked Simone. "And what is going on with those sharpened branches back there? Are those spears or something?"

"It's a pit trap. I'm sure you've seen them in cartoons," Lewis said, making his way over. "You dig a big hole, large enough for a man-eating tiger—or in this case, a man. Then, you line the bottom with sharpened sticks and cover it with refuse, and when a raider attacks, blammo! He—or she, pardon me—falls right into the pit."

Grace looked horrified. "What if someone from the compound falls in?"

"Ah, yes. Of course that's the risk with any security device you employ." Lewis steepled his fingers ponderously. "But I've selected an area that's rarely used by the compound residents. In fact, I'm growing poison ivy along the gate there. I think it looks rather pretty in the summertime."

Grace still looked dubious, but she climbed down with Lewis to complete the pit, and Simone returned to the compound to check on Perla, who was still in bed and blessedly Monty-free.

Later that afternoon, Simone and Grace set out across the valley on horseback; Simone in search of food, Grace in search of the men who killed her family. The search yielded no unusual tracks in the area, but Simone was glad to have the company and the chance to show off the valley, thawing under the warmth of the white spring sun. But even the brightness of the day and the two juicy rabbits in her snare couldn't banish the sense of unease that nagged at the edges of her brain. She felt like something was watching them, something unseen and malignant. Something dangerous.

The craggy pine waved their branches in warning. The wind whimpered and begged them to go home. "Beware," the forest groaned. "Beware!"

The women made it back to Elwood's moments before the valley plunged into darkness. Simone felt her body relax as the gate was bolted shut behind them, a reassuring sound that made her feel like she was being tucked in for the night. When they reached the house, all was silent within, except for the discovery of Elwood asleep at the dining room table again, snoring loudly. It appeared dinner had already been served, and the residents, having supped, had departed to their respective beds for the night. To Simone, the stillness felt like a luxury.

RAID!

Simone awoke with a start; her heart was racing. She looked around the room in confusion as her mother slept, searching for the nameless terror that had crawled under her skin and shaken her from her dreams. Then she heard it: the trumpet was sounding from the guardhouse. Another raid had begun.

Downstairs, the acreage house jumped to life with shouts and doors slamming, feet running swiftly through corridors. Simone peered out the window; she could see Doug and Bob in the yard below, wielding a torch and rushing to reinforce the gate. She threw her shotgun sling over her shoulder and grabbed her hat for luck.

Perla was awake now and thrashing against her bindings in bed, frightened by the commotion. Simone tried to calm her, smoothing her bristling hair away from her forehead and murmuring softly to her, but it had little effect; Perla's eyes were wild with terror.

"I'm so sorry," Simone whispered. "You deserve better than this." She kissed her cheek and then turned and hurried away, her guilt thickening like bile in her stomach. Emerson would have handled their mother's illness better; she knew that. But Simone was the caregiver now. She was the one who had survived long enough to watch everything fall to pieces.

Grace was waiting for her in the hall. "What's going on?" she asked, shivering in the night air.

"Warning from the guardhouse," Simone replied, throwing her jacket to the young woman. "It's a raid. We gotta go."

"Really?" Grace cried. She pulled the coat on and limped after Simone, who was bounding down the stairs, two at a time.

"We've got to get the Parson boys to the basement," Simone called over her shoulder. At the bottom of the staircase, she grabbed Grace's arm to speed her up and pulled her, limping, through the foyer, then the sitting room, then down a long, black hallway stopped by a muscular wooden door. "Usually Doug takes care of the kids, but he's reinforcing the gate," she huffed. "They must be trying to break through."

"Who's trying to break through?"

"Don't know yet. Hopefully we'll live to find out." Simone said, before pushing open the door. Inside Elwood's old library, broad-shouldered bookshelves circled the room like giants guarding two sets of bunk beds in the center of the room. A lone candle was lit, casting a pall on the fearful faces of the Parson boys, who were huddled together in one bed, clutching each other for protection. The youngest boy, Max, was crying, rubbing at his eyes with his hands.

"Hey, guys," Simone said awkwardly as she began loading blankets into her arms. She had none of her mother's knack with children. "Are you ready to go to the hideout now? We have to be quick."

"I saw fire in the window," Max cried. "It's waining fire on us!"

"It's not raining fire," Simone replied. "Come on, Max, you've been through raids before. We'll put you in the hideout, and you can try to sleep. Then we'll come and get you when everything's OK."

"I miss Mom," said Harry, the second-youngest Parson, pausing from a reflective suck of his index and middle finger. He looked down sadly, and a lock of hair fell across his wan forehead. "I want Mom now."

This comment set off the rest of the boys, who all began to cry for their dead mother, a woman Simone envied at this very moment.

"Oh, boys, stop. Please stop crying." She pleaded with them, trying to regain some control. But it was about as effective as yelling into a windstorm; the boys continued to weep, their howls reaching a fevered pitch.

Feeling anxious and frustrated, Simone hurled the bedding to the floor.

"Stop your damn crying!" she yelled at the top of her lungs. "Now!" The boys stopped midcaterwaul and looked up at her in surprise.

She gave them all a tight-lipped smile. "What I meant to say," she continued on in a softer tone, "is that Grace will be staying with you in the hideout tonight."

Grace tried to smile at the boys, but it looked more like a snarl. "What are you talking about?" she asked Simone, without moving her lips.

Simone shrugged her shoulders and gestured to the Parson boys, who were looking at her with interest. "Do me a favor," she said.

"Can you pick another favor?" Grace asked.

Simone's face darkened. "I really need this one."

Grace nodded her head, worked her jaw, and turned toward the boys. "Fine then." She brought her hands together in a loud clap. "Looks like I'll be staying with you guys tonight." She glanced defiantly back at Simone. "Even if I miss the only chance to avenge the murder of my family."

"What's murder?" came Max's feeble voice.

Grace looked at the child and raised her eyebrows. "Are you serious, kid?"

"I'm pretty sure he is," Simone said. "We don't use the *m* word around here." She gave the young woman a long, assessing look. "Can we count on you, Grace?" she asked.

"Of course you can," came the young woman's answer.

It sounded reluctant, but it was good enough for Simone, given the circumstances. "Great, then let's go."

They began shepherding the flock of Parsons through the gloomy house, down the stairs, and into the unfinished basement where old appliances and electronics sat on display like a museum of past civilizations. The effect was both sad and eerie. It made Grace feel nostalgic for an instant, though the sensation soured quickly into sorrow, hate, and a thirst for revenge. She was emboldened by the feeling. "Please reconsider," she said to Simone, pleading with her again. "These kids don't need me. They're old enough to look after themselves."

Swiftly, Simone turned and handed her the candle. Her expression wasn't angry, as Grace thought it would be. Instead, it was softer than usual and full of understanding. "Grace," she said quietly, "if the compound falls, it will be up to you to get them out. There's a secret tunnel in the room, behind the TV. You'll see what I mean. The tunnel's supposed to lead out to the forest—it doesn't yet; we haven't finished the project. But you can hide in there if you need to."

Grace made no reply; her face remained expressionless. "Getting them out of the house is a really important job," Simone said, placing a hand lightly on her shoulder. "You know that. Of all people, you know that."

The young woman nodded mutely.

"Listen, if I don't make it back, Perla's upstairs," Simone continued. "She's too unpredictable to keep with the kids. Grab her if you have time; otherwise there's a loaded revolver in the closet of our room. I don't want her to be at the mercy of the raiders, so make it quick."

Upstairs, there was the sound of shattering glass, setting off another wave of Parson hysterics. Simone dashed to the rickety hutch against the basement wall and ran her hand behind it, finding the lock and releasing it. Then she turned the hutch out like a door, revealing the hidden room it had been so effortlessly concealing. She motioned the children inside; they didn't need further convincing.

"Another one of Lewis's inventions?" Grace asked as she climbed in after the Parson boys.

"Sure is," Simone replied, and Grace was mollified by the look of appreciation in her eyes. "Thank you," Simone said. "After this is over, I promise to make it up to you." She extended her hand, and Grace took it, and for the second time in as many days, the women shook hands. And for the second time, Grace was filled with a surge of hope that coursed through her body, even after Simone had closed the secret door, and she was alone with the Parson boys.

Simone, however, felt no such hope as she hurried back upstairs in the dark. Instead, she was filled with the terror of a hunted animal, provoked into defending itself. She hated raids, and there hadn't been one in so long. She felt rusty, yet the heart-pounding, mind-numbing sensation of going into battle returned to her as if it had never left. There was nothing she wanted more than to run upstairs to her bedroom and her mother, but she didn't. She couldn't. Exiting the house through the kitchen door, Simone rushed headlong into the arms of the night.

DE-FENCE

Screams and shouts cut through the darkness; there was an ominous thumping at the gate. Somewhere, something was burning—Simone could smell it. She whirled around to face the house. Was it on fire? In an instant, the yard brightened and a handful of fiery streaks came whistling over the fence, before plunging into the orchard and garden below. She watched Felicity Walker's bony silhouette rush over to beat out the flames, before retreating back to the safety of the garage.

The whistling noise came again, and fire rained down upon the compound as Simone sought shelter on the porch. One blazing streak stabbed the earth a few yards away from the house. Once the sky looked clear, she ran into the open and toward the flame, smothering it with her hat before kneeling down to inspect the source: a crudely carved arrow that smelled of pine resin, a highly flammable substance. She muttered a few choice obscenities and got back on her feet. The raiders were improving their tactics; this could only make their existence far, far worse.

A gunshot rang out from the guardhouse, a deep, primal boom that cut through the chaos in the yard; it was Zeff's revolver. Simone ran to the guardhouse and climbed up the ladder, flinching as a burning arrow flew past her head, coming so near she could smell the resin burning and feel the heat upon her face. Inside, Barbara sat hunched in the bowels of the tower, peering through the sights of Zeff's revolver. She turned her head slightly as Simone approached.

"What are we dealing with, Barbara?" she asked. "Where's Zeff?"

"It's so hard to see out there," Barbara replied; her voice was calm, but the fear in her eyes shone in the dark. "I don't know where Zeff is, but I've counted seven or eight archers and four men at the gate. I think there's more out there."

"That's a big raid." Simone peered out the window. "Who the hell are these guys?"

"That's what I want to know," Barbara muttered. "We've never had archers before. And just my luck, the bastards are out of range." She had taken a few pot shots to rattle them; she knew Zeff would disapprove of the waste of ammunition, but who was going to tell him? She smiled nervously to herself. It was like she was whizzing through the night in a speeding car, high on fear and giddy to be alive.

There was a terrible splintering sound as the battering ram forced its way through the front gate. Shouts and cries filled the air.

"Good luck, Barbara. Keep 'em at bay," Simone said, before slipping down from the guardhouse. She ran toward the noise.

"Thank goodness you're here!" Doug Parson yelled as she reached the gate. "They're getting through!" His gentle face was twisted into a mask of distress. If the gate fell, the compound would fall. Then, they would be done for—the children and Perla included.

The battering ram retracted from the hole in the gate as the raiders swung it back again, preparing another blow.

"Let me!" Simone cried, motioning with her shotgun. Doug stepped aside as she forced her muzzle through the hole and fired. On the other side of the gate, they could hear the battering ram falling to the ground with a muffled thud. A man was screaming.

"Simone! Simone!" she heard Zeff cry. Looking wildly about the yard, she spotted him by the far west corner of stockade; he looked like he was struggling with something. Without hesitation, she handed her shotgun to Doug. "I gotta go," she said.

"But, Simone—" Doug's voice wavered.

"Just keep shooting!" she called over her shoulder. "There's extra buckshot in the sling."

Arrows peppered the compound as she sped across the yard; she felt the force of them plunging into the ground around her. When she reached Zeff, he had his head tilted back, squinting at the top of the stockade. A large ladder was settling into place, the top rung peeking over the sharpened spikes.

"Is that a ladder?" he shouted to her. "We gotta bring it down!" More arrows came shrieking into the stockade, arcing over the far side of the fence. Hearing their terrible cries, Zeff pulled her to the ground, shielding their bodies with two large garbage-can lids. As they huddled together against the fence, they heard a man's voice on the other side. "Get to the walkway!" he was yelling. "I need archers on that walkway!"

Simone craned her neck and looked up at the shaky wooden gangway that spanned the interior perimeter of the compound stockade. She thought Lewis had been crazy when he suggested they build it, but it had certainly come in handy from time to time—as long as the rotten gangway planks held firm. Simone had put her foot through more than a few of them.

"How do they know about the walkway?" she wondered aloud.

"Must have spies in the area," Zeff answered. "You can see right into the compound from Braggart Hill." He furrowed his brow. "Think it'll hold?"

"I have no idea," she replied. "But it's all over if they get archers up there. They'll be shooting fish in a barrel." A distinct clumping sound was coming from the stockade behind them. She sprang up. "The stairs are by the front gate."

"But I'm right here." Zeff jumped to his feet. "I'll give you a lift. And maybe a catch too, in case the walk don't hold." He laced his fingers together and leaned against the fence. "You got this?"

"I do."

"Take a lid."

With a practiced jump, Simone sprang onto his interlaced fingers. Zeff lifted her up, and she threw the lid onto the walkway first before stretching her hands up and grabbing on to the side railing, holding on tight. Grunting, she pulled herself up onto the shaky wooden structure as it trembled underneath her and she feared it might give way. But she didn't have much time for fear. As she scrambled to her feet, a raider's face came into view: hawkish, grimy, and mean. He had reached the top of the ladder. And he had a knife.

With his free hand, the raider grabbed the top of the stockade. He gripped the knife in the other and slashed at Simone's face with the blade. She ducked and the swipe went wide, throwing the raider off balance. She scrambled for the lid behind her, grabbing it by the handle. Savagely, she began smashing at the man with it, concentrating the blows to his hands and face. The raider tried to block her assault as he clung to the fence, until Simone leaned forward and bit his hand, sinking her teeth into his pine-tar-tasting skin. The man yowled and swiped at her again with his knife, this time catching her on the arm and drawing blood. The wound was deep, and it throbbed and yawned as she dropped the lid and rocked her weight forward, smashing the heel of her hand against the raider's nose. With a sudden cry, he grabbed at his face with his hands.

That was his mistake, and one was all she needed.

Her body pulsing with adrenaline, Simone seized the ladder and shook it with all her might until the raider fell backward, sinking through the air like a heavy stone, his arms open wide in a gesture of surrender. He let out a desperate cry before hitting the ground with a wet-sounding crunch. Simone pushed the ladder down on top of him.

"Incoming!" Zeff yelled. "Get down!"

Simone threw her lid to the ground, then leapt over the side of the walkway, dangling below it until Zeff grabbed her legs. They toppled to the ground together, before seizing their lids again, huddling behind them like shields. They listened to each other breathing as the terrible humming began, followed by the thwack, thwack, thwacking sound of arrows piercing the cold soil nearby. Pine-tar smoke forced its way into their noses and clawed at their lungs.

"We gotta get those archers!" Simone cried.

"You've got that right." Zeff coughed and wiped at his eyes. "They have 'em on both sides." The two friends slouched back against the stockade. There was silence and a heartbeat.

"Think that catapult's ready to go?" he asked.

"We might lose a section of fence," she said. "It's risky."

"They keep firing those arrows, and we might lose the whole house."

Simone thought of Perla, tethered to her bed as the house burst into flames around her. "Let's go," she said, breaking into a run.

They darted across the yard toward the catapult, a dark silhouette against the radiant stars. But before they could reach it, the inventor himself intercepted them as he jauntily emerged from the depths of the garage.

"Hullo, you two!" Lewis hooted at them. "Look who I found hiding."

Monty came trailing out behind him, wearing long under-wear, a blazer, and a bowtie and carrying a large cast-iron pot with some difficulty. "I wasn't hiding," he sneered. "I was conducting a risk assessment. See for yourself." With some effort, he used one hand to retrieve a piece of paper from his blazer pocket and handed it over to Simone. As she unfolded the worn page, she could see it had been separated into two columns by a crooked pencil line. One column had been labeled "Risks," and there were indeed a number of entries below: arrows on fire, men with ladders, gate rammers, compound collapse. The second "Mitigating Strategies" column, however, remained woefully blank.

"Resource managers do the mental heavy lifting." Monty sniffed. "That's the job, and I am fully committed to it."

"Monty, my boy, if you want to live through the night, I recommend you do some *actual* heavy lifting," Lewis said drolly. "Some throwing might be good, too."

"Who are you to tell me what to do? I *own* this compound!" Monty snapped. He shifted the heavy pot in his hands; the contents seemed to be emitting a sharp, acrid smell that seemed familiar. And concerning.

"What's that smell?" Simone asked.

"What? Oh, that's the lye," Lewis replied. "It was left over from the last round of soap making."

"You're dumping lye on the raiders?"

"We are." Lewis tugged at his moustache. "I hope this batch is corrosive enough to do the job."

"We just came from the west side of the stockade," Simone said. "They're putting up ladders."

"Excellent. We'll start there," Lewis replied. "As a famous general once—"

"We want to use the catapult against the archers," Zeff briskly interjected. "Does it work?"

"Of course it works," Lewis replied. "Everything I create works. If I had sired this little fellow," he pointed to Monty, "even he would work."

The little fellow in question smoldered with rage.

"Steady on, lad," Lewis said with a smile. He turned back to Zeff and Simone. "Bring the catapult to the driveway. I shall escort this gentleman to the western wall and will join you presently."

The two war parties went their separate ways, and it wasn't long before Simone heard a thin wailing coming from the stockade. The lye had met its mark.

Zeff and Simone positioned themselves behind the catapult and with some effort, began pushing it forward. The winging wheels began turning, slowly at first, then faster and faster as the massive weapon picked up speed on the slight downhill slope of the yard. By the time they reached the guardhouse, Lewis was already there, waiting for them, hunched over a large, ornamental rock he had rolled from the garden. With an impressive display of huffing and puffing, the inventor eased the boulder into the payload of the catapult and then walked around the great machine, pushing it forward, then pulling it back, moving it slightly to the left, then to the right. He cast an appraising look over his shoulder toward the stockade before leaning down and locking the wheels into place.

The sky behind the catapult glowed auburn. The whistling hum was coming again.

"Now!" Zeff yelled. "Fire the catapult now!"

Lewis took his place by the catapult lever. "I believe it was the esteemed Carl Sagan who once remarked, "Somewhere, something incredible is waiting to be known," he began as the arrows ripped into the earth around them. "Although I certainly thought I understood the meaning of that quote before as a humble physics professor, now, as we are about to step off into the void of the unknown, I truly feel this is the greatest test of my abilities as a man of science. This is, without a doubt, the—"

"Now!" Simone and Zeff shouted in unison.

Lewis shot them a blistering look before pulling the lever. The catapult beam swung high into the air, and the boulder cleared the spikes of the stockade before disappearing from view. Cries of surprise and pain erupted from the other side of the stockade, and more arrows came wobbling over the gate, but there were fewer this time.

Zeff and Simone scrambled around the yard, looking for projectiles as Lewis loaded the catapult again and again. More decorative rocks went over, along with an old toaster oven and the laptop computer Barbara used to prop the kitchen door open when the weather was nice. The catapult made a glorious booming sound each time the beam went high, sending the payload whizzing out of sight.

They fought this way for what seemed like an eternity: ducking, grabbing, running, hauling. They changed the catapult's position four times, chasing the archers, always watching for their arrows until they finally stopped coming. Soon, the sun began to emerge in the east, sending a blaze of red rippling across the sky. The fog crept in across the valley, blanketing the compound in a cotton-wool quiet as the three figures stood by the catapult, waiting, afraid to break the inhaled breath of dawn.

It was a relief to everyone when the trumpet finally sounded from the guardhouse. The raid was over, but assessing and repairing the damage to the compound had only just begun. Soil from the garden was scattered about the yard in clumps. Trees in the orchard had charred boughs and arrows lodged in their trunks. The front gate would need replacing, and wide sections of the stockade had been badly burned. But Simone was starting to feel tired and shaky, and she had to check on Perla. The repairs would have to wait.

As she moved toward the house, she overheard Zeff congratulating Lewis.

"That catapult saved our damn lives," he said.

Saved our damn lives. Damned lives. The words repeated themselves over and over in her head like a song. *What are we saving our damned lives for, anyway?* she wondered. *More of this?* She left the yard and her entire body shuddered as she walked toward the house. Entering through the back door, she thumped down the stairs with legs and eyelids that felt like poured concrete. The adrenaline was leaving her system; apparently it was leaving her with nothing.

In the gloom of the basement, she heard a muffled shriek and experienced one final, strained surge of it. Racing across the room, Simone dove for the hutch, fumbling for the release button to the hidden room. It swung open heavily, and visions of the dead Nowak family flashed through her mind; she reached for her shotgun, expecting the worst.

But that's not what she found in the hidden room behind the wall. Instead, she found a gaggle of Parson boys, alive and well, smiling and sprawled across the bedding in the middle of the room. Little Max was in the midst of getting tickled by Grace and was screaming in delight.

"Is it over?" Harry asked. He almost looked disappointed.

Simone smiled. "It's over. You can come out now." She looked at Grace. "Thanks for watching them."

"The boys were awesome," Grace replied, her face bright with laughter. "Hey, guys—what do you say to Simone?"

"Thank you, Simone," the boys chanted in unison.

"Anything else?" She winked.

The boys licked their hands then put them under their shirts and into their armpits. Flapping their arms up and down, they emitted a chorus of juicy farting noises.

"That's lovely," Simone said.

Grace laughed as she made her way through the room, patting a couple of rumpled heads as she passed. "Now fold the blankets, guys. You gotta put the 'bro' in 'brother'." She looked happy, amused, as if she didn't have a care in the world. But by the time she reached Simone, Grace had dropped the facade and her gaze was all business. "Did anybody from the compound get hurt?" she asked in a low voice. "Who were they? Did you capture anyone?"

"No major injuries," Simone replied, feeling as if she was running from the flaming arrows again. "At least, I don't think there were. We didn't capture anyone—we just held them off. And we don't know who they are."

Grace's eyes rolled in frustration. She pressed her face against the wall and issued a single, unmistakable profanity.

"Gwace?" Max said, tugging at her shirt. "Are you aw-wight?"

She mustered up a smile. "Never been better, kiddo," she said, but nobody in the room believed her.

"OK, boys, back to bed," Simone said, ushering the children out of the room and up the basement steps. They chattered to one another as they flew through the corridors of the house like a flock of chickadees, casting the occasional anxious glance back at Grace. But everything seemed forgotten by the time the Parsons were deposited back in their room in the library. After winning a nonconsensual wrestling match and tucking the boys in, Simone and Grace found themselves in the hall again. Alone.

"Look, I know what you're going to say," Simone began.

"Come on, Simone! You were a park ranger—you can track those guys!" Grace cried.

"It's foggy. And dangerous," she said, slumping against the wall to preserve what was left of her strength. She tilted her head and looked at Grace. "Are you insane?"

"The fog will burn off soon enough," Grace replied, ignoring the question. "We need to find these guys. They could be attacking another compound right now; they could be regrouping for another attack—who knows?"

Simone emitted a low groan. She staggered down the hall toward the stairs, but the younger woman followed her doggedly. "I need sleep, Grace, not another battle. Please just let me sleep."

"No! We'll lose their tracks if we wait any longer!" Grace leaped in front of her. Her eyes were raw with pain, fear and a single, throbbing request. "Please," she said one more time. Then she threw down the last card she had to play. "Do me a favor."

Simone stopped and sighed; she lowered her head. "Can you pick another favor?"

Grace grinned. "But I really need this one."

DISCOVERY, PROPHECY

The women wrapped their faces in bandanas and rode out of the stockade, taking two horses and two guns with them. Grace led the way on Zeff's horse, Peaches, feeling fresh for a fight as Simone lingered behind with Alfred, looking for signs of the war party in the area. But the cold and shifty fog was as persistent as they were, swirling around their ankles and haunting the tree line. It seemed to have no intention of "burning off" and fulfilling Grace's earlier and apparently wishful prediction. Indeed, its only interest that morning seemed to be in getting them lost before summoning large, heavy rainclouds as backup.

Grimly, the women continued their search, and Simone almost fell off Alfred twice, due to the state of extreme exhaustion that had crept into her body. Grace finally suggested that they return to the compound before it started to rain. Then it did—quite hard. They were shivering and sopping wet by the time they made it home again.

Late afternoon brought a storm that prowled around the house like a burglar, rattling at the windows and the heavy wooden doors. The rain drove long and hard across the valley, soaking everything in its path. This would not be a good day for tracking, nor would it be a good day for repairs. So after changing into dry clothes and enjoying a nice long nap, Grace and Simone passed the worst of the storm in the snug farmhouse kitchen, playing cards with Lewis and sipping on roasted-sunflower-seed tea. Perla sat nearby with hands clasped, looking quietly out the window because even now, she still loved a good storm. The other residents did not stir from their quarters, remaining elusive as ghosts. Tired and fearful from the raid the night before, they stayed in their beds, forgoing the pleasure of the woodstove for the bliss of unconsciousness.

"Where is Barbara anyway?" Grace asked, shuffling the soft deck of cards as the rain pounded at the window. "I haven't seen her once today."

"Who knows with you women?" Lewis threw up his hands in mock confusion. "She could have lady issues, you know. Female problems. Could be that blasted Monty. Could be anything."

"Why? What's Monty done now?" Grace asked eagerly. She put the cards down and gave Lewis her full attention.

"It seems the fellow tried to throw lye over the fence last night," Lewis said, as if it was the first time he had ever heard of it. "Apparently some of it dumped on his leg in the process."

Simone almost fell out of her chair. "What? You never told us that. Did you see it happen?"

"Of course I saw it happen." Lewis sniffed. "I was right there. He spilt it climbing the walkway. But I couldn't stay—I had to assist with the catapult, as you know. Barbara tells me he's in terrible pain."

"Oh, God," Grace's eyes were wide. "That sounds gruesome. Do you think I can see him?"

"I dare say you will," Lewis replied. "He's got to come out of his room sometime."

When the storm finally passed, it left behind an indigo sky and a fresh breeze that lured the card players outside. The garden was a mess from the night before, worse than Simone had remembered, and they set about removing arrow shards while Lewis went to have a look at the gate. Before long, Simone could see him walking back across the yard, his face set in a worried frown. Even his moustache seemed to droop with displeasure.

"What's the matter?" Simone called over to him.

Lewis had thrust his hands deep in his pockets; his shoulders were up around his safari hat. His mouth moved, but no sound came out.

"Oh, for heaven's sake!" Grace cried. "What is it?"

"It's…" Lewis started; his voice was high and tentative. "It's…I think…it's possible that…the pit trap caught someone."

"Why do you think that?" she asked.

"I heard moaning." A queasy look spilled across Lewis's face.

"Let's go look!" Grace shouted, grabbing him by the arm with a muddy hand before pulling him toward the gate.

"Wait!" Simone yelled after them. "It may not be safe! Goddamn it." She grabbed a length of rope from the garage and tethered her mother to her side. By the time she had reached Grace and Lewis, they were already on the other side of the gate. The ground beneath them was swollen with rain, and it squished and gurgled with every step they took. Grace led the charge, marching toward the trap. Simone walked a short distance behind her, slowed by Perla, who almost lost her shoes in the mud. Even further behind them came Lewis, who was starting to regret the whole pit-trap idea. He should have never listened to Simone…

"I can definitely hear something!" Grace called back to them.

"Let me check first," Simone said. She tethered her mother to a nearby tree and pulled her gun from its sling before approaching the pit and peeking cautiously over the side.

At first, all she could see was blood comingling with the rainwater from the storm. The sharpened sticks inside the trap were broken and splintered; several held snatches of fabric that fluttered casually in the breeze. Then she noticed a man huddled against the side of the pit, caked in mud and mire. A pair of wide hazel eyes met Simone's as he struggled to breathe.

Beside her, Grace stared at the man with shameless curiosity. "Lewis, you should come see the fruits of our labor!" she called over her shoulder. The resident inventor approached the pit, cast a frightened glance over the side, and stumbled backward, clutching at his safari hat and retching soundly.

Amused, Grace returned her gaze to the man in the pit. "Why did you attack this compound?" she asked, the smile vanishing from her face. "What's your motive? You like killing people, you sick fuck?"

"Take this off," the man said faintly, grabbing at the torn neckline of his shirt. "Get it off me. Sssss'hot."

Curling her upper lip, Grace put her hands on her hips and gave the man a long, hard look of disgust. Unfortunately, he was too far-gone to appreciate the white-hot hatred in her stare, and she knew it. Inconvenienced but undeterred, she spit on him instead.

"Was that really necessary?" Simone said, shaking her head.

"I wouldn't say necessary—but it just felt right," she answered. "Look, this guy's got hypothermia. If we're going to get any answers from him, we better get them now."

Simone looked back at the man in the pit, his face twisted in mud and pain. He might be a raider, but now that she saw him, she pitied him. "Maybe we should try and help him," she said. "He must have been in there for hours."

Grace looked at her as if she'd just proposed a threesome. "Are you kidding me?" she cried. "If we help him, he'll kill us. C'mon, Simone, don't be such a baby."

"He won't kill us. Maybe he knows something about your family." Simone watched the man pulling weakly at his clothes and muttering to himself. "If we make him more comfortable, maybe we can get some answers."

"If we make him less comfortable, we can *definitely* get some answers," Grace snapped.

"Are you ladies having a catfight?" Lewis chimed in. He was seated beside Perla under the tree, a safe distance away from the pit, and had regained some of the color in his face.

"Shut up, Lewis!" the women yelled in unison.

Lewis smiled.

"Fine. Let's pull him up," Grace said, annoyed. "But it's better than you deserve!" she shouted at the injured man.

The women grabbed the man's arms and tried to hoist him from the pit, but his screams of agony convinced them to try another approach. The second attempt was better; the man cursed and moaned, but they managed to pull him onto the grass. Simone turned him on his side and covered him with her jacket as Grace rolled her eyes and sighed a lot.

"Why did you come here?" Simone asked the man gently, kneeling beside him. She could see his teeth chattering in his skull; his lips were blue.

"Horush," the man weakly replied, slurring his words. "Horush."

"Horus?" Grace asked.

The stranger flinched.

"Is that your name?"

He shook his head. "He is coming," the man murmured. "He's coming for you, *slaves*. And there will be no mercy. Only pain." As these last, ominous words dropped from his lips, the man's body began to violently twitch and contort. Then the shuddering stopped just as suddenly as it had begun, and the man's head lolled to the side. He was gone.

"Wait!" Grace cried. "Do you know about my family?" She grabbed the man by the shoulders and shook him. Large circles of blood oozed through Simone's jacket, coating her hands with rust.

The women looked at each other across his body in silence. Only the wind still whispered through the trees, rustling fat pearls of water from their boughs. Simone turned her head and stared across the dripping valley, wondering if anyone was out there, watching them right now. The emptiness rushed in to meet her like an enemy.

"We should get inside," she said. "And we should get that gate fixed right away."

"What was he talking about?" Grace asked, furrowing her brow. "Slaves?"

"I don't know," Simone replied. "But I don't like the sounds of it." She removed her coat from his body as Lewis made a few tentative steps in their direction.

"Is the…individual…er…dead?" he asked.

"He is," Simone murmured; something had suddenly caught her eye. When she removed her jacket, some of the dirt had rubbed away from the dead man's neck, just enough to reveal the contours of a tattoo that was becoming horribly familiar: a single, stylized eye, trickling blood.

"This thing again," she said out loud. "But what the hell is it?"

Lewis peeked over her shoulder.

"That's interesting," he mused. "I haven't seen one of those in a while."

The inventor now had her full attention. "One of what in a while?" she asked.

"The ancient Egyptians called it a *wedjat*," Lewis replied, inspecting the tattoo carefully. "It's also known as the 'Eye of Horus'—god of war. God of the hunt."

THE ANIMALS RETURN

Time trudged on in a slouching, messy fashion, undefined by clock or watch or calendar. Simone felt it pass as the green returned to the valley and the meadows ran riot with wildflowers. At Elwood's Compound, the orchard exploded into a sea of shivering blossoms, and the kitchen garden sprouted shy little seedlings that trembled under the sun. The season was alive with promise; it shone in the rushing rivers and brooks, it glistened in the dew on the leaves.

There had not been any more raids on the compound, nor had there been any further mention of the mysterious Horus. Each day passed in a flurry of activity as the residents worked vigorously around the compound, each person with a separate job to do, as designated by Barbara, who went over her assignments every evening after dinner with the air of a general preparing for battle. Summer had just begun, but winter was already on everyone's minds.

Monty managed to survive the lye incident, albeit just barely. The wound on his leg had blistered and become infected. It wasn't long until gangrene set in, and the smell of the disease roamed the hallways of the house, sending the other residents hurrying outside to escape it. Elwood avoided the room completely and committed himself to drinking as much hard cider as he could. Barbara, on the other hand, remained devoted to her festering son, smothering him with love instead of the pillow she so longed for as she tried in vain to meet his ceaseless demands. Aside from Barbara, Grace was Monty's most frequent visitor, and she was obviously more interested in the wound than the patient.

In a matter of days, it became evident that the leg would have to be amputated in order for Monty to survive—evident to everyone except Monty, that is, who put up a horrified resistance to the idea. Elwood eventually came to the rescue by getting his son drunk. Then Zeff sawed off the leg and cauterized the wound while Simone and Grace held him down, suffering his howls.

Somehow Monty survived the rustic operation, and once the wound began to heal, Grace administered a homemade bee-balm poultice to the stump. Before long, Monty was hobbling about the compound using a branch as a crutch, snooping into the affairs of the other residents and sniping about the quality of their work. The senior resource manager had returned.

Grace, for her part, fit well into compound life, working in the orchard and foraging for wild medicinal and edible plants. On foraging days, she and Simone would ride out into the valley, scouring the hills and wood for all manner of food and game. Simone had begun to look forward to these expeditions, amused by Grace's bright, lively conversation and her impressive knowledge of plant secrets. But Grace's knowledge did not merely extend to plants; she also had an in-depth understanding of the many strange and disturbing diseases of the body, cooped up in a house as she had been with only her father's medical books and journals to read after the storms. Yet Simone had the feeling she hadn't minded it: she seemed fascinated with wounds and injuries of any nature.

Simone could imagine a younger Grace, running her candle low into the night as she devoured the "Tropical Diseases" section of an old textbook.

Over time, the two women developed a friendship that improved the quality of compound life for the entire household. Simone began to feel less wary when she was out hunting and began setting more snares, grateful to have another set of eyes with her. While Grace, emboldened by Simone's steady presence on their rides, tumbled into any thicket of wood, returning with delicate strands of purslane, mushrooms, and fistfuls of mint leaves.

"How'd you know that was in there?" Simone would always ask her.

"You just have to think like a plant!" Grace would always reply.

Like Simone's mother, Grace was keenly observant but in a much different way. While Perla had turned her eye toward artistic expression, the younger woman was far more interested in the external world around her and the people who inhabited it. She was particularly interested in Simone, who was so different from anyone else she'd known. So mysterious! Something about her quiet reserve made Grace wish for her approval. She wanted to make her laugh. She wanted to impress her. She wanted to know everything about her. And it was a good thing Grace loved a challenge, because she found her friend remarkably tight lipped when it came to sharing personal information, always changing the subject when it rested on her for too long, flipping the conversation like a pancake.

But that was all right. Grace understood stubborn personalities. She happened to have one herself.

"You never talk about Emerson," she said one day, out of the blue, surprising herself with the comment as much as Simone. Instantly, she regretted it and chewed at her lip, wishing she could gobble up the words that hung in the air and made her friend look so upset.

"I don't?" Simone's voice was soft, hesitant.

"Well, you talk about, you know, his jokes and when he worked at the ranch and everything. But you never...it's just..."

"You want to know how he died—don't you?"

"I'm not trying to be morbid or anything. But that's something important that happened in your life, and you never talk about it."

"My brother was murdered." Even now, Simone could taste the vomit that had filled her mouth when the policeman had come to the door that night. "He pulled over to help a man with car trouble. That man thanked him by stuffing him in his trunk, shooting him dead, and stealing his car."

"Emerson was murdered before the storms?" Grace asked in surprise.

Simone nodded. "You almost forget that there was crime back then. It was such a peaceful time."

"Did they ever find the bastard who did it?"

"His name was *Harvey*." Simone spat out the word. "Harvey Miller— just some loser who escaped from prison and went on a crime spree. The police caught up with him a few weeks after he killed Em." She stared into the distance so she wouldn't have to look at Grace's face. "When the case finally went to trial, we went every day—it broke mom's heart. But we made it through to the guilty verdict and the sentencing. Last time I heard, he was doing life in Ely Max."

"I hope they tore him apart in there," Grace replied with such savagery that Simone was touched. Emerson would have gotten a kick out of her. Hazen certainly had, and he'd been Emerson's best friend his entire life.

Zeff was often away during this peaceful time, attending seed exchanges with other compounds and looking for livestock. This was no simple task, as many other compounds had eaten all their livestock during the long winter. But Zeff rode up and down every inch of valley, investigating rumors that there was livestock in the area. And when he finally came home, he returned bearing five little brown hens, a rooster, and three goats, secured for the satisfactory price of two hundred candles, twenty-nine shotgun shells, and four good pairs of work boots.

The news that there were animals back at the compound filled the other residents with wild surges of joy. They had eggs now and goat's milk, and one day they would have chicken and goat's meat. Even better than that, they had something to watch at the compound—other than each other. The residents had learned in previous years that animals were as good as TV.

The night of Zeff's return, the residents gathered outside the house, watching as the animals explored the yard, the chickens bobbing about and scratching at the dirt, the goats capering about with the Parson boys, who couldn't resist giving them a good chase. The communal joy and excitement that enveloped the residents at that moment was soon doubled by the arrival of Hazen's caravan as it plodded its way through the gates, bearing a fresh supply of flour, honey, and grain alcohol to Elwood's compound. It was a good time to be alive.

Dusk was just beginning to fall, and the purple cloak of twilight was settling upon the valley when Simone and Grace returned home for the night, their packs jammed full with frog and rabbit meat, wild strawberries, and garlic mustard. Tired but satisfied with the day's yield, the women heard the shrieks and shouting coming from the other side of the gate and froze in their tracks. They looked at one other with worried eyes. An unspoken question hung in the air between them: Was it another raid?

Abruptly, the gate opened, and Zeff appeared on the other side, an irritated look lining his tanned face. "Evening, ladies." He touched the brim of his hat in greeting. "I thought you two would never get back. Most of this house is drunker than a peach-orchard pig and without half the sense."

"What's going on?" Simone asked.

"I'll tell you what's going on," Hazen said, as he sauntered through the gate, hugging Zeff around the shoulders with one arm, and reaching for Grace with the other. "A celebration! That's what's going on!"

Grace struggled to conceal her pleasure at the sight of the tradesman, who had been absent from her life since she'd scorned him in the spring. They had quarreled; she thought of it often, turning the memory over and over in her mind. She'd decided that she'd been justified in her dealings with him but perhaps a bit blunt. And as the days passed, she wished for the sight of his patchwork caravan to come rolling into the yard so they could start over again. Now he was here. Hazen had come back, and he was standing beside her, looking bronzed, shaven, and oh so fine.

"What are we celebrating?" Grace asked coyly. "Your return to the compound?"

"Seeing your beauty, here, in the moonlight—that itself is worthy of celebration," Hazen replied in a husky voice, gazing into her eyes.

Zeff coughed dryly.

Once they entered the gate, the scene that met them on the other side made Simone wonder if they'd returned to the wrong compound. In the middle of the yard, a squealing Max Parson bounced up and down on a large bedsheet held at the corners by Barbara, Doug, Felicity, and Max's eldest brother, Gregory. Simone could see Barbara laughing as Max tumbled through the fragrant dusk, high above their heads. The other Parson boys were running through the orchard after the goats, amid the leafy inlet of trees and the glow of the fireflies.

Drawing closer to the house, Simone spotted her mother tethered to the steps of the porch, petting a lone hen who sat hunched below her, spreading her wings trustingly under Perla's trembling hands. Simone felt her throat constrict at the sight of her mother's tenderness; it had been absent from their lives for so long. She stopped to give her mother a kiss on the cheek.

"Ah, look! The gang's all here!" Lewis called from the porch. "Come one! Come all! And drink from the cup of the immortal Dionysus!" He gestured grandly to an empty glass carafe sitting on the table before him. Slumped in a chair to Lewis's left, Elwood let out a grating snore, a snore that continued as Monty burst out the kitchen door, wheeling wildly on his crutches. A glossy black rooster followed him outside, pecking at the stump of his leg.

"Where the hell did you get this bird?" Monty screamed as Zeff shooed the rooster away. "This chicken is a monster! A monster that is *obsessed* with *me!*" The rooster fluttered to the bottom of the staircase, where it puffed out its chest and swaggered about. "And what the hell is that?" he asked, pointing to a mild-mannered goat that was seated at the table to Lewis's right and blinking at him with benign interest. "That's my seat!"

"All right, very well," Lewis said somewhat resentfully and turned to the goat. "Good day, Master Cornelius," he said, tipping his hat to his silky tablemate. "Monty requires his seat now." By way of response, the goat leaped down from the bench and trotted off in the direction of the garage.

Sitting down felt good after a hard day's ride, and the grain alcohol was swift and sure, melting Simone's legs into something that felt fuzzy and warm. As the dusk deepened into night, they cooked the frog meat over the fire, and the residents sat outside, eating the greasy dinner with their hands. Barbara suggested they sing camp songs, but the only songs everyone remembered were old advertising jingles, so they sang those instead. Then Hazen told ghost stories until the Parson boys started to cry and were taken to bed.

Warm and with full bellies, the compound residents smiled at each other across the fire, and it seemed, for once, that they were all thinking the same thing: "We will get through this together. Someway. Somehow." It was a feeling almost like true happiness.

When Simone met Zeff in the guardhouse later that night, he took a few swigs from a flask and glumly confided that he'd come across more empty compounds on his travels. It was the same story: the residents were gone, and the properties had been ransacked. Zeff was shaken up about it, but the news angered Simone. By the fire, she had been feeling so hopeful about their future. Now she was gripped by fear, and it caught in her throat; she was choking on it.

PERLA GOES

Perla died when the moon was full.

The morning had dawned clear and bright, and Grace and Simone had left the compound for the day, drawn out by the fair weather to venture further into the valley than they normally dared. Overhead, a faint moon watched their progress from the hazy summer sky. Simone had often noticed this lunar companion on their travels, peering down on them as they rode across the valley. She liked how timid and uncertain this queen of the night appeared in the brash light of day, how demure and discreet she could be. But on this day, as they tramped through muskegs harvesting skunk cabbage and cow lily, their astral friend appeared swollen to Simone, almost rotten—a hideous death's head floating in a crystal summer sky.

Later, Simone would realize it had been an omen.

"Oh, my dear! I am so sorry!" Barbara cried once she had returned home, dabbing at her eyes with her handkerchief. "I left Perla in your room this morning. She seemed happy enough there, lying in bed, and you know how I hate to tether her. I went to feed the chickens, and when I came back across the yard, I saw her go tumbling out the window." She pressed the faded floral material against her eyes. "I can tell you it was quick, Simone. She didn't suffer. The poor dear died right on impact."

"Where is she? I want to see her," Simone said. Her voice sounded muffled to her own ears, like she was caught outside in a storm.

"She's resting in the orchard," Barbara said; pressing a small, hot hand against Simone's forearm. "We moved her body there. I'm sure you'll have your own plans for her."

True to Barbara's word, Perla's body had been laid out on a few planks of wood under the shade of an apple tree. The injury from the fall had affected the back of her head; her face wore a look of serenity, and the corners of her lips almost looked as if they were turned up in a slight smile. Simone realized it had been a long time since she had seen her mother with a happy expression on her face. Maybe somewhere, Emerson was making her laugh.

Simone knelt quietly by her mother's side and took her hand. The lithe artist's hand had become a claw, cold and rigid, yet it provided comfort to her still. She studied her mother's familiar form, lifeless and stiffening in the afternoon heat. She leaned over and hugged her, holding her as Perla had once held Simone as a child. She realized she was crying.

My mother is gone. My brother is gone. Now I am alone.

Simone felt an overwhelming urge to return home to Valkyrie House, the place where they had all been together once, so long ago. She should have gone sooner. She smoothed her mother's hair away from her forehead as she so often did and slowly got to her feet, wiping her tears with the cuff of her shirt. When they kept coming, she slapped herself across the face and took a couple of deep breaths. By the time she returned to the house, she had herself together again. Better yet, she had a plan.

Once the Parson boys had been sent to bed, Simone burned her mother's body on a pyre under the dancing northern lights. Most of the residents stayed inside, choosing to avoid the grisly bonfire, except for Zeff, who never strayed from her side, and Grace, who tried to look disinterested as the flames consumed Perla's body.

"I'm going with you to Valkyrie House tomorrow," Zeff said eventually, breaking the silence he knew Simone wanted.

"I'll come too!" Grace offered. "It'll be an adventure."

"I'm not in the mood for adventures," Simone said, keeping her eyes on the flames until they stung from the heat. "As a matter of fact, I'm not in the mood for company either. I'm going alone."

"This isn't a matter of company," Zeff countered. "It's a matter of safety. Have you been closing your ears when I've been telling you what's going on around here? Are you bringing your mother's ashes home, Mona, or is this a suicide mission?"

His face was full of concern, but Zeff's good sense and reason were annoying to Simone. She turned on her old friend, her grief boiling into anger. "Goddamn it, Zeff, I don't need a father, all right? I've never had one before, and I don't need one now. I'm living my own life, and I'm the one who calls the shots concerning it. Do you understand me?"

"You're not thinking straight," he snapped. "You're caught up in your own grief, so you figure you'll do whatever you want to do right now. But we're the ones who'll bear the consequences if something happens to you. You remember that, Simone," he said abruptly before stalking off, disappearing into the darkness.

"You should go easier on him," Grace said, watching Zeff go. "He loves you, you know. He just wants you to be safe."

"Grace?"

"Yeah?"

"Fuck off."

"Fine," Grace evenly replied. "I will 'fuck off.' But just so you know, I'm giving you a pass because of your poor momma." She kissed Simone on the cheek, then turned and went back to the house. Once she reached the kitchen door, she looked back at Simone. "I'm coming with you tomorrow, you know!" she called. "You can't get rid of me that easily!"

We'll see about that, Simone thought as she turned her eyes back to the fire.

THE BALLAD OF OLD BILL

The next morning Simone had Alfred fed, watered, and saddled as the chilled blush of dawn began to creep across the sky. She tipped her head back and shielded her eyes against the sun, wishing its rays would ward off the relentless damp of the morning. But it was too early for that. She thought the sunrise seemed begrudging today, almost lazy. She didn't like it.

"That better not mean rain," she muttered under her breath. The ride back to Valkyrie House would take all day. If she got soaked, she could bank on a fever following.

She made her way to the remains of her mother's funeral pyre and scooped up the cooled ash with her hands. She funneled fist-fuls of it into an old yogurt container and snapped the lid closed, tucking it into her saddlebag as she used to tuck her mother in at night. As her mother used to tuck her in at night.

A chipping sparrow trilled in the trees, and Simone realized she was crying. She was alone with her grief. She was alone. Throwing her shotgun sling over her shoulder and tipping the brim of her hat low over her eyes, she slipped out the compound gate and closed it quietly behind her. Mounting her horse, Alfred, she sat soundlessly in the morning hush, listening, waiting. Hearing only the steady ins and outs of her stallion's breath and nothing more, Simone took her leave of Elwood's Compound.

Assumption Valley, thick with mist, was haunting in its beauty but difficult to navigate as familiar trails became unrecognizable to Simone in the fog. Thickets of wood and scrub seemed to leap out at every turn, sometimes startling both horse and rider, but they continued to trudge their way through the cold-nosed morning.

By early afternoon, the mist had dissipated, and the day grew warm and breezy. Encouraged by the sunshine, Simone stopped in a friendly-looking meadow to let Alfred have a rest. But the fine weather was short lived. By the time she was back in the saddle, the wind had picked up, and the air was bristling under a darkening sky. When the rain finally came sweeping across the valley, the sky was alive with bright flashes of lightning and the steady growls of thunder. They had to seek shelter.

Simone guided Alfred toward an old ramshackle barn she remembered from her wildlife enforcement days, the house beside it long since fallen to pieces. Like all abandoned barns, this one had been a great attraction for wannabe graffiti artists, curious arsonists, and paranoid pot smokers. Once she got lucky and caught a poacher in there, still butchering his kill.

Ahead, the barn came into view, sodden and humped under the teeming rain. It looked so fragile to her now as it trembled and shuddered against the wind. She began to reconsider the wisdom of seeking shelter in such an unstable building as this, but a clap of thunder sounded at her heels, urging her on.

Simone rode straight through the gaping maw of the barn, the doors long since hauled away, and brought Alfred to a halt. He stood panting in the gray light as she dismounted, waiting for her eyes to adjust.

Then a terrible scream filled the air. Alfred's reins jerked hard in her hands as he reared back on two legs, throwing her off balance. Bewildered, she could see the whites of his eyes before something hit her on the back of her head, and there was a blinding flash of stars. Then, there came the dank grittiness of the floor against her cheek; a pair of bloodied feet swam before her eyes. After that, she was pitched into oblivion, and there was nothing more.

When Simone awoke, she was lying on her side atop the rotted floorboards of the barn. As her mind raced to remember where she was, she came to the shocking realization that she was naked, with her hands and feet bound tightly behind her. Somewhere to her right, she could hear Alfred stamping his hooves; he let out a high-pitched whinny that sounded like a woman's cry. The sound sent chills down her spine.

"You seen her wake yet?" a man's voice asked.

Simone fluttered her eyelids shut and lay very still, trying to keep her breathing slow and even. Peeking out from under her eyelashes, she could make out the forms of three men sitting at a rickety fold-out table in front of her, silhouetted against the sheets of rain that tumbled in through great holes in the roof. Bearded and frail looking, the men shivered in their rags as they pushed a pile of decrepit playing cards around the table. One man appeared to be wearing Simone's boots, another, her hat. The rest of her clothing and her small cache of weaponry lay in a pile at their feet.

"Naw, she's out cold," a hoarse voice answered. It was the man who was wearing her hat—Emerson's hat, the one he bought the day he got the cattleman job at Bing Ranch. "I'm going to be a real goddamn cowboy!" he'd hollered as he bounded into the house, tugging on the brim of his new hat. Em had looked so happy then, so healthy; it was strange to see his hat on a man who was neither of those things. In fact, the man bore a closer resemblance to a lizard than her brother, with flitting, reproachful eyes and a thin, bloodless mouth. The lower half of his face sprouted clumps of facial hair that climbed his cheeks like Spanish moss.

"I say we just leave her," the man wearing Em's hat continued. "We can just drag her somewhere and leave her. We got her stuff, why waste a shell? We already said we wouldn't waste shells if we got 'em again."

"Old Bill's gone soft," sneered the man wearing Simone's boots. "Just because you knew her before, don't make no difference now."

Old Bill? Simone's mind raced to recognize the filthy stranger who was silent now as he stretched his legs out under the table.

"You're right, Lyle," Old Bill answered. "I hardly knew her. I mean—we weren't close or anything."

"We should fuck her," the third man suggested. "Hey, dealer, I need another card here."

"I don't have the energy to fuck. Hell, I don't even have the energy to think about it," Lyle said, tossing a card across the table. "I'm too goddamn hungry. Why haven't we killed that horse yet?"

"If you want to try and lead him out of here, be my guest. The bastard already gave me one hell of a bite. But we don't want no more holes in this place." Bill gestured to the leaks in the roof. "It's bad enough as it is." Looking back at his cards, his face grew cunning, and his lips stretched into a wide grin. He threw his hand down on the table. "Read 'em and weep, boys—I got a royal flush! Hand it over!"

Cursing, the other men threw down their cards. The man wearing Simone's boots tossed her shirt to Bill. He snatched it out of the air greedily, pulling it over his torn shreds of clothing with a sigh.

On the floor, Simone gently moved her hands behind her, rubbing her bindings along the rotted floorboards until she felt a jagged edge catch at her thumb. She moved her arms slightly and began to saw her bindings against the snag, worrying the knots against the sharp edge of the wood. The men at the table ignored her as she worked, only glancing down at her once or twice as they gambled for her things. With every hand, the pile grew smaller and smaller, until there was nothing left at all.

"Well, that about does it," Bill said at last, gathering the deck of cards together. "That's all her stuff, and the rain's stopped. I think it's about time we had ourselves some grub." He rubbed his hands together as he spoke. "I'll shoot the horse, but Lyle, you gotta help. That stallion's a two-man job."

"I'll shoot the horse," the third man offered. "I love shotguns. There's nothing better."

"It's my gun now, and I'll shoot him." Bill's voice was commanding as he rose and slowly shuffled toward the door, clutching the shotgun as if it weighed a thousand pounds. "You stay here, Carl, and watch her. She's going to wake up any minute now, so keep your knife handy. She's feistier than you think."

A light bulb flashed in Simone's head. *Bill.* She recognized him now. It was Billy—Billy Cruikshank, a fellow wildlife enforcement officer from her division. They had even worked a few cases together. She remembered liking Billy as a coworker. She had found him to be pleasant and professional, a real animal lover. But the proud and well-groomed man from her memory no longer bore any resemblance to the emaciated creature that was about to kill Alfred.

Carl shambled after Bill and Lyle, whining feebly about shooting the shotgun. As they approached the door, the horse kicked and lunged at the men.

"Goddamn it!" Bill cried. "That horse-fucker bit me again! Grab him!"

A brief struggle ensued, creating just enough of a diversion for Simone to sit up and free the bindings at her ankles before gathering them together in her hands. Lyle tightened the rope that held Alfred, and she watched Bill smash the stallion's neck with the muzzle of her shotgun again and again as the horse shuddered in pain. She tore her gaze from the wretched sight; she had to focus if she had any hope of saving him.

Simone looked around the barn. An impressive scrap-metal collection lined the walls, giving her countless places to hide. The men probably eked out an existence as scavengers, trading their wares for food at local compounds now that the barricade business was booming. Ducking low, she scurried over to a collection of rusted car doors and hid behind them, carrying her bindings with her. Leaning against the wall, she worked feverishly, knotting the bindings together to make one long rope as Bill continued his attack on Alfred. The horse's screams were like a dagger to her heart. She loved that horse, and she had led them into this mess. She was the reason there was no help coming. She would be responsible for his death and her own.

Through the doorless doorway, the gray light spilled into the derelict barn, casting a pall on Alfred and his abusers. The gentle stallion had grown quiet and still; he seemed to have accepted the violence as his fate and no longer fought against it. Finally Bill grew tired and stopped the beating, his body heaving from exertion. He caught his breath and left the barn with Lyle, pulling the broken horse into the open air. They would shoot him and cook him out there; there was nothing else she could do. Simone wanted to scream with anger.

Her wrathful eyes settled on Carl, the man who had been left behind. With gritted teeth, she watched his slow, shuffling return to the center of the room. Then the skeletal figure stopped and looked around; he'd finally realized she was gone.

The man lunged forward and pulled a knife from his pocket. Simone instantly recognized it as one of her own—her sharpest one. *Damn.* Carl held the weapon out in front of him as he moved about the barn in wide circles, glancing about, wildly at first. But Simone noticed he was looking more and more in her direction.

Carl and the knife drew closer, eyeing the amputated car doors with a suspicious gaze until he was only a few feet away from her. Peeking through the pile, she could see his grizzled face. She could smell the rankness of his breath.

Outside the barn, her shotgun went off, and Carl turned toward the sound. Silently, Simone emerged from the pile of car doors and came rushing out of the shadows at him, lowering her shoulder and ramming Carl's body from behind. As he fell forward, she gripped him by the knees and pulled him to the ground. The knife slid free of his grasp and skidded across the floor.

Carl turned and brought his fist down on her head, and they both yelped in pain as she used her legs to kick the knife further away. Although her nudity made her feel vulnerable, it gave Simone an advantage on the ground as she became slick with grime, wriggling out of his grasp as they struggled together on the barn floor. She knew she was better fed and healthier than Carl was; she could feel it. So she bided her time, using the minimal amount of energy required to block his blows and keep him at bay. Once Carl had weakened, she used her full strength to pin him face down on the ground, grinding her knee into his back as he shrieked in pain. She grabbed the rope she made from her bindings and pulled it around his throat, choking off his cries. She held the rope tight as he wiggled and thrashed beneath her, his fingernails scratching at his neck. She kept the rope taut until he became blue in the face. Then his movements stilled completely.

She left Carl's body where it lay, legs askew and hands up around his face. Simone retrieved her knife and ran toward the opening of the barn where the doors once stood, pressing her body against the wall. She waited, listening, her knife at the ready and her heart in her mouth, focusing on nothing except the open doorway and the moment Bill and Lyle would step through it.

Fate would have it that Lyle came through the doorway first, wearing her boots and her pants. The instant the tip of his foot came through the entrance, Simone lashed out with her knife, striking him in the neck with the blade. The man doubled over, making a wet wheezing sound as she withdrew from the doorframe, preparing a second strike.

"Holy shit!" a woman's voice cried out in surprise. There was the ear-splitting crack of a revolver, and Lyle dropped like a possum. Before he was dying; now he was dead.

"Lyle! Oh, Jesus!" Simone heard Bill cry.

"Simone?" It was Zeff's voice, and it sounded alarmed. "Simone, is that you? Are you all right?"

"I'm here!" she called from the doorway. "I'm alive."

"Thank God." He sighed in relief. "Grace, you're a goddamn fool," he said, his voice becoming hard and admonishing. "You could have killed her, shooting your gun off like that. I knew you couldn't handle that revolver. Put the damn safety on before you kill somebody."

"I'm sorry! I wasn't expecting her to jump out of there," Grace replied. "She scared me half to death."

Simone tilted her head around the corner and peered out at her friends, standing under the clearing afternoon sky. Zeff had Simone's shotgun in his hands, and it was trained on Bill, although it didn't seem necessary at the moment; the man couldn't stop staring at Lyle's body.

"I guess I did need some help after all," she said with a ghost of a smile.

Zeff turned in the direction of her voice, a relieved grin cracking his sun-worn face. "I'm glad to see you, Mona. When Grace and I came across these boys about to shoot Alfred, we thought you were already dead. Then they shot at us, and we were almost dead. Good thing this guy's got lousy aim," he said, prodding Bill with the shotgun.

Grace put her hands on her hips and looked at Simone. "You didn't *really* think we were going to let you go alone, did you?"

Simone, who had desperately wanted to be alone and hide away with her grief, now felt overwhelmed by the loyalty of her friends. In the midst of her mourning, she was cared for and protected. More than that, she was lucky, lucky to have that kind of love in her life, long after her family had gone. Her eyes welled with tears; embarrassed, she cast her gaze to the hills in the distance, scrubbed green from the afternoon rain.

"So are you coming or what?" Grace asked, looking at the barn. "This place is beyond creepy."

"Well, I would," Simone said. "But I'm naked. And I'm starting to get cold."

"You're naked?" Zeff said; his dark eyebrows knit into an angry V across his forehead. He grabbed Bill by the shoulders and punched him in the face. Whimpering, Bill fell to the ground and curled into a tight ball, hugging his knees to his chest.

"Zeff, stop," Simone interjected. "They didn't rape me. They just took my clothes. Look—he's wearing my hat and shirt."

"I'll give it back," Bill bleated, struggling to sit up. "I'm sorry. I never meant for this to happen." He got into a seated position and began unbuttoning Simone's shirt with some difficulty. Blood dribbled from his nose onto the collar.

"This guy says he doesn't know anything about the disappearances in the valley," Zeff said, looking hard at Bill. "He even claimed that he knew you."

"He does. We used to work together," she replied.

"OK, so what do we do with him?" Zeff handed her bloodied shirt through the doorway.

Simone studied Bill, her former coworker and current enemy. It was a predicament. "I guess his friends are dead," she replied. "They didn't have much weaponry in there, other than a few dull knives. I say we leave him. He won't do any harm." She finished buttoning up her shirt and came out of the doorway, the garment hanging to midthigh. She grabbed her hat off Bill's head while

Grace tugged her boots off of Lyle's body. Simone's pants, however, were unsalvageable.

"Don't leave me here," Bill begged her. "I can't make it on my own."

"Simone, I have an extra pair of pants in my saddlebag," Zeff said, steering her away from Bill. "Let's grab those and git. It'll be dark soon."

She retrieved the last of her weapons from the barn and returned to the horses with Zeff and Grace. Bill stayed seated where he was, slouched against the front of the barn, his face crumpled in despair.

"Simone, please," he pleaded with her.

"We can't take you with us," she replied. "You hurt Alfred, and you would have killed me. Anyway, we'll have a hard enough time getting food for ourselves out there. But I will leave you some of my rations— for old time's sake." Simone turned awkwardly to go; she couldn't meet Bill's desperate gaze.

"Just shoot me then!" he yelled after her. "Shoot me then, and give me peace! Don't leave me here all alone!"

Simone made no response. She couldn't shoot a man in cold blood, even if he was asking for it. She nuzzled Alfred when she reached him, careful to avoid his neck, which she knew would be sore. She checked the saddlebag and was relieved to see that her mother's ashes were still in there. As she did this, Bill watched her, quietly, hopefully.

Simone pulled out the raspberries and smoked fish Barbara had wrapped for her in skunk-cabbage leaves. She set the food on the ground before mounting her horse, and only Bill's cries followed them down to the river.

RETURN TO VALKYRIE

T he stars were bright enough to guide the travelers on but cast no further light on the path before them. They moved cautiously through the darkness, one horse in front of the other, keeping to the tree line. Sometimes there were noises from the grasping and twisted woods beside them, great cracking and rustling sounds that made Simone jump in her saddle, still shaken as she was from the ambush earlier at the barn. When she tried to think about other things, her mind filled with mountain lions, wolves, and bears, predators that stalked through the darkened undergrowth, sight unseen, licking their beastly chops, watching, waiting. Waiting for the perfect time to lunge from the bushes, pull her from her horse, and tear her to pieces. Her limbs ached at the very thought of it.

Holding her breath, Simone listened. Behind her, Grace was humming something that sounded like a hymn. In the distance, a pack of coyotes yipped and howled. Zeff, as usual, didn't make a sound. He was listening too, and that made Simone feel better—for a little while at least. Then the gates of Valkyrie House came into view, and she was filled with a dizzying combination of relief and despair. They had made the journey in one piece, and that had been harder than she'd thought. However, the destination, her childhood home, looked desolate in the dark. The gates themselves were a miserable sight, overgrown with weeds and badly deteriorated. Only one half of the gate remained standing, held open by an athletic-looking clematis vine that twisted and wound its way through the ironwork. The other half lay defeated as a corpse in the shadows. Simone knew the house would have fared no better.

"Welcome home, Simone," Zeff said after the group had dismounted in an uncertain silence. "You too, Perla," he added and winced, feeling like that was a stupid thing to say. Grace noticed his discomfort and squeezed his shoulder sympathetically, but Zeff only grabbed for his revolver and moved forward, shaking off her hand.

"I'd like to go first," Simone said, her shotgun at the ready.

"Of course, Mona." Zeff courteously stood to the side as she passed. "After you." He looked at Grace. "You watch that revolver now," he grumbled. "For God's sake, keep the safety on."

"I'm keeping the damn safety on," Grace replied. "I know how to handle a gun properly."

"You do? Well, I'd love to see it sometime."

"As if you've never made a mistake in your whole entire life!" Grace snapped. "I forgot I was talking to John Wayne fucking Junior over here."

"Guys, please," Simone whispered. "Let's keep this quiet." With a feeling of nervous anticipation and terrible nostalgia, she walked through the ruined gates and approached her old house, leading Alfred along. She passed the spot where the vegetable garden had once stood, unrecognizable now in its untended and animal-scavenged state. If any people were living in Valkyrie House now, they hadn't been there long—or they weren't living on fruits and vegetables.

She reached the house and led Alfred around to the backyard, hoping the darkness was thick enough to hide him for the night. She stepped back and took a long look at her childhood home, shining dully in the soft starlight. No flames flickered in the windows; no cooking smells lingered in the air. The place looked empty and abandoned. But then she had thought the same thing about the barn.

She motioned for Zeff and Grace to stay where they were. Hunching low, she tiptoed up to the porch and picked her way across the rotting planks until she reached the back door. The wooden door was gone, although the screen door was still there, minus the screen. She tugged at it with her hand. It wasn't locked.

She beckoned to Grace and Zeff, and they joined her on the porch. Taking a deep breath in to quiet the alarm bells ringing in her head, Simone reached for the handle and turned. As she pulled the door open, it released a high-pitched shriek that pierced the very heart of the night. Everyone stood still, afraid to move in the heavy seconds that followed, but only silence stirred in the blackened bowels of the house.

Feeling Simone hesitate, Zeff squeezed her arm and moved through the door first, holding his revolver out in front of him and advancing with a muscular ease. He expected she might be feeling skittish after everything that had happened earlier. Besides, he felt at home in the darkness; it had been descending upon him for months. Darkness was something other folks had to get used to.

Other folks like Grace, for instance, who was walking close at Zeff's heels. She was frowning, simultaneously concerned about dying in this creepy old place as well as killing someone in this creepy old place—at least, if she happened to stumble and shoot the revolver she was carrying by accident. Grace was familiar with rifles, but revolvers were different beasts, and almost shooting Simone had rattled her. She was starting to feel uncertain about herself. That was why she was walking behind Zeff, not Simone.

At the rear of the group, Simone fumbled her way forward, almost overcome by the wave of emotion that had engulfed her the instant she stepped through the door into Valkyrie House. There had been so much laughter here, so many cozy, firelit nights with board games and snacks and scary movies; these walls had been her home. But Simone had to struggle to remember all that. The first memories that came to mind were the bodies of the butchered Nowak family, the blood on the walls, her mother's screams. Simone closed her eyes and willed the terrible thoughts away.

When she opened them again, all she could see was an impossibly dark house, filled with the unfamiliar scent of burned hair and human waste and the mawkish aftershave of filth and decay. But what did she expect? Her family didn't live here anymore; they didn't live anywhere any more. They were gone now, and so was her home; all that remained was its skanky shell, dirty, infected, and sick. It was a place filled with rats and garbage, not love. It was a place where people were murdered.

They were making their way toward the staircase when Zeff stopped suddenly and listened, tipping his head. Then he continued on, moving faster this time, feeling his way forward. Someone was inside the house with them—or something. His finely tuned ears could detect a shallow, rhythmic breathing coming from somewhere nearby. At least he thought he did...

There. He'd heard it again.

Turning toward the wall, Zeff felt the outline of a door with his left hand. He waved to Grace and Simone behind him before getting balanced on his feet. With one swift motion, he kicked the door open.

In an instant, the hallway was filled with screaming—so much screaming. Simone shuddered as the grotesque memories heaved themselves back into her brain. She found herself staring at Irina's dead body again, her blood-hemorrhaged eyes rolled up toward the ceiling as if asking *why?*

"Quiet!" Zeff barked, and the shrieks subsided. "I've got a gun here. Got a couple, as a matter of fact. So I'm asking you to come out, one at a time, with your hands in the air. We don't want to hurt anybody."

After several long breaths, a man stepped through the doorway, holding his hands up in front of his chest. He was stooped and nervous looking and moved wearily, as if he expected a hard kick to the backside.

"What's your name?" Zeff asked him.

"Have mercy on us, sir," the man pleaded in a desperate voice. "They didn't mean any harm! It was my idea to escape! My son is only a child. He was just doing as he was told! You can understand that, can't you?"

There was a brief silence. "What's your name?" Zeff asked again.

The man looked confused. "It's Lloyd, sir. Lloyd Lawson."

"Well, Mr. Lawson," Zeff said, "I have a question for you, so I need you to listen. Who else is in that room?"

"My family—my wife and son."

"Is there anyone else in this house? Anyone at all?"

Lloyd shook his head.

"Well?" Zeff pressed, sounding impatient. "Yes or no? Say it out loud."

"No," he answered, his voice quavering.

"Thank you. Now call them out here."

"Please," the man begged.

"Call them out here," Zeff growled, his voice growing low and menacing. "Now." He squared his shoulders, ready for a fight. He didn't know if he could trust this character, and Simone had already lived through an ambush that day. He didn't want her to have to face a second one so soon, not if he could help it.

"I'm sorry our friend is acting like such a *macho asshole*," Grace interrupted. She holstered her revolver, grateful for an excuse to put it away. "We don't know about any escape," she said, approaching

Lloyd and holding out her hand in greeting. "My name's Grace. We aren't going to hurt you. We just need to see who's in there— it's a safety precaution."

The man's breathing steadied as he looked at Grace. He took her hand as if he were unsure of what to do with it. His fingers felt so thin in her grasp; Grace could feel the bones with startling intimacy as they settled around her own. "Never seen a woman general before," he muttered, turning his head to the open doorway. "You can come out now!" he called over his shoulder. "It's OK."

A woman emerged from the bathroom in a filthy dress that was torn in unexpected places. Her shoulders were exposed; they looked spectral in the darkness and as sharp as two crescent moons. She held the hand of a young boy who clung to her in fear. His belly was bloated with starvation.

"This is all of you?" Zeff asked. The family nodded, their heads moving up and down with varying degrees of vigour. "Yes?"

"Yes," the man answered.

"Are you taking us back to Horus?" the woman asked quietly.

There was that name again. Grace and Simone exchanged looks of surprise. "Who *is* Horus?" Grace asked.

This time, it was the family who looked surprised.

"If you've never heard of Horus, you've been living in a goddamn paradise," Lloyd replied, and his voice sounded strange and bitter in the dark.

THE REFUGEES

Lloyd Lawson introduced his wife, Claire, and their young son, PJ. Starving and in rough condition, the family had sought shelter at Valkyrie House after traveling for days on foot. Standing closely together, the Lawsons clutched at each other and gripped hands. They seemed like good people, with kind eyes and honest intensions, but there was also a feeling of anguish that hung over them, as if suffering clung to their skin like the lingering smell of wood smoke.

And they had mentioned that name again.

That mysterious name.

That terrible name.

Horus.

But the family was famished and weakened, and their hoarse voices made it clear that it was too soon for them to talk very much. Putting an end to Grace's mountain of questions, Zeff retrieved his canteen from his pack and gave it to the family, which they passed between themselves with a thirsty urgency. Then he produced his salted-meat rations and divided it into three portions, dispensing it to the Lawsons in small portions so they wouldn't get sick

"Now let the food sit a little," Zeff instructed the family once they had finished. "We won't bother you. It can be hard to wake your stomach back up."

Leaning against the mantle on the other side of the room, Grace frowned and thought about Horus, the man whose name had been spoken with such terror. Was he one of the men who had murdered her family? Was he somehow responsible for their deaths? She longed to ask the Lawsons more about him, but Zeff did not want them to be disturbed until they had *digested*. That was so like him. Grace wanted to shriek with frustration and pummel the air with her fists.

Catching sight of little PJ, she watched the boy until he felt her gaze and grew anxious, drawing closer to his mother. Feeling guilty, she quickly looked away. She knew in her heart that Zeff was right to be patient with them—PJ in particular. If she wanted answers, she would have to wait. With a relenting sigh, Grace decided to make herself useful. Holding her nose and emitting the occasional gagging sound for effect, she cleared the debris from the fireplace by opening a window and hurling it outside. Then she set about making a decent fire.

As she was doing this, Simone decided it was time to face the vestiges of Valkyrie House and all the ghosts that might be lurking there still. Treating herself to the luxury of a candle from her saddlebag, she walked upstairs in the direction of her old room. Reaching the door, she took a deep breath and pushed it open with some difficulty, revealing the squalid state of the room inside. She took an involuntary step back and drew her candlelight over a pile of feces that looked human.

"What was I expecting?" she said out loud. The windows had been shattered, and the room was damp and smelled savage. Bags of garbage and tin cans littered the window ledges and the floor.

There was something in the far left corner that resembled a giant mound of hair, and suddenly Simone felt herself slipping back there again, back to the afternoon it had happened, back to finding the bodies of Irina and the Novak children on the floor. Back to all that blood, congealing in an afternoon patch of sun.

Rubbing fitfully at her eyes, Simone ventured down the hall to her mother's room, before being bowled back by the rancid smell of urine. She covered her nose with the sleeve of her jacket and pushed her way inside. Her mother's bed was gone, her bookshelf was gone—even her big wooden desk was gone, probably burned as kindling in the fireplace downstairs. Breathing through her mouth, she picked her way across the piles of animals bones and teeth to search her mother's closet, but not a single scrap of Perla Hardy remained anywhere.

The root cellar, on the other hand, had not been discovered and had a far better yield. Simone found their old blankets and bedding, moldy and speckled with spiders, but they could be shaken out upstairs. The rough wooden shelving in the corner still held a few jars of food that they had left behind in their haste to leave Valkyrie House. Canned plums and briny pickles pressed their bright colors against the glass. There was also a small jar of wild-raspberry jam, and behind that, an elderly can of sardines they had been keeping in case of an emergency sat unopened. Simone smiled; there was some comfort here after all.

By the time she returned to the living room, the floor had been cleared, and the house smelled less feral. A fire was crackling in the fireplace, and Zeff, Lloyd, and Claire were seated in front of it, deep in conversation. Grace appeared to have found and killed several rats in her absence and was busy dismembering them in front of PJ. He watched with great interest as she grabbed a three-pronged stick and pierced the chunks of rat meat with it.

"And now," she said to the child, "the rat kabob is complete. Seriously, you have to try it. It's way better than it sounds." Raising her eyes, she caught sight of Simone. "Welcome back," she said with a smile, raising her bloody trident. "We've got rat kabobs on the menu tonight!"

"I found a few treats as well," Simone said, setting the pile of blankets down and exposing the jars of canned plums and pickles, the jam, and the little tin of sardines. PJ stared at all the food in astonishment but made no movement toward it. In the firelight, she finally got a good look at the boy, noticing with a shock that he had a nasty wound on the side of his head where his left ear should have been, but wasn't. She opened the tin of sardines and held it out to him. His expression grew anxious, but he took a few faltering steps toward her before snatching the tin from her hands and backing away again, keeping his eyes down.

"I'm sorry about that," Claire said in a tired voice. "Old habits die hard. Small bites, PJ!" she cried as he gulped back the fish like a starved pelican. She smoothed her red hair back from her face as she made her way over to her son. "You don't want to get sick again, sweetheart."

Simone retrieved the yogurt container with her mother's ashes and placed it carefully on the mantle before taking a seat in front of the fire. The warmth chased the damp from her bones, and she felt almost a violent pleasure from the sensation. After a brief struggle, she managed to get the jars of plums and pickles open, and it wasn't long before the group had huddled together on the floor, grabbing at the slippery meal with their fingers and devouring it happily.

"I can't remember the last time I ate something this good," Claire said, slurping the juice from her fingertips. "I forgot I loved plums."

"There are a few plum trees out back," Simone said. "We can see how they're faring tomorrow in the daylight."

"That would be wonderful," Claire replied. "Horus didn't permit laborers to eat fruit."

Grace, who had been prowling the room like a caged lion, perked up noticeably; she had her opening.

"Who is Horus?" she asked Claire. "What can you tell us about him?"

PJ looked tearful and leaned his head against his father's shoulder. Lloyd pulled the boy against him and cradled him in his arm.

"We lived just east of Saint Kitts," Claire began, her voice sounding hollow and out of tune. "After everything went dark, we lived on what we had in our pantry until it was empty. Then we starved. The children...the pain of it at first was too much for them. Scavenging for food became impossible. There were mobs, rioters. It was dangerous..." Claire pressed her lips together until they turned white. "There was a rumor about a settlement—a few days to the east by foot. They said there was food and water there, even jobs. It sounded so pleasant, so *normal*." She gave a harsh-sounding laugh and shrugged. "We thought it was being run by the government, so we left our home to find it on foot. We had a daughter then, Maizy. But she died on the way." Tears began dribbling down Claire's hard-lined cheeks. "When we buried her, I thought that was the worst day of my life, but you know," she swiped at her face with her chapped hands. "It actually wasn't. I used to think about that day all the time. It brought me comfort, knowing she would never have to experience the cruelty of the New Empire."

"The New Empire?" Grace repeated.

"That's what Horus calls it," Lloyd said angrily. "I call it hell on earth."

"When we got to the settlement, we knew we'd made a mistake," Claire continued. "We dragged ourselves into a field...that field..." she began to shake with the memory of it. "He calls it Deserters' Row. But we didn't know that at the time. We didn't know where we were." She started crying again. "Everywhere we looked there were heads on spikes, bodies that had been propped up like scarecrows.

Naked torsos...staring, glassy eyes—hundreds of them it seemed, hundreds and hundreds and hundreds of them. The grass under our feet was dead, drowned in blood, and birds circled the sky above us, screaming like demons." She covered her eyes and swallowed hard. "We were trying to leave when they attacked us. They beat us...even PJ," she said with a sob. "They beat all of us."

"Who beat you? Horus?" Grace asked, ignoring Zeff's look of reproach.

"No, his generals," Lloyd replied, as Claire struggled to compose herself. "The generals police the New Empire and report everything back to him. You can identify a general by his neck tattoo."

"The Eye of Horus," Simone murmured.

"They run the show at the New Empire—more or less," Lloyd said. "As long as Horus gets what he wants, they have free rein."

"And what does Horus want?" Grace asked.

"Power," Claire replied. "The man calls himself an emperor, for Christ's sake."

"He wants something more than that," Lloyd said quietly, looking at his son. "Something far worse." When he looked up again, his face was grim. "Once we were captured, we were split up. I tried finding Claire and PJ, but no one would help me. That's how I found out about the 'Redemption Sessions.'"

"What's that?"

"*That*," Lloyd said, "is Horus's punishment for bad behaviour. If you step out of line at the New Empire, he would torture you—in front of everyone, like some sort of show. I always looked for my family in the crowd, but I never saw them." He grimaced. "Until one day they brought PJ up on the stage. A general had reported him for food hoarding. But before I could think of what to do, Horus had strapped him to a table and hacked off his ear with a hunting knife."

A collective gasp filled the room. Lloyd hugged PJ closer.

"They wrapped some filthy bandages around his head and sent him back to his house, but I followed him back and memorized the address. After I was promoted from meat grinder to wagon driver, I began driving generals out to hunts and raids, and I got to know the area. One day on a trip through town, I saw Claire coming out of her house. The next morning I was assigned to pick up a shipment of prisoners, and I knew it was time to go."

"He was so courageous," Claire said, smiling at her husband. "I found him waiting outside the front door of my house that morning when I left for work. I remember it was a gray day. I was so tired; I didn't know how I was going to survive it. Then I heard Lloyd's voice say, 'Miss? Please come with me.' And we got in his wagon and left."

"We stopped at PJ's house next," Lloyd said. "Claire went in and got him."

"Simple as that?" Grace asked.

"Well..." Lloyd and Claire looked at one another. "His supervising general was there. We had hoped he wouldn't be."

"And?" Grace said, hanging on their every word.

"Let's just say," Claire said flatly, "he learned that you don't take my boy and leave a knife lying around."

"Cool," Grace breathed.

"Of course, escaping was the easiest part," Lloyd said. "The generals started hunting us right away. We weren't far from the Empire before they were already on our trail. They've never stopped chasing us." He looked up at his audience with haunted eyes. "And if they catch us again...we end up in Deserters' Row."

A hush fell over the group as they considered the full horror of that final statement. Faintly, the crickets sang outside under the silent stars. The fire rustled quietly in the fireplace like an obedient child at play. Then there was the squeal of the back door opening and the sound of heavy footsteps coming down the hall.

HATCHING A PLAN

*T*hump...*thump*...*thump.*

These were the sounds of a stranger, an intruder. An attacker. Simone readied her shotgun and pressed her body into the corner of the room, surrendering to the shadows that waited for her there. She cursed quietly under her breath; they should have never built that fire.

The footsteps continued their slow, almost languorous procession toward the living room as Grace covered the Lawson family with the blankets from the root cellar. Then she sauntered over to the fireplace and leaned against the mantle as if she hadn't a care in the world. Casually, she unsheathed her knife and examined the blade in the flickering firelight.

The footsteps drew closer still.

In her darkened corner, Simone shook her head at such recklessness. Nervously, her eyes searched the room for Zeff and found his familiar form hiding in the corner across from her, revolver at the ready. She almost smiled at the reassuring sight.

The footsteps were upon them now.

By the warmth of the fire, Grace planted her feet and gripped her knife. Her face was set and determined, her jaw jutting ever so slightly. This time, she would not let revenge escape her. No, this time she would grab it by the throat and beat the living hell out of it.

"Well, now, Miz Grace," a velvety voice drawled from the doorway. "I know we don't always see eye to eye, but that's no reason to hold a grudge."

It was Hazen. Unmistakably, undeniably Hazen.

Breaking into a smile, Grace tucked her knife into its sheath and ran across the room, throwing herself into the tradesman's arms. He lifted her off the ground, crushing her body against his until she accidentally knocked his hat off while she was peppering his face with kisses. Hazen laughed, pleased by the onslaught of affection.

Once he'd put Grace down again, Zeff stepped forward to greet him. "Hazen, I'm glad you're here," he said. "I hope you will settle for a handshake from me." And the two men shook hands, friends for the time being.

When Hazen saw Simone, his handsome face grew sorrowful. "Oh, Mona, honey," he said, giving her a long hug. "I'm so sorry to hear about your momma. She was one heck of a lady."

"Thank you," Simone whispered.

Hazen squeezed her shoulders and took in the vestiges of the old living room. "When I heard you were coming back here, I thought it'd be nice to see the place again." Releasing her, he walked over to the fireplace mantle and ran his fingers along the molding. "Probably the last time I was here was when—"

"Em was still alive," Simone said. "I was just thinking that."

"Hazen, this is Lloyd, Claire, and their son, PJ," Grace said as the family emerged from the blanket heap. "They're staying here. You actually missed out on a jar of plums. We've just finished eating it."

"Good thing I didn't come empty-handed then," Hazen said, retrieving two flasks from the interior of his jacket. He grinned. "And something for PJ, of course." He handed Claire a small green apple, and she smiled with pleasure, tucking it into a pocket of her dress.

Soon everyone was seated on the floor in the living room, roasting rat kebobs and passing around Hazen's flasks to keep their innards warm. The Lawsons recounted the story of the New Empire again for Hazen's benefit, and after hearing it, he looked like Simone felt—frightened. For a long time after that, he didn't speak. No one did. Until he said, "I heard Horus was ruthless, but I had no idea he was so evil."

Grace stared at Hazen. "You knew about Horus?" Her expression was growing dark and angry.

"I'd heard rumors on the trade route," Hazen sputtered. "I didn't know he was torturing people!"

"You are such an asshole!" Grace looked at him scornfully. "You knew about the New Empire, and you didn't tell anyone about it?" Agitated, she stood and began pacing the room. "I never saw my family's bodies, you know. The flames were too high." She looked at Simone. "Is it possible that they're still alive? Could they be at the New Empire?"

No one answered.

Grace turned toward the Lawson family in desperation. "Did you meet any Gatemans when you were there?" she asked. "A Lora or a Bruce?"

Claire and Lloyd looked at each other and shook their heads. "Sorry, sweetheart. Doesn't ring a bell."

"Grace, listen." Hazen reached for her, but she pushed him away, and his eyes grew cold. "I didn't tell you about the New Empire because I knew you couldn't handle it, OK?"

"What the hell are you talking about?" Grace asked.

"I was worried you'd come up with some ridiculous plan to go there and get yourself killed." He raised a pair of well-groomed eyebrows. "Well? Am I wrong?"

"I'm not leaving my family to die!" she shouted at him. "You selfish bastard!"

"You don't even know if they're at the New Empire!" Hazen yelled back. "You must be bat-shit crazy!"

"She's loyal; there's a difference," Zeff interjected, looking up from the revolver he'd been cleaning. He scowled at Hazen. "Grace is sticking by her family, right through to the end. I wouldn't expect you to understand something as profound as that, Hazen, given your history. When there's trouble, you like to cut and run. Ain't that right, son?"

"Not this again." Hazen clutched at his head with his hands.

"Emerson's best friend for twenty-five years, and where were you after his murder? Consoling his family? Checking up with Perla and Simone? No. You were gone, baby, gone. I barely caught sight of you at his funeral."

"Why do you always bring that up?" Hazen said sadly. He shrugged his shoulders. "This situation has nothing to do with Emerson. And Em's murder…" his voice wavered. "Em's murder really fucked me up, OK? I wish you'd stop talking about it."

"I'm talking about it because I'm making a point," Zeff said, refusing to back down. "You can only handle reality when it's pretty enough for you, Hazen, when it looks as good as you do. Once things get ugly, you're out of there. There's only empty space where you used to be, and empty space doesn't help anyone. Do you understand what I'm telling you?"

"Listen, I didn't think we'd have to worry about Horus," Hazen said. "I thought he would stay to the east. I didn't know he'd be so ambitious."

"What do you mean by 'ambitious'?" Lloyd asked, looking at Hazen intently.

Hazen stuck his tongue in his cheek and pressed on with the bad news. "On my last run, most of the compounds on the eastern route had been ransacked; some of them had even been burned to the ground. Elwood's Compound is one of the few left standing in the area."

"What are we going to do?" Claire cried.

"I'll tell you what I'm going to do," Grace said, putting her hands on her hips. "I'm going to the New Empire, instead of waiting for it to come to me."

"Be reasonable!" Hazen cried in exasperation. "Even *if* your family is there—and that's a big *if*—you can't sneak yourself into the New Empire, find them, and sneak out again. Haven't you heard a word the Lawsons have been saying? The generals will hunt you for the rest of your life!"

"How can I live with myself, wondering if my family is still alive?" Grace snapped. "Wondering if they're being tortured!"

"That's right, *live* with yourself," he replied. "The key word here is *live*, Grace. You won't be living with yourself—or anyone else, for that matter—if you go." He grabbed her hand and enveloped it with his own. "Just think about it," he pleaded.

Grace shot him a look that smoldered with rage. "I have thought about it." She bit off every word as she spoke. "If my family's still alive, I will find them, whether anyone comes with me or not."

Hazen threw up his hands and shook his head. "Well, I for one will not be going with you," he said. "I refuse to watch you serve yourself up on a platter to Horus and his generals."

"You just don't want to get any blood sprayed on your nice sweater," she retorted. "Zeff got you right. You're a damn coward!"

Hazen jerked his head back as if he'd been slapped. He grew pale as he worked his jaw back and forth, grinding his teeth. Simone was astonished; she'd known Hazen all her life, and she'd never seen him this angry. But Grace didn't appear to care. She looked at the other faces around the fire. "Does anyone want to come with me?" she asked.

"I'm sorry, Grace. I understand how you feel, but we won't be going back," Lloyd said. Claire nodded in agreement, careful not to wake PJ, who was sleeping with his head in her lap. "I think it's best for us to keep moving."

A silence fell.

Simone cleared her throat, and everyone's eyes were suddenly upon her. "I'll come with you," she said.

"Oh, thank you!" Grace cried, grabbing Simone by the shoulders. "I really think we can do this!"

"You just might," Zeff said thoughtfully. "If you kill Horus." He turned to Claire and Lloyd. "What can you tell us about the generals?" he asked.

"From what I've heard, Horus is an extremely paranoid man," Lloyd replied. He rubbed at the hook in his nose. "He thinks his men will assassinate him if they become too powerful, so only he and a few other generals have guns. Most of them carry clubs and knives."

"Really?" Zeff was surprised. "The New Empire doesn't have guns?"

"The New Empire has lots of guns, but only Horus knows where they are," Lloyd replied. "He doles one out to a general every now and then—he calls them the Berserker Class. The rest of the stash is hidden away somewhere."

The conversation died away again, giving Simone time to consider their position. Even if they made it out of the New Empire alive, the generals would hunt them. And Horus's men had already attacked the compound once; next time it might fall. On the other hand, the women had the element of surprise in their favor, an asset that had often tipped the balance of war. If they could get to Horus, they could cut the head off the dragon; that would certainly hinder the expansion of his empire. And if the man was as paranoid as Lloyd claimed he was, they could use that to their advantage. Horus would be so busy with his invisible enemies, he would never see the real ones coming.

Simone looked at Grace. "If we kill Horus, we'll never get out of the New Empire alive."

"Yeah, but neither will he." Grace smirked. "We'll make damned sure of that."

"What about Elwood? What about the compound? They rely on you!" Hazen cried. "There are generals all over this valley! With you two gone, the compound will fall!"

"How do you know the compound will fall?" Grace wheeled on him angrily. "The other residents are capable defenders. And the catapult is working now. They're well protected."

"Would you like to stay at Elwood's Compound for a bit?" Simone asked Claire. A look of panic spread across the woman's haggard face. "It's behind a huge stockade, and they have lots of supplies," she continued. "Just stay a night or two, and see how it feels. You could get some food and rest at least for the time being. And there are other boys there. PJ might like that."

Claire looked at the dozing child in her lap. He whimpered in his sleep as the firelight licked at the dark hollows around his eyes. Lloyd was just as concerned about him as she was; he told her last night that he didn't know how much more running the poor boy could take. The long days of traveling, the bitter pains of starvation, the all-consuming fear they would be found—it was unbearable for her. And PJ was just a child.

"Lloyd, let's go to the compound, at least for a few days," Claire said finally. "It might help him."

"All right," Lloyd agreed, but his eyes still looked weary and fierce, and Simone thought he looked like a featherless eagle as he pushed his face toward the fire. "We'll try it out and see how he adjusts."

"That's great. I think you'll like it there," Simone said, in an overly cheery voice that in no way reflected her emotional state.

She was relieved they had found a safe place for the Lawsons for the time being, but the wolves were circling.

"It's late," Zeff announced. "We should hit the road early tomorrow. Hazen, can you take the Lawson family back to the compound with us? We should probably pick up a few supplies before we leave for the New Empire."

"*We?*" Grace smiled.

"That's right," Zeff said. "I'm coming too. And we'll need to introduce Elwood to his new tenants before we go."

"Fine," Hazen said in a manner that suggested it wasn't fine at all.

"Thank you for your cooperation," Zeff tipped his hat in Hazen's direction. "So there's our plan. Now let's get this fire out before it attracts any more *unwanted* visitors."

Hazen bristled at this, but Zeff ignored him. "Simone, how's the old root cellar holding up?" he asked.

"Snug as a bug," she replied, as the place was definitely snug, and there appeared to be many bugs. "Doesn't look like anyone's been down there since we left."

That night, Zeff, Simone, and their five new guests slept in the root cellar for one last time.

It was dreadful.

HIGH OAKS

The sleeping arrangements in the root cellar were cramped; the blankets, sodden with mildew. After a fitful slumber, the weary travelers awoke the next morning, anxious to depart for Elwood's Compound. While Hazen was hitching up the horses, Grace and Simone foraged in the yard, picking Labrador tea and early plums and cherries from the overgrown orchard. Finding a rusted shovel under the porch, they dug up patches of sorrel and chickweed from the rangy, thistle-choked garden.

"Hazen's got some containers we can use as pots," Simone said. "Barbara's going to love this. She's got a thing for sorrel. It reminds her of lemons."

Grace took her friend's arm. "Are you going to scatter your mum's ashes here?" she asked gently.

Simone's expression grew drawn and sad. "I was just thinking about that. She was proud of this garden. I thought it would be a perfect resting place for her. But seeing it now…it seems so lonely. I don't think I can leave her here."

Grace looked around the yard. "Do you know a better place?"

"I think so," Simone replied. "But Zeff isn't going to like it."

When they returned to the caravan, it was already loaded and ready to go. Even the Lawson family members had been packed up and were hanging their heads out the back, eager to hit the road.

"How was the ash scattering?" Zeff asked when Simone was close enough, peering at her with concern. He willed his betraying eyes to see her face, to see her expression, but it remained a blur. "Is everything OK?" he prodded. "Simone, are you all right?"

"She still has the ashes," Grace said. "She doesn't want to leave them here."

Simone waited for Zeff's reaction, but it was Hazen who spoke first. "Em's grave. High Oaks Cemetery. That's what you're thinking, right? That's the perfect place for Perla."

"Now, Simone," Zeff said, "you know how much I cared for your mother, but we've got to get going. We can't be making any more stops. We should already be on the road by now."

"Zeff, you're so worried about dying, you're not living anymore," Hazen said. "Perla is dead, and Simone's grieving her. C'mon, old man, you're the judge and jury of appropriate expressions of grief around here, right? You should understand."

Zeff glowered in Hazen's general direction.

"We'll only stay a minute," Hazen reassured him. "It's practically on the way."

Simone gave the tradesman a look of gratitude, and as their eyes met, she remembered the feelings she had for him once, when he was her brother's best friend. Even as a boy, Hazen had known how to talk to women, always saying hello to her and inviting her on their adventures, giving her ponytail a playful tug whenever he walked by. But those were the days when Emerson was alive. Hazen had been different back then. She had been different too.

Once they were on the road, it didn't take long to reach High Oaks, even with Hazen sticking to the back trails to avoid ambushes. Passing acres of woods, they turned into the cemetery entrance, and the wagon bounced its way down the winding drive, past the sobbing stone angels clothed in ivy. Then they were among endless rows of headstones, just visible above the heads of wildflowers that seemed to turn and watch as they passed by. Simone climbed up to the driver's seat with Hazen so she could get a better view. The graveyard was neglected and overgrown just as Valkyrie House had been, but it seemed more peaceful there, more inviting. Leaves and petals shone with the morning dew; songbirds whistled in the trees. Perla had come home.

Hazen and Zeff accompanied her to Emerson's grave while the rest of the party remained in the caravan. It was on the perimeter of the cemetery, close to the surrounding woods, and in deep shade. Plumes of grass concealed her brother's headstone, but Simone still found the grave with ease, resting in its familiar place under a sprawling linden tree. She tore at the blades of green that obscured his name, plucking them from the earth before she knelt forward and touched the engraving with her fingertips:

In Loving Memory of Emerson Hardy
In Life We Loved You Dearly
In Death We Love You Still
You Haven't Been Forgotten
What's More, You Never Will.

Hazen and Zeff stood behind her, staring at the grave they had both visited countless times before but always alone. The breeze rushed through the cemetery like a ghost train, stirring the trees and the wild grasses that swayed around their knees.

"We need to get moving," Zeff said nervously. "We've already stayed longer than we should."

"Zeff, why don't we head on back to the caravan now?" Hazen said. "Simone will come along when she's said good-bye." He put his arm around the older man's shoulder and led him away, leaving Simone to scatter her mother's ashes alone, amid the steady hum of the cicadas. Crouching back on her heels, she surveyed her work. Her family was together again.

"Hold it," a man's voice said at her back. "Don't make any sudden movements. Get up slowly, and put your hands in the air."

Palms open, fingers spread, Simone rose slowly from her brother's grave. Raising her eyes from her brother's headstone, she looked over her shoulder and was disheartened to see a giant of a man with a brown beard and a black eye. He wore thick leather pants in the morning heat and a mangy vest with no shirt underneath, exposing his pimply, barrel-shaped chest. He had a handgun trained on her—a Colt .45, by the looks of it—but Simone was far more shocked to see the man's beer gut jutting over the waistband of his pants. His well-fed appearance was unusual to see—almost obscene. She knew in an instant he was a general, and not only that, he was Berserker Class. He must have been hiding in the woods.

"What are you doing?" Simone asked, stalling for time.

"I was going to ask you the same thing, sugar bear," the man replied. "Since I have the gun, you go first."

"I was visiting my brother's grave."

"How touching. All alone?"

Simone searched the general's face; how much did he know? Had he already seen the caravan? Was he alone? Had he captured everyone else? Was the question a trap?

"All alone," she replied.

"Ain't that something?" the general grinned. "Lucky thing I came along when I did." Unhurried in his movements, the man removed Simone's shotgun sling from her shoulders, slipping it off her body like a dress. He licked his lips, and the tip of his tongue protruded grotesquely from his mouth. He moved further behind her. "Start walking," he said poking her in the back with his gun. "Slowly."

But Simone hadn't taken a single step before she heard the muffled cries behind her, accompanied by a series of sharp slapping noises. She turned in time to see the general's body slump to the ground. And there was Zeff, standing in his place, retrieving his knife from the man's throat.

Throwing her arms around the rancher, Simone laughed with relief. Surprised, Zeff looked down into her face, squinting and smiling. He was trying to see her, as much of her as he could, wringing his faded vision for familiar shapes and lines. He could feel her body trembling with adrenalin; then she stilled in his arms.

"There's a second general coming!" she shouted, breaking away from him. "He's running! We better cut him off before he gets to the woods!"

Zeff could hear rustling in the grass; he could tell something was coming, and it was big and fast. Then he caught the shadow of a man's form running past, and he bounded after it. Simone retrieved her shotgun and the .45 before chasing after them. Small, squeaking creatures scampered to get out of the way as she sprinted through the unkempt cemetery, vaulting over headstones and weaving around graves. She soon passed Zeff, who, to his utter humiliation, kept running into grave markers and tangling himself in the grasses.

The chase spilled out onto the cemetery's sloping drive where Hazen's caravan stood at the ready. In the distance, Simone could see Hazen and Grace in the driver's seat.

"It's a general!" she shouted ahead. "Shoot him! Shoot him!"

Hazen's eyes widened with surprise as he spotted the approaching general with Simone and Zeff close behind. Grace leaned behind the driver's seat and grabbed the old hunting rifle he kept there in cases of emergency. Then she loaded it with ammo from the first-aid kit and handed him the rifle.

"Here you go," she said curtly, still mad from their fight the night before.

Hazen looked at the gun like he'd never seen it before.

"Shoot him!" Simone cried again. The general had almost reached the caravan; then he would be past them, out of the cemetery, and lost in the woods. They would never find him after that. Chances are, he would probably find them—with a war party in tow.

"Come on," Grace said, prodding Hazen with her elbow. "You've got to bring him down! Wake up, Hazen! *You've got to bring him down!*"

The tradesman aimed the rifle and fired, but the general kept running. He'd missed.

"Try again!" Grace shouted, bouncing in her seat. "You can get him this time!"

Hazen fired the rifle again. This time, the man jumped in the air with a shout before falling to the ground.

"Great shot!" Simone cried. She gave Hazen a thumbs-up as she ran past them to retrieve the body.

Grace looked at Hazen. He had already lowered the rifle and was staring at his feet; his mouth was set and straight. At that moment, she thought he looked like one of those cherub angel figurines her sister, Lora, used to collect. He was a cherub angel that was all grown up. And sad.

"You OK?" Grace asked, touching his arm.

"I don't like killing," Hazen replied. "I try to do as little of it as possible. But that's pretty fucking hard to do these days." He met her eye. "Does that make you think I'm not a man?"

Hazen's honesty touched Grace's heart. She took his hands in her own, last night's quarrel completely forgotten. "You're a pacifist. I think it's cool." She grinned at him. "Somebody's got to respect life around here."

"Exactly, honey," Hazen said, flashing his dimpled smile. "I'm a lover, not a fighter."

"That's good," Grace said, her voice low and throaty. She leaned in a little closer. "Because I'm both." Hazen was laughing when he kissed her. Her lips were soft and welcoming as he entwined his fingers in her hair.

"The general's dead," Simone interrupted, watching the embracing lovers from the ground. "You got him with that last shot of yours, Hazen. That should make you good and horny."

"I'm not horny!" Hazen said. "Killing people doesn't make me horny!"

"We should get going before the gunshots attract more generals," Zeff said. "That would make Hazen even hornier."

"I'm not horny!" Hazen protested as Zeff and Simone climbed into the back of the caravan. He looked at Grace and wiggled his eyebrows. "Well, not because of that."

"What happened?" Claire asked them, once Simone and Zeff were seated again. She and Lloyd were huddled around PJ, trying to look as small as possible. "Are there generals out there?" she asked. "What's going on?"

"There were two generals in the cemetery," Zeff replied. " But we killed them both."

"Good," PJ said in a small and brittle voice. It was the first word Simone had ever heard him say.

BON VOYAGE

The return trip from the cemetery was delightfully uneventful, and even the weather was on the travelers' side. The river at midday was low enough to cross with ease, and the sky was a gauzy blue, dappled with fat, friendly-looking clouds as far as the eye could see.

"I guess Lady Luck is finally smiling our way," Zeff said, but he kept poking his head out the back of the wagon just the same, keeping an ear out for trouble. He didn't trust Grace and Hazen to keep watch, mooning all over each other like a couple of rutting gophers; they would never spot an ambush like that.

But an ambush never came.

Once Hazen guided Esmeralda through the gates of Elwood's compound, Claire let out an audible sigh. "Today's been a blessing," she said with a rare smile. "It's been so nice to rest our feet. And now, to come to a secure house with a gate…it's wonderful." Her eyes misted with tears as Lloyd and PJ hugged her, and the little family clung together, trembling with relief.

Barbara was happy to accept the Lawson family into the compound, especially after hearing about Horus and their escape from the New Empire. They didn't mention what had happened to PJ's ear. Simone had noticed Barbara looking at the wound on the side of the boy's face and was relieved she didn't ask about it.

However, Barbara was not happy with the second part of their plan.

"You're not going to the New Empire!" she tearfully shouted in Zeff's face. "And my girls…" She started to cry harder, and he gave her a dishrag to dry her tears.

"We'll be fine. We'll come back," he said. "Barbara, this may be the only chance we've got."

"Well, I appreciate what you're doing, but I am absolutely heartbroken," she said, folding her arms across her impressive bosom. "We were getting to be like family."

"We are family," Grace said, kissing her on the cheek. "We'll be back. You'll see."

"Baby, you're sweet as pie, but you're a damned liar," Barbara said, laughing and dabbing her eyes with the rag. She pulled Simone and Grace to her and embraced them in her matronly way. "I wish the rest of the compound was here to see you off, but they went to Myrtle Pond for the day. Elwood's here…somewhere, but he's impossible to find when you need him." She consulted the grosgrain-lined bulletin board. "Oh! Monty's on watch!" she said. "I'm sure he'll want to say good-bye."

Simone was sure Monty did not want to say good-bye, but she promised to stop by the guardhouse anyway. As she walked out the kitchen door for the last time, hearing it swing shut behind her, she felt sorry that Lewis wasn't around. He had amused her many times when her spirits were low, and even though she had often strained her back doing heavy labor for his projects, he had been a good friend. She wondered how he would fare in the New Empire, if Elwood's Compound fell.

Thankfully, Hazen had capitulated somewhat and had agreed to take them most of the way in his precious Esmeralda. "But this bus ain't going to Crazy Town," he'd said, and it sounded like he meant it. So they readied the caravan for the journey ahead with Lloyd and Claire's assistance. Even PJ helped, folding blankets and towels over his pointed little knees.

Barbara appeared with salted meat and several baskets of berries, handing them up to Grace, who popped a strawberry in her mouth.

"Hey," Simone said, swatting at her with her hat. "We've got to save those." Grace pulled a face and gave one to PJ whose expression didn't change, although his eyes shone, ever so slightly.

"Mother!" Monty squealed from the window of the guardhouse. "Are you supplying the deserters with our provisions?"

"Good-bye, Monty!" Simone said sweetly, waving up at him. "I'll miss you!"

"Not as much as I will!" Hazen cried in a high, falsetto voice. They both laughed, and Monty held up his middle finger.

"I guess you told him we're leaving," Zeff said to Barbara. "Did you tell the little darlin' about Horus?"

"Not quite," Barbara said. "We'll get to that soon enough. I just told him you were going on a long trip for now. I didn't want to worry him. You know his artistic temperament."

"I do indeed," Zeff replied.

Hazen finished hitching up the horses, adding Simone's horse, Alfred, and Zeff's horse, Peaches, to his team. Then he climbed up into the driver's seat. Grace hopped up beside him and settled in the passenger's side, her long blond hair streaming out behind her like a banner in the breeze. Zeff and Simone took their now customary place in the back of the wagon.

"I know the perfect place to stop for the night," Hazen called back to them. "I was just there a few days ago. It's a bit hidden, so it's a harder target. Hopefully it's still in one piece."

Barbara opened the compound gates, and Esmeralda rolled forward with a bump, bump, bump. One of the goats in the yard chased after the caravan halfheartedly for a few feet, before stopping to munch on some of the grass that grew along the side of the stockade. The travelers shouted their farewells to Barb and the Lawson family, waving from the wagon with forced cheer. Then they were gone, out the compound gates and out of sight.

In the shade of the orchard, Elwood awoke from his nap with a start. He smacked his lips, let out an elephantine sigh, and rolled into a more comfortable position. He had been dreaming of his old professor days again, when he had been the most published member in the faculty and a respected expert in his field. And the parties, the soirees, the food! Students had begged to be in his classes. Begged!

Those were the days when a man could really make a difference, Elwood thought. Then he dove again, headfirst, into a pit of slumber.

TERROR AT THE TAYLORS

"One more bend in the road, and we'll be there," Hazen said, smiling at Grace, who was riding beside him in the driver's seat. "The Taylors are good people. If they're still alive, they'll take us in for the night."

Grace smiled back, a beaming smile that lit up the lush and dappled glade they were traveling through. The trees here were enormous, each with its own labyrinth of roots that snaked across the ground, ancient and thick limbed. Their leafy canopies sighed and trembled as the little caravan bounced past like a ladybug scuttling through a vegetable garden. She took a deep breath in. The air was sweet and fragrant, and the breeze felt soft on her sunburned cheeks.

She cast a look over her shoulder into the wagon behind her. Zeff was staring at his boots with a look of fierce concentration, his neat salt-and-pepper beard framing a worried frown. Simone was seated beside him, her chin cupped in her hands, her hat tipped low over her eyes. Grace knew they were thinking about Horus. She'd been thinking about him too; more specifically, the possibility of her family in his clutches. They had to figure out a plan and a good one. But they had a ways to go before they would reach the New Empire, and Grace was determined to feel the lightness of the day, to soak it in like a sponge and carry it with her into the dark.

The caravan hugged the final bend in the road, and as promised, the Taylor Compound came into view. Sheets of metal, scavenged car parts, and weathered pieces of wood had been twisted together to form a barrier around the property, bound with chicken wire and spiked with shards of glass. Grace wished Lewis were here to see it. He would have loved it.

Hazen drove the caravan up to the doors of a ruddy-colored barn, flanked on either side by the scrapyard barricade. He hopped down to the ground and strode up to the tidy structure, ringing the large copper bell that hung above the door, just as he always did. But this time there was no response. Frowning, he stepped back, looked up at the barn, and rang the bell again, holding his breath. He did not want to make camp in the open tonight.

At last, Charlie Taylor, red faced and panting, threw open the second-story window and peered out of the barn, blinking down at them in obvious confusion.

"You're here again?" he shouted. "I'm sorry, Hazen, but we're terribly busy right now. This isn't a good day for trade. Take care now; see you next time." And he pulled the window closed and hurried out of view.

Hazen rang the bell once more, louder this time. Charlie reappeared at the window again, looking more frustrated and disheveled by the second.

"Charlie!" Hazen called up to him, cupping his hands around his mouth. "I'm not here to trade. We're seeking shelter for the night. I can give you some provisions for your trouble."

Charlie appeared to consider the offer before his eyes alighted on Grace. She offered him a breezy little wave from the caravan.

"You have a woman with you?"

Hazen was surprised. "We have two."

"In that case you'd better come in. And hurry!"

Charlie disappeared from the window again, and moments later, there were various clicking and locking noises on the other side of the barn door. It swung open, and Hazen drove the caravan through.

Warm afternoon light filtered through the building, illuminating the golden motes of dust that orbited through space like a miniature solar system. By the time the caravan rolled to a stop, Charlie had already secured the barn door behind them and was standing beside the wagon, his body stiff with nerves.

"Charlie Taylor, it's been a while," Zeff said, climbing out of the back of the wagon and lowering himself to the ground. He could feel their host's anxiety quivering in the air. "You're more skittish than a cat in a bag. What's going on around here?"

"Anya's in labor!" Charlie blurted out, his hands bunching the seams of his oversized khaki trousers. "None of us knows what to do. You should hear her hollering. It's like she's getting murdered in there! Something's gotta be wrong, a woman screaming her head off like that."

"Sounds like a normal labor to me—a normal labor with no drugs," Grace said, jumping down from the front of the wagon. She extended her hand to Charlie. "Grace Gateman. Pleased to meet you."

Charlie put his hand out like a child expecting to be slapped, and Grace squeezed it reassuringly, trying to pump some life back into the clammy appendage.

"I assisted with a neighbor's labor a little while back," she said warmly. "She came through it fine. Had a beautiful baby girl."

Charlie looked like he was about to cry. He twisted his mouth as if he was trying to say something, but no words came out.

"Maybe we should go to Anya now," she suggested, giving him a little pat on the back.

Charlie led them to a modest stone cottage tucked at the back of the property. They kept to a cobbled pathway surrounded by hills of thick, shiny potato plants that stretched toward the sun. Leafy cucumber and tomato plants climbed up an ornamental trellis placed at the front of the house, while homely raspberry bushes peeked shyly around the corner. On the porch, dwarf blueberry bushes grew in chipped yellow planters. Beside them, a rocking chair tipped and groaned in the breeze.

Charlie opened the screen door and bounded up the stairs. Grace heard a thin wail coming from inside and ran after him. She was halfway up the stairs before she realized she was alone. Zeff, Hazen and Simone had remained downstairs looking uneasy, Simone in particular.

"Well?" Grace called down to them. "Aren't you coming?"

"Seems a bit intimate for all of us to be there," Hazen said. "You know, with all the liquids and.... juices and such." He swallowed. "We should probably wait somewhere else."

"That seems more appropriate to me," Zeff agreed.

Grace rolled her eyes. "Fine. We don't need you anyway," she said. "Simone and I can handle it."

"We can?" Simone asked, her voice breaking.

"Aren't you going to help me?"

"Help you? What am I going to do? I don't know anything about childbirth."

There was another shriek from upstairs, a long, gusty cry that set Simone's teeth on edge. It sounded like someone was being tortured.

Grace put her hands on her hips. "Simone, pull yourself together. I'd expect this kind of thing from the man-babies here—"

"Hey!" Hazen exclaimed.

"But not from you," she continued. "I've seen you kill and butcher an animal, for God's sake. Don't tell me you can't help another woman at her hour of need. You'd better grow a set, Simone. And by that I mean ovaries."

With her admonishment still ringing in the air, Grace turned on her heel and vanished upstairs, although she should still be heard stomping down the hall. Simone took a deep breath before running after her, feeling the chill that lingered in her friend's wake. When Grace got mad, you knew it; the atmosphere of the room changed.

Simone found Grace at the end of the hall, standing beside a closed door. She was conversing quietly with Charlie and two other men who looked pale and nervous.

"Just try to stay calm," she heard Grace say. "I'll let you know if we need anything. Simone, I'm glad you're here. We're going in."

Grace moved to the door and placed her hand on the knob. She turned back to Simone and gave her a reassuring smile. "Buck up," she said. "This kind of stuff separates the girls from the women."

She opened the door. Simone focused on remaining conscious.

The inside of the room was stuffy and hot. The rank odour of blood comingled with something sour and primal. It was the smell of fear, but Grace couldn't tell if it was coming from the woman writhing on the large canopy bed or the man who knelt beside it, pressing a wooden crucifix to his lips. He rose to his feet as they entered the room.

"Who comes unbidden to this birth?" he asked in a low voice.

Grace was taken aback. "Well, um, hello. I'm Grace—this is Simone, and actually we were…bidden? Is that a word? Anyway, Charlie asked us to help."

The man stared at her from a pair of brooding, close-set eyes that looked down a long, aquiline nose. "Are you a believer in the righteousness of the Lord and in the goodness of Jesus Christ, his only Son?" he demanded.

"I will be if this lady pulls through all right," Grace answered briskly.

"You don't understand," he said. "This child is a sign from God, just as the olive branch was brought to Noah on the wings of a dove. Anya must give birth undisturbed and *uncontaminated*."

"And *you* don't understand the mother-infant mortality rate these days," Grace retorted, before brushing past him and moving to the side of the bed to examine the woman. "You must be Anya," she said, smiling down at her reassuringly. "We're going to help you through this. Just try and stay calm, OK? I'm going to check where you're at with the contractions."

Anya nodded, her face slick with sweat. Grace placed her hand gently on the woman's abdomen, feeling the muscles rippling before she even began counting. One Mississippi, two Mississippi, three Mississippi...

The man grabbed her by the wrist and pulled her away. "I cannot let impure hands touch the child!" he shouted, his eyes wild with anger. "This is God's most blessed gift! He has not forsaken us!"

"Hey!" Grace shouted, wriggling in his grasp. "Let me go!"

Simone, who was still standing by the door, frozen by the sight of the bloodied bedsheets, felt herself return to reality. She walked over and detached the man's grip from Grace's arm.

"Calm yourself," she said in a strange, robotic voice. Her eyes were on the bedsheets again.

"Trinity," Anya called from the bed, struggling to sit up. "Darling, I'm frightened. Let the women help. Perhaps they were also sent by God."

"Anya." He sniffed. "Need I remind you of Psalm 27? 'The Lord is my light and my salvation; whom shall I fear? The Lord is the stronghold of my life; of whom shall I be afraid?'"

"Easy for you to say, bud," Grace interrupted. "Listen, Anya's still got a ways to go. We should be making her more comfortable..."

"What do you mean she's still got a ways to go?" Trinity asked. He suddenly looked less stern and more frightened.

"Am I dying?" Anya asked.

"No, you're not dying. Simone, come help me," Grace said. She eyed Trinity standing beside the bed: tall and gaunt, leaning over Anya with a feverish look on his face. He could easily pass for the specter of death himself.

"Excuse me, uh, Trinity, can you get some clean towels or sheets or something? We also need a few other things," Grace said, listing an assortment of items. "Oh, and while you're out there, make sure you update everyone about Anya's progress. I bet the other guys are shitting in their pants right now."

Trinity stared at Grace in disbelief.

"Uh, we kind of need that stuff now," she pressed.

"Woman, your tongue is like sandpaper," he pronounced, before stalking from the room and slamming the door behind him.

"I can't believe you had sex with that guy," Grace remarked to Anya, as she strained through another contraction.

"I rarely do!" Anya screamed. After the contraction passed, she looked up with pain-filled eyes. "Please excuse my husband," she said with a weak smile. "Years ago, the doctors told us we were infertile. This birth is a miracle to him." Her face contorted as another contraction took hold, and she cried out in agony.

Her wails were getting thinner; Anya was tiring. She needed water; maybe she could even be coached into eating something. Grace looked at Simone across the bed, awkwardly patting the woman's hand and wearing an expression of dazed horror on her face. She choked down an urge to laugh.

"OK, Simone. Your job is to be Anya's personal cheerleader. Keep her motivated, and keep her breathing through the contractions. Anya, when your husband gets back with the sheets, we're going to move you to the floor and get you more comfortable."

Anya looked up at the women standing over her: one blond and fiery as a Viking, the other brunette and armed to the teeth. She began to wonder if these strange women were even real. Could they possibly be pain-fueled hallucinations? Could she actually be alone in the room with poor old Trinity? Then she felt another contraction take hold, wrenching at her insides. She felt hands holding her, she heard a coaxing voice, and then she pushed, pushed, pushed, pushed, pushed.

BELABORED THOUGHTS

The mood in the hallway was a somber one. A silence had fallen among the men, punctuated by the sound of Anya's screams through the door. Zeff felt so damn awkward and uncomfortable he had to work at sitting still. Across the hall, he could vaguely make out the figure of his compatriot Hazen, sitting next to Charlie. Charlie's younger brothers, Jason and Jared, sat nearby; Zeff could tell by the sound that one of them was chewing his fingernails. The two weren't twins, but he could never remember who was older and by how many years. As with most folks in the valley, he'd known the family for a long time, and even when his vision was sharp as a hawk's, he could barely tell the two apart. They were both big-toothed, broad-shouldered boys, with no discerning features and no irregularities to add interest to their forms. But he remembered their eyes were kind. And they were always willing to help a friend.

Not a bad bunch of fellows, he thought. *Except for that nut, Trinity.* He wondered how Grace and Simone were handling him. More than that, he wondered how Simone was handling the labor. He turned his head toward the closed door and strained his ears, speculating with a smile how long she was going to last in there. Not too long, by his estimate.

Zeff had made the mistake of asking Simone to assist with the birth of one of his calves once, back when his ranch was still standing and humming along with the throb of electricity. He often asked for her help in those days; she was an expert with the lasso and was reliable and steady in any situation—or so he had thought.

But the birth in question had been a difficult one. The mama was a saint, but the calf had her head tipped back in the uterus, and Zeff had to hook her jaw with a chain to straighten it. He also had to do this alone, as Simone had been vomiting in a corner of the barn at the time. When the calf started to emerge, she had taken one look at that sticky head emerging from the dam and fainted straight away. Poor Simone. He would have felt sorry for her if it hadn't been so damn funny.

When the bedroom door opened again, Zeff turned his face toward it, certain it would be her, but it wasn't. He could tell by the heavy footsteps that it was a man. Trinity.

"What's happening in there?" Charlie cried, struggling to his feet. "Is Anya all right?"

"Clean linen!" cried Trinity. "The baby requires clean linen!" He paused for a moment. "Does anyone know where Anya keeps it?"

The Taylor boys looked at one another, each one shaking his head.

"Maybe the hutch downstairs?" Jason suggested.

"Or the shelving in the basement?" Jared added.

"Or the blanket chest in the sunroom," Jason continued.

"I was going to suggest the blanket chest." Jared said, looking peevish.

"Then you should have suggested it."

"I was going to, but you interrupted."

"I did not interrupt." Jason's lower lip sagged into a pout.

"Yes, you did. You always do. I can never finish my sentences around you."

"Maybe that's the Lord's way of telling you that you need to talk faster."

Jared inhaled sharply. "Have you forgotten his holy words, *brother*? Love is *patient* and *kind*. It does not envy or boast. It does not *insist* on its own way."

"Do nothing from rivalry or conceit!" Jason shouted back at him. "In humility, count others as more significant than yourself!"

"To you, O Lord, I lift up my soul!" Jared yelled, trying to drown out his brother. "Let me not be put to shame! Let not my enemies exult over me!"

"Silence, you fools!" Trinity cried, and Jared and Jason stopped squabbling. "We must find clean linen immediately or face the wrath of God."

"Actually, I think her name's Grace," Hazen joked, and the Taylor brothers gave him four sour looks in return. "You can't believe everything she tells you," he finished lamely.

"Maybe you should just ask Anya about it," Charlie said, turning to his brothers. "Instead of scaring her with all your noise."

"We will locate the linen ourselves," Trinity declared, with a dramatic wave of his hands. "This is our lot to bear, and we will meet the task with patience and enthusiasm. Charlie, wait by the door in case Anya needs assistance. Jason, Jared, you will assist me, please."

Once the brothers had gone, Charlie sat back down in the hallway. His round face drooped like a caved-in jack-o'-lantern, and his forehead shone with sweat. He rubbed his eyes with short, calloused fingers, exhaling deeply.

"C'mon, don't look so glum," Hazen said, patting him on the back. "Anya's in good hands. Grace and Simone will get her through it all right."

Charlie stared hard at the floor. "What if this baby isn't a sign from God?" he asked. "Maybe saying that it is…might…curse it. Do you think that could happen?"

"Well, maybe the baby is a sign," Hazen said. "Who knows, right? Trinity thinks it is. He's told me before that he and Anya couldn't conceive."

"It's possible that he and Anya didn't conceive," Charlie replied.

Hazen looked at Charlie sharply. "What are you saying?"

"I love her," he whispered. "I have always loved her."

There was a sudden commotion on the stairs. The brothers were already returning from their quest: Trinity with a bushel of blueberries, two more lanterns, and a vintage bottle of whiskey, Jason and Jared with piles of sheets and towels that wobbled high above their heads as they made their ascent. And by the sounds of it, they were still quarrelling.

"You only suggested the linen closet. *I* was the one who looked in it."

"We both looked in it."

"I looked in it first. You looked in it *after a time.* There's a difference."

"There is no *after a time.* There is no difference. We found the towels together."

"A false witness will not go unpunished!"

"He who breathes out lies will perish!"

"What's that for?" Charlie asked as Trinity sloshed by with the whiskey.

"I believe it's for that horrid blond succubus," his brother replied. Charlie hung his head in his hands.

Hazen couldn't bear Charlie's nerves anymore or Jason and Jared's bickering, which had become as insistent as the drone of mosquitoes in the hall. He had to get Charlie away from Anya's door and out into some fresh air. It was the best way to clear the mind.

"Charles, sir," he said. "What say we take a walk? Zeff too. We've been sitting awhile, and I need to stretch my legs."

"I don't know," Charlie answered. The hesitation was evident in his voice. "What if something happens to Anya? We really should be here."

But Hazen's charm was as fluid and relentless as water; it found a way around every impasse. Moments later, Charlie was leading them down the stairs, out the front door of the cottage, and into the star-spun night. He led the way with a lantern, but the light did little to ward off the darkness that huddled around them and nipped at their heels as they walked through the yard of the compound. They stopped in front of the detached garage that was adjacent to the house. With trembling hands, Charlie opened a small side door.

The interior of the garage was as black as coal and still smelled of gasoline. The familiar scent circulated through Hazen's nostrils and, rather unexpectedly, made him want to cry. Charlie swung the lantern in front of them, revealing a car covered in bedsheets, peeking out at them like a frightened child. He placed the lantern on the ground and, with one swift motion, swept the sheets off the vehicle, revealing a silver Mercedes-Benz in pristine condition. It could have been in a dealership showroom, if there were any dealerships or showrooms.

"Beautiful," Charlie said with reverence, stepping back to admire the car. Like a lord returning to his manor, he opened the door on the driver's side and seated himself comfortably inside. "Make sure your boots are clean," he said, before closing the door.

Hazen and Zeff clumped and banged their steel toes on the ground before getting in the back, settling themselves on the plush leather seats.

"Sometimes I like to come out here and sit," Charlie said, staring ahead, his hands hugging the wheel. "Saved all my life for this car. Now she's just an expensive thinking stump at the end of the world."

"Sorrow, loss, death," Zeff replied. "That's always been humanity's burden to bear. Take away our creature comforts, and it's magnified."

"You know what gets me?" Hazen asked. "Not knowing anything, you know, never getting any answers or any explanation for this whole breakdown. Is it possible that there's electricity somewhere else in the world, and they've just forgotten about us? Have you guys ever thought about that?"

"All you need to know is what's in front of you," Zeff said. "Asking who or what or why doesn't change anything."

"Asking questions is an important part of life," Hazen retorted. "A man's entitled to his natural curiosity and philosophy on the subject. Back me up on this, Charlie. You boys are Christians; you understand."

"We are Christians, you're right about that," Charlie drummed his fingers meditatively against the wheel. "Don't tell Trinity, but I think my faith is slipping." He looked in the rearview mirror and laughed harshly. "Of course, his has never been stronger. According to him, this is God's way of testing us. It's his 'greatest test.'" Charlie turned so he was facing Zeff and Hazen in the backseat, his face flushed with emotion. "I've seen some terrible things since the blackout—neighbors starving to death. Murders. Families slaughtered in their own beds. I guess I'm wondering what's so great about this test."

In the backseat, Hazen and Zeff were lost for words. The man of faith had lost his faith and found another, more complicated love to replace it. It would be a hard road ahead for him, and both men pitied Charlie in different ways—Zeff for his unattainable love, and Hazen for the sad desperation that swam in his eyes and made him look older than his years.

THE DELIVERY

"Oh, hell! What is that? What's happening?" Simone cried.

"*Relax*—you're going to freak Anya out," Grace muttered out of the corner of her mouth. She readjusted the towels on the floor where the expectant mother was crouched on all fours, panting in pain.

"It's just the top of the baby's head!" Grace called to Anya in an upbeat voice. "Everything looks good. Keep breathing."

"I can't stop staring at it," Simone murmured. Her eyes were fastened like snaps to the dark head that was beginning to emerge into the world. She felt a wave of nausea and scrambled to her feet, desperate for air. The room suddenly seemed hot and putrid; it was stifling. She gasped for breath.

Grace grabbed the pot of boiled water, long since cooled, and hurled the contents at her. The tepid water splashed across Simone's face and chest, dousing her shirt. She froze, blinking in shock.

"Get it together," Grace said, her hands cradling the head. "I can only handle one baby at a time. That's why I sent Trinity away."

Anya let out a thin, high wail. "It hurts! Oh, God, it hurts!"

Chastened, Simone knelt down and grabbed for her hand, keeping her eyes on Anya's face this time. "Squeeze, Anya. Squeeze through the pain."

"The shoulders are coming. Here we go. Keep panting, Anya. I'll tell you when; then you push," Grace encouraged her.

Anya screamed again. She was gripping Simone's hands like a vise.

"OK, now!" Grace cried. "Push, Anya! *Now!*"

Anya's face contorted as she locked eyes with Simone. Then, the caterwaul of a newborn baby filled the air, and she went limp, collapsing onto the padded floor.

"It's a girl!" Grace exclaimed. "Anya, you have a beautiful baby girl!"

"A girl?" Anya asked.

With some reluctance, Simone tore her gaze from Anya's face as Grace showed her the sticky, mottled child. "What a miracle," she said softly as Anya held her baby for the first time. Then Anya smiled and expelled the placenta, and she fainted straightaway.

When Grace announced the safe arrival of the new baby girl, the hallway erupted in cheers. Charlie grabbed Hazen and wrapped him in a big bear hug, choking back his tears of joy. Jason and Jared gave each other a series of elaborate high fives. Only Trinity, who'd expected the sign from God to have a penis, looked disappointed.

When he held the child in his arms, he still looked disappointed, but less so.

"Don't look so forlorn," Grace patted him on the back. "A woman can change the world. Just look at how a woman changed yours." She pointed to Anya, but the exhausted woman was oblivious to this; all she could see was Charlie, standing in the doorway with all that love in his eyes. For his daughter. For *her.*

Jason and Jared got a fire going in the fireplace downstairs, and everyone joined them in the living room to celebrate, everyone except for Anya and the baby she'd named Mary. But Trinity joined them and appeared to be in better spirits, raiding the pantry to set out a modest feast of cheese, thin slices of smoked fish, and fresh berries with honey. To everyone's delight, Charlie contributed a small supply of instant coffee powder that he mixed with water and simmered in a large kettle over the fire. Hazen donated a jug of cider and gifted Trinity with a few pieces of baby clothes he had for trade in the caravan.

The night had been long and exhausting, but everyone felt too joyful, too hopeful to sleep. The excitement of the evening coupled with the dizzying combination of coffee and cider left Grace feeling bolder than usual, and her body throbbed with a restless, prowling energy. Once Trinity brought out his guitar and tuned it, he played the chords to his favorite hymn, "Great is Thy Faithfulness." He also played "Proud Mary" to honour his child, and Grace sang along with him, her voice as clear and high as a bell.

Hazen watched Grace's performance from across the room, hanging on her every note, hooked by the unexpected beauty of her voice and the soft curve of her face in the firelight. Simone, in turn, watched Hazen, concerned by the wolfish look in his eye and his slackened, drooling chops as he watched Grace sing her heart out. Jared watched Simone, thinking how pretty she was. Jason watched Jared, thinking how annoying he was. Charlie watched the ceiling, because Anya and Mary were up there, sleeping in the bed above them.

Zeff, alone, was in his own world, and it wasn't a pleasant one. Under the brim of his hat, his eyes throbbed terribly, and his back was sore. The day's events had taken a toll on him, or more specifically, Charlie's impossible love for Anya had taken a toll on him. It had almost given him hope that one day, Simone—

Zeff banished the thought before it had the chance to unfold itself. He didn't need hope now that he was as used up and ornery as an old tomcat. No, he was defeated and wanted solace. Every fiber in his being urged him to slip out of the room, to escape to the dark barn where he could close his eyes and be alone with his thoughts. Maybe Simone would even stop by and visit. This thought cheered the rancher up a bit; he cast a hopeful glance at her blurred form and took another swig of cider.

Grace and Trinity performed a few more songs they both knew, and everyone except Zeff joined in on the chorus, giggling and shushing each other, trying to keep their voices low so Anya and Mary could sleep upstairs. Preoccupied with his thoughts, Zeff missed the performance altogether, fidgeting in his seat and casting dark scowls across the room that everyone else chose to ignore. It was a clear relief to him when Trinity put away the guitar for the night and gave Grace a friendly bandmate handshake. Hazen was on his feet clapping and looking at the young woman with such admiration that she skipped over to him, giggling with pleasure. With a low laugh, he gathered her in his arms and spun her around the room, knocking over a chair in his jubilation.

Upstairs, baby Mary awoke with a squawk.

"I should go!" Trinity said, smiling. He looked at Grace, then Simone; his face was beaming. "Thank you. You were both a blessing here tonight." He turned again and bounded up the stairs.

"We can set you up on the sofas to sleep," Charlie said, pulling his gaze away from his brother's retreating back. "We've got some clean blankets left."

"Don't worry about me," Hazen said, casting a look of sympathy at their host. "I like to sleep in my caravan. It's my home. And it sleeps two, Grace, if you're interested." His handsome face split into a wide smile. "Now, before you say anything, shall I tell you about the caravan's best feature—just so you can make an informed decision?"

"Let me guess. The best feature is you?" she answered with a laugh, her cheeks pink with excitement.

"Would I say something so uncouth to a lady who is as fine as the summer sunshine?" he asked in mock outrage. "No, I am a gentleman, darlin'. But I do feel obliged to tell you, in the interest of full disclosure, that you can unzip the wagon cover and open it right up to the night sky. You can watch the stars from the comfort of a luxurious bearskin bed."

"Hazen, if you lay it on any thicker, we'll all be gagging on this shit," Simone interrupted.

"Aw, come on," Grace said, still looking at him. "I think it's a pretty good offer." She smiled and smoothed a curling forelock away from his face. "I've never seen the stars from a bearskin bed before."

"Er, Grace, may I have a word with you?" Simone asked, beckoning to her. She nodded and gave Hazen's hand a squeeze before bouncing over, her tread upon the floorboards as light as air.

"You aren't seriously considering this, are you?" Simone asked quietly, looking over at Hazen with a disapproving frown. "He's a nice guy and everything; he means well. But he's a flirt. And I worry about you."

"Oh, come on—don't be so uptight," Grace said. "Listen, I don't play around, all right? We don't know how much time we have left. So when something I want presents itself to me, I reach out, and I grab it. And right now, I want to forget about what might be happening my family just for one night. And that *something* just happens to be a sexy man with a fur bed. Is that the worst thing in the world?"

Simone had to admit it wasn't.

Once the room had emptied and the sounds of festivity had fallen away, she and Zeff were left alone by the dying fire. But tonight, the two friends sat awkwardly together in a strained silence. Simone knew something was bothering him. Tension was emanating from his high-held shoulders and his wrinkled brow, but for some reason, she found herself unable to ask about it. She couldn't form the words—any words for that matter.

Zeff finally broke the silent spell by uttering a terse "Good night, Simone," before rushing from the room and out the front door, stumbling down the stairs in his haste to leave. As he felt his way along the path to the barn, he was forced to pass the caravan, already shuddering from side to side with the force of the lovers' rapture inside. He heard Grace's passionate cries and Hazen's voice, hoarse with sex, as they moved together in ecstasy.

I hope that damn caravan tips over, Zeff thought as he groped for the door to the barn. He already suspected he would get very little rest that night and soon proved himself right. Every time he closed his eyes, his thoughts circled back to Simone. She was always there; he could never reach her.

THE HAUNTED FOOTHILLS

"This Boris must be the devil himself," Jason murmured, his pebble eyes shining in the morning sunlight, his nose moist and pink.

"It's *Horus*." Jared elbowed his brother snidely in the ribs.

"That's what I said."

Zeff and Charlie picked up their pace ahead, leaving the bickering brothers behind as they continued their stroll about the yard. The rancher's neck was sore, and he hadn't slept a wink, but the luxurious boiled-egg breakfast provided by the Taylors had energized him. In the long hours of the night, he had gotten over feeling sorry for himself. There were more pressing matters at hand.

"So does anyone know who this Horus really is?" Charlie asked, running an anxious hand through his thinning blond hair. "I mean, who is this guy? He couldn't have just come out of nowhere."

"I haven't heard anything about that." Zeff shrugged. "But he's the only person I know who seems to be benefitting from the storms."

"Do you think he'll come here?" Charlie surveyed the barricade with a look of concern and glanced back at the house.

"I'd be surprised if he didn't," Zeff said. "He appears to be colonizing the entire valley, so be ready for an attack. Have a guarding schedule, and stick to it. And make sure you have some means of escape: a hideout, a tunnel, somewhere you can go if the compound falls. Don't let them take you to the New Empire."

Charlie thrust his hands into his pockets and pursed his lips as he considered this advice. He looked up at Zeff. "And you?" he asked with a worried frown. "Where are you folks going?"

"We're headed east. I have an aunt in Smyth we need to check on." Zeff's voice trailed away, and he fought the urge to flinch. He hated lying; it was cowardly and dishonourable in his opinion, but they had agreed not to tell anyone where they were going. The element of surprise was all they had at the moment, and if the generals captured the Taylors…well, it was best not to think about that.

Ahead, Grace, Hazen, and Simone waved to them as they emerged from the cottage, chatting about their visit with Anya and the baby. Anya had looked tired but seemed to be recovering well and was in good spirits, holding little Mary in her arms. Sprawled across the bed beside her was Trinity, who had slept soundly through the good-byes. The visitors had left him dreaming, promising to come back to see them one day and wondering if they ever would.

Once the caravan was packed up and ready to go, the war party moved east, keeping off the highways and main drags where they might attract unwanted attention. They moved at a brisk pace, determined to travel as far as they could by daylight so they could make secure camp by nightfall. Simone and Zeff rode ahead of the wagon on their horses, scouting out the safest route, but the wet, rainy summer made the terrain difficult to cross, and they had to stop a handful of times to push the caravan out of the various ruts and bogs that had ensnared them along the way. Yet throughout all the heaving, pushing, and bouncing, the sturdy Esmeralda re-mained intact, never losing so much as a wheel in the muck. She was performing beautifully, and Hazen beamed and flashed his teeth like a proud papa.

Simone, on the other hand, took little notice of the caravan's performance, even when she was leaning into it with her shoulder and pushing it out of yet another mud hole. She was filled with a dreamy nostalgia that day, induced by the blazing purple loose-strife and citron strands of St. John's wort that peppered the land-scape around them. There was so much beauty here. She could even catch glimpses of it in the silent, ramshackle houses they passed by on the road and the birds that perched in their unblink-ing, windowless eyes. It made her think of her mother and her famous stormscapes, her eye for dark splendour.

"Zeff! Hey, Zeff!" Hazen called, startling Simone from her day-dream. "When are we stopping?"

"I know a fella out here," Zeff replied, his voice husky with dis-use. "Man by the name of Joey VanCleave. I've traded with him before; just keep following the road."

"How long till we get there?" Hazen asked, looking concerned.

"Not long now," he answered.

And it wasn't long before they reached the place where Joey VanCleave's home had once stood. Now it was nothing more than a dilapidated garbage heap, seated quietly at the end of a long drive-way, among the shushing trees. The house had been burned to the ground, but one side remained standing, although it was sagging, warped, and speckled with mold. It was clear the house would not be fit for camp. It wasn't even fit for firewood.

Still seated in the wagon, Grace started to tremble.

In her slow and deliberate manner, Simone cautiously ap-proached the house and jumped down from her horse. Shielding her eyes from the setting sun, she walked around the house into the backyard. There, she found a vegetable garden that looked as if animals had gotten to it, but other than that, it appeared to be have been recently cared for. At the back of the house, she found a neatly kept brick oven and fire pit. Crouching low, she placed her hands above the ashes. They were still warm.

"It doesn't look like much, but someone's been using this place. Probably left an hour or two ago," she said when she returned to the group. "The fire pit's warm, and the vegetable garden has been weeded. Think that's Joey?" she asked Zeff.

"Could be," he mused. "Or it could be someone else altogether." His tired eyes found the dark blur of the foothills in the distance. "Let's go there," he said, pointing to them. "If we can't find Joey, we can use the hills to hide the caravan for the night."

They moved off the road and cut across the countryside as the sky turned a dark, lusty red. The landscape pulsed crimson under the melting sun as long shadows flickered across the foothills. It was so quiet, even the sound of birdsong had fallen away. Simone shivered in the soft air and glanced over her shoulder at the burned wreckage of the VanCleave house. The solitary standing wall was still visible in the distance, a deformed and lonesome figure. She cast her gaze toward the wagon and noticed Grace staring back at it from the driver's seat, her eyes shining with tears.

Suddenly the wheels of the wagon made a sharp cracking sound, and Grace's face froze. The horse team dashed forward in a panic, and Simone could hear Hazen cry "Whoa!" Curious to see what the wagon wheels had kicked up, she rode up and dismounted, her eyes already scanning the ground. It wasn't long before she had found the object of her search: a rusted shovel lying across the path, its wooden handle snapped in two. She got on her knees to take a closer look in the dying light and immediately noticed how trodden the ground was. She couldn't believe she hadn't picked up on it sooner. She had to warn the others.

Simone got to her feet and was still holding the shovel in her hands when she felt the presence of a stranger nearby. By the time she'd spotted him, it was already too late; he was coming down the side of the hill at her like a bowling ball. And he was pointing a gun.

"I hope you have another shovel," the man growled when he was close enough. "I sincerely hope—for your own safety—that you have another goddamn shovel." He tightened his grip on the weapon.

Simone straightened her spine and looked at him, taking in the man's scrawny stature and his scowling, sunburned face. "I don't know what to tell you," she said, casually reaching a hand up the loose folds of her shirtsleeve and freeing her knife from its sheath. "But I don't have another shovel," she said.

"Drop the gun," Grace said, startling the man. She'd snuck back from the wagon with her revolver and had it trained on him.

"This bitch owes me a new shovel," the man said, lowering his gun until it was pointed at Simone's feet. "Do I look like a man who has extra shovels to you? You think I can afford to lose one?" His free hand rubbed at the mist of dirt and sweat that coated his face. A long, straggly clump of hair at the back of his head hung limp with grime.

"Father, as always your logic is breathtaking," a new voice remarked. Grace and Simone were startled to see a young woman emerge from a carefully concealed shelter that had been dug into the nearby hillside. As she approached, her black hair ruffled, and her long navy skirt blew in the breeze, making her appear dirt-swept and determined under the darkening sky.

"Hold it," Grace ordered without moving the revolver. "Stay where you are, or I'll shoot him."

But the young woman only lifted her lovely, high-boned cheeks and laughed. "You think I care?" she asked, pulling a meat cleaver from her skirt. She walked past Grace, giving her a wide berth, along with a look of imperious disdain. Once she reached the man, she raised the cleaver to his throat.

"His gun's not loaded, you know," she said in a bored tone. "We have no ammunition."

"What the hell are you doing?" the man snapped.

"Teaching you some manners." She smiled at him unpleasantly. "You obviously don't know how to treat guests." She lowered the knife and looked at Grace and Simone. "Please excuse my father. He's a brute."

The man cursed angrily and hurled the gun to the ground as Zeff arrived on horseback, and Hazen appeared not soon after.

"What's going on here?" Zeff demanded.

"My father was rude to your friends," the young woman replied. "I was just explaining that to him."

"She broke my shovel!" the man cried, pointing a stubby finger at Simone.

Zeff furrowed his brow and pricked his ears up. "Joey?" he said, squinting at the hunched figure in front of him. He dismounted and took two small steps toward him. "Joey VanCleave? Zeff Davis, remember me? I wondered if you were still alive."

"Oh, hello, Zeff," Joey said darkly. "Don't worry about me; I'm alive." He glowered at his daughter. "And spending every day in hell."

"Allow me to introduce myself," the young woman said, ignoring the remark. "I'm Carmen, Joey's daughter. Please, let me invite you to share a fire with us tonight." Her delicate features adopted a tragic expression. "We've been through so much already. And it would be nice to have the company."

"Carmen, I'm Hazen." The tradesman reached forward to take her hand. "We saw your house down there—at least what was left of it. I'm so sorry."

The exquisite creature looked at Hazen, smiled, and then looked away. "It has been hard," she said.

"I have a few extra provisions in my caravan." Hazen's face was flushed, his smile, eager. "We can get you extras of anything. Anything you want to get you and your dad back on your feet."

Grace watched Hazen; her mouth was drawn into a fine line.

"Why don't we go over there now and pick out some supper for tonight?" Hazen continued, oblivious to the third-degree stink eye that was pointed his way. "Your choice."

"Thank you; that's so kind of you," Carmen replied. "You must be a very special group of people." The beautiful young woman was addressing everyone, but her eyes never left Hazen's face. "Charity is so rare nowadays."

"Thank you," Grace cut in, resting an arm on Hazen's shoulder. "We are *truly* very special people." She cast a poisonous look at her new lover. "So, are *we* going to get some grub or what?"

In the meantime, Zeff and Simone followed Joey back to his shelter to admire his handiwork. It was certainly makeshift, no more than a muddy hovel hacked into the hillside, reinforced with planks of wood and sticks, with large pine boughs to cover the entranceway. As Simone inspected the structure, the branches across the doorway began to move, and a second young woman exited the shelter, causing her to gasp in surprise.

"That's just *Libby*." Joey rolled his eyes. "Libby, we have company."

The woman may have been Carmen's sister, but the two looked nothing alike. Where Carmen was dark eyed and delicate, Libby's eyes were cornflower blue and set in a sturdy, raw-boned face. She wore a pair of filthy sweatpants, a T-shirt, and sneakers, and though she was taller than her sister, she stood in a stooped, slouching manner—a far cry from Queen Carmen indeed.

"Don't look anything alike, do they?" Joey remarked, his voice crass and ugly. "And yet their *mother* expected me to believe they're both mine." He laughed.

Libby raised her head and stared at her father with unchecked hatred. "How dare you mention Mom? How dare you!"

"Don't get sassy, kid," Joey growled. "We may have company, but I'll still give you a wallop."

"You wife-killing scum bucket!" Libby cried. "You murdering piece of shit!"

"Shut the fuck up!" Joey roared at her, and the veins bulged in his neck like electrical cords. Then he looked at Zeff and Simone and twisted his roasted-tomato face into an appeasing smile. "She's still grieving her mom. It's making her loony," he said. "Listen up, Libby, your mother died when the house burned down. You know that. You think I organized a bunch of strangers to burn down our house and chase us around the foothills, just so I could live in a fucking dirt hole with you?"

"You locked her in!" Libby screamed. "You locked her in when they set the house on fire! You trapped her inside!"

"Goddamn it, Libby, I did not," Joey insisted.

"Goddamn it, Joey, you did," Carmen said serenely, sashaying back from the caravan with a wicker basket loaded down with food. She smiled at her father. "You know we'd kill you if we didn't need you, right?"

"OK folks, let's all just take a moment to cool down here," Hazen said, laying on his easy charm. "In fact, what can be more cooling than a couple of swigs of cider?" He raised the jug he was carrying and swilled the contents around enticingly. "Plus, we've got eggs, salted meat, and a few veggies. I can make omelettes tonight."

"We'd be happy to accept your offer of food," Carmen interjected. "But please, let us make dinner for you as a token of our gratitude."

"You don't have to do that." Hazen ducked his head and shuffled his feet.

"It would be our *pleasure*," she replied, drawing out the final word.

The effect on Hazen was immediate. "All right." He blushed. "If it means that much to you."

"You have no idea," she replied with a strange smile.

DOWN THE RABBIT HOLE

After assuring them that he hadn't seen anyone in the hills for weeks, Joey started a small fire in a concealed pit. Soon everyone settled around it, and muscles loosened, as did tongues; that was the way of the fire. Or maybe it was the way of the cider.

Simone kicked off her boots and stretched out her feet, feeling the warmth on her damp, woolly socks. She stared up at the night sky where the swirling stars glittered like confetti thrown across the universe. Lewis once told her it took tens of thousands of years for the light from some stars to reach earth. She wondered how many stars up there were already dead, shuttered in a cosmic darkness yet still emitting a ghostly light.

Grace moved over and sat beside her, leaning her head against Simone's shoulder. "Hey, babe."

"Well." Simone raised her eyebrows. "Haven't seen you around lately."

"I've been busy." Grace smiled sheepishly. "Are you mad?"

"Of course not. How's lover boy?"

Grace glanced across the fire at Hazen, who was in deep conversation with Joey. "I really like him, you know. Everything's been going so well. But it seems like he's flirting with Carmen or something." She tugged at the sweater she was wearing, and Simone noticed it was one of the chest-hugging, cable-knit sweaters the tradesman was famous for.

"I could see that," she replied.

"You could see that?" Grace repeated; she looked alarmed.

"He was smiling at her a lot." Simone patted her arm. "But Hazen's like that; he loves flirting with women. Just play it cool. Don't let him get to you."

"Like…flirt with other guys?"

"If that's what it takes." Simone laughed. "But there's only Zeff and Joey here, and I don't know if they're your type."

"Zeff's hot, in a rugged-old-man kind of way, but he's obviously in love with you." Grace pouted. "I don't know why you don't make a move. Put him out of his misery."

"Because we are on a mission to assassinate someone," Simone replied. "Maybe start some kind of civil war. Maybe be tortured, killed, I don't know. I don't think that *now* is the time to worry about love."

"Then when is the time?" Grace asked. "Because we may not have a whole lot of time left. You know that as well as I do."

Carmen and Libby returned to the fire with one of Hazen's bowls; the omelettes were ready to be cooked. A flat stone was laid across half of the fire pit, and once it was hot enough, Carmen cooked the eggs on it and added the filling. A respectful silence fell over the group as the first omelette bubbled and hissed over the fire.

"Any ideas about who burned your house down?" Zeff asked suddenly.

There was silence again; this time it was strained.

"We saw 'em," Joey said, staring at the steaming omelette on the cooking rock. "Didn't recognize anyone, though."

"Notice anything unusual about these individuals?" Zeff persisted.

"Yeah, they were a bunch of fucking tough guys, you know, scary sons of bitches." He moved his jaw around as he thought about it, revealing a significant underbite. "They must have been a gang or something. Black leather, lots of tattoos."

"Any weird eye tattoos?"

"Excuse me?"

"First omelette's done!" Carmen shouted. "And it's a damn good one." Her words were beginning to slur from the cider.

"I'll have it," Joey said.

"The first one will be split amongst our guests!" she shouted drunkenly. "That's called being polite, dummy." Carmen returned her attention to the omelette again, quartering it with some effort before handing the portions around to them. Still hot and bubbling with juices, it tasted heavenly.

As they ate, Zeff told the VanCleaves about Horus and the New Empire and then moved on to the fictional story of his aunt in Smyth. This time Simone tuned him out, focusing her attention instead on the softness of the eggs, the bite of cheese they were given by the Taylors, and the juicy bits of tomato. In her opinion, the mushrooms were tasteless and chewy, but she didn't mind; she could have eaten forty omelettes just like it.

By the time dinner was over, a heavy drowsiness spread over the group like a favorite blanket. The only sound was the fire snapping its kindling and flinging clouds of smoke up into the darkness. A coyote howled nearby.

Still seated by the fire, Simone felt happy, despite an insistent thudding that had started behind her eyes. The evening air felt so nice on her skin, so smooth. She raised her face to the sky as the breeze swept her hair off her cheek. The sensation reminded her of her mother, and she felt a great sadness welling up inside her, growing bigger and bigger and bigger until it burst, and then she was laughing, laughing, laughing. Bent over, her sides in stiches, Simone laughed until she was physically exhausted. Then she laughed some more.

Wiping the tears from her eyes, she leaned back and caught sight of Hazen and Carmen in a passionate embrace on the other side of the fire. Libby and Joey sat a short distance away, watching the two lovers until Carmen rose to her feet and led the handsome tradesman into the darkness.

Simone laughed again.

On the other side of the fire, Zeff stood and made his way over to her as if he was balancing on a tightrope. With great care, he lowered himself to the ground.

"What…the hell…is going on…here?" Zeff asked her. "Something's weird."

"I know," Simone said, still laughing. "I can feel my heartbeat in my eyeballs."

"You're so beautiful," Zeff said in a rush, the words tumbling out of his mouth before he could stop them. "I wish I could see you right now." The world seemed to be flickering like a strobe light around him. He felt so strange. *Was this how it felt to go blind?*

Simone stared at Zeff. "Why are you so sad?" She leaned forward and lightly stroked the beard that darkened his weathered jawline. He pressed his face into her hand, closing his eyes against her touch.

"Because I care about you," he murmured. "I don't want to be a burden. I want you to be happy."

Simone could hear Zeff speaking, but she was having difficulty following his words. She was looking at the stars again. Like magic, the twinkling lights above her head seemed to spin together, taking the form of a beautiful goddess reclining in the heavens. The female deity smiled at Simone and gave her a roguish wink. Flattered by the divine attention, Simone winked back.

It was at that moment that Grace appeared naked before the fire, the soft curves of her body bathed in the gold-spun light. She carried three well-patched blankets in her arms that she threw on the ground next to Zeff, bending down on all fours to smooth the pile into a makeshift bed. As she worked, she arched her back and wiggled her rump invitingly.

"See anything you like?" she crooned, then crawled, catlike, to his side, grabbing his calloused hands and placing them on her breasts. Not satisfied with this, she leaned down and covered Zeff's mouth with her own.

At first the rancher was confused; he felt odd and out of sorts. Even breathing seemed difficult. For months, maybe years, he had steeped away in his own loneliness, pining for a woman he had no right to love. Perla had been his friend, and he wasn't a cradle robber, so he'd sought out Simone very carefully, taking great pains to manage his feelings for her. This strategy had sort of worked when he was her neighbor and they had miles of wilderness between them. Then they'd lived together in the root cellar for months, and Zeff had been forced to find time alone every day to keep his head on straight. Now they were traveling together, and the burning physical proximity of Simone's company was wearing him out. His heart felt charred and weak, his eyes betrayed him at every turn, and his presence of mind, which had once been quiet and serene, now heaved and roiled like sun-scorched earth.

Zeff felt soft curves under his hand, and the ground seemed to give way beneath his feet. He was falling through a never-ending darkness, but he wasn't afraid. *She* was there too, beside him; they were falling together. His Simone, beautiful Simone. They had found each other here, in the abyss, and she loved him too. He gave in to the demands of the warm flesh covering his body. His hands began moving on their own, and soon he had thrust himself between Grace's thighs, penetrating her deeply, as Simone sat nearby, wearing a vacant expression on her face.

Joey and Libby observed their guests with satisfaction across the fire.

"I'm pissed she used the last of my 'shrooms, but you gotta hand it to her, spiking the omelettes was a good plan," Joey said. "Good thing I saved them from the fire."

"It was the *only* thing you saved from the fire," Libby retorted. "Actually, I'd stop mentioning the fire if I were you."

"Did the trick, didn't it?" Joey was smug. "Be honest. Who would you rather be tomorrow? Them or us?"

"Us."

"Damn right you would," he said.

SMOKE SIGNALS

S imone awoke the next morning as the sun began peering into her eyes. A bird choir was singing in the treetops; nearby, a sparrow perched in a dogwood and began cleaning his plumage. She watched this and wished she could feel so industrious. Instead, she felt like a slug. Her teeth ached, her back was stiff, and her mind felt hazy. She was thirstier than hell, and worse yet, there was an uneasy feeling in the pit of her stomach, and she wasn't sure why.

Something's wrong. She threw the blanket aside and shivered. *Something's happened.*

She fumbled around for her shotgun. Finding it tucked under the blanket at her side, she breathed a sigh of relief. She next sought the comfort of her long leather jacket, and it was then that she discovered Zeff and Grace's naked bodies beside her, still entwined in a lover's embrace. With a grimace, she pulled her jacket out from under Grace's curvaceous rear end and shook it out, watching the two sleep. Curious, she leaned over and looked at Zeff's face. In Grace's arms, his sharp features were softer, his twitching eyebrows stilled. Even his mouth was relaxed. He had never looked more handsome. Simone supposed she should have felt jealous. But all she really felt was the nip of the cold and a strong urge to hit the wilderness commode. But there was still something else…

"Simone?" Zeff said in a strangled voice. He had awoken in Grace's sweaty arms and instantly recalled the events of the night before. They had…but why? He didn't have any answers, but he knew Simone had seen them. What would she think of him now? Sitting up, he stared at her, but her expression was a blur to his aching eyes. Was she angry? God—could she be disgusted? Zeff felt nauseated as he considered all the ways he had debased himself in front of her last night. Simone. Of all people. At that moment, he would have given his life just to see her face.

Grace stirred beside him, stretching under the blankets. "Good morning, tiger," she said, running the palm of her hand along Zeff's back. She caught sight of Simone and stopped. "Oh! Morning, Simone."

Hearing her name overwhelmed Zeff with frustration and shame. He turned towards Grace, scowling. "Goddamn it!" he shouted, pulling the blankets around his waist. "You bewitched me with something!"

Grace's sleepy kitten smile melted into an irritated frown. "First of all," she said, "I didn't have to do much convincing. Second of all, your pal Joey obviously drugged us."

Zeff let out a long, hissing sigh. "Where's Hazen?"

"Who cares?" Grace answered without missing a beat.

There was an anguished howl in the distance. For Simone, it suddenly clicked into place. "The caravan!" she cried, running toward the sound.

She found Hazen standing by the little thicket of wood where he had hidden his wagon the night before. But this morning, the colorful Esmeralda was nowhere to be seen. And the horses were missing.

"Oh, Hazen, I'm so sorry," Simone said, her heart sinking into the sole of her boots. "We'll find her again...somehow." Her voice faded as she thought about Alfred, and her stomach coiled into knots. She had little faith in the kindness of the VanCleave family and their ability to take care of animals. What if they mistreated Alfred? What if they ate him? He must be so scared.

"What are we gonna do?" Hazen asked bleakly. "We've lost every-thing. Our weapons are gone. Our supplies are gone. We'll be lucky if we can survive a week out here, never mind getting Esmeralda back." His handsome face was clouded with misery; the theft of his pride and joy had left him a broken man. He had lost his home. He had lost everything he had worked for. It was all gone. Covering his face with his hands, Hazen released a wracking sob.

"My shotgun's got a few shells left," Simone said halfheartedly. "That's something at least."

"Looks like your little girlfriend screwed us all last night," Grace said, striding into the clearing with Zeff close behind her. She finished buttoning up her shirt. "Guess you're nothing special, Hazen."

"Come on, Grace." Simone shot her a withering look. "Give the man a break. I think we can all agree that we were drugged last night. Some things happened, and that's that. Let's just forget about it."

"Wait a second—some *things* happened?" Hazen asked Simone. "Things? As in the plural of 'thing'? Wait...did you and Zeff...did *Grace* and Zeff?"

Grace shot Hazen a rebellious look. Zeff just kept his head down and looked like he was eating something sour.

"Oh, Christ!" he exclaimed. "You two had sex?"

"So did you and Carmen!" Grace shouted. "At least Zeff isn't a bloody Judas!"

"No, he's just as old as Judas! Hey, Zeff, all this time I thought you were in love with Simone. Who knew you were so fucking easy!"

Hazen tried to punch Zeff in the face, but the rancher had been waiting for that. Feeling the force of the tradesman's hand rushing toward him, Zeff grabbed the offending appendage and twisted it behind the younger man's back until he yelped in pain.

"Don't let your hands make a fool outta you," Zeff growled, without releasing his grip.

"Get a hold of yourselves!" Simone cried; she could bear her mounting frustration no longer. The VanCleaves were getting farther and farther away with each passing minute, with Alfred and the rest of their stuff. "We're wasting time," she continued. "They could have killed us last night, all right? They took everything, but they left us alive. If we want to get out of this mess, we've got to pull together and start thinking like a team."

"I agree with Simone. And I think our first team activity should be heading over to that old stump where I hid our guns." Grace smiled. "I also hid a few provisions, of course. I knew that family was devious, but nobody listened to me."

After locating Grace's hidden loot, stashed in a large knapsack and stuffed under the cavernous roots of an old tree, the group packed up what they had left and hit the road on foot to recover Hazen's stolen caravan. The wagon tracks were easy to find and led them east anyway, toward the New Empire. Joey appeared to be driving the caravan down the deserted highway, trading stealth for speed. That was the kind of recklessness Simone feared and did not follow. She checked the road every so often for tracks, but the group traveled far more carefully than the VanCleave family did, keeping to the forests and fields that ran parallel to the highway so they would be harder to ambush. Anxious to recover Alfred, Simone kept a brisk pace in the lead, crashing through the foliage with her steady stride and snapping off any branches that had the nerve to get in her way. With his poor vision and terrible sense of shame, Zeff had neither the capacity nor the desire to keep up with her, so he trailed morosely behind, feeling his way along the path she made, stumbling over roots and counting his regrets. To further his punishment, Hazen and Grace followed closely at his heels, sniping and quarrelling with each other. It was the Jared and Jason show all over again.

They traveled east all morning, making good time on foot. Gradually, the coolness of the dawn faded away, and the heat became relentless, turning the bleached-out highway into a dusty ocean that rippled and swayed in the heat. Adjusting her course, Simone led the group deeper into the shade of the forest, but the mosquitos they found there were blood crazed, attacking every inch of exposed skin and launching kamikaze strikes into their nostrils and mouths. When the group came across a small stream, they fell upon it with something akin to desperation, dipping their hands into its brimming waters and scraping out layers of skunk-smelling mud. This, they applied liberally to their arms and faces to ward away the desperate insects. In fact, the mosquitos were so bad that even Hazen spread the pungent goo across his face, and without once remarking on the acne-inducing properties of smearing muck on one's face. There was a first for everything.

Fortunately the mud from the stream had its desired effect, and the group had some reprieve from their winged tormentors. They dug a hole along the riverbank, letting the water filter through the mud until it was clean enough to drink. Then they filled their canteens. Nobody spoke. Nobody felt like it.

"The caravan's still traveling east," Simone reported when she returned from her brief reconnaissance of the highway. She'd found fresh wheel tracks in the gravel and trampled-down flora where the caravan appeared to have veered off the road. From the looks of things, Joey was not taking care of Hazen's wagon. She took a swig of water from the canteen Grace handed her. "I think I saw smoke in the distance. Looks like the VanCleaves have made camp already. If we keep going at this pace, we might be able to catch up."

"Why would they stop so early?" Zeff asked, furrowing his muddy brow. "Aren't they worried we'll catch up with them?"

But the news brought a smile to Hazen's dirty face. "Well, let's get moving!" he said, scrambling to his feet.

Hazen took the lead for the second leg of the journey and moved at an enthusiastic pace, eager to set eyes on his beloved Esmeralda again. He whistled softly as he went, bounding over fallen trees and ducking under low-hanging boughs as Grace walked behind him, feeling angry and confused. Their disagreement had passed from shouting into silence, and Hazen didn't enjoy this new development. But once he got Esmeralda back, everything would be better. He would forgive Grace, she would forgive him, and they would be back in the lap of luxury with food, blankets, and horses. Plus, he would have his stuff back, which was timely because he needed his special stinging nettle tonic to wash the river junk off his face. (God knows what it was doing to his pores.)

By the time the column of smoke was clearly in their sight, the sun was high in the diaphanous sky. It looked to be early afternoon, and even Hazen was beginning to wonder why the VanCleave family would have made camp already, especially after fleeing with a stolen caravan in the night. Were they having some kind of extended lunch? He thought of Charlie Taylor, weeping over his faith in his gasless Mercedes, and wondered: *Could this be divine intervention?*

When the air was thick with the smell of campfire, Hazen felt like he had reached the end of the rainbow. The forest path was too dense to see the campsite, so he motioned for everyone else to wait in the woods while he snuck a peek. Once they knew how Joey had set up camp, they could determine the best way to attack it. At least, that's what Simone said, and she was generally right about these things. He was just anxious to see his caravan again.

And see her he did; cutting his way through the forest and moving down to the highway, he found the charred remains of his beautiful Esmeralda, still smoking in the sun. There wasn't much left of her, just the remnants of a wooden frame and a sagging cover, blackened and billowing in the hot breeze. Behind the burning wreckage on the other side of the highway, Hazen caught a glimpse of something that he couldn't identify but seemed to draw him in. Once he'd noticed it, he felt like he couldn't look at anything else, even his poor Esmeralda. He didn't even realize he was walking toward it, until he was standing a few feet away from the object and staring at it with mounting terror.

He felt himself falling to his knees. The earth seemed to spin around him as he stared up at what he now recognized as a badly mutilated corpse, still dripping blood onto the dirt below. Bloated, nude, bearing horrific wounds, the legs dangled limp in the breeze. With a sudden wave of queasiness, Hazen realized the body had been cruelly impaled on a large wooden stake that had been thrust through the anus, emerging through the corpse's silently howling mouth. The eyes had been cut out, leaving the ravaged face streaked with gore. A terrible wound marred the pubic area of the body, making it impossible to determine the gender at first devastating glance. Only the small patch of ragged hair at the back of the head could serve to identify the body as Joey VanCleave.

Hazen put his hands on the ground to brace himself. Making a low moaning noise, he trembled violently in the sun before vomiting into the dirt. Taking a big inhale and wiping at his mouth, he looked up and watched a glossy black crow settling on the corpse's head. Scornfully, it set midnight eyes upon him and began pecking at the anguished face beneath its feet.

"Stop!" Hazen screamed. His feathered foe looked surprised but flew off anyway, and settled in a nearby pine.

"Hazen! Your caravan!" Grace cried. She had left the forest and was making her way onto the highway, staring at the smoking wreck. She caught sight of him on his knees and ran across the road to him, her long legs making short work of the distance between them. Once she reached his side, she threw herself to the ground and wrapped her arms around him.

"Let's get out of here," she whispered, staring up at Joey's body, her face stark with horror.

"You're right," Hazen said faintly. "We should bury him and go."

"We have to leave him. We have to get out of here." Grace said casting a terrified glance at the woods behind them.

"We can't leave him like this." Hazen wept. "It's not right."

"No, it's not right. It is *definitely* not right. But generals did this." Grace pointed to a familiar-looking wound carved into Joey's face. "The Eye of Horus—they know we're out here. Joey probably told them about us during…this." She gestured to the wounds that covered his body. "If we take him down, they'll know we came this way. Right now, they think we're headed toward Smyth. That's the only advantage we have."

Grace helped Hazen to his feet and pulled him away from the grisly sight. As they walked past the smoldering remains of his caravan, he looked over his shoulder at what was left of his sweet Esmeralda. But he didn't feel anything then. He didn't feel anything at all.

GONE FISHIN'

They found a small clearing in the woods and made camp for the night, but Simone was restless. She couldn't stop worrying about Alfred's fate at the hands of the generals. Horses were prized commodities these days, but so were finely crafted wagons, and look at what they had done to Hazen's caravan. Simone shook her head; she didn't understand these men. They were far more savage than strategic, which made them difficult to predict. She hoped they would see Alfred's value and treat him decently. She hoped she would find him again and steal him back. All she could do was hope.

But hope doesn't fill an empty belly, and Simone was starting to realize that she was hungry. Ravenous actually. She hadn't eaten anything all day, and it was making her edgy. She sat down to preserve her energy and mull over their food options. They could dip into the provisions Grace had hidden, but they still had a long way to go, and the weather was good; it was better to save them for an emergency. Furthermore, the hunting and fishing looked promising in the area, and Simone was confident she could find them something for dinner. In fact, she was as starved for alone time as she was for food. Zeff had been downcast and mournful all day; she felt it would be a blessing for the both of them to have some space.

She looked at Hazen and Grace, sitting together under an old spruce tree. Grace held the head of her scorned lover in her lap and was murmuring quietly to him. Around them, the air was filled with white poplar fluff that caught in the needles of the tree boughs above their heads and covered the ground around them. The scene was beautiful and tranquil; it served as an unnerving contrast to the terrified look on Hazen's face and his unrecognizable, hollow eyes. He hadn't spoken a word since they'd returned from the highway. Grace said they had found Joey's mutilated corpse down there.

"We can't let them take us alive," she'd said. "Better to be killed in the fight than go out like that."

Now Grace's eyes scanned the wilderness as she held Hazen in her arms, her revolver close at her side. She would probably want everyone to stay together at the camp. But Simone felt her stomach growl, clench, and roll over, and she decided to risk it. *Hot food always lifts the spirits*, she thought, grabbing her shotgun. *And Grace and Hazen need all the help they can get.*

"I was thinking about going on a hunt, maybe catch some fish," Simone said to Grace. "We need to eat." Standing up, she shook poplar fluff off her hat.

Grace stared up at her in surprise. "Simone—are you crazy? We can't split up now! It's too dangerous!"

"We need to save our rations for when we really need them," she reasoned. "I'll just go down to the river and see if I can catch some fish. I'll even cook 'em there."

Begrudgingly, Grace's mouth began to water. Her belly throbbed with hunger pains. She looked down at Hazen; he had closed his eyes. He would be hungry too— once the shock wore off. "You can't go alone," she said finally.

And that's how Simone and Zeff ended up at the river together, silently appraising its depths from the shore. The water was still, but the tension between them crackled in the air like an oncoming storm. Under the brim of his cattleman cowboy hat, Zeff's brain was working overtime, searching for something to say. He was so damn embarrassed about the night before, so embarrassed about Grace. The shame he felt cut deep, and there was no escaping it; it was as much a part of him now as the marrow in his bones, as his own shadow, which he couldn't fucking see but knew was still there. He squinted hard at the fuzzy figure of Simone; she seemed to be seated. He recognized the clicking sound of a knife; she must be sharpening a branch into a spear.

He moved away from the river and began clearing a spot for a small cooking fire, feeling the ground with his hands to remove the debris. Dried grasses crunched and snapped under his fingers as he worked. They would make good kindling.

"Good prospect for fish," Simone said, her voice higher than usual. "Maybe we'll catch a turtle if we're lucky."

Zeff didn't reply for a moment, and Simone wondered if he had heard her.

"I need to say something to you," he blurted out. "I didn't know what I was doing last night. I know we were drugged, but that's no excuse for my behavior with Grace. Not when I love you."

He regretted the confession the instant it came out of his mouth. He had no business telling her such things. She was a young woman with her whole life ahead of her, and he was a worn-out old bachelor whose chance at love had faded years ago. Now his eyesight was leaving him too. He squinted at Simone, desperate to read her face, but for once his aching eyes were kind to him, and he was spared the sight of her obvious discomfort.

A noise in the bushes behind them saved Simone a reply. The rustling sound was too heavy and deliberate to be the wind. Something big was coming their way, prowling through the brush in the direction of the river. The tiny hairs rose along the nape of her neck as she pulled her shotgun from its sling. Beside her, Zeff stopped what he was doing and tilted his head, listening.

A black bear emerged from the willows down the shore. Gingerly placing one paw in the river, then the other, the animal waded into the water. He took several big gulps before submerging himself in the river and paddling away from shore, his dark head cutting through the reflected trees and sky. Reaching a rock that jutted out from the riverbed, the bear climbed out onto it, balancing his sizable mass with an athlete's grace. He stood there for an instant, listening, watching, before suddenly plunging back into the water and emerging with a wiggling fish in his jaws. When he returned to shore, he gazed meditatively about his surroundings before his brown eyes settled on Simone, and she gazed back at him without fear. Woman and bear regarded each other in a semifriendly fashion before the bear turned and ran back into the bushes with his dinner. She smiled. He had been a welcome diversion, and not only that, he had showed them the river had fish. Which it did—fish aplenty.

The conversation fell away again as Simone hunted with her makeshift fish spear, and Zeff roasted the catch over a small cooking fire. She caught an even dozen before wrapping the last four in leaves, then clay from the river. After that, they buried the fish in the coals of the fire; they would leave them there to roast until morning.

The cooking eased the tension between the two friends, but it was still there, crackling at the edges of their sparse conversation, and whispering, "Things will never be the same."

HAVENBROOK

The sky was overcast the next morning, and conspiratorial black rain clouds gathered low on the horizon. The trees moaned and shook, and the air felt thick with the coming storm. This time it was Grace who woke them early. Aside from Hazen, who was still in shock, she had been the only member of the group to see Joey's body, and she desperately wanted to keep moving and leave the violence on the highway behind. After retrieving the last of their fish, she led the group for most of the morning, dragging a dazed-looking Hazen behind her. The entire party seemed to be making good time on foot; at least, before the sky opened up and started dumping buckets of rain over their heads. After that, progress slowed to a crawl. The wind was inescapable, howling in their faces from every direction and pelting them with fat droplets of water. The trail became slick with mud, and everyone lost their balance at least once. All they could do was put their heads down and travel through the bush in a gloomy silence, inching toward an even grimmer place.

The rain still hadn't stopped by evening, so they sought shelter in an old-growth forest. Grace found a dry spot at the foot of a large spruce tree, and they erected a respectable shelter out of fallen branches. The few possessions they still had were soaked, and they couldn't get a fire started, despite Zeff's best efforts with a flint rock, then a bow saw. This disappointment forced them to spend the night in the wet and chilly darkness, huddled together for warmth and sharing the intimacy of survival.

Sullen gray showers met them again in the morning when the outfit roused themselves and found their bodies sore and shivering. Drab specters of cloud scuttled across the sky as Simone assessed the weather with a sinking heart; they were in for another day of hard traveling. Zeff dispensed the last of the fish, and they all choked on the cold, rubbery food, satisfying their bellies but nothing more.

They pressed on until the shelter of the forest soon gave way to open sweeps of meadowland where wild roses grew along fallen fence posts, filling the air with their heartbreaking sweetness.

"Looks like horses have been grazing here," Simone observed, pointing to a cleared patch of field.

Hazen looked hopeful. "Think they're ours?"

"Could be." She thought of Alfred and crossed her fingers.

The field came to a stop at a ragged country road. Stepping out onto the concrete and peering down the street, Simone could see a weather-stripped sign in the distance, squeaking in the rain. *Welcome to Havenbrook*, it read.

"Havenbrook?" Grace stepped onto the road behind her. "I've never heard of this place before."

"You might have," Hazen replied. "It housed a huge slaughterhouse and meatpacking plant in its day."

"There's a cheerful thought," Grace said, her teeth chattering. "Think anyone's left in town? Maybe we can find some provisions."

"Dry clothing would be aces right now." Hazen shivered. "I think I'm getting hypothermia."

Both Simone and Zeff were hesitant about going into town and leaving the planned route for the day, but they too were chilled to the bone. They knew they had to warm up before the situation became serious.

"Keep your weapons handy," Zeff said.

The group proceeded down the street and turned down the next, traveling furtively so they would not be discovered, moving among the imitation clapboard houses that lined the road. The houses must have looked the same once, when they were new. They all had the same shape, the same pastel siding. Now, the extent of the damage set each house apart, each one bearing the signs of a ruthless attack that must have happened some time ago. Windows had been smashed in and broken. Front doors were completely torn away, leaving empty entranceways in their place. There were scorch marks, bullet holes, and bleached-out bloodstains everywhere. The very earth felt haunted beneath their feet.

Passing a sign that read *Main Street*, the wartime housing gave way to a patch of small downtown businesses. Moving like animals of prey, they crept past a mostly burned-down post office, overturned fry truck, and vandalized jewelry store, then on to the Havenbrook Diner with its smashed-in windows and sodden carpet of leaves and plastic wrappers.

At the end of the road, they found a park that held the remains of a children's playground. In the thigh-high grass, a pair of rusted swings moved in the wind while saddled pigs and frogs bobbed metallically on their springs. Beyond the playground, the wild tangle of grassland fell away, and the slaughterhouse could be seen in miniature below, calmly outwaiting the rain.

"Who puts a children's park in view of a slaughterhouse?" Grace scoffed. "This place is beyond creepy. We should get out of here."

"Hold on," Simone said in a low voice. She gestured in the direction of the playground equipment, where a small figure was wading through the grass, making its way toward them. It was a boy: thin, soaking wet, and hunched with the cold.

"Help me! Help me, please!" the child implored them. He huddled by some lilac bushes, clutching his hands together, too frightened to come any closer. "My mom needs help! She's going to die!" he cried tearfully, before rushing into the bushes and disappearing from sight.

"Wait!" Grace called. When the boy made no sign of returning, she started running after him.

"Grace! Stop!" Hazen shouted, but she kept running. "This isn't safe!"

"He's a little boy!" she called over her shoulder. "He needs helps!" Then she, too, disappeared from sight.

"Goddamn it," Hazen cursed before hurrying after her.

"We should stay here," Zeff said to Simone. "We don't know anything about this place."

"You can stay here if you like," Simone said, breaking into a sprint. "But I'm going!"

Zeff scowled, but he followed after her. No one wanted to be left behind in Havenbrook.

They waded into the dripping lilac patch, which soon gave way to a scrubby thicket that grew down the side of the hill. Chasing after the boy, they crashed through the wet foliage, tripping over tree stumps and snagging their hair and shirt sleeves on wayward branches and thorns. The boy was small and shoeless, but he could scamper through the bush like a mouse, zipping through the undergrowth with ease, as they struggled along after him.

At the bottom of the hill, they found themselves in a landscape that had become sprawling and industrial. An old auto-body shop stood looted and empty. Parking lots were filled with all manner of debris. A doe bolted out of a storage-locker business and ran into the street with them until suddenly shying off down another alley-way. Ahead, the slaughterhouse loomed before them like a rough, dark-hearted beast. Simone was starting to feel nervous.

"He better not be taking us to the slaughterhouse," she muttered to Zeff, who was just behind her. The place looked dark and foreboding, and she had no interest in visiting. Nonetheless, the boy led them to the front gate at the edge of the waterlogged parking lot, making sure everyone was still following him before dropping to the ground and wiggling underneath. But before he could disappear completely, Zeff grabbed him by the legs and pulled him back out.

"Where are you taking us?" he demanded, holding the boy by his shirt.

"Let me go!" the boy cried. "My mom needs help!"

"You live in the slaughterhouse with your mom?" Zeff persisted. "Just the two of you?"

"We have to go!" the boy sobbed. "We have to go right now! She's going to die!"

"Let him go!" Grace shouted. "Jesus, Zeff! He's just a kid!"

Zeff reluctantly let the boy go, and he wriggled under the gate like an eel.

"Some compassion would do you good," Grace said with a frown, before neatly scaling up the gate and jumping down on the other side.

"Girl thinks she's got the world by the tail," Zeff grumbled to himself as he climbed over the gate after her, feeling his way as he went.

The boy led them down a gravel path before veering into the long, curving cattle ramp that led to the entrance of the slaughterhouse. Simone had once read that cattle ramps were meant to calm the cows, to keep them oblivious to the squealing, mechanized slaughter that lay before them. But now, as she raced down the oppressive passage, wondering what could be lurking around every corner, the device seemed anything but calming.

The cattle ramp ended in a holding pen inside the slaughterhouse that had a slippery floor and smelled musty and stale. Hoisting themselves over the sides of the pen, the group ran further inside after the boy. Simone noticed the slaughterhouse walls were covered in thick plastic sheeting. A derelict conveyor belt wound its way through the terrible shadows of the room. Monstrous hooks and chains hung above the boy's head as he darted to a door ahead and pushed his way inside.

With Grace still in the lead, they followed after him, stumbling into an unbearable darkness. The door swung shut behind them and gave a final-sounding click. Simone groped for the handle, but it only confirmed what she already knew: the door was locked. She turned and waited for her eyes to adjust, but there was nothing to adjust to; the blackness was infinite and unyielding.

There was a shallow panting sound.

"Hey, kid, where'd you go?" Grace's voice echoed in the dark. "Where's your mother?"

"This is a trap," a low voice said. "I thought you might have figured that out by now. Go ahead and drop those weapons you're holding. And just so you know, Daddy's watching."

There were the sounds of fumbling and unstrapping. Clink, clank, thud; everyone dropped their weapons to the ground.

"Hey, old timer, I'm talking to you too. Drop that knife, or I'll kill one of your friends."

Clank.

"OK. It took some time, but we finally got there. Boys, give the idiot savants a round of applause."

The room shook with the roars of men. The clapping was deafening. The four companions drew closer to one another and clung together. There was a feeling of dreadful resignation between them. It seemed this must be their fate—to come here and be torn apart in the darkness by an army of unknowns.

When the shouts and applause had faded away, there was a sharp snapping noise. Then the voice spoke again: "Otto, show the good people what they've won. Light 'er up."

A match flared in the blackened room, and a single torch flickered to life. The light it gave off was watery and uncertain, but it illuminated the gravity of the situation they were now in. Unfamiliar, unfriendly men with bats and knives lined the edges of the room around them. Several brandished guns. They looked tough and pockmarked, a sea of black leather and facial scars. And neck tattoos.

The center of the room seemed to yawn into some kind of pit. Beside it towered a man with an executioner's mask on his face, bare chested in the cold, wearing a pair of bloodied parachute pants. He held a Glock .34 in his left hand. At his feet, a woman was perched on her knees, gagged and blindfolded, trembling violently.

"Solar-powered night vision," the man said, gesturing to the goggles that hung casually around his neck. "We used to invent such interesting things!" He laughed, flashing a strong set of carnivorous teeth, and then turned to face the boy cowering before him.

"Here's your darling mother," he addressed the child. "I've been taking care of her while you were gone."

The boy took a few tentative steps toward the woman, his eyes filled with concern.

"Well?" the man barked. "Aren't you going to thank me?" He pointed his gun at the boy, who froze where he stood, staring at the barrel.

"Thank you," the child said in a quavering voice.

"Thank you *what?*"

"Thank you, Emperor H-H-Horus."

Simone stole a glance at Grace beside her. The bastard was here! They were close enough to kill him. The only problem was, he would probably kill them first. She scrutinized the man in the mask. He was an intimidating, frightening figure, but there was something familiar, almost predictable in his manner or his voice. There was something about him, something she just couldn't put her finger on.

"Now," Horus continued, advancing upon the boy like a spider with a fly. "I believe I said if you led these people to me, I would spare your mother. Is that correct?"

The boy nodded.

"Do you know what a lie is?"

Worried, the boy nodded again.

"Good. You're not as stupid as you look." Lips curled in a smile, the self-proclaimed emperor raised his gun and shot the blind-folded woman in the chest. She pitched forward with a muffled scream, struggling on the floor before her body stilled, and she fell silent. Zeff roared with outrage, prompting a nearby general to slash his arm with a dagger before pressing it to his throat.

Horrified, the boy stared at his mother, unable to speak.

"You win some, you lose some, buddy," Horus said, ruffling the child's hair.

The boy shook himself free from his grasp and reeled backward, his face contorted with hatred and wet with tears. The emperor watched him with some curiosity, smiling as the boy tried in vain to stop crying. When the child hiccupped loudly, Horus's eyes hardened behind his mask.

"Get him out of here," he snapped, pressing his fingers to his temple. "I think I feel a migraine coming on."

Two generals stepped forward and began to pull the weeping child from the room.

"Wait, wait," Horus said. He stared at the boy; there was a strange, reptilian light in his eye. "Leave the boy. Stand down. I said *stand down, Goddamn it!*"

The generals let the boy go and backed away with their eyes on the floor.

"Listen," Horus said to the boy. "I shouldn't have lied to you. Let me make it right." He smiled and for a moment; his eyes seemed to soften. "Come here," he said and stretched out his arms.

Still weeping, the boy took one tiny step forward, then another.

Like a rattlesnake, Horus struck quickly. He drew his gun, aimed, and shot the boy in the head. Without a sound, the tiny body lurched forward before collapsing on the ground beside his mother.

Grace screamed.

With a casual disinterest, Horus sauntered over to the bodies of the dead woman and child. A small smile played over his lips as he surveyed his work. Then, without warning, he laid into them, kicking at the bodies with an unrestrained brutality until they flopped into the pit below. The smear of blood they left on the floor looked sinister in the torchlight.

"Next on the docket is what to do with *you*." Horus turned to face his four guests, his eyes glittered in his mask; they were cold, dead, impenetrable. Simone stared at them in shock. They had awoken a chill of recognition in her. It finally clicked into place.

This man killed my brother.

Hate hardened like a lump in her stomach; blood sang in her ears. Thoughts of Emerson flashed in her mind: a handsome young boy, looking for frogs in the creek; a kindly older brother, bandaging her knee when she fell off her bike; the two of them, together, goofing off as they washed mom's car in the driveway. Em got older and older in her mind, until suddenly he didn't. Because he couldn't.

Because of *him*.

The ground seemed to heave beneath her feet. Her body trembled with years of pent-up anger and loss. "Harvey Miller." Her voice sounded coarse to her own ears. "Still nothing but a goddamn murderer, I see. Tell me, is there anything else you can do?"

Horus turned toward Simone abruptly and stalked toward her with the ease of a jaguar, grinding his formidable jaws. "Who the fuck are you?" he demanded, thrusting his head forward until it was inches from her own. He sniffed the air dramatically through his mask. "I smell dyke. Let me guess, former parole officer?"

"Wildlife enforcement, actually."

He circled around behind her. Simone could feel his breath on the nape of her neck. His malignant gaze spilled across her body like acid, and she straightened her shoulders, refusing to be intimidated.

"You look familiar to me. But where do I know you from…"

He didn't form the sentence as a question, but she answered him anyway. "You don't know me; I know you. I made it my business to know you after you murdered my brother." With one fluid motion, Simone pulled her knife from her arm sheath and turned on Horus, striking him with the dagger. She went for his throat, trying to drive the blade deep into his neck, but he lowered his chin, and she slashed at his face instead, cutting his mask like butter.

The room erupted into shouting. Dimly, Simone was aware of Zeff and Hazen nearby, fighting with a group of generals who were struggling to get to Horus.

"Kill him!" Grace screamed, biting a bearded general on the cheek.

The torchlight sputtered, hurling the room into darkness as Horus made another grab for Simone. Slipping on the bloodied floor, she darted past him and tightened her grip on the dagger. The room brightened again, and she turned the same moment he did, running at him, holding the blade high, this time aiming for his cold, black eyes.

A jolt ran through her body before she could make contact; there was a bright explosion of light, and suddenly she could no longer stand. Simone felt herself tipping toward the ground, dropping her knife so she could brace herself against the stained concrete floor. Something heavy hit her across her back, and she curled up in a ball to protect herself. Then there was another explosion of pain; the blows came again and again until she couldn't move and couldn't think.

The beating stopped abruptly, and Grace was suddenly standing over her, howling with rage. With tigerlike ferocity, she tackled Simone's assailant, who turned out to be a bat-wielding general almost twice her size, but she went for the man's knees, pulling him down with her as she fell. Thrown off balance, the beefy man fell backward, and the two went rolling across the floor together, cursing and struggling. Grace grabbed the man's pinkie finger and pulled it back until it snapped, and he dropped the bat with a shriek. Seizing the opportunity to disadvantage her opponent further, she raked at his eyes with her fingernails, and the man lunged away from her, squinting. She leaped on top of him as he wiped at his eyes, and the two dropped back to the ground. Struggling to the top of the pile, Grace wrapped her legs around the general's neck, squeezing them tight. The general gasped for air, kicking his legs and clawing at her thighs until he drew blood, but Grace wouldn't release her hold. Other generals moved in to intervene, but Horus waved them back with an impatient swipe of the hand. He moved closer to the skirmish, crouching down on the floor and watching as the general struggled for breath. Licking his terrible and sensuous lips, Horus smiled as his man went purple, then blue, then white as Grace squeezed the life from him. The attack wore on for some time, filling the room with the sounds of a prolonged and relentless choking.

Eventually, the general's arms went limp, and the last of his oxygen bubbled out of his throat. The room went painfully silent and still as everyone regarded Horus with some confusion. But the man in question appeared to be full of confidence as he rose to his feet and cocked his head, looking at his generals as if he dared one of them to say something. No one did.

"Well done," he said to Grace. "Very well done." He smiled smugly. "Are you disappointed to know that you've done me a service?" This thought seemed to amuse him, as he chuckled like an indulgent father. "I'm afraid you have, although I can't quite bring myself to thank you for it. You see, the herd, as it were," he gestured to his generals, "must be culled from time to time. It's a simple fact of life. They know it, and I know it."

Horus pulled off the satin mask and grinned at his men; the effect was disturbing. His long black hair, receding slightly at the temples, was pulled back into a low ponytail, framing a strange, angular face. His scarred cheeks and high forehead appeared to have been painted with war paint, although it had become smeared under his mask, giving him the look of a demented clown. The struggle with Simone had left a long gash across his jutting cheekbones that still oozed blood and yellow fatty tissue. Thick rivers of gore trickled into his grinning, fleshy mouth.

At his feet, Simone stirred slightly, trying to pull herself upright, but she was too dizzy. Her brain had been tossed like a ship at sea, and she felt nauseated. She moved her hands to her face and realized that her hat was gone. Without warning, Horus reached down and yanked her up by her ponytail, pulling her upright until she was standing in front of him, hunched in pain.

"Now, you listen to me," he said. "When you address me, it's Emperor Horus. Or Emperor. Or Horus. I will accept any of those titles." He grabbed her face and squeezed it hard. "But call me Harvey again, and I'll cut your tongue out. You got that, *Simone?* See, I do know you." He smiled. "You were that little maggot's sister, Wordsworth or Shelley or whatever his name was. I used to see you in court all the time. I even had a special nickname for you. That's right, you were the Sad Sister. Sad Sister Simone sitting still in court. So much has happened since then, wouldn't you agree, sis?"

Horus released her from his grasp and took a few steps back, spinning wildly on his feet. "I was sent into exile by the dregs of society and rose again, a god, baptized by the sun, and with an army of outcasts at my command. I am Horus now." He turned to face her, his eyes shining with madness. "The last hope for humanity."

"Humanity." Simone snorted. "That's just *one* of the things you're missing."

"You think the word 'humanity' means weakness?" he asked. "You think the human race should be defenseless as piglets, suckling at the government's teat, fattening up the weak at the expense of the strong?" With a look of contempt, he moved away again, stalking the perimeter of the room. As he paced, generals dove out of his way, desperate to not fall across his path.

Drawing to a stop on the other side of the pit, Horus gave his men a long hard stare. "*I* always knew we were capable of so much more, and I was imprisoned for my troubles. Meanwhile, our nation of parasites continued to breed weaker and weaker strains, until look what happened: we lost electricity, and we crumbled. *We crumbled!* Yes, man, lord of the beasts, could no longer survive on his own when every other creature in this world could. We had become less capable than fly larvae, and we finally realized that. Can you tell me what else we learned during this *unfortunate* event?" Horus glanced around the room with strange, agitated eyes. "We learned that man is *not* created equal!" he thundered. "That assertion is ideological claptrap! A fallacy! A bald-faced lie told to us by our nanny-state government. You witnessed for yourself that domestic man could not survive in the wild. And yet savage man prospered." He held out his arms. "*I* prospered. You see: Mother Nature is a great equalizer. She has her ways of cleansing the earth and restoring it to the natural order."

Lecture concluded, Horus came back to Simone and put his hands on her shoulders. He looked at her as if she was expected to say something. Simone stared back at him; darkly glaring into his face until she suddenly leaned forward and bit him on the nose as hard as she could. With a low grunt, Horus punched her in the jaw and Simone fell backwards, reeling from the blow. She landed on the ground hard, but she didn't care. There was something vengeful and fatalistic pounding in her head. At this exact moment she felt no fear and no pain; all she wanted to do was hurt this man as much as she could.

Jumping to her feet, Simone charged at Horus again, and it took five generals to restrain her. This time Horus made no attempt to call them off.

"Throw that trash in the can," he ordered, spitting blood on the floor.

Simone thrashed against the generals, but there were too many to resist. A knee was jammed into the small of her back, and she found herself airborne, hurtling into the pit. She hit the ground below, winded but still in one piece. She felt Horus watching her as she drew herself to stand.

"Such a spirited one, aren't you?" he remarked. "So different from that crybaby brother of yours. 'Don't kill me! Don't kill me! I was trying to help you!'" he shrieked to the laughter of his men. "Too bad the girl got all the balls in the family," he said, and the generals howled and jeered. The sound was loud and obviously forced, but Horus didn't seem to mind. He had retrieved his gun from his holster and was stroking it with his other hand, enjoying the moment before pointing it at Grace.

"You're a little wildcat too, aren't you?" he murmured. "My men are going to love you in the New Empire brothel. In fact, *unlimited* brothel access is one of the perks of being a general." He stalked closer to her, looking her in the eye as he ran the barrel of the gun along her cheekbone. "Personally, I find the brothel to be an interesting study in submission: the longer a woman survives there, the more obedient she becomes. Eventually it gets to the point where she'll do anything she's told. *Anything.*" He sighed. "And yet, the process of breaking them in seems to be what every man really values: the reward of watching a woman struggle against her pain and realizing that there's no escape— that she's trapped." He licked the side of her cheek, a long stroke of the tongue that made Grace cringe involuntarily. "Somehow her tears are more exciting when they fall, so salty with defeat and humiliation."

Without warning, Horus smashed Grace across the face with the barrel of his gun. She stumbled on her feet, blinded by the sudden surge of blood in her eyes. The emperor beckoned to one of his generals, and Grace was also sent hurtling into the pit. Below, Simone rushed over to break her fall.

"It's funny how slaughterhouses always attract rats," Horus said, looking down at the two women. "Even now, years after the last cow has been disemboweled, the rats are still here. Once they get a taste of blood, they always want more. They're like people that way." He gave them a cruel smile and gestured to the broken corpses and the pool of gore that subsumed the floor of the pit, black and endless and terrible to behold.

"Let's see how you ladies handle the rats tonight. In the morning, we'll take what's left of you back to the New Empire." With a smirk, Horus kicked the dead general into the pit. The body landed hard, splashing the women with blood.

"Something else," he said, "for the rats."

THE INTERVIEW

The rusted machete at Hazen's throat was beginning to nick his skin. He stole a furtive glance down at the blade before looking away in disgust. The steel was sticky with someone else's blood and matted with strands of long blond hair that rubbed against his neck. He fought back the urge to gag, but the effort seemed unnecessary. The grizzled old general on the other end of the knife was paying little attention to him anyway. His eyes were on Horus and that horrible pit...where Grace was.

Hazen felt useless as he thought of her in there now, with the bodies and the unmistakable smell of death. He fought back another urge to gag. *Grace is tough. She can handle it,* he reassured himself. *And she's got Simone. They'll make it out of there.* But somewhere even deeper in his mind, a soft voice whispered: *Better her than you.*

Zeff was right. He was a goddamn coward.

Feeling guilty, Hazen looked at said compatriot, but he too was looking at the pit. Behind Zeff stood a general with a meat hook and deep, watchful eyes. But the old rancher didn't look frightened; he looked enraged. Zeff's lean frame was coiled as tight as a spring, his eyes narrowed into slits. His fists were clenched and held rigidly at his side, and the expression on his face suggested he would love to use them on somebody. With both of their fates hanging by a thread, this made Hazen feel extra anxious. *I may have my faults, but I know people,* he thought. *And now is not the time to lose your cool.*

"Hey—take it easy," he whispered. "We're in this together, remember?"

"I'll skin that son of a bitch!" came Zeff's heated reply.

"Wait for the right time," Hazen said. "Don't lose your head."

"Shut up," the general muttered behind him, pressing the machete closer to his throat. Hazen shut up immediately.

"Let's go," Horus commanded, casting a final look of disgust at the pit. He turned toward his men, who were headed for the door. "Mitch, you stay here," he said. "You're on guard duty."

From the black bowels of the slaughterhouse, a muffled noise was starting to get louder and louder, muffled but utterly terrifying. It swelled into a tormented roar before dying away again, leaving an electrified silence in its place. Hazen's heart hammered in his chest. *What the hell was that?*

His captor nudged a fellow general with his elbow. "Hear that, Ricky? Sounds like Grinder caught a bear after all. I guess you'll be giving him that apology."

A bear?

"Shit," Ricky replied with a grin. "I guess I'll be giving him my cider rations too. I'd be mad about it if it wasn't the best goddamn thing to happen all week. Too bad Hooper ain't here to see it."

"Poor bastard," another general muttered.

Zeff and Hazen were herded down a long corridor and onto the killing floor, where they stood together uneasily until Horus strode out of the gloomy shadows of the room. He approached them at once, moving with the brawny confidence of a powerful predator, wearing Simone's shotgun and sling like a prize. By the time he'd reached them, Hazen had buried his hatred of the man deep inside and was looking at Horus with an open curiosity he hoped would be more acceptable—and life prolonging, given the circumstances. But the more Hazen looked at the man before him, the harder it was to look away. Horus's gaze was magnetic; his dark eyes shone with a strange and frantic light. He could almost be considered attractive, except for a certain malignancy in his facial features that oozed out of his wild expressions, and tainted every word that he spoke. In stature, he was tall and broad shouldered, muscular, with a sizable beer gut. Yet his well-developed physique only emphasized the peculiar hollowness around his eyes and the bulging, angular cheekbones that tautened the skin across his face.

"I suppose you think I'm ruthless," he said, looking at Zeff and then Hazen. "In the old world, they called me a *psychopath*." He grimaced when he said the word, as if it tasted foul. "But they misunderstood me. The slave class and its herd morality could never appreciate what I am."

"You're nothing but a murderer," Zeff said. "They locked you up like the animal that you are."

"Things are different now," Horus replied. "Or haven't you noticed, *Zeff*? I'm starting to get the sense you're not very open to change."

"How do you know me? Who told you my name?"

"That's not important. What is important is that I know things about you—you too…Hazen, I believe that's your name. That's not really a man's name in my opinion, but not your fault, I suppose." The emperor looked them up and down and then smiled a dreadful, hungry smile. "You see, I'm the kind of man who likes to know who he's dealing with. And you two have impressed me. You're capable. You're survivors. You get things done, and that's why I need you at the New Empire. I'm looking for men who have certain skills, aside from raping and pillaging."

"Grace and Simone are skilled," Hazen offered. "If you get them out of that pit, they'd be a real help to you. Simone's an excellent hunter, and Grace knows everything about plants and diseases—"

"No women," Horus replied. "We lost our way in the old world. We indulged the weaker sex, and they lost their fear of us. Their exquisite helplessness decayed into self-entitlement and sloth, the very symptoms of an ailing society." He frowned; his mouth formed a crooked fissure across his paint-smeared face. "I will not make the same mistake."

"And what happens when the power comes back, and the army rolls into town?" Zeff asked heatedly. "You'll suffer for this."

Horus straightened his spine, and Hazen flinched, half expecting to be struck for Zeff's insolence. But the emperor stayed his hand; his eyes glittered with a demented glee. "It will take a lot more than an army to bring power back to the valley." He smirked. "You can thank my men for that."

"You blew up the hydro plant," Hazen said.

"The hydro plant was a little project of mine." Horus's lips drew back from his teeth. "The explosion was hot enough to make your balls blue."

"You've thought of everything," Hazen pronounced in what he hoped was an admiring tone of voice. "You must be a genius to execute these ideas *and* manage a growing city."

"It hasn't been easy," Horus admitted. He puffed out his chest. "And if I am to live as an emperor should, I need improvements in key departments. For instance, the soap I have to use is ash-riddled lard. I can never get completely clean from it. I'm left feeling grimy all the time, and it preoccupies me. As for the cider from our orchards, it's barely fit for beasts."

"Zeff has experience making cider and moonshine," Hazen volunteered before the rancher could open his mouth. "And I could offer some assistance in the soap-making department. I've been making my own and trading it around Assumption Valley. It's pretty popular stuff."

"Excellent." Horus smirked. "Then here's my offer to you: come work for me at the New Empire, or I'll blow your brains out, right here, right now. You decide."

"What's to decide?" Hazen forced a smile. "Consider us employees."

"That's what I thought you'd say." The emperor smiled before turning to his generals, the torchlight snagging against the sharp angles of his face. "I am going hunting," he addressed the men. "These two," he gestured to Zeff and Hazen, "will be returning to the New Empire with us in the morning, and I want them to be watched while I am gone."

Several generals nudged one another, grinning and snorting.

"I said *watched*, not *hurt*." Horus drew his eyebrows together. "No beatings, no torture. As long as these men are useful to me, I want them to be treated like guests. If they're harmed while I'm away, if they receive even so much as a scratch, I will find the man responsible, and I will tear him to pieces with my bare hands. Do you understand?"

The generals nodded.

"Mercer, Wertz. Step forward."

In the sprawling hydra of men, two generals cringed as they heard their names called. Mercer and Wertz stepped forward, careful to keep their eyes on the floor.

"Congratulations, you've been promoted to Berserker Class." Horus gave Zeff's revolver to Mercer and Hazen's hunting rifle to Wertz. "Don't fuck it up. Now take these men to the wagon."

The bear roared again in the distance.

RAT CITY

Darkness fell like a hungry wolf once the generals and their torchlight had gone. Mitch had a single, stubby candle to keep him company as he guarded the captives, but it offered no consolation tonight. He wanted to see the bear.

This wasn't a new desire for Mitch, nor was it an interest sparked by the sheer novelty of the situation. He had been listening to the men's bear-baiting stories for months now, ever since he had become a general himself, though he had never witnessed a fight. But he'd spent countless hours thinking about it, daydreaming about how *he*, Mitch, the lowliest of generals, would one day become an expert bear baiter. He just needed that first fight to prove himself, and he was ready for it. He could just imagine himself stepping into the arena as a hush fell over the crowd. The other generals would press together and crane their necks to get a better look, astonished to see him, simple Mitch, a man they never thought could be so courageous, readying himself for battle. In a thousand waking dreams, Mitch vanquished a thousand snarling bears, in barns, old factories, on a stage. His attacks were always quick and clever, leaving his adversary to whimper in pain and pull at his chains, bawling like a baby. The generals in the audience would yell and stomp their feet, begging for the beast's death, and Mitch would give it to them. After a few preliminary jabs and several deep thrusts of his blade, he would end the miserable creature's life, removing its head to the cheers of the crowd. He could already hear them chanting his name, and it sounded so sweet.

The only problem was there had never been a bear to bait since Mitch had come around. Until right now—in this slaughterhouse, and he was stuck on guard duty. Mitch lowered himself to the ground and slumped against the wall, glaring at the pit in the center of the room. He spat on the ground in anger.

"Don't worry, Mitch," Ricky had whispered before leaving with the others. "The rats always come when there's blood in the pit. All you have to do is wait and see."

Mitch considered Ricky to be a mentor of sorts, and he'd never led him astray before, so he trusted his prophecy enough to seek some solace in it. The man was a veteran general, and he had done a lot of pit duty; he knew rat attacks. Personally, Mitch had never seen one before, but the idea had some vague appeal. He was curious to know how it would happen. Would a horde of teeth and claws descend upon the women and begin savaging them at once? Or would the rats start off slow in their attack, darting out of the darkness one at a time to bite at their victims' soft and flinching flesh?

Mitch stretched his legs out and gave a wide yawn. The candlelight beside him was soft and warm, and he hoped his clothing would dry from the rain. Maybe then the rats would come. Before long, like any tired animal in a warm, dark den, he fell asleep, his mouth hanging open, his head tilted jauntily to one side.

"Simone," Grace whispered in the blackness of the pit. "I think the guard's already asleep. We've got to do something."

"I'm working on it," Simone murmured. "I'm working on it." She was feeling the sides of the pit with growing anxiety; they felt smooth to the touch, though badly scratched by the clawing, desperate fingernails that had come before her own. Clearly, they were not the first to be condemned to rat city.

"Hey, this guy's got a knife!" Grace pulled the weapon from its sheath, still strapped to the dead general's ankle. She squinted at it in the dark. It looked like it had a decent-sized blade.

"Good stuff," Simone mumbled. She was reaching higher now, her arms reaching above her head, her fingertips searching for any means of escape. Then she felt it: a slight groove in the wall. She inched along the wall to the right, then along to the left before finding another groove.

"Grace," she whispered. "I think I've found something."

Balancing on her tiptoes, Simone's fingertips detected another set of grooves further up the wall. Jumping as high as she could, she detected two more. They seemed to run up the entire length of the pit. It appeared a ladder had once been mounted here; Horus must have had it removed. She felt again for the first set of grooves; they were pretty high up the wall. It would be difficult to get a toe in, but difficult wasn't impossible.

"I'm going to have to jump for it," she said.

"Just keep it quiet," Grace cautioned. "We don't want to wake Sleeping Ugly over there."

"OK," she answered and looked nervously around the pit. "You watch for rats."

The two women fell silent, and Simone thought she could hear faint squeaking sounds in the distance. The rat army was approaching.

She removed her steel-toed boots and gently tossed them out of the pit. They landed on the ground above, rolling and knocking together as they flopped to a stop. She waited to see if this had awoken the guard, but his deep and steady breath suggested it had not. Tucking her socks into the pocket of her jeans, she waded barefoot through the warm pool of blood until she reached the far side of the pit. Next, she turned and half hopped, half ran back to the other side, moving as quickly as she could before leaping at the wall and stretching her arms high.

Thud.

Connecting with the side of the pit, she grasped for the grooves in the dark. Her fingers made contact, and for one victorious moment, she thought she had a good grip. But her hands were wet and slippery, and they couldn't hold her. With a low groan, Simone slid back down to the ground.

At the far side of the room, Mitch awoke with a start. His heart was pounding, and he didn't know why. He'd been dreaming of bears again. Bears and glory. Maybe the noise of the baiting had woken him. Beside him, the flame in the roly-poly candle stump jumped up and down in excitement. He smacked his lips and got up; time to check on the bitches.

Clutching his candle, he trudged to the edge of the pit and looked down at the women below—the women and the trio of gnarly, busted-up corpses that lay scattered around them. Once, Ricky told him that the pit used to be a garbage disposal in the slaughterhouse. It was where they threw the diseased and low-grade animal meat. Mitch smiled; it seemed the pit was serving the same purpose today.

"Well, it's nice to see you too," the blond woman said, and Mitch stopped smiling immediately. He looked down at her and scowled. He didn't like the way she was looking at him—and did she just wink?

"What the fuck are you looking at?" he shouted at her.

By the time Mitch noticed the glint of the knife, it was already on course, flying through the air toward him. He jumped back, but it was too late; the blade had already swiped his neck. Blood sprayed from the wound as he reeled back on his feet, his eyes widening with surprise. Then he collapsed, his candle falling with him and rolling to a stop at his side. The flame dimmed, then flared to life again, bathing the pit in its welcome, if somewhat uncertain glow.

"Nice throw," Simone said.

"Not really," Grace replied. "I was aiming for the heart."

Simone rolled her eyes and surveyed the side of the pit once more. The candlelight was faint, but it gently illuminated the grooves on the wall, making them easier to see this time. With confidence, she wiped her hands on her pants and moved to the other side of the pit again, taking a running start. She ran as fast as she could, balancing on her toes and skimming across the pit before leaping high into the air, her fingers reaching for the grooves she already knew were there.

Thud.

She hit the wall hard, winding herself, but this time she managed to get a good grip. Hanging by the tips of her fingers, Simone forced her toes into the indents below until she had balanced herself, clinging to the side of the pit like a human inchworm. Moving ever so slowly, she reached for the next set of grooves above her head, making sure she had a firm grasp before pulling herself up and repositioning her feet; then she reached for the next set. She continued crawling up the side of the pit this way, a caterpillar escaping her confinement, until she was surprised to find herself at the top.

Pulling herself out and beaching herself on the ground with a celebratory grunt, Simone rolled the dead general's body over and took out a dry bandana she found in his pocket. Then she dangled her legs over the side of the pit as Grace scaled her way up, wiping her feet before putting her socks and boots back on.

"That was fun," Grace said, upon reaching the top. She groaned as she hauled herself over the edge, waving away Simone's offered hand. Seeing the dead general, she wasted no time in retrieving her newly acquired knife and rifling through his clothing. She found a crust of something breadish in a little pouch that she sniffed and popped into her mouth. It was gross. She swallowed it, then wished she hadn't, then gagged a little.

Simone was able to locate her hat in a far corner of the room, and she popped it on her head with a sigh of relief, but it was a fleeting feeling. She could hear raucous laughter coming through the door. Listening hard, she could hear other things too: the crack of a whip, a bear whimpering in pain, the sound of rattling chains.

"So what now?" Grace asked.

Simone narrowed her eyes. "Now we even the playing field for the bear."

Grace grinned. "Let's go."

They made their exit through the same plastic-sheeted door Zeff and Hazen had been taken through. Creeping further into the slaughterhouse, they followed a hallway strewn with bones and apple cores until they could see the killing floor from the shadows. A dozen generals surrounded a gaunt grizzly bear that was leashed by a chain to a conveyor belt. The bear had reared up on its back legs in an attempt to defend himself, although his left paw was badly injured. The creature kept it tucked close to his chest as his dark head turned from side to side, waiting for the next strike to fall. Just out of the animal's reach, a general with a whip strutted back and forth with unconcealed arrogance.

"Give 'im another!" a general called in an unsteady voice, drawing Grace's attention. He was a straggler, standing alone at the back of the crowd, jostling a filthy travel mug in his hands. Her gaze moved lower. *Jackpot.* He had a leather holster strapped to his waist; he must be Berserker Class. She watched the man a little longer, almost disappointed by his drunken, slovenly appearance. She had been expecting more.

"If that's one of Horus's best men, his HR department sucks," Grace said out of the side of her mouth and darted forward before Simone could stop her. She skirted the edge of the room, approaching the berserker from behind and grabbing the gun from his holster. It was a Colt .45, and it was loaded.

"Nice," she breathed.

"What the—" the man looked at Grace in complete bewilderment, prompting her to smash him across the temple with the gun. She bear hugged his body as he fell, quietly heaping it on the ground.

At the front of the room, the bear baiter raised his whip again; all eyes were on him instead of Grace and the fallen berserker. The sight of the cowering bear captivated the generals as they looked on, enjoying the collective sadism of the event. Every man was waiting for the lash to fall, waiting for the creature to cry out in pain as the leather bit into his skin.

The bear reared back, ducking his head, trying to protect himself. Without mercy, the baiting general advanced upon him, snapping at the floor with the whip.

Grace took aim and fired at the conveyor belt.

There was a loud bang, instantly followed by a metallic rendering noise and a terrible crash. Spooked, the bear ran forward and found himself not only dragging his chains but also a large section of the conveyor belt after him as he continued his panicked flight across the killing floor. He rounded a large pillar in the center of the room, and the machinery wrapped around the concrete support, snapping the chain and freeing the bear completely.

The brutalized beast made a loop of the room before turning and charging at the crowd. This time, the bear was snarling. The men scattered and yelled as the bear charged the baiter first, knocking the whip out of his hands. The general tried to run, but the bear was on him before he got far, biting into his head like a Granny Smith apple.

The room erupted into pandemonium. Generals were running everywhere. A small group of men confronted the bear; others chased Grace and Simone across the killing floor as they fled for the door at the far end of the room. Both women had spied light coming in from underneath it; they knew the door would lead them outside. As they ran for the exit, Grace could feel the generals behind them, closing in. Thirty feet from the door, she turned and shot at their pursuers. Two fell, two continued their chase. That's when she noticed the bear.

With a muscular lunge, the grizzly sprung forward, knocking the pursuing generals off their feet. The men yelped with fear as the animal reared up and stood over them. Balancing on his hind legs, the bear bristled his blood-soaked fur until the entire slaughterhouse seemed to be filled with his terrible mass and his growling, carnivorous face.

Simone backed away from the animal slowly, stumbling over a pipe that had fallen to the ground in all the chaos. Retrieving the object, Simone pulled Grace toward the exit, feeling a sense of elation as she pushed at the fire doors, and they opened with relative ease. The women hurried out into the soggy world, where the endless gray sky appeared startling and beautiful to them now. It had stopped raining. Still squinting, Simone pushed the fire door shut behind them and jammed the pipe through the handle, locking it from the outside. There were other exits in the slaughterhouse, but this one was not in service today.

Recognizing Alfred's anxious nicker, Simone was overjoyed to find her stallion tied up with the other horses behind the slaughterhouse. Alfred looked weary but was otherwise in good health, and Zeff's horse, Peaches, seemed as friendly as always. Hazen's caravan horses, Dolly and Molly, hadn't fared as well, each one bearing wounds to her flank and around her mouth, but they were superficial injuries and they would heal in no time. After deciding it would be too difficult to escape with nine horses, Grace and

Simone released the five other nervous-looking animals that were tethered alongside their own, removing their saddles and harnesses before turning them loose. And that's how the mistreated creatures began their new lives: drinking from the river and sampling some of the finest grasses they had ever tasted.

MAN TO MAN

Zeff and Hazen were marched out of the slaughterhouse and into the dullness of the day, pushed and prodded by the generals at their back. Hazen was relieved to see the rain had stopped, but that was the only comfort he had, and it was short lived at best. He didn't trust these men, and he wasn't sure he trusted Zeff either; Simone's beating at the hands of the generals had done something to him. Hazen stole a glimpse at the rancher's face as they trudged along. His salt and pepper eyebrows were knit into a severe V, his nostrils were high and flaring. He was making a clicking noise as they walked, and Hazen realized he was grinding his teeth.

They passed an open strip of field where three-foot dandelions had gone to seed, and the sky seemed to sag down to the earth. Further along, they reached a derelict building that was missing a good portion of its front wall. The roof slumped inward like a deflated blimp; the door had been torn away. The place seemed miserable, as if it were mourning its own neglect.

"In here, boys," one of the generals said, and Zeff and Hazen found themselves being pushed toward the shabby structure. Zeff almost lost his balance, and Hazen caught his arm, steadying him as they continued to walk.

Inside the building, a misshapen caravan lurked in the shadows. The wagon was larger than Esmeralda had been, but it wasn't nearly so elegant. It was humped and stooped and even pointy in some places. And the entire rig looked too big and too heavy to be useful; Hazen pitied the horse team that had to drag that thing around.

The generals pushed them deeper into the gloom, and they walked toward the wagon with small, hesitant steps.

"Get in," Mercer said. He thrust the revolver between Hazen's shoulder blades.

"OK, OK," he said, raising his hands higher in the air. "I'm getting in."

Hazen climbed into the back of the wagon, but he almost needed a running start to do so. Inside, the air was rancid with the smell of urine and blood. He got to his feet and fingered the wagon cover with disdain. *Common tarps,* he scoffed inwardly. *Definitely not breathable.* This monstrosity was nothing like his glorious Esmeralda.

But Hazen's self-satisfaction grew black and turned to horror once he saw the rest of the interior. A tall and foreboding cross ran from the floor of the wagon to the crossbeam ceiling, filling the space with its dreadful size. Chains, bungee cords, and shackles had been fastened to it at varying heights; handcuffs had been lashed to the crosspiece. It was a sinister sight, and stepping back from it, Hazen tripped over a pair of restraints that had been welded to the floor.

"Where are the seats?" he asked in a daze. "Where do we sit?"

"There are no seats." Mercer sneered. "We're chaining you up."

"Move it, you miserable old prick." Wertz shoved Zeff forward, and he stumbled toward Hazen until he was standing shoulder to shoulder with his compatriot—at least he assumed it was shoulder to shoulder. The rancher turned his head slightly and glanced at the shadowy form beside him, raised his eyebrows once, twice, and hoped to God Hazen got the message.

Wertz pushed Zeff against the cross, putting the hunting rifle aside so he could use both hands to shackle him. The general only took his hands off Zeff for a moment, but it was the moment the rancher had been waiting for. With lightning quickness, he swung at the general with his fist, striking him on the chin, then delivered a powerful uppercut to the man's throat. Choking, Wertz fell back, clutching at his windpipe as his eyes filled with tears. He fumbled for the hunting rifle at his side.

Bang!

A shot was fired. Confused, Wertz thrashed for his gun and only succeeded in knocking it further out of reach. Zeff struck again. This time his aim went wide, but he recovered and hit Wertz in the jaw. The wagon shook as he continued the assault, beating the general about the head and stomach until he collapsed. Breathing heavily, Zeff felt around for the weapon, but his hands located a pair of restraints instead that had been attached to the floor. He slipped the unconscious general's wrists into them and locked them in place. Then he located his hunting rifle.

Hazen, on the other hand, was not pleased with Zeff — not in the slightest. He hadn't been planning a physical attack. "Damn it!" he'd cried when he heard Zeff attack Wertz. Mercer had heard it too, and when he attempted to go to his friend's aid, Hazen tucked his shoulders and bent low, ramming the general into the heavy wooden crosspiece behind him. Mercer smashed his head on the wood before turning in a bellowing rage, pointing the revolver at Hazen. The tradesman threw himself to the ground, rolling across the wagon floor. Mercer pulled the trigger; the shot went wide, but he still pursued Hazen. Mercer tried to kick him in the head, but missed. When he tried kicking at him again, Hazen seized his foot and pulled him to the floor, trapping the revolver underneath his body. He grabbed the general by the hair and smashed his face into the floor.

Suddenly Zeff was there with his rifle; he hit Mercer across the head with it as Hazen fumbled for the revolver. He managed to pull it out from under Mercer's chest.

"Got the gun," he said to Zeff.

"Good." Zeff stood up and leveled his gun at the general. "Get up." Bleeding profusely from the head, Mercer stared at him hatefully. "Now," Zeff ordered.

The general struggled to his feet.

"Up against that cross," Zeff commanded. "Tie him up, Hazen."

Hunched in pain and clutching at his face, Mercer staggered to the cross and leaned against it. Swiftly, Hazen cuffed him to the crosspiece and tied his feet at the ankles. Mercer remained compliant as he was bound, but once Hazen had finished, he began struggling against his restraints.

"Let me go, you little maggot!" he roared; the scars that crossed his chinless face were white with anger. "When I get outta these handcuffs, I'm going to murder you!"

"What should we do with these guys?" Hazen asked.

"You decide," Zeff said. "Just do it quick before the others get here. They must have heard the gunshots."

Hazen looked at Mercer; the general glared back.

"Let's just leave them," Hazen said. "At least they'll be out of the way for a while."

"All right. Your choice," Zeff conceded, though his tone suggested it wasn't the one he would have made. The two men switched guns and climbed out of the wagon, enjoying the smell of fresh air.

"You think I'm thankful?" Mercer shouted after them. "I'm going to skin you alive, you son of bitches! Your mothers were whores!"

"Some folks just don't know when to say thank you," Hazen said when they were outside the building again. They could still hear Mercer screaming.

"Hold on," Zeff said. "Got any extra fabric on you?"

"I've got this bandana," Hazen offered, pulling it off his head.

"Great." He grabbed the cloth and swished it around in a muddy rain puddle.

"Hey!" Hazen protested.

"It's for a good cause," Zeff replied. "Consider this a lesson in manners." He took the filthy bandana and returned to the wagon. After a few long seconds, Mercer's cries fell silent.

When Zeff returned, his face was grim. There was no bandana in his hands.

"Did you…" Hazen's voice trailed off.

"He's still alive," Zeff said. "As long as he can breathe through his nose." And he patted Hazen on the shoulder, grinning in spite of himself.

Retracing their steps, the men returned to the slaughterhouse at a run. As they drew closer to the dark and sprawling building, Hazen's eyes were on the heavy fire door ahead; it looked like there was something jammed in the handle. Then there came the sucking sound of hooves galloping over waterlogged ground, but he couldn't tell which direction it was coming from.

"Zeff!" he yelled.

"I know," Zeff yelled back. "I hear it too."

"Here," Hazen said, gesturing to several derelict wheelbarrows that had been discarded nearby. "We can hide behind them." He grabbed Zeff and pulled him down.

But Grace and Simone had already noticed the two men as they rode in on Peaches and Alfred with Hazen's horses in tow.

At that moment, Hazen was glad he was already on his knees, because he doubted they could withstand much more excitement. "Looking good, girls!" he called to them.

"You're looking at a couple of women, sunshine," Grace replied, laughing. She tossed Dolly's reins down to him. "Long story, but the bear's loose. We gotta split."

Zeff and Hazen didn't need any further convincing. And the four horses and their riders were only specks in the distance when the last general fled the slaughterhouse, followed by an angry, three-pawed grizzly bear.

WIN SOME, LOSE SOME

The area around the slaughterhouse had been well traveled, and it was impossible to tell which tracks, if any, belonged to Horus.

"Busy place," Simone remarked as she crouched in the dirt. The sky was beginning its slow roll into night, and Havenbrook had lost its charm hours ago, so the outfit decided to travel east along the highway, going as far as they could before dark. Now that they were closer to the New Empire and Horus was still at large, they dared not travel in the open. Instead, they made their way through the tangled wood that bordered the roadway, hacking their way through the bush with their knives. It was slow going at first, but the forest soon thinned, and they came to a clearing where a dozen deer grazed in the dusk. Perturbed by the intrusion, the animals arched their necks and bounced off, the whites of their tails flashing under the setting sun.

The group moved on. Zeff passed under a low tree branch that he didn't see, and was knocked off his horse, landing on his tailbone in the dirt. Embarrassed and aching, he struggled to his feet.

He felt like a fool—a used-up, clumsy old albatross. And he was getting mighty tired of feeling that way.

"You all right there, old man?" he heard Hazen say behind him. He was further mortified to hear the younger man stop his horse and dismount; he was walking toward him. Zeff's humiliation surged into anger.

"I don't need any help." He scowled. "Especially from the likes of *you*."

"I'm just trying to be a friend! No need to get so testy!" Hazen cried indignantly.

"Then be a friend, and leave me be."

Grace and Simone carried on ahead at a steady pace, oblivious to the fact that Zeff and Hazen had stopped and were quarreling behind them. Simone was in "the zone," as they called it in her wildlife-enforcement days. She could feel something, some inexplicable current carrying her on, and she knew better than to fight it. There was a sour wickedness in the air that she could almost touch. The birds had grown quiet; even the wind had fallen away. All that was left was the movement of the horses, panting and galloping across the slowly spinning earth.

Bursting into a curry-colored field of goldenrod, she spotted a lone, muscular figure ahead, walking beside his horse. She noticed her shotgun sling hanging between his shoulder blades and clenched her jaw.

Without warning, the figure turned. Catching sight of her approach, it flung itself on its horse and began galloping away.

"We've got him! We've got Horus!" Simone shouted to Grace, pointing to the horse and rider ahead.

"I've got Hazen's rifle!" Grace cried, but Simone was already gone, flying across the field with a speed that took her friend's breath away. Grace pressed her heels into Peaches' flank and chased after them.

"Come on, slowpokes!" she called to Zeff and Hazen, who had finally struggled into view. "The emperor's waiting!"

The horses plunged through the gilded meadow. Ahead, they could see Horus clearing the field with Simone and Alfred close behind. Without slowing, the man drove his horse into a wall of bush and shrub, forcing the animal to crash its way through. Simone followed soon after, picking an easier route for Alfred's sake.

In her sights again, Horus turned in his saddle and closed one eye, holding her shotgun close against his shoulder. With a wide smile, he shot at Simone twice, the slugs missing their mark by inches. From the treetops, a jay shrieked and whistled as Simone tucked her head and continued her pursuit.

The undergrowth was becoming sparser. The trees were growing further and further apart. She could hear a steady rushing sound in the distance, and soon the forest floor gave way to a patch of grassland that led to a riverbank. The river itself wasn't wide, but the bank was high, and the water looked fast and deep. One glance at it, and she already knew it would be difficult to cross the horses. Yet Horus was racing toward the river with reckless abandon, whipping his stallion's flank to ribbons with his crop. Astonished, Simone watched him drive the poor creature over the riverbank, and they both disappeared from sight.

Without waiting for Alfred to come to a full stop, she lunged off his back and ran to the river's edge. Horus's horse was struggling in the foaming waters below, the whites of his eyes rolling with terror. Indifferent to the animal's suffering, Horus reached the other side of the river, holding Simone's shotgun above his head as he climbed up the bank like a wet and spiteful cat. Then he swiftly dropped to his knees and lay flat on his belly, pointing the shotgun at her.

"Oh, God!" Grace cried, reaching Simone's side. "We've got to get that horse."

"Wait." She pointed to Horus. "He'll kill you if you go down there."

The struggling horse weakened and was finally swept downstream, his dark muzzle disappearing under the frothing waters that had grown pink with blood.

"You motherfucker!" Grace screamed across the river.

Still on the ground, the soaked emperor appeared to be struggling with the shotgun.

"He got it wet," Simone whispered to Grace. "Now's our chance!"

Grace planted her feet and aimed her rifle. Click. "Shit! I'm out!" she cried.

"Dammit! We're going to lose him!"

"Oh God," Grace said softly. "I think Hazen's carrying the ammo."

Simone threw her hat to the ground in frustration as Horus heaved himself to his feet and disappeared into the forest beyond. When Zeff and Hazen arrived, they didn't have to ask what happened. Horus had escaped them.

"Let's follow the river," she said, trying to hide her disappointment. "We can cross the horses at a calmer spot. Maybe we'll pick up his tracks again."

They doubled back and followed the river upstream. There they found a more serene side of the waterway, placid and shallow, where the horses crossed without incident. They journeyed back down the other side, looking for Horus's tracks, but evening had all but arrived, and the dark forest was growing darker still.

"This is useless," Simone said, squinting her eyes as she looked for fresh tracks. She stood up and brushed the dirt off her trousers. "We might as well be looking for a needle in a goddamn hay stack."

"Then let's give up for the night," Hazen suggested. "Horus is on foot. We can round him up tomorrow."

"I don't want to sleep in this forest," Grace said wearily, wiping her eyes and leaving a smear of gunshot residue across her face. "There are too many stinkin' roots around here."

"We've got to find a safe place," Zeff said. "Horus is out here somewhere, so we better set up a watch, too. That man is crazier than a shithouse rat."

They were still looking for a spot to make camp when night finally settled in. It was another damp, black evening, but the sky was clear, and the pearly stars glimmered above their heads, whispering the promise of a rain-free slumber. Deciding not to venture too far into the forest, the group followed the animal trails that ran along the river, cutting their way through the willow and thrush. Finally they found a clearing in the trees where the ground was somewhat flat, and there was grass for the horses to graze on. It was perfect.

Zeff set out the remaining blanket they had left while the horses were turned out. After this bit of work was complete, the outfit threw themselves down to sleep, with the exception of Hazen, who was on first watch. But it wasn't long before he dozed off too, dreaming about blood and murder. And rats.

When Hazen woke again, the sky was streaked with dawn. He sat up with a start; he had slept through his watch. He had slept through the entire night! Grace, who was still sleeping next to him, burrowed closer to his body, seeking warmth against the nip of the morning. He peeked over at Zeff and Simone. They were still asleep.

Well, we made it through the night, he thought. *No harm, no foul.* But he knew he had gotten lucky. If the others found out he had fallen asleep on watch, he would never hear the end of it.

A short distance away in the small meadow, the caravan girls, Dolly and Molly, nibbled at the grass as Alfred and Peaches watched the sunrise. Hazen was about to curl back up with Grace and shake off the cold when one of the horses—a new horse—caught his eye, standing with the other four. The creature was black and muscular, although his mane hung in pitiful straggles around his face. As the horse moved haltingly to another patch of grass, Hazen could see a nasty-looking wound on his flank.

My God, it's Horus's horse, he thought. Hazen hated the man, but he still couldn't believe anyone would use a horse so cruelly. It just wasn't good survival sense. Then another thought entered his mind: *Grace is going to love this.* He tipped his head back and sighed, elated with their good fortune. Living through the night had never felt so good.

"You awake, Hazen?" Zeff said suddenly, sitting up and blowing into his hands for warmth. He fumbled around for his hat. "You never woke me for watch. You didn't fall asleep, did you?"

The smile faded from Hazen's face.

A SURPRISE

"We've been looking all damn morning, and there's still no sign of him," Hazen grumbled, unable to hide his irritation. "Let's give up this wild goose chase and go get some grub. I'm hungry."

Earlier that morning, when the tradesman had realized he'd been given the gift of another day, he had decided to use it wisely and do everything he could to catch Horus. With the loss of his beautiful Esmeralda, he'd accepted the fact that he was going to be dragged to the New Empire with the rest of the nut jobs, and he didn't want to survive the night only to get impaled later. No, not that. He certainly did not want that.

Besides, the bastard had killed Em. *Now it's his turn*, he'd thought. And he had meant it, at the time. But then he had gotten hungry, really hungry. As a successful tradesman, he wasn't used to starving or doing without the comforts of his wagon.

"It's not break time yet," Zeff replied. "I know you're tired from being *on watch* all night, Hazen, but we're on a manhunt here."

He couldn't see Zeff rolling his eyes, but he could feel it. He wiped at his face with his shirtsleeve, pretending not to hear him. Sometimes that was the best way to deal with the old jerk.

They searched the entire west side of the riverbank for what seemed like an eternity. Finding nothing, they continued east, away from the river and the traitorous, thickset forest and toward the gently winding country roads, as friendly to them now as oatmeal on a cold winter's day.

They decided to stop behind the first building they came across: a white, weather-beaten church with a modest spire and a field behind it where the horses could graze. The church itself seemed dark and in poor repair, but the stairs had been cleared of debris, and a vegetable patch was growing in the garden by the stairs. Someone was living there.

"There are tracks all over this place," Simone said, returning from a survey of the field. "Human tracks and horse tracks. Some of them are quite fresh." She moved on toward the church, peering in the back window, but the curtains were pulled down.

Grace tried the back door. "It's locked."

"Shoot the lock then!" Hazen cried; hunger was gnawing at his patience.

"Wait," Simone said. "This is someone's house. And they may have nothing to do with Horus or the New Empire."

"And living so close to that viper's nest in Havenbrook?" Hazen snorted. "I doubt it."

"Look at that vegetable garden," Simone said. "It's immaculate. Can you imagine Horus or his generals weeding that thing?"

"Fine. I'll shoot the lock." Hazen grabbed Zeff's revolver and marched up to the door. "We'll get to the bottom of this, one way or another."

"Maybe we should knock—" Zeff began, but he was interrupted by a violent crack as Hazen shot the lock and threw the door open, stepping inside. "He wasn't kidding when he said he was hungry," the rancher muttered.

"Downstairs first," Hazen ordered, assessing the two flights of stairs that met them directly inside. "It'll be cooler there. That's where I'd keep my food."

He led them down a set of wooden stairs that sagged and squeaked as they made their way into the basement. Greeting them at the bottom was a long, dark hallway with four closed doors, two along each side. There was a fifth door at the end of the hall, also closed, but far more interesting to all concerned due to the patch of light peering from underneath it and reflecting dully on the hardwood floor.

"Looks like somebody's home," Grace whispered.

"Looks like a trap," Simone said grimly.

They tiptoed into the shadows, passing every closed door with a tangible sense of unease. The hall was filled with a strange darkness that smelled like sewage. The hardwood floor creaked and groaned under their feet. It was a relief when they reached the end of the hallway without a single door flying open or a net tumbling down around their heads.

Creeping up to the fifth door, Simone put her ear against it and listened intently. Hearing only silence on the other side, she motioned everyone aside. With one swift movement, she brought her leg up and kicked the door open.

"Great Augustus! Who's there?" a familiar voice boomed. "Come out, you scoundrel! I am armed! And I am infuriated!"

Simone paused. "Lewis?" she called.

There was silence. Then: "Simone? Is that you?"

She stepped into a candlelit room whose windows bore no natural light, overrun as they were by the grass and weeds growing outside. In the middle, sat their old friend Lewis, wearing his trademark safari hat and seated comfortably in a high-back chair with a pistol in his hand and a book at his knee. He lowered his weapon, placing it carefully on a side table before rising to greet her.

"My God, there's more of you? Grace! Hazen—oh my, and Zeff! What an unexpected reunion!" he cried as the others entered. "Welcome! Welcome to my study! It may not be much, but it is my little den, befitting a humble historian busy with his work."

Everyone looked around the crowded and colorful room with muted awe. The walls were lined with bursting bookshelves; piles of books were stacked around the floor. There were peculiar gatherings of patterned footstools and overstuffed pillows on the ground. The only clear space in all of the chaos was immediately in front of the blackboard at the front of the room, and even that particular item was covered in Lewis's pinched scrawl. At the back of the room, a large writer's desk held court, surrounded by admiring stacks of paper and mugs jammed with pens. A bust of Nietzsche scowled at them from a shelf nearby.

"My God, Lewis! Why are you here?" Zeff's face was lined with concern. "What happened at Elwood's? Did the compound fall?"

"Not that I know of, my good man," Lewis replied. He stroked his moustache fondly. "You see, I was…shall we say…forcibly removed from the area."

"What are you talking about, Lew? What's going on?" Grace gestured around the room. "What is all this stuff?"

"My dear Grace, you are right to ask so many bluntly worded questions, and I will answer them all, I hope, to your satisfaction. Perhaps you could say this all started with my abduction." Lewis leaned toward them, his eyes gleaming. "I went down to the pond for a swim with the Parsons and the Walkers—I'm not sure where you folks were. Anyway, I decided to take a stroll in the woods when I was hit over the head with something rather hard and taken away in a wagon. Oh, and Hazen, that wagon didn't hold a candle to your beautiful Esmeralda."

"Thank you," Hazen whispered, bowing his head to hide his sudden surge of tears.

"Horus took you?" Zeff asked.

"Absolutely correct," Lewis said. "Or rather, it was the emperor's henchmen who took me, if we're splitting hairs. What do those fellows call themselves?"

"Generals," Simone said.

"Right again. My word, how do you know so much about all of this?" Lewis smiled at her like a favorite student. "You know, I was held captive for a day before I was taken to meet the man himself. The emperor."

"They took you to the New Empire?"

"No, they took me to some desolate town, I don't know where. They said the emperor heard about me and wanted to meet me. He actually *heard* about me, if you can believe it." Lewis beamed with pleasure. "Apparently, my catapult made quite the impression among his men."

"So what happened?" Zeff asked.

"I met the fellow, of course." Lewis sniffed. "He ended up being a very decent chap, despite the aggressive nature of his men. We ended up chatting the night away like a couple of boarding-school boys."

"Then he asked you to build him a catapult," Zeff said. "Right?"

The inventor looked surprised. "Why do you ask?"

"Just answer the question, Lewis."

"Well, he did. But it came up organically in the conversation. I practically offered to make it for him."

Simone put her head in her hands. "And did you?" she asked.

"I drew him the blueprints," Lewis said proudly. "The emperor liked them so much he gave me this church and a handsome supply of food and firewood." He was smiling again. "The sheer amount of resources that man has is astonishing. Now that I don't have to provide for myself, I can design weapons full time—and as if that doesn't keep a man busy enough!" He cupped one hand around the side of his mouth, as if he were telling them all a juicy secret. "I'm also the official historian of the New Empire. You

know, Horus has so few men he can trust. Now I'm one of them."
Lewis smiled at his friends.

But no one spoke. A candle made a loud popping sound.

"Well?" Lewis asked. He looked at Simone. "Isn't this exciting?"

"Exciting?" Zeff repeated in bewilderment. "Lewis, have you
gone mad? The man is a monster!"

"A *monster*?" Lewis repeated, incredulous. "I think that's a rather unkind comment, Zeff. I expected a more insightful perspective
from you." He shook his head and seemed to wag his moustache at
them admonishingly. "The emperor is working for peace in a time
of civil war and food scarcity. He admits he's employed a few puni-
tive measures for the sake of the greater good, but when you think
of the lives he's saved—"

"Horus is a psychopath!" Simone cried. "Can't you see that,
Lewis? He abducts people! He abducted *you*, for Christ's sake!"

"I could have been treated much worse." Lewis replied. "I've
read several POW biographies in my day, and I think my time
in the hole stacked up rather well. I wasn't terribly harmed." He
grinned. "And we had cigars."

"He's a murderer," Simone cried, exasperated. "Listen, his real
name's Harvey Miller. I know that because he murdered my brother in cold blood—before the storms. He was serving a life sentence
for it in Ely Pen."

"What? Your brother?" Lewis furrowed his brow. "How can that
be true?"

"It *is* true," Hazen said.

"But he's such a considerate and gracious host!"

"Oh, yeah?" Grace said. "Well, yesterday we watched your 'considerate and gracious host' murder a woman and her child. Then
he threw us in a pit to be eaten by rats."

"A woman and a child?" Lewis echoed. "And a pit? Are you
quite sure?"

Grace scowled at him. "Of course I'm sure."

"Guys?" Hazen said.

"We're going after him, Lewis," Grace continued. "You should come with us."

"Guys?" Hazen said again.

"The emperor told me he was returning to the New Empire," Lewis said. "He told me this morning when he came to take my horse. Of course, I wasn't thrilled about the whole thing. I understand that he *gave* me that horse, but it's very difficult being out here without any means of transportation. Am I to tramp about the countryside like some kind of hobo?"

"Guys, I'm really hungry," Hazen said.

"So will you come to the New Empire with us?" Simone asked Lewis.

"I don't know," he replied. "I don't know what to think about all of this." His buoyant moustache seemed to droop, and he thrust his hands into the pockets of his clean corduroy pants. "The emperor and I are friends. He trusts me. He's confided in me."

"Really?" Grace inquired, perking up. "What kinds of things did he tell you?"

"Like where he keeps his weaponry," Lewis bragged. "He keeps his men lightly armed, you know. It's quite a progressive tactic."

Zeff's face brightened as Grace and Simone looked at each other with mounting excitement. Finding Lewis was like hitting the jackpot. If he could lead them to Horus's hidden weapon depository, they could deprive the New Empire of its firepower and turn it on the generals—and Horus himself.

But this conversational subtlety had been completely lost on Hazen, whose thoughts had never left his empty stomach. He felt it clench and then unclench for the umpteenth time, causing him to shout: "I'm fucking starving!"

This time the conversation stopped, and everyone looked at him. "Do you have any food, Lew?" he asked in a quieter tone. "I feel like I'm about pass out."

"Dear me, yes!" Lewis said, looking surprised. "I *am* the official historian and inventor for the New Empire. Of course I should be provided for! I have a stocked larder that I beg you to loot. And I have a few vegetables..."

Busying himself immediately, the inventor went to his pantry before setting out an impressive spread of cheese, meat and bannock, carrots, and romaine lettuce, puffing his chest out further and further with every item that emerged from his pantry. He even had some sort of butter-like substance to generously spread on it all, although nobody knew what it was, and nobody cared to ask. They washed the feast down with *real* Earl Grey tea and *real* sugar, and the granules crunched on their tongues in the most delicious way.

"Horus has scavengers that patrol the area," Lewis said, knocking bannock crumbs from his moustache. "You wouldn't believe the things they find. Can you believe they recently found an unopened bag of sugar?"

"Have you seen the New Empire yet?" Hazen asked.

"I have not yet visited," Lewis answered. "My work has been here. 'Away,' as Horus would say, 'from the wretched sounds of humanity clawing its way back from survival to revival.' That's rather good, isn't it?"

"Well, the official historian of the New Empire should *see* the place, don't you think?" Hazen said. "That way you can capture the true essence of it in your writing. It's important research for you."

"You're right," the inventor said, still stroking his moustache. "It's a milestone along the path of civilization. And once you visit, I know you'll change your mind about the emperor."

As they were packing to go, Simone was gratified to find her shotgun and sling in the larder, left behind in Horus's haste to return to the New Empire. Lovingly and with much care, she polished it with a rag as she reflected upon the matter of Lewis and their unexpected reunion. He was such an intelligent man, yet his opinion of Horus was so flattering, so bizarre. How could he not see the man for what he was? How could he not recognize evil when it was staring right at him and chomping on a cigar?

Perhaps the emperor's charisma was too much to resist.

Perhaps it was just another way to stay alive.

TO ELY

They left the wilderness church with Lewis in tow, riding on the back of Horus's discarded horse. Grace had already cleaned the animal's wounds and dressed them with club moss and a clean bedsheet, and the horse appeared to be in perfect health. In fact, he had behaved like a perfect gentleman when she had tended to him, blinking his warm brown eyes and lowering his head for pets. Grace called the horse Basil, and the name seemed to suit him as he trotted soberly through the afternoon, taking great care in the placement of every hoof and shying away from the wetter, swampier patches of the path.

Although Basil's meticulous nature caused Lewis to fall behind the rest of the group, it didn't stop the man from making conversation as he trailed along at the rear, making observations that ranged from criticisms of the scenery to shapes he saw in the clouds, which included a grandfather clock, a shark, an abacus, Pangaea, and later (after some mulberry wine), a woman's thigh, a pair of buttocks, and Geraldine's nipple. Lewis did not say who Geraldine was.

The day passed in travel, and the weary outfit stopped at twilight to make camp by a derelict gas station. The adjoining convenience store smelled thick with death and buzzed with insects. Something had been festering in the small, glass-scattered store in the heat of the day, but no one was in the mood to investigate the matter further, so they made camp on a patch of weeds behind the self-serve carwash and pitched the optimistically labeled "four-man tent" Lewis had brought.

After turning out the horses, Simone found the inventor nodding off by the campfire, waking each time his head pitched forward onto his chest. She pulled off her boots and sat down beside him, her knees creaking in protest. Leaning forward, she felt the warmth of the fire on her face. It was only a small cooking fire, but it was warming nonetheless. She had been cold these days, colder than she had been all winter. The days of rain had seeped into her body, and now it felt like she had rivers instead of marrow running through her bones. She pulled her knees up to her chest and hugged them tight, watching the smoke from the fire disappear into the dancing night sky. The northern lights had come again, fluttering their unearthly ribbons across the glittering oblivion. Their colors were beautiful to behold, but Simone preferred the simple constancy of the stars.

"I'm sorry your brother died," Lewis said, and his voice startled her. He seemed more awake now, and was blinking at her as he straightened his back. His eyes had lost some of their bleariness from the wine.

"I miss Emerson every day," she said softly.

He nodded. "Time heals all wounds."

"Not all of them." She tipped her head back again, watching the sky roll with color. "Hearts don't just break, you know. Sometimes they get beaten beyond all recognition."

Lewis fell silent, and the cicadas hummed. "So, what would your brother think about all this?" he asked. "About our lives now?"

"He'd probably think it was an adventure." Simone laughed. "Em found the silver lining in everything, even when we were kids. If you were ever having a bad day, he'd always say—"

"Now you can show the bastards what you're really made of," Hazen said, walking into the light of the fire. He settled beside Simone and looked at her and smiled, thinking about the best friend he'd ever had. She grinned back, just like she used to. Hazen put his arm around her and kissed her cheek, and the childhood friends sat together for a little while, remembering the old times without saying anything at all.

The rest of the evening lingered on under that tumbling, Rorschach sky. When dinner was finished, Zeff lay under a tree for the night, leaving the tent to Grace and Hazen, who shivered and laughed in the dark, clinging to one another for warmth under a scratchy woolen blanket. Lewis fell asleep by the fire (this time for good) and was snoring in crescendo, the tips of his moustache rising and falling with his breath. Simone covered him with a blanket before settling down for first watch, with only her brother's ghost for company.

When the northern lights faded away and the long, inky night disappeared into a deep-blue morning, Simone woke Lewis for next watch. As she flopped down by the cooling embers of the fire, Lewis handed her the blanket. She covered herself with it immediately, feeling herself warming. Smiling, she felt the angel of unconsciousness rise up to meet her.

Then: "Simone, I want to tell you something." It was Lewis, and he sounded worried.

She opened one eye.

"The catapult isn't the only blueprint I've drawn for Horus. There are others—I thought you should know."

Simone sat up again, looking at Lewis with concern. "Oh no. You didn't—"

"Yes," Lewis said, grasping his soiled safari hat with both hands. "I drew the blueprints for the flamethrower."

Simone felt sick. Lewis had always been talking about inventing some kind of flamethrower, but then, he'd talked about inventing a lot of things.

"When did you draw them?" she asked tersely.

"Three nights ago," he answered, hoping to find salvation with honesty. "Horus took them right away. He told me he was returning to Ely—that's where I was first detained—I remember that now."

Simone said nothing; she continued to glower at him as he examined his hiking boot.

"The town is close," he said. "I may be able to recall where we stayed. Perhaps I can retrieve the blueprints before…well…before."

Simone put her hat back on.

They packed up camp and left for Ely just as dawn was beginning to break. The rising red sun looked like the eye of something wicked as it watched them on the road to Ely. By the time they reached the outskirts of town and the Ely Maximum Security Penitentiary, it had turned a sour yellow and radiated an unpleasant heat.

"What the hell happened here?" Grace asked, staring ahead at the torn-up parking lot and what remained of the prison. The concrete building had been burst open, picked clean, and left to loll in the sun like a dead whale. The entire structure had been blackened and charred. Most of the perimeter fencing had been torn down and dragged away. The vegetation in the area had grown back some time ago, filling the abandoned lot with rangy weeds and cabbage moths. But it had been the site of an explosion once—multiple explosions from the looks of things.

"This was the prison they sent him to," Simone said. "Horus—Harvey."

Grace shivered. "He blew the place to smithereens."

Zeff took a sip of water from his canteen and listened to the crows and blue jays announce their arrival in town. "We'd better tread carefully from this point on," he said, frowning.

"Yeah." Hazen glared at Lewis. "They've probably got a *flame-thrower* by now."

The inventor hung his head and trailed behind the others as they left one scene of despair for another.

THE BUNKER

"There it is!" Lewis whispered triumphantly, lowering the binoculars. He pointed to a nondescript little townhouse in the distance, nestled along the tree-lined avenue. Ely had hundreds of these streets, apparently, where abandoned houses huddled together under beefy tree boughs and gardens grew wild in the absence of their keepers. But the house to which Lewis now directed their attention was different from the others they'd been creeping past all morning; 1527 Crabtree Lane was swept, kept, clipped, and cleaned. It was a shrine to order in the encroaching wilderness.

"We'd better leave the horses where they are," Lewis said. "They'll be fine in that yard back there. The town isn't used much by the generals, but if they come, they will come to this house."

"Oh, really, traitor?" Grace replied in a furious whisper. "How can we believe anything you say?"

"Yeah!" Hazen chimed in. "Mister freakin' flamethrower over here!"

Lewis looked hurt. "As I have already told you, I was only trying to help. He certainly gives the impression of being a sensible man."

"*You*, on the other hand…" Grace glowered at the inventor.

"Binoculars, please," Simone whispered loudly. Lewis handed them to her in a wounded manner that didn't interest her. She peered through the lenses and focused in on the house. "There's a guard on duty," she said. She lowered the binoculars again and looked at Lewis. "You deal with him."

"What?" Lewis squawked in surprise. He raised his eyebrows and his moustache at the same time. "I can't possibly deal with a guard. I don't know how!" He looked at the others for support; there wasn't any.

"Don't worry, we'll cover you," Simone said. She gave him a small knife. "Here, hide that somewhere. And stay in broad view. Make sure the guard sees you coming."

Lewis stared at her wordlessly.

"Go," she said. "*Now.*"

"But—"

"You heard her," Zeff said.

Feeling somewhat like the infamous Adam after he had been cast out of Eden, Lewis scrambled down the tree they were hiding in, hugging the trunk as he made his slow-footed descent. Once he reached the ground again, he stared up at the canopy and gave it one last, lingering look in case his hidden comrades changed their minds. When they didn't, he shuffled to the exit of the overgrown park and down the hill to the sloping street. It was the street that would lead him to the emperor's bunker—eventually. Seeing no incentive to hurry, he plodded down the sidewalk, trembling with fear as he approached the house. Sweat trickled down his back and dampened his shirt until he was soaked in it. Finally, he took his hat off and started fanning himself with it until he arrived at the tidy driveway with its handsome flower planters. They appeared to have recently been watered.

Lewis looked around for the guard but he couldn't see one. Sick with nerves, he walked up the drive until he was standing by the house. "Hello?" he called. "Is anyone here? It's the official historian!" He paused. "I'm here on important business!"

The back gate swung open, and a long-armed, small-nosed general marched out, carrying a nail-studded bat over his shoulder. He had a wild look in his eyes and a contemptuous curl to his upper lip as he advanced on Lewis.

He took a few steps back. "Sir, have you been charged with watching the place?"

The general didn't answer as he continued his approach. As he drew closer, Lewis noticed he was wearing a necklace made out of human teeth.

"Excuse me, sir, but I am under Emperor Horus's protection!" Lewis cried, moving back until he found himself standing in the middle of the lush, hand-trimmed lawn.

"Don't know nothing about that," the general said, continuing his advance. Once he was within striking distance, the man raised the spiked club in the air.

Lewis closed his eyes and hunched his shoulders under the expected blow—which is why he felt rather than witnessed Grace's knife flying past his head. He also missed watching his would-be attacker collapsing onto the grass. But when he opened his eyes again, and saw the dead general before him, he knew his friends had come. Overwhelmed with relief, Lewis fainted.

When no further generals emerged, Zeff, Hazen, and Simone crept out from behind an overgrown hedge and moved the body to an abandoned garage. They cleaned up the crime scene as best as they could, with a little help from a fully filled watering can they found nearby. In the meantime, Lewis regained consciousness and sobbed quietly into Grace's shoulder. Once he had composed himself again, they regrouped in the yard next door to plan their next move.

"What do you think, Lewis?" Grace said once they were in their huddle; she had softened considerably toward the shaken inventor.

"I think we should enter through the back door." Lewis's voice quivered. He had stopped crying, but he still looked misty eyed and dispirited. "The guard probably left it unlocked," he said, and this thought seemed to pluck him up a bit because he added, "I'll take you there."

"You better," Hazen scoffed, not so quick to forgive. "You're the one who got us into this mess."

Lewis led them to the side of the house and through the white picket fence that guarded the shaded and beautifully landscaped backyard, speckled with foamy plumes of astilbe, rosebushes, and great dogwood shrubs. Bees drifted lazily about, droning in the afternoon heat. A light breeze shook the leaves on the trees, bringing with it the scent of cedar woodchips and floral perfume.

"This garden is completely ornamental?" Simone asked in disbelief.

"It's the garden of an emperor," Lewis replied. "It's not a garden of necessity."

When they reached the back door, the curtains were drawn. The place appeared to be dark and silent—a far cry from the house Lewis had entered as a captive, but left as a valued guest, and possible friend. He recalled how the place had been so noisy, overrun with carousing generals. In the end, the emperor had sent them all away so Lewis could concentrate on his work—but not, he warmly remembered, until every man had personally apologized for disturbing him. Lewis knew the emperor had forced them to do it, but he appreciated the gesture nonetheless. The mass apology had made him feel respected in a way he felt he deserved and yet seldom experienced.

As Lewis walked to the door, he saw the emperor's death unfold in his mind: Zeff kicking in the back door, Simone rushing the entrance, gunshots in the living room, Horus lying dead on the green velvet sofa—the very sofa where they had spent several pleasant evenings together, sipping cognac and discussing issues of great import.

Maybe he didn't murder Simone's brother after all, Lewis thought. *The justice system isn't infallible.*

He stole a glance at her over his shoulder. Simone was waiting quietly by the door, her jaw set and locked, her eyes blazing in a manner that worried him. She did not appear open to discussing his idea of not killing the emperor and instead having supper with him and sampling some of the tremendous jams he kept in his pantry.

Lewis's eyes next alighted upon Grace. She was leaning against the side of the house and sharpening her knife with a rock. This was not encouraging. Lewis fondled his moustache as he snuck a peek at Hazen. He considered appealing to the man's pacifist side, but he still seemed bent out of shape about the flamethrower blueprints. And Zeff secretly terrified him.

"What's taking so long?" Zeff hissed.

He fumbled noisily at the back entrance. As the door pushed open, Lewis felt another stab of anxiety and then calmed. The emperor wouldn't be here. Deep down inside, he knew that. Wasn't that the reason he had suggested they had come here in the first place?

He stepped inside.

The interior of the house was quiet and still; the air smelled stale with disuse. With Lewis in the lead, the group cautiously made their way into the kitchen before moving into the living room, where sunlight filtered through the heavy woven blinds, leaving pale scales of yellow to pool across the carpet.

Lewis made his way over to the green velvet couch and fondled it tenderly. The emperor wasn't here; the couch was unmolested. He breathed a quiet sigh of relief.

"Who are these people?" Hazen asked, with a soft chortle. He was standing beside a table, holding a framed picture in each hand. In the first picture, a sleeping, middle-aged man sported colorful butterfly barrettes in his hair as two little girls laughed with delight. The second picture featured the same man, posing with a woman in front of Niagara Falls; both wore serious expressions on their faces. The woman held up a garden gnome.

"I don't know. I've never looked at these pictures before," Lewis answered.

"There's something I'm not getting here," Grace said, squinting at a mahogany hutch in the corner where an impressive collection of cat figurines sat on display. "Horus collects these things?"

"Heavens no," Lewis replied. "He said everything came with the house. He's had this place for some time—that's the only reason this stuff wasn't stolen or scavenged. When I was a guest here, one of those horrible general men broke a lamp. Well, the emperor was terribly angry about it. Over a broken lamp! Imagine that—when they're all broken to us anyway!"

"Why would he choose this place?" Grace asked, examining a lace doily in her hands. "Ely's in the middle of nowhere."

"It's not the middle of nowhere for him," Simone replied. "He was being held at Ely Pen before the solar storms. When the prison fell, he must have fled into the town and ended up here somehow."

Zeff walked into the front hall. Passing the coat closet, he jumped when he noticed a movement in the shadows. He drew his revolver from his holster.

"Relax, Zeff," Simone said, putting a steadying hand on his shoulder. "It's just a mirror. That's the closet."

His grizzled cheeks burned as he lowered his gun. "Someone should open those doors," he muttered. "Make sure no one's hiding in there."

She pushed the closet open, sliding the mirrored door along its track with a slight whooshing noise. It was packed with coats and ski jackets and a well-stocked shoe rack covered in dust.

"Wow!" Grace said, coming over for a closer look. "There are some really nice jackets in here. My God, look at this!" She fingered the sleeve of a women's pea coat. "This is almost new! There is no way we are leaving this stuff here. These jackets should be used."

"Don't touch those!" Lewis cried and Grace looked at him sharply. "The emperor is quite particular about his things," he said in a calmer tone. "He doesn't like anyone touching them."

"I don't care!" Grace shot back. "He probably doesn't like anyone killing him either!"

"Can it, you two," Zeff said. "We'll talk about the jackets later. Right now, we should be searching the house."

The group made their way through the rest of the downstairs, moving through the formal dining area, past the nautical-themed washroom and the cozy guestroom where Lewis had slept. The upstairs was more of the same: a linen closet, a few children's bedrooms filled with toys, a compact bathroom, and a comfortable master suite. Finally, one last room remained to be searched. Hazen tried the handle, but the door was locked.

"What's in this room?" Simone asked Lewis.

"That's the emperor's private room," he replied. "I've never been insi—"

Before the last word was out of his mouth, Simone kicked the door in, revealing a small study behind it. In the middle of the room was a large wooden desk that faced the door. The surface of it was completely clear except for a novelty beer stein that held several pens. "*Ely Curling Club Championship*," the inscription on the glass read. "*Because Curlers Have Big Stones.*"

The wall behind the desk included a generous window and a large bulletin board with a map of the valley and surrounding areas, covered with an impressive collection of pushpins linked by lines of red thread.

"Who is Lester Jackson?" Hazen asked, examining a framed university diploma that was hanging on the wall.

"That name sounds familiar," Simone replied. But her thoughts were interrupted by a horrified gasp.

"Look," Grace said, her voice catching in her throat. Following her gaze, Simone discovered the object of her dread—or objects rather. For there, stuffed and mounted on the wall, were the heads of two little girls; they looked like the little girls from the picture downstairs. Simone felt her body begin to shake

"Shit. They're on the other side too," Hazen said, covering his eyes with his hands.

Facing the desk, just above the doorway, the heads of a man and a woman had been stuffed and mounted in a similar fashion. All the mouths had been sewn shut, as were the eyes. Only the eyes of the man had been stitched open so that they were staring straight ahead, staring at the little girls across from him for all of eternity.

"Does he have no mercy?" Grace cried, smashing her fist down on the desk, making the beer stein and everyone else in the room jump.

"The eyes are glass," Simone said quietly, inspecting the man's head. "Looks like they've been to a professional taxidermist. And there's a name engraved here—our Lester Jackson."

In a flash, the memory returned to her. She remembered that man, alive and sitting in that oh-so-familiar courtroom in his suit and tie, giving testimony against Harvey Miller, who had escaped from Ely Pen before going on to murder Emerson and several other innocents.

"In his escape from the penitentiary, Harvey Miller grievously injured four of my guards," the man had said. "They're lucky to be alive."

"Warden Jackson, did Mr. Miller's behavior come as a surprise to you?" the prosecutor asked.

"No, it did not," he had replied. "Mr. Miller has been a prisoner at Ely Pen for the past three years, and I was often forced to deal with him for various acts of violence and brutality against my guards and other prisoners."

"This is Warden Jackson from Ely Pen," Simone said. "I remember him now." She looked across the room at the two little girls. "I assume that's his family. This was probably the first place Horus stopped when he broke out of prison."

Grace grabbed Lewis by the shoulders and shoved him closer to the little girls. "Look at that!" she yelled. She pushed him even closer until he was staring up at them. Their faces were stitched up like pincushions; their golden curls streamed past alabaster cheeks.

"Take a good look," she said. "This is your man's handiwork—your *emperor*." Grace spat out the last word in disgust.

Then, there was a clicking sound downstairs, followed by the gusty squeal of the back door. Someone had entered the house.

AN INTRUSION

"Darnell! Git yer dirty ass over here!" shouted a low, guttural voice downstairs.

"I'm coming! Fuck!"

The back door shrieked again. There were thumping sounds.

"Where's Hooch?" a gruff voice demanded. "Ain't he on guard?"

"Hooper? Are you shitting me?" replied a male baritone. "Hooper ain't on guard—not after what happened to him."

"I said *Hooch*, not Hooper. Hooch is supposed to be here. Now where is he?"

"How should I know? I ain't fucking him."

There was a long pause; feet thudded around the living room.

"Place looks fine. That's all that matters."

"Shit, you got that right."

The back door squealed again.

"It just seems really messed up," a young voice said.

"No, man, it makes sense if you think about it," another youthful voice replied. "The emperor is a smart dude."

"Take your goddamn boots off! You know the rules," the gruff voice admonished them. "You leave one thing out of place, you leave one speck of dirt, you die."

There were more thumping noises.

"Good, now grab a drink. And use a fucking coaster, all right?"

A top was twisted free. Liquid gurgled into glasses.

"Here's to one hell of a life!" the hoarse voice continued. "We're generals, and we do what we want, always upholding—"

"The natural law of the empire!" the voices shouted in unison. Glasses clinked together, but not very loudly. There were careful sipping noises.

"Don't you guys find it hard to believe this 'natural law of the empire' shit?" a voice said, after a spell. "All that 'discipline of suffering,' 'art of exploitation' nonsense? I don't know. Do you guys ever wonder if the emperor's crazy?"

There was a long silence.

"Listen, sweet pea," the rough voice croaked. "You're going to get yourself in trouble by asking too many dumb questions, so shut the fuck up. Quit while you're ahead, as the fucking Frenchies say. Do you understand what I'm telling you right now?"

"C'mon, Lowry, tell the kid the truth," another voice said. "We know the emperor's crazy. He's always been fucking crazy. I watched him castrate a man with a pair of scissors in the clink, OK? He's not normal. But it's a new world, and there are new rules now. That's the beauty of the situation."

"That's the beauty? The *beauty*?" The young voice was querulous. "At the last Redemption Session, Horus whipped a pregnant woman for stealing food."

"It's an offense to steal, and it's an offense to criticize the emperor, Cody," the gruff voice said. "You know that."

"I'm not trying to criticize the emperor. I just…I just wanted to know what you guys thought about it."

"Let me tell you what I think about it. I think the emperor has clothed you, protected you, promoted you to general, and it's still not enough for you. No! Not for some newly minted, sniveling little cocksucker who doesn't have balls hairy enough for the job." The coarse voice grew more threatening. "Sounds like you need to see a pair, son—a nice, hairy pair with lots of juice."

There was laughter.

"Caskin! Gorman! Take Cody outside."

"No! Stop!" the voice cried. There were the sounds of a scuffle. "Darnell, help! Don't let them do this!"

"They warned you, buddy. Oh, don't look upset. It ain't gonna kill you...long as you relax, that is." Darnell sounded like he was smiling.

The back door opened, and there were screams as the young general was dragged outside.

Upstairs, Simone leaped to the window of the study and parted the blinds so she could see into the backyard. There was a wagon parked there now, sitting in the middle of the lawn. In the shade of the large carrier, two generals held a third man by the arms as an enormous fellow smashed him in the face with his fist. When the youth collapsed, his captors dropped him on the lawn in a heap. The redheaded giant leered at his victim, grinning from ear to ear.

"I can't take much more of this today," Lewis pronounced, looking pale. "If anyone needs me, I'll be in the closet," he said, ducking inside and closing the door behind him.

But Lewis wasn't the only one who was sickened by the sight. Simone eased her shotgun from her sling. This one was worth a shell or two.

"Want me to hold the window open for you?" Grace asked, hurrying over to raise the blinds for her. "We don't want glass flying in your face."

"Can't we just outwait these guys?" Hazen whispered. "Just close the door. They'll never come in here."

"Hazen." Simone turned to him frowned. "We can't hide up here and let them tear that poor kid apart." She patted Zeff's shoulder. "Can you cover the hallway? By my calculation, there's one general left downstairs, and he'll be up here once I start shooting."

Zeff gave Simone a curt nod and headed for the doorway, suppressing a small smile.

Outside, the bearlike general had pulled his dick out of his pants and was wielding it like a weapon. The young man was trying to crawl away from him, but he was moving slowly, dragging his body behind him. With one fluid motion, Grace hoisted up the heavy glass windowpane, and Simone took aim and fired. The blast was loud, and the men below looked at one another in confusion before the hulking general crumpled forward, his lifeless penis still clutched in his large paw.

"Holy shit!" came the cry from downstairs. "What the fuck was that?"

"There's someone in the house! He's got a gun!" yelled one of the men. The horses galloped from the yard in a panic, and the two generals raced after them. Simone watched them through the scope, but she didn't take the shot. She just couldn't.

"You can't let them get away!" Grace shouted. "Here, gimme that."

Simone handed her the shotgun.

There was the familiar sound of Zeff's revolver in the hall. It came again and again and again.

Grace flew across the hallway to the bedroom window and smashed a hole in the windowpane with the butt of the gun. The generals were in front of the house now, right where she wanted them. She took two shots: one man fell in the driveway; the other sprawled across the weed-ridden sidewalk, spilling blood into the deserted street. She lowered the gun with grim satisfaction and looked at Simone in the doorway.

"It's OK," she said. "I don't mind doing it."

They met Zeff in the hallway. He had finished rifling through the fallen general's belongings but hadn't found much, save for a pocketknife, a few bullets, and four large rubber bands. It wasn't a bad haul—they could use all of those things. And Zeff could certainly use the extra bullets. *To replace the ones you wasted killing one single man,* he thought darkly.

"Thanks for taking care of that general, Zeff." It was Simone's voice, her shadow.

"I apologize for wasting so many bullets," he replied. "I think I need to adjust the sights."

"You're too hard on yourself." He felt Simone's hand rest lightly on his shoulder. "You didn't let him get to us—that's what matters."

Once they had dragged the body out of the hallway, they returned to the office, where Hazen was attempting to coax Lewis out of the closet. "Come on, Lew," he said in a gentle voice, rapping on the door. "Why don't you come out now? Your friends miss you."

Lewis was silent as he absorbed the word "friends." Maybe they weren't mad at him anymore. "Is everything all right?" he asked, his voice muffled by the door.

Hazen glanced at the mounted heads one more time. "Of course it is," he said, but it was a lie. How could everything be all right? How could anything ever be all right again?

TWIN TERRORS

"Who the hell are you?"

The wounded young general used the wagon to hoist himself to his feet and looked resentfully at the strangers in front of him. With some difficulty and much laboring of breath, he leaned to his side and picked up a wooden club that had been lying on the ground, abandoned by one of the other generals in his haste to escape the yard. Once the weapon was firmly in hand, the young general shook it in a weak and somewhat hostile manner, but only the pink-and-white blooms of astilbe trembled under the midsummer sky.

"I'd like to have a word with him first," Simone addressed the rest of the group. "Wait here where he can see you. We don't want him doing anything stupid."

Making eye contact with the young general, Simone slowly removed her shotgun sling and placed it on the ground. With her arms in the air, she began her approach, taking small, deliberate steps forward. The general raised the club again, but she smiled reassuringly. "We don't want to hurt you," she said. "We just want to ask you some questions."

Behind her, Grace switched off the safety on Hazen's hunting rifle as a mere precaution, but the click carried over to the young general, who startled like a deer in the open. He raised the club higher.

"Be a sensible fellow!" Lewis called over to him. "We're only trying to help you! Anyone can see that!"

"Who said I needed help?" the young general yelled back and then immediately felt deflated; the effort of shouting had drained the last of his energy. He tried to sneer, but his face was puffy and sore. He could barely move it, and he was so tired. Actually, he was exhausted. If only he could rest for a while, if only he could sleep, then things would be better.

Slick with sweat and blood, the club slipped in his hands.

"No one said you needed help," Simone said.

The young general squinted at the woman as she made her way over to him. She was tall and lanky, and he noticed tendrils of long brown hair peeking out from beneath her soiled cowboy hat. When she got closer, she smiled at him with no inch of malice, and he felt his guard slacken. It had been a long time since he had felt any warmth from another human being. He'd missed that.

"We're the ones who need help, actually," she continued in a pleasant tone of voice. "We've been tracking Horus, and we think he's returned to the New Empire. Can you help us get there?"

"That depends," he replied. "What are you going to do once you find him?"

"Kill him," she said.

"In that case, count me in," he said with a feeble smile. The young general reached out and shook her hand. "Cody Coately, at your service." The effort of talking was becoming too much for him and he winced in pain. "Just let me sit down for a minute."

After the introductions were made, Grace whisked Cody back to the house to have a look at his injuries, and the young general went with her quite willingly, content to have someone fuss over him. All the attention made him feel warm inside, like a good pull of cider.

"Simone? Hazen?" A thin voice asked, tentative and husky. Simone wheeled around. It was coming from the wagon.

They looked at each other in surprise as Simone threw open the back of the caravan, revealing Libby and two young women lying inside. The women were sprawled in a tangled heap on the floor, dressed in ill-fitting lingerie and bound at the wrists and ankles by coarse lengths of rope.

"Get us out of here!" Libby cried.

"Oh, Jesus," Simone breathed, climbing into the rickety structure. With a knife, she cut away Libby's bindings, exposing wrists and ankles that had been rubbed raw by their restraints. The last time she had seen Libby, she and her family were on the verge of stealing Hazen's caravan. They'd found the body of her father, Joey, but where was Carmen?

Hazen and Zeff freed the other two women, who lay meekly on their sides as the rope fell away, their expressions never changing. Two pointy chins tucked into the hollow of two slender necks; two sets of eyelashes smudged two pale and wearied faces. The women's faces were like dolls, lifeless and staring.

"Hey, are you two twins?" Hazen asked, but neither woman answered him. They didn't seem to hear his question, although they did sit up.

"What happened, Libby?" Simone asked anxiously, helping her down from the wagon. It had only been several days since they'd seen each other, but the young woman was even thinner than before, and bearing a violent black eye. Simone observed a sinister-looking bite along her collarbone, and when she took her hand, she saw Libby's fingernails had been bitten down to the quick. Without warning, Libby collapsed in Simone's arms and wept.

"I'm sorry we stole your caravan!" she sobbed. "It was Carmen's idea."

"That's OK, Libby. We found the caravan. Well—what was left of it."

"And Joey…I mean Dad?" Her voice wavered.

"We found him too. Did you see that…happen?"

She nodded, covering her anguished face with her hands. She shivered as Simone gripped her shoulders and began steering her back to the house. The other two women followed them without question, without seeing, and possibly without caring.

"Libby?" Grace asked in surprise, as they came through the back door and into the kitchen. She was seated at the table, dabbing at Cody's wounds with the whiskey she had found on the table. Her eyes fell upon Libby's attire: the garish lingerie, the bestial wounds that savaged her body. Then she noticed the two women standing with her; they looked even worse.

"Help me get them upstairs," Simone said. "They need some decent clothing." Without another word, Grace joined her friend in shepherding the women upstairs and into the master bedroom where they found a closet jammed with clothes. Libby grabbed eagerly at a T-shirt, a fleecy jacket, and a pair of sweatpants, sighing happily as she discarded her New Empire lingerie and pulled the clothing over her brutalized flesh. The pants were a little short around the ankles, but she didn't care. She was warm, she was covered, and she was in paradise.

Grace looked at the other two women still sitting vacantly on the king-sized bed. Their faces were lined with suffering, and neither one of them had uttered a single word yet. "Come on, ladies," she said encouragingly. "You don't want to sit in that stuff all day."

"I'd just leave them alone for now," Libby said quietly, moving toward the closet again. "Maybe it's better to pick something out for them."

"Do they talk?" Grace asked. She watched the women with concern. Their eyes shone glassily.

"I've never heard them say a word," Libby said. "The other girls said they were twins—Ruby and Raven. I guess they've been at the brothel for a while."

"The New Empire brothel?"

Libby looked away. "You know about that place?"

"We've heard about it." Grace sat down on the bed. "What happened to you, Libby? Where's Carmen?"

"After we stole your caravan, Horus overtook us. He set the wagon on fire. We ran, but his men hunted us down and brought us back to him. At first he thought we'd escaped from the New Empire, but then he realized we'd never been there before."

"So he killed Joey?"

"No." Libby grew pale. "He was going to send him back to the New Empire with us. Carmen convinced him to kill Joey. She hated him for what he did to mom—I did too. But to kill your own father...like that?"

"Impaling him was *Carmen's* idea?" Simone asked.

"Yes," Libby replied. "He tried to cooperate. He told Horus about you. He even said he would work at the New Empire. It was Carmen who mentioned impalement." She rubbed at her arms, like she was trying to rub something off her body. "After it was over, he sent us to the brothel." She sobbed bitterly. "He made Carmen the madam there. She has all the power at that place. She could have helped me. She could have protected me. Instead, she sent me to the generals in the field." Libby was biting at her nails again. "Carmen had no problem pimping me out. She just didn't want to see it."

Grace and Simone looked at one another in disbelief.

"I met Ruby and Raven at the brothel first. One of the girls told me they were favorites with the generals. They get requested all the time because they're twins."

But the twins in question never heard this remark. They were both far away, someplace soft and full of light, where nothing ever hurt, and they were finally warm. In the distance, there was the muffled buzz of conversation, like a fly bumping against a window in another room. And like a fly, the twins paid no attention to it. It had nothing to do with them. Such trifles didn't matter. Now that they were away from their bodies, matters of the physical realm were no longer of any interest. Those things caused pain and humiliation. Those things defiled your sisterhood. They made you hate the very nature of your twinship when you had prized it all your life. No. It was better here, in this hazy world where they had all the control. The twins had escaped the generals, and the fools had never even realized they were gone.

Grace watched the sisters across the room. "They need help," she said, sounding determined. Simone and Libby exchanged dubious glances as she moved toward the bed and pulled a blanket over the women's sharp-looking shoulders. She sat down beside them and looked into their faces. When she received no response, she pulled a hunk of salted meat from her pocket and ripped it into pieces. She held shreds of it out to the women, offering it to them. When they still didn't respond, Grace sat even closer and pressed the food into their hands. After some gentle enticing, the two young women began looking at her and returning her gaze. Then Raven crammed the salted meat into her mouth and chewed shyly, motioning to her sister to do the same. As they ate, Grace talked softly to them, smiling, pulling the blanket closer around them.

Across the room, Libby gasped when Ruby quietly answered a question. "It's a miracle!" she whispered to Simone.

Several more minutes passed, and Grace led the women to the closet.

"She's so good with them," Libby murmured. "I've never seen them like this before."

Grace was showing Raven and Ruby several pairs of pants that looked too big for them. But the clothes were in good condition, and they looked comfortable. It wasn't long before Raven and Ruby picked out two oversized tank tops and large flannel work shirts to layer on top. Raven selected a wide brown belt with a gold buckle to hold up her pants, while Ruby opted for a pair of red suspenders that seemed to please her enormously.

By the time the women returned downstairs, Raven and Ruby were finally beginning to understand that their immediate nightmare was over. They weren't brothel women any longer; they were free—at least, for now.

"Dinner's ready!" Hazen called. By the time they had all trooped into the living room, he was standing by the fireplace, tending to a pot suspended above the flames. He stirred the contents and then sniffed at it inquiringly.

"What is that?" Grace asked, peering into the pot at the greasy brown substance that bubbled and squeaked over the fire.

"That's stew, my sweet interrogator," Lewis boomed, appearing from the kitchen with a plate of sandwiches in his hands. "Let's call the flavor 'brown,' shall we? I suspect the meat is coyote, but it's impossible to know for sure. Also on the menu," he set the plate on the coffee table with an elegant bow, "are grilled cheese sandwiches. I found some bannock in the back—still good, for the most part. Then I added some reasonable-looking cheese and toasted it over the fire. Take one, and ye too shall know the delights of heaven."

Raven, Ruby, and Libby snatched at the warm sandwiches and tore into them with grunts of satisfaction. Simone and Grace each grabbed one as well and slouched out across the green velvet couch.

"I also have dessert coming, so save room," Lewis warned. "It's one of my own inventions, and it may be my best one yet." He chuckled. He felt like a veritable Michelangelo these days, an artist with many canvases. One day he was designing weaponry, the next he was an impromptu gourmet.

Zeff shuffled into the room, holding a stack of bowls in his hand. Cody followed him with an armful of glasses, and Ruby gasped at the unexpected sight of the battered young general. Cody's face reddened, and he looked down at his feet, letting his long, dark hair fall across his eyes. Once he put the glasses down on the table, he squared his shoulders and walked over to the chaise lounge where Raven, Ruby, and Libby were perched, clutching at the remains of their sandwiches and watching him intently.

"I want to apologize for everything," Cody said. He grimaced. "I hated how those guys treated you, and I should have said something. I should have stood up for you." His shoulders dropped. "But I can't change that now. I can't change what happened. But I promise I won't ever hurt you. I'm not like the others. I just.... I just want you to know that."

Ruby's eyes filled with tears, and Libby put a reassuring hand on Cody's arm. "We know you're not," she said. "You never hurt us. And the other generals were so cruel to you."

"Yeah, I guess." Cody gazed out the window into the backyard, the scene of his recent assault. "They say rookies get hazed pretty bad in the Empire. But I don't think I was general material anyway. Those guys are messed up."

Horrific images flooded Ruby's mind, and she quickly blinked them away. Raven, knew what she was thinking and gave her sister a reassuring kiss on the cheek. They reached for each other, and their hands intertwined like roots nourishing a tree.

"Well, there's no better way to make peace than by enjoying a nice meal together," Hazen said. "Or, in our case, a weird stew." He went over to the fireplace and started doling the steaming concoction into bowls, which were then passed around. Surprisingly, the mystery stew proved to be delicious and the talking soon gave way to slurping and the clink of spoons against bowls.

"What are we going to do with them?" Zeff said in Simone's ear as she slurped at her meal. "We can't bring them to the New Empire. They'll be killed."

Simone nodded in agreement, but remained hunched over her bowl like a lion over its kill. She gave the matter some thought as she finished the last spoonful and then dragged a crusty piece of bannock around the bowl, soaking up the last of the juices. "Maybe we could take them back to the Taylors," she suggested, although turning back from the New Empire was the last thing she wanted to do now. But what other choice did they have?

Grace shoved closer to Simone on the sofa. "They should come with us," she said. "We need their help."

"Exactly," Hazen chimed in on the conversation, his mouth full of bread and cheese. He joined the small huddle. "We could use more people. The odds are already stacked against us."

"These women are traumatized. They can't help us," Zeff replied, in a frustrated whisper. "They need to go someplace and get better."

"We want to come with you," Raven said suddenly, startling everyone in the room. All eyes turned towards the twins.

"You're going to the New Empire, aren't you?" asked Ruby. "To kill Horus?"

"We're going to try," Zeff answered. "But it's extremely dangerous, you know."

The sisters looked at each other. "We know how to shoot," Ruby offered. "Mom used to take us to a shooting range."

Grace grinned. "I rest my case," she said.

"I want to come too," said Libby. "But I don't know how to shoot."

"Well, Libby," Simone said with a thoughtful expression on her face, "want a quick lesson?" She looked out the window. "We better hurry though—the sun will be setting soon."

"A shooting lesson?" Zeff asked; he looked incredulous. "We can't waste ammo."

"We can focus on form, theory, loading, and unloading. Besides, there's that weapons cache that Lewis knows about—right, Lew?"

"You know where the gun cache is?" Cody gasped, turning to face the inventor. "I thought only Horus knew that."

"The cache is in the library of Sonoma Heights Secondary School," Lewis pronounced, trying not to look too pleased with himself—and failing miserably.

"I know where that is!" Cody replied, jumping to his feet. "The Redemption Sessions are held at the school, in the auditorium."

"Horus knows we're coming," Zeff said. "Let's hope he doesn't empty the cache before we do."

"In the meantime, shooting lessons in the backyard," Grace said, picking up the pistol and Zeff's revolver. Libby, Ruby, and Raven followed in her wake as she made for the back door. Simone and Cody brought up the rear, and she let the young general carry her shotgun.

"Focus on form! Do you hear me? Save the ammo, for Christ's sake!" Zeff hollered after them. "We haven't found that gun cache yet." He followed the crowd out into the backyard, where his reprimanding soon became a lesson on the importance of gun safety.

When the light began to fade and the air grew cool with the coming night, Lewis returned from the kitchen proudly bearing the dessert he had promised. However, he was deeply disappointed to find that everyone was still outside—well, almost everyone. Hazen was seated in the living room, alone, looking into the fire. The tradesman's lack of enthusiasm for guns had left his mind unoccupied, and so it had wandered down a twisted, root-choked path in his head. He saw the hell of the New Empire and its dark agonies. He saw suffering; more specifically, he saw his own suffering. Stabbing, fire, impalement, crucifixion.

"I don't want to die." He groaned out loud.

"Are they still doing gun stuff out there?" Lewis asked, placing the dessert on the table. Hazen continued to stare morosely into the fire until the inventor poked his large, safari-hatted head in front of his gaze.

"I suppose that's fine by me," Lewis continued. "More dessert for us, then. No offense old boy, but it looks like you could use a little extra cheer." The inventor went to work with a ladle before handing Hazen a bowl of something yellow floating in something pink. "I present to you: power-out pudding," he said. "I took Twinkies from Horus's pantry and paired them with a strawberry coulis. I think you will be delighted with the result."

To Hazen, the result looked like a bloated corpse, lolling in its own blood in the sun. "Looks great, Lew," he said with forced bravado. "Give it here."

But the first bite was so sweet and creamy, Hazen tucked into the rest of the dessert with utter abandon, slurping and licking at his spoon and then the bowl itself. When he finally came up for air, his cheeks felt sticky, and there was fruit syrup in his hair. Somehow, he felt happy again. He gave Lewis a wide smile. There was no doubt about it—power-out pudding was the man's best invention yet.

HELLO, GOOD-BYE

For some, sleep was fitful that night; for others, it never came at all. For Raven, a deep and even slumber consumed her as soon as her head hit the pillow, a dreamy smile playing upon her bow-shaped mouth. Yes, she was returning to the New Empire, a place where she and her sister had experienced cruelty, violence, and prolonged confinement. But this time they were returning with a vengeance to match their terrible mistreatment.

Raven had felt everything change the instant Simone had given her the rifle to hold in the backyard. She'd used a handgun before at the shooting range. But this—this was different; it *felt* different. The weight and size of the rifle was impressive to her; it made her feel dangerous. She'd never felt that way before, and she delighted in the sensation. It reminded her that she was alive, that she was a person and not some strip of land that could be owned and rav-aged on a whim. With the regularity of passing clouds, the gener-als had moved over her and her sister, over and over them again, with their hitting, their spitting, their slaps and smirks and grunts, their filthy, mangy bodies with their sickening, rotten smells. In her dreams Raven saw all those men again—through her riflescope.

The next morning, the entire outfit was up early. The summer air still felt brisk and fresh, and fat droplets of dew sparkled like gems in the grass. While the others packed up the generals' wagon with food and supplies from the bunker, Grace and Simone buried the ashes of the bonfire from the night before, where they'd ceremonially burned the brothel lingerie in the flames. After that was destroyed, the group removed the taxidermied heads from the study and laid them across the fire as well until they were burnt to ashes. This had given the evening a solemn and sober air, and reminded everyone of what they were up against.

Back on the road again, the war party kept to the secondary streets for most of the morning, using their horses to pull the wagon. They couldn't travel too far off the beaten path because, as Hazen pointed out on a number of occasions, the requisitioned New Empire wagon was an inferior build to Esmeralda, and they would have to take it easy on the "hunk of junk." As they traveled, Simone and Alfred scouted the woods ahead, while Zeff and Peaches followed the wagon. Everyone was nervous of an ambush; the closer they got to the New Empire, the more likely they were to find generals—or for generals to find them.

In the early afternoon, Simone found a copse of trees that sheltered a small, rushing stream. She dismounted to let Alfred have a slurp of water when the sounds of beating hooves thundered into the shady grove behind her. She knew it was a stranger in an instant; she could recognize the sound of Zeff's horse. She turned in the direction of the sound, brandishing her shotgun and planting her feet, when two riders came into view, hats tucked low over their eyes and filthy bandanas concealing their faces.

"Hold it!" she cried.

"Simone?" the first rider shouted; it was a female voice. The rider brought her mount to a stop and pulled the bandana from her face. "It's Claire—Claire Lawson!" she said, smiling and rubbing at the dust around her eyes. "Thank God we found you."

"I almost can't believe it!" the second rider cried; it was her husband Lloyd.

"What are you doing out here?" Simone asked with concern. "Is everything all right at Elwood's?"

"Well…" the Lawsons looked at one another. "Things are all right," Claire said quickly. "The compound fell. The generals have it now."

"But the Parson boys!" she cried. "And PJ! Are they…"

"Everyone's alive," Lloyd said. "We managed to escape. The rest of them are living in a secret dugout in the woods for now." He looked at Claire. "But we couldn't stop wondering how long it would take for the generals to find us again." He jumped down from his horse and walked toward Simone. "We realized you folks were our only chance. And we want to help in any way that we can." He held out his hand to her and she shook it gratefully.

"You don't know how good it is to see you," she said. "I know it must have been hard leaving PJ."

"We're doing this for PJ," Claire replied, her voice hard and low. "We're going to tear that damn Empire apart."

Lloyd and Claire's arrival brought good cheer to the convoy once they'd returned to the wagon with Simone. The addition of two more people to their small war party seemed like fortune was smiling in their direction, and a strong dose of fortune was just what they needed right now. They would be reaching the outskirts of Trafalgar City soon; it was only a matter of time before they would have to abandon their horses. The New Empire wagon had been drawn by two horses, so only Dolly and Molly would remain in their service. They would be the ones to pull the wagon through the city and into the heart of the New Empire.

Simone was dreading the inevitable separation from Alfred, her loyal steed; they had been through so much together. Before Grace had come along, he had been her only company on hunting trips in the valley, but he was good company to have. Patient and understanding, he'd always done what she'd asked of him, even when it was cold and there was little to eat. He'd never let her down.

How she would miss him.

When they reached a field of rolling hills and long, ruffled grasses, Simone knew it was time to say good-bye. The lush, green meadow looked like a horse's paradise, and Alfred gave an exultant nicker when they stopped nearby, his eyes fixed longingly on the virgin field and the swaying delicacies that awaited him there. Simone took off his saddle and packed his reins away, patting his neck for the last time.

"You've been a good boy," she whispered, rubbing his muzzle affectionately and finding her face was wet with tears. Alfred gazed down at her as she wept, blinking at a forelock that kept falling into his eye. He rubbed his face against her hand, and Simone sighed heavily, taking his great head in her arms. Another good-bye. Eventually, she released him and returned to the wagon without looking back.

Everyone was sorry to leave the horses, but Simone was the most affected by it, slouching inside the wagon and emanating a deep and sorrowful silence that even Lewis feared to penetrate.

No one told her that Alfred had followed along after her, hanging behind the wagon for miles, until Zeff finally shooed him away.

BARRICADE

By the time the crowded wagon had huffed and puffed its way to Trafalgar City, Simone had gotten a grip on her melancholy. She knew she couldn't afford to be swept away by emotion at a time like this; she needed to focus.

"Open the back!" Cody called from the driver's seat. "You should see this."

The wagon was clip clopping through the financial district of the city, once the vibrant hub of the rich and elite. Now, silent office towers loomed out of the ground and leered at them like gargoyles. Refuse and burned-out cars lined the streets, forcing Cody to maneuver around them. The wagon turned a corner, and a flock of indignant pigeons took to the skies, their whinnying wings disturbing the uncanny quiet of the city.

"Where is everyone?" Grace asked. "Are they at the New Empire now?"

"A few of them are," Cody said. "But I heard most of the city starved to death in the first winter, and sickness took the rest. The generals said there was no resistance when they got here. They just rounded up the survivors."

"And the survivors went to the New Empire?"

"Yup. The poor bastards."

"Talk about from bad to worse." Grace leaned forward in her seat. "The New Empire used to be Sonoma Heights, right? That fancy town?"

"That's the one," Cody replied. "The river runs right through the middle of town, so there's a reliable water source. And the residents had big yards, which they turned into cooperative farms. The Meadowlark Golf Club became a rye field. They were growing hemp—they even had granaries." He frowned suddenly. "It was a complete slaughter when the generals got there."

The wagon passed a faded green sign, riddled with bullets holes. Sonoma Heights—Next Exit. The luster of the bright, sunny day had faded, and the sky had become dark and brooding. Storm clouds bulged in the distance, hanging ominously over the New Empire. The wind had gained strength, and what started out as a pleasant breeze had mutated into a howling poltergeist, scratching at the wagon tarp and hurling dirt through the air.

Simone poked her head out of the sanctuary of the wagon and into the rising wind, handing Cody a bandana to protect his face from the flying debris.

"Thanks!" he said, pulling the fabric over his nose as road grit beat into his eyes. Drawing the wagon, the miserable Dolly and Molly kept their heads down, hunched over and flat eared against the weather. Simone gave a discouraged sigh and let the flap fall shut again.

Outside the wagon, there was a muffled gasp.

"Everyone keep quiet," Cody said; he sounded nervous. "There's a barricade ahead. Damn it—they've already noticed us."

"How many men?" Simone whispered through the tarp.

"Two. Both armed," he replied.

"Don't let 'em see your fear, Cody," Zeff encouraged him. "Just relax, son. And remember: we've got your back."

Cody was heartened to hear Zeff's voice. He tried to relax; he wanted to make the gruff old rancher proud—he truly did. In the driver's seat, he bent double against the wind, his eyes burning under the gritty assault. But no amount of wind-flung debris could conceal the barricade ahead and the two hooded figures that were now stepping out into the road.

Cody lowered the bandana that had been covering his face and brought the horse team to a stop. He hopped down from the wagon and approached the generals in what he hoped was a causal manner. When he spotted their assault rifles, his mouth went dry. He hated Berserker Class.

"Back so soon, Cody?" one of the men taunted. "What the fuck happened to your face? You talk back to Lowry?"

"Yeah," Cody mumbled. Squinting at the hooded man, he was crestfallen to see the unmistakable mug of Decoy smirking back at him. Decoy had been a favorite of Horus's as long as Cody had known him, infamous among the generals for his vicious temper and disturbing sexual appetite. His face, completely covered by a tattoo of a spiderweb, drove fear into the hearts of those who trembled before him, begging for mercy. But begging was always a futile exercise with Decoy; it was like pleading your case with a shark.

Decoy smiled, and the web on his face rippled. "Hey, Arms—guess who?" he called to his partner. Armson pulled his hood down to stare at Cody, revealing a face that looked like it had been punched too many times and probably deserved it.

"What's the barricade for?" Cody asked, raising his eyebrows in feigned surprise.

"Haven't you heard?" Armson sneered.

"Heard what?" Cody was starting to sweat.

Armson looked at him closely. "There was a rebellion in Havenbrook." His large, hooked nose seemed to sniff at Cody inquiringly. "But I guess a little worm like you wouldn't know anything about that, now would you?"

"A rebellion? Yeah, right," Cody replied, embarrassed at the insult. "Who'd want to rebel against the emperor?"

"No one, that's who," Decoy said. The spiderweb twisted into an expression of rage. "Because I'd rip his arms and legs off first. I'd gouge out his eyeballs and piss into his skull. I'd end that motherfucker's fucking world!"

"Yeah, like you could rip somebody's arms and legs off," Armson said snidely, pointing his butter-knife nose at Decoy and then back at Cody. "So where are the rest of the boys? Is Lowry with you?"

"He's in the back," Cody said, vaguely motioning to the wagon. "They all are. They're not going to ride up front in a wind like this."

Armson remained silent. He stared at Cody, narrowing his yellow, pitiless eyes.

"We just got sent back," Cody continued uneasily, trying to fill the silence. "Message by rider. I guess now we know why." He gestured to the barricade.

"You'd think the rider would have given you a reason." Decoy moved closer. Alarm bells began to ring in Cody's head. He was very close to danger; he could feel it.

In the back of the wagon, Raven and Ruby looked at each other with concern. Both sisters had a long and terrifying acquaintance with Decoy. They knew what he was like when he was in the mood to hurt someone.

Ruby took a deep breath and screamed the ragged, pain-filled scream she knew so well.

"Yell, 'Take it, you little bitch,'" Raven whispered to Hazen. "Do it now!"

"Take it, you little bitch!" Hazen hollered roughly, and his cheeks flushed.

Outside in the swirling wind, Decoy looked sharply at the wagon. He gave Cody a knowing smirk.

"Sounds like the twins are getting a workout today," he said. The spiderweb split into a leering smile as he looked at Cody. "OK. Get the fuck out of here."

"We should check the wagon," Armson objected as Cody quickly turned to leave. "We were told to check *every* wagon. He could be hiding something."

"You kidding me?" he heard Decoy reply. "Interrupt Lowry with the twins, and you'll get yourself shot. Besides, Cody couldn't hide his own shit in the woods."

Cody climbed back up to the driver's bench with a powerful sense of relief. The wind was still driving in his eyes, but it didn't seem that bad now; in fact, it was almost refreshing. Armson and Decoy moved the barricade out of the middle of the road, and he drove the wagon through before they could change their minds.

This was Round One; and it went to the underdogs.

INTO THE EMPIRE

With Armson and Decoy far behind them and wreathed in the rust-colored dirt from the road, the war party found themselves breathing a little easier. A few miles further, and Grace pushed the wagon flap to the side so they could take turns peeking out at the first signs of the New Empire. At first it was just forest—forest which quickly gave way to acres upon acres of deforested and denuded land on either side of the road. It was wasted land, as far as the eye could see, a desolate and miserable sight. Stumps jutted out of the earth like broken teeth and pools of murky green water pooled around them like weeping abscesses. The wind fluttered into the wagon, and with it came the smell of human waste, burned garbage and death.

Drawing closer to town, the wagon trundled past a dozen head of skinny looking cattle standing in a front yard, confined by barb-wire fencing. Ramshackle vegetable gardens sprawled along the ground in side yards and boulevards, bug infested and begging for water. The houses themselves were sadder still, laced with bullet holes and windows boarded up with planks of wood. What were once elegant manors were now hovels of despair. They were cages now, not houses.

"Here are more ranches!" Cody called from the driver's bench. "That's a barn right there." He pointed to a rambling bungalow with an attached garage that had been fitted with a barn door. "Most of the ranches are located in this area, but the Empire doesn't have much for cattle. There's a horse ranch, a little further out. There's even a few sheep, but they keep them at the golf course."

The wagon passed a line of skeletal men and women shuffling bleakly along the side of the road, carrying pails of water. All of them kept their heads down as the wagon passed. Anguished and sunburned, they bore their loads on bleeding feet.

"Those are the ranchers," Claire said, noticing Grace's shocked expression. "It's a high-stress job. If an animal dies before it's due, the rancher goes to a Redemption Session. And they don't usually come back."

One of the women on the road behind them began staggering. Suddenly, she stumbled forward and collapsed to the ground. The water from her pail poured out around her, soaking her clothes and the pavement beneath her. She slowly got back up as the other workers passed without stopping and without looking as they stumbled on with their heavy loads.

"She needs help," Grace said, watching the woman and her pail grow smaller in the distance. "We should stop."

"That will draw attention," Zeff said. "We've got to push on. C'mon, close the flap."

They closed the flap, leaving Cody to ride alone upfront. And this made him the only human witness to the horrors of Deserters' Row when he drove the wagon passed it, Horus's message to any would-be escapees from the Empire. The young general had seen the evil sight many times and could never get used to it. He looked away from it now as the wagon went by, away from the severed limbs dangling from tree boughs like rotten fruit, away from the impaled heads of people he once knew, away from the hordes of carnivorous birds circling the field, screeching like demons. He gagged at the smell of rotten, festering meat and covered his nose. Then he pulled on the reins. The horses had started to quicken the pace on their own accord; they were frothing at the mouth, and snorting in fear. Cody turned the wagon down another street, and Deserters' Row was soon behind them, leaving man and horse to breathe a little easier. Once they were even further away, Cody started to feel pleased that no one else from the wagon had been exposed to that sight today. Something told him it wouldn't be good for morale.

They journeyed on, meandering down winding residential streets with names like Rose Briar Lane and Magnolia Avenue, where Tudor-inspired mansions and boxy modern homes sat side by side, displaying ragged vegetable-patch lawns that were as tragic and worn out as the workers who tended them. There always seemed to be a general around, sporting a curled lip and a suspicious gaze, strutting around the dejected workers like a tyrannical rooster. Cody winced at the sight every time, terrified that one of them would order the wagon to stop. But it was midsummer, which was a busy time of year in the New Empire. The overseers were more interested in antagonizing the workers than watching the road.

"What do you think, Cody?" came Zeff's voice through the tarp. "Think Horus has ramped up the firepower?"

"I see a few more guns around, but not many."

"Hmm." Zeff paused and peeked out the front of the wagon, squinting as he tried to make sense of the landscape that swam before his eyes, but it was no use. All he saw were strange shapes he couldn't place in his mind. Cody followed the rancher's gaze to the remains of Schaeffer Park, stripped of most of its trees and pitted with stumps and hollows. It was a sadly pockmarked piece of land, barren and dead.

"The forest was culled for firewood," Cody said. "Horus thought the land could be tilled, but the roots were too deep. Then he thought they could be dug out by hand, but he was wrong about that too."

The Schaeffer Park wreckage gave way to the Sonoma River and the squat limestone Traffic Bridge that spanned across it. From a distance, the river appeared littered with debris, but once the wagon drew closer, it became clear it was not debris but children who speckled the water, beating laundry on rocks under the waning sun. Cody noticed a general kick one of the children, a small, stern-faced girl, rubbing a piece of fabric with a nugget of soap. The child went tumbling into the river without a cry of surprise.

Passing over the bridge, Cody guided the wagon down River Avenue. Like a phantom, the Sonoma River Market appeared on the horizon. Tucked in the back of the wagon, Ruby and Raven held hands; they could feel themselves drawing closer to the brothel. Their pounding hearts bruised their ribs; every breath came hot and fast.

Libby chewed her nails. Grace chewed her bottom lip. Lewis chewed the tip of his pencil.

"Here we are," Cody said in a low voice from the driver's seat. He looked at the V-shaped strip mall designed to look like an old ski lodge, now thoroughly soaked with suffering and human misery. Along the storefront, the signs had been stripped from the building, leaving behind white strips of plaster that arched like eyebrows over barred windows. In the parking lot, two horses at a hitching post blinked sleepily. Cody guided the wagon to a parking spot and hopped down from the driver's seat with a nonchalant look around.

The terrible wind seemed to be falling away with the setting of the sun. Draped in shadows of the early evening, the parking lot seemed quieter than usual, almost deserted. Cody cast an anxious

look at the brothel before walking around to the back of the wagon and poking his head in.

"All right." Simone was addressing the group. "So everyone
knows the plan. Taking the brothel should be the easy part, so
don't get too nervous. Raven, Ruby, and Libby"—she gave the
women a long, meaningful look—"think of this as payback time."

The three women nodded, expressionless.

"Also, and this goes for everyone, but try not to die. Cody, we're
ready when you are."

Wiping his hands on his pants, Cody nodded and hitched
the horses before walking to the front door of the brothel. He
had been to this place once before—before the storms, when the
place had been a popular coffee shop called River Grounds. His
dad had taken him there when he was twelve and bought him his
first mocha. "Don't tell your mother!" Dad laughed, and he had
laughed too, happy to share a secret with somebody so important.
Cody hadn't been back since; he didn't want to sully that cherished
childhood memory. Also, he might have had a general's privileges,
but that didn't mean he had to use them, especially if he disagreed
with what those privileges included—and violently so.

Cody opened the door with effort. The planks of wood that
had replaced the glass panels were heavy, weighing it down. Once
inside, the door closed with a heavy bang behind him. It sounded
final, like a gavel.

Inside, a dozen young women sat at cheap bistro tables, wobbling on their wrought-iron chairs. As he walked in, a dozen pair
of eyes looked fearfully in his direction. Somebody muttered a
prayer. Cody looked around, noticing the painted cinnamon buns
and steaming cups of coffee on the butterscotch walls of the shop;
he remembered those. The front counter from his memory was
still there too, although it had been constructed into something
that looked more like an office cubicle with a pastry case serving
as a window.

"Well, hello there," a breathy female voice whispered in his ear. "Welcome to your fantasy."

Cody wheeled around and recognized Carmen immediately from Libby's description of her. She was wearing a smart pinstripe blazer and carrying a clipboard in her hands. With her hair pulled back into a chic French twist and her fingernails filed and manicured, the young woman was a mirage of effortless glamour in a ragtag, filth-encrusted existence. The young general stared at her in surprise. He knew Carmen was Libby's sister, but the two sisters looked nothing alike. Carmen was so…well…beautiful.

"H-hello," he stammered, red to the tips of his ears. "Is the brothel busy today? I have some friends outside, and I wasn't sure…"

"Yes, of course," Carmen purred throatily. "You were just checking. That's very sensible of you." She gestured to the bistro tables around her where the terrified women hunched in their seats.

"As you can see, we have many women available to you and your friends to meet all whims and desires. There are only three women at the moment who are *occupied*." Her smile parted her lips, but it never reached her gleaming eyes.

Cody looked again at Carmen's well-cut suit, her flashing diamond earrings, and her predatory smile, then at the women behind her, wearing tattered and cheap lingerie and cowering in their seats. He felt a strong wave of revulsion run through his body. Carmen had lost her charm in a hurry.

"Great," he said. "I'll go get my friends." He heaved opened the heavy front door again and stuck his head out into the fading light, giving the wagon a thumbs up. He held up three fingers.

Instantly, the wagon flap burst open, and Libby, Ruby, and Raven rushed out. By the time Cody had turned around again, Libby had already cornered Carmen and was waving Darnell's gun in her face.

"Libby!" Carmen cried, looking at the gun, then her sister, then the gun again; she forced a smile. "I've been so worried about you!" She opened her arms for a hug.

"Shut up, Carmen," Libby curtly replied. Her mouth was as thin as thread, the puffiness under her eyes shone blue. "I don't need to hear any more of your lies and I certainly don't need a fucking hug."

Carmen winced.

As the VanCleave family reunion continued, Raven and Ruby took Zeff's revolver and Hazen's hunting rifle to the back rooms of the brothel. By the time the others made it inside, there had been three gunshots.

The rest of the brothel women were beginning to come to life now, staring at the newcomers with unabashed curiosity, and whispering excitedly to one another. Although Carmen had only been a madam for a short period of time in the New Empire, she had already become feared and loathed by all the women in the brothel, without exception. She had flogged their flesh with an enthusiasm she never bothered to conceal—and one they never would forgive. Seeing their enemy now, with her back against the wall, stirred something inside the women. It was hope, and it rained down on the scorched gardens of their minds.

"Hazen." Carmen beseeched her former lover with wide doe eyes. "Do something."

The tradesman looked at Carmen and then looked away and spit on the ground.

"Don't get them involved," Libby said. "This is between you and me."

"I really don't know what you're talking about," Carmen said, smoothing her coiffed hair. "What's between you and me?"

"You pimped me out!" Libby yelled. "You killed our father!"

"Now don't exaggerate—"

"All of our lives you were the favorite daughter, the pretty one, the smart one! They gave you everything and forgot about me." Libby's voice cracked. "But no matter what they did, it was never enough for you, was it, Carmen?" she drew closer to her sister. "You always wanted more, even though the rest of us never had enough. And in the end, you bargained our lives away for trinkets! Bloody trinkets!"

Carmen looked at Libby and arched a perfectly plucked brow. "This is exactly what I was afraid of, Lib," she said. "You don't understand everything I've done for you. I've been protecting you, dummy. That's why you've had it so easy here."

In a flash, Libby was in her sister's face, pressing the barrel of the gun against her head. "You think what I've been through is easy?" Her voice sounded like it was tearing at the seams.

Simone moved behind Libby, placing a steadying hand on her shoulders. "Take it easy, Lib," she murmured. "She knows where Horus is."

"Horus?" Carmen smiled; her lifeline had arrived. "So that's what this is about. I guess that explains all the guards I noticed stationed around his manor." She paused a moment to let the comment sink in. "Of course, I could get you past them easily enough."

"You can take us to him?" Simone asked.

"I can take *you* to him," Carmen replied, looking at Simone with hard brown eyes. "I know you might not think much of me, but I want that man dead, just like you do. He's a monster."

Libby snorted.

"Listen to me," Carmen continued. "You pose as a brothel girl, and I can walk you right past the guards. It wouldn't be unusual for me to bring Horus a girl in the evening. But more than one, and the generals will get suspicious—that's not the emperor's thing. Besides, it only takes one bullet to kill him, right?"

By now, Simone almost doubted that, but she privately weighed their options. There weren't a lot of good ones.

"You got a wagon we can use?" she asked.

"The brothel wagon is in the parking lot," Carmen replied.

There was excited shouting as Raven and Ruby returned from the private rooms with three blood-spattered young women who were wrapped in sheets. "We got 'em," Ruby said, to the cheers and applause of the other women. "We got those bastards."

"I'm going with Carmen," Simone said to Libby, raising her voice above all the noise. "It's the best use of our resources, and we just can't pass that up right now."

Libby paled. "Are you sure?"

"I'm sure. This plan will free up the wagon, so put it to good use." Simone threw her sling over her shoulder. "We need to get moving."

Libby reluctantly lowered her gun. "OK. Well, good luck, Simone. I really hope I see you again. Carmen, on the other hand"—she gave her sister a murderous look—"feel free to die horribly."

"Whatever," Carmen replied.

"Are you sure about this?" Zeff said, when Simone came over to say her good-byes.

"It's the best way, Zeff," she answered. "I'll meet you at the school when it's over." She leaned over to give him a hug and he could feel the energy coiled in her body.

She's preparing herself for it, he thought, *for Horus, for death.* He wondered if this would be the last time they would ever be together. "I don't like this plan," he said in a voice that sounded angry to his own ears. "You shouldn't be going alone."

"I won't be alone," Simone said. "I have Carmen."

Zeff frowned. "That's what worries me the most."

CACHE ME IF YOU CAN

The clattering of horses' hooves outside was the sound of Zeff's heart breaking.

He knew Simone was alone in the back of the wagon with Carmen. Only God could help her now.

Clip clop, clip clop. To him, the sharply hollow noise sounded like *good-bye, for-ever.* Sick with worry, he listened to the steady gallop until the noise faded, and a heavy silence swept across the brothel. He looked around the room with his wasted eyes, but that didn't tell him much. Everyone was still; the air felt choked with anticipation. They seemed to be waiting for something, but waiting for what? For him?

With some effort, Zeff pushed his fear for Simone to the back of his mind. She was doing her part. Now he needed to do his.

"Grace, see that the women get some proper clothing," he said, drumming up his old air of authority. "Libby, I need you to get your colleagues ready to leave this place. Hazen, Lewis, Claire, and Lloyd, distribute the food; everyone must be fed. Cody, ready the wagon. We're going to the school."

Zeff's orders reenergized the group, and soon everyone had an assigned task or chore to do. The newly liberated women were lively as they nibbled on salted meats and bannock with jam. There were tall and petite women there, blondes and brunettes, all shimmying out of sordid lingerie into jeans, shorts, and sweatshirts, excited by the favorable turn of events. Each woman had wept in fear, slept in fear, gone for days consuming nothing but fear, and now there was a light, tiny and tremulous in the distance. It was an uncertain light, but it was there. And now that they could see it, they would do anything to reach it. Something primordial filled their brains. An ancient desire for revenge surged through their bodies. The women seemed to throb with excitement as Zeff explained he would take a small group to the school. If they found enough weaponry there, Lloyd and Claire would ride through town, sending residents to the school to launch a defense. In the meantime, Libby would lead an attack on the general's clubhouse to thwart an organized response, as well as hurt, maim, and kill as many generals as possible. When she asked for volunteers, every woman in the brothel raised her hand; better yet, most knew how to shoot a gun.

Zeff charged Libby and the twins with keeping the brothel on lockdown while the caravan was sent ahead to the school. "We won't be long now," he said, turning to go. "If we find that gun cache, we'll send some firepower. Then you'd better turn Claire and Lloyd loose."

"Zeff, hold on." Libby stopped him. "What if you don't find that gun cache?"

"We're leaving you with Hazen's rifle, the general's pistol, and half a dozen daggers," he replied. "Do what you do best—fight for your lives."

Zeff, Lewis, and Hazen made their way to the parking lot where Cody and the caravan were waiting. Grace was the last to leave, murmuring words of encouragement to the women as she passed.

When she reached Libby and the twins by the door, they wrapped her in their bony arms and pressed their faces to her cheeks.

"We'll make you proud," Ruby whispered in her ear.

"I already am," Grace said. She put her hands on Ruby's shoulders and gave them a squeeze. "Remember, when you're done with the generals, come to the school." Then she was gone, passing through the brothel door and into the night, where the first stars had already appeared, peeking through the clouds to watch the violence swelling below.

The wagon maneuvered through the streets of the New Empire, jangling over the crumbling roadways with Cody at the reins. The wind had calmed, and night had fallen in its entirety. There were no more workers along the road, no more cocksure generals. The streets were empty, and this made Cody feel self-conscious; the wagon must stick out like a sore thumb tonight. He swallowed a startled gasp as they rounded a corner and passed a group of generals ambling down the sidewalk with jugs of cider. He gave them a friendly wave, and the men stared as the wagon rumbled by. Soon, the black outline of Sonoma Heights Secondary School came into view.

With a few clicks of the tongue, Cody slowed the team and peered at the school from the road, searching for the guards he knew would be posted there. He heard a faint clinking noise in the dark; the generals on duty were drinking.

Navigating the wagon past the school, he turned down a quiet side street, where decaying mansions loomed in the dark. A single general was on patrol, torch in hand, his hawkish features illuminated by the glow as he watched them pass. Cody turned the wagon again, and when the back of the school came into view, he urged the horse team off the road and across the overgrown athletic track, skirting the portion of the field that had been planted over with flint corn. He drew the team to a stop along the edge of it, hoping the shadows would be enough to conceal their presence from the guards. Jumping down from the driver's seat, Cody stopped and listened. He could hear the hoot of an owl. That was all.

He retrieved a crowbar from the front of the wagon and walked around to the back, parting the flap. Zeff exited the wagon first, followed by Grace, then Hazen and Lewis, who carried unlit lanterns in their arms. Leaving the shadow of the corn, they moved quickly across the field in the dark, with nothing more than the high grasses to hide them. Once they reached the back of the school, Cody gestured to a broken window that had been boarded up with bowed sheets of plywood. He gave his crowbar to Hazen, who began prying it from the window as Grace and Lewis struggled with the lanterns.

Nearby, Zeff stood with his back to the rest of the group, listening for trouble. He felt someone move beside him and knew it was Cody; he could tell by the hesitant step and the shaky inhale of breath. "How you doing, kid?" he asked.

"Not too bad, sir," Cody whispered. He looked at Zeff shyly. "Maybe a little nervous."

"You're doing great," Zeff said, placing a careful hand on the young man's shoulder and giving it a squeeze.

"I'm going to take care of the generals out front for you guys," Cody said in his ear. "I'll meet you inside."

"Cody, wait," came Zeff's immediate reply.

But it was too late for that. Cody was already gone, racing away from the warmth of Zeff's reassuring presence and toward the pale, moon-dappled staircase from where even now, he could hear voices calling from its shadows—raucous male tones, uneven as the sea, getting louder and then quieting again, rising into laughter and jeering. There was the boozy scent of cider in the air. He ran blindly toward it all.

At the back of the school, Hazen pried the plywood from the window, deftly cleaning out the shards of glass that still spiked the pane. Grace raised a lantern to light the room inside. The light flickered and sputtered, revealing a squalid place filled with dingy plastic chairs and soiled cafeteria tables covered in debris. There was a rustling sound as something scurried through the garbage on the floor.

Grace leaned through the window with great care, placing the lantern on a table below before pulling the rest her body through. Inside, thick, stale air assailed her nostrils, and she almost choked on the smell. Putting a hand over her nose, she surveyed the filthy floor, and the battered furniture, overturned and lying at awkward angles across the room.

"What's that stink?" Hazen asked with disgust, climbing through the window. "Is this an abandoned cafeteria or something?"

"Actually, I believe this is a functioning cafeteria." Lewis's voice cut through the rancid closeness. He had already climbed inside and had ventured over to the kitchen, where maggoty produce and piles of strange gray meat shone under the light of his lantern. On the counter to his left, a number of large industrial-looking pots caught his eye. On further inspection he determined that the pots housed some kind of weevil-infested gruel. This must be breakfast in the New Empire. With an air of disappointment, he pulled out his notebook to record his observations, then mopped at his head with his handkerchief as if he could wipe away the nausea rumbling in his stomach

"Let's keep moving," Zeff said as Lewis rejoined the group. Holding her lantern high, Grace pushed one of the cafeteria doors that led into the hallway of the school. With a groan, the door opened to a dark, locker-filled corridor.

Everyone paused at the door.

"Think Cody got rid of the generals out front?" Hazen whispered. "They're not in here with us—are they?"

"That's what we're about to find out," Zeff said in a low voice. "Everyone stay close. Now where's the library?"

"I volunteer to lead," Lewis said. "I have a knack for sniffing out libraries."

"By all means," Zeff replied. "Just get us to that gun cache."

The small war party moved down the hallway, and past the defaced lockers that shone faintly like sarcophaguses in a looted tomb. Lewis led the group through the winding corridors of the school, locating the library with relative ease. But when he found the door unlocked, he began to worry. If Horus had gone to such lengths to hide his weapons, surely he would have secured the door.

He entered the room. In the bright flame-ups of the lantern, Lewis scoured the room for weaponry, but the library looked just as a library should, with its surgical-looking checkout counter, reading cubbies, and freestanding bookshelves. The rest of the group filed in behind him. No one said a word, but it was clear they were all thinking the same thing: *oh, no.*

The group split up.

At the front of the library, Grace tore apart the circulation desk in her search. Finding nothing at all, she turned the small break room upside down, kicking in the bathroom door and throwing open the cabinets below the chintzy porcelain sink. But all she found was a rat's nest on the bottom shelf and rat shit everywhere. She cursed and slammed the cabinet doors shut again.

At the center of the library, Hazen was seated at the table, and covering his face with his hands. He had given up hope that they would get out of this rotten scheme alive. He never should have come here—that was his first mistake. His second mistake? How about trusting Lewis? Yes. That was a good one. They had made their plans, they had gambled their lives, upon the idle speculations of a man wearing a safari hat. What the hell were they thinking?

Hazen began ruminating about his fate; surely it would be a grisly one and no doubt quite painful. Last night, Lloyd had told them Horus would actually *resuscitate* people he'd tortured to death at the New Empire. The man was so depraved, he'd perform CPR on some of his victims and bring them back to life—just so he could subject them to further cruelties. It was as if he saw death as a disapproving mother who had whisked her child away from a party too soon. The tradesman's eyes filled with tears.

Elsewhere in the library, the search continued. Zeff felt his way along the stacks of books with his hands, sniffing the air for the familiar whiff of gunpowder as he went. Finding the gun cache was the linchpin of their plans, and he knew it. There wasn't much of a Plan B. Across the room, Lewis checked every aisle, every table, every reading cubby for the weapons, desperate to believe the emperor had been telling him the truth, that he truly had confided in him, that their friendship really had been genuine. Both men searched long and hard, and with different motivation. Both men returned empty-handed.

They met at the back of the library.

"It ain't here," Zeff said to Lewis, slouching against an over-stuffed bookshelf. "What the hell do we do now?"

THE EMPEROR'S MANOR

B ound for the emperor's manor, Simone tried to take stock of her surroundings. She peered out the back of the wagon and watched for landmarks as they traveled through the fetid, sewage-soaked streets. Even in the cool night air, the place smelled like disease, and she felt like retching as she struggled to concentrate on the road. They must be going north now. Northwest?

The horses lurched around a corner, causing the wagon to fish-tail crazily. Simone felt her stomach flip, and she choked back the urge to vomit.

"Damn it," she cursed. "I'm about to get seasick in the suburbs."

Carmen leaped to her feet, shaking the rickety bench they had been sharing, and moved to the front of the wagon.

"Phil, get your act together, or I will have you killed! You hear me?" Carmen screamed at the unseen driver up front. "We're getting our asses kicked back here!" She turned, flashed an apologetic smile at Simone, and returned daintily to her seat. "You know what they say: good help is hard to find."

"Yeah, it's too bad you only have one sister," Simone replied. "You seem to have no problem employing her in your service."

Carmen hung her head at the remark, and her body visibly drooped. "You must hate me," she said, keeping her eyes on her shiny leather shoes.

"Yeah," Simone replied, returning her gaze to the road. "I'm pretty sure everyone does."

"You're right." Carmen paused. "I even hate myself. But I'll make it right again, you'll see. After what that bastard did to my father…"

"What? The impalement—that you suggested?"

"Suggested?" Carmen looked stunned. "Why would you think that?"

"Libby told us."

"Listen, Libby is obviously upset about what happened at the brothel, but she's making that up. Dad and I had our differences, but I didn't really want him dead. I'm not a total freak."

Simone looked dubious.

"I'll admit it—I've done some fucked up stuff," Carmen rushed on. "What happened with Libby in the New Empire wasn't right— but he made me do it. Horus said I could either pimp her out or kill her." She started to cry. "I couldn't kill her! I couldn't kill my own sister. And I couldn't kill my own father, either. Even after what he did to mom." Snuffling, Carmen wiped her eyes delicately on the sleeve of her blazer. "Libby wanted to turn you all against me. She's been through hell so I can understand why, but I'm not a bad person. I'm really not." She trembled as she spoke. "I'm just a normal person who wanted a normal life, you know…to go away to college, live in an apartment, have a cute boyfriend. That's all I ever wanted. I never thought that at twenty-one, there would be an apocalypse, our house would burn down, our mom would die, and we'd be forced to live in some kind of slave camp." Tears were openly rolling down Carmen's cheeks, and she no longer bothered to wipe them away. "And you know what the worst part of it is? I can't stop living—you know, surviving. I've thought about killing myself...I think about it all the time, but I could never go through with it." She sighed heavily. "I'm so scared of death and pain I'll do anything to avoid them. And now that I know that about myself, I'll never be able to forget it. I'm a coward in every sense of the word."

Simone looked at Carmen closely. Her hands clutched her face; her shoulders heaved beneath her blazer. Thin beams of moonlight filtered into the wagon, catching on her tear-stained cheeks, and Simone felt a twinge of sympathy for this survivor, for this woman who fought tooth and nail to save her own life.

"We've all done things we're not proud of, all right?" she said. "Sometimes you have to make tough choices to survive."

Carmen looked at Simone, and her face brightened. She threw her arms around her. "Thank you," she whispered. "I just needed someone to understand."

"I don't completely understand, OK. You owe your sister something, some kind of restitution for what you did," she said, working herself free from Carmen's arms. "You're going to have to think about that."

Bang!

The wagon lurched to a stop, tipping the women off the bench and onto the ground below. "Goddamn it, Phil!" Carmen hollered at the driver before helping Simone to her feet. "We're here. Are you ready?"

"This is the manor?" Simone asked, suddenly feeling anxious. She'd lost track of where they were. She threw her shotgun sling around her shoulders and began to climb out of the wagon. She would have to orient herself using the stars.

"Wait!" Carmen cried; the frantic note in her voice stopped Simone in her tracks. "You can't go out there like that!" she said. "The guards will know you're not from the brothel. You're going to have to put that lingerie on." She pointed to the far corner of the wagon, where a lump of artificial lace and satin sat like a spider in the shadows.

"Come on," Simone protested.

"You'd better hurry up and put that damn uniform on," Carmen ordered. "I'm not kidding around. Horus has at least ten generals stationed here, and I'd be surprised if they're not all Berserker Class. You're probably the bashful type, so I'll wait outside while you change." She exited the wagon, and Simone watched her go, somewhat bemused. Gone was the tearful, brokenhearted woman she had just been consoling. Carmen had regained her swagger in no time.

"Hey, Phil—take a break!" Carmen yelled to the driver. Simone heard her coming around the back of the wagon again. "Here, give me your gun," she whispered through the tarp. "Brothel women don't pack heat. I'll bring it into the manor for you."

Simone hated the thought of handing over her shotgun, but she could hear the low muttering of the generals nearby. Carmen was right. She couldn't walk into the manor armed; she would be killed before she got very far. Simone handed her shotgun and sling out the back of the wagon and hurried out of her trousers and flannel shirt before jamming her legs into the fishnet stockings. Once those were on, she attacked the corset with a mixture of fear and curiosity.

"How do you get this thing on?" She grunted in frustration, running the tips of her fingers down the tiny metal clasps that lined the bizarre contraption. Not to be deterred, she threw the corset around her body, contorted her arms like a monkey, and tried to fasten the clasps from the front as the wagon rocked back and forth with her efforts.

"What's going on in there?" Carmen whispered.

A victorious Simone emerged from the back of the wagon, dressed in full brothel uniform. But the victory was short lived.

"Oh, no. No, no, no, no. Lose the boots," Carmen said, catching flashes of Simone's legs in the darkness. "And that cowboy hat's got to go. Brothel women don't wear…items…such as those."

"They do tonight," Simone replied. "You can talk us past the guards. Don't pretend those general boys are any match for you."

"I'd accuse you of flattery, Simone, but in this case, you're right."

They walked together to the front of Horus's sprawling home, an elegant Colonial brick mansion, hairy with ivy and set back graciously from the road. As they drew closer, Simone noticed the carefully manicured lawn and blooming rose bushes, illuminated by the freestanding torches that lined the front of the house. From the porch, silhouettes of generals watched them approach.

Time seemed to melt away into something slow and sluggish, and for an instant, Simone felt acutely aware of her environment: the lick of the evening breeze on her legs, the reassuring weight of Em's Stetson on her head, the sharp odor of pitch from the torches. She could also feel the absence of the shotgun sling across her back; the weight that should be there, but wasn't. Her gaze flitted over to Carmen, who was carrying the weapon under one shoulder. *It has to be this way*, Simone reminded herself. *There's no other choice.*

Then Carmen was beside her, clutching Simone's arm with her hand and pointing the gun in her face. "Evening, boys," she called to the generals ahead, smiling a charming, kittenish smile. "Special delivery for the emperor."

She shoved Simone forward. As Simone stumbled up the path through the fragrant torch smoke, she counted seven generals: five leering from the porch, two standing at the foot of the stairs.

"Is that a new brothel girl, Carmen?" one of the generals called. "What's with the hat? Is it western-theme night or something?"

The other generals laughed and whistled lewdly.

"Why so surprised?" Carmen asked as she ascended the stairs, pushing Simone along in front of her. "You know the emperor likes variety, and we just got this one in yesterday." With one arm, she wheeled Simone around and pressed the shotgun against her face. "Every cowgirl needs to be broken in. Right, honey?" she cooed, before casually moving the barrel away.

"Now wait a sec," one of the generals said; it was the one nearest to them, a squat, angry-looking man with cropped blond hair and pale, colorless eyes. "Where'd you get that gun, Carmen?" he asked.

"Yeah," a second general chimed in. "Are you Berserker Class now or something?"

The guards began muttering to one another in doubtful and unmistakably dubious tones. "A fee-male berserker?" one said. "The emperor would never allow it."

"No way, no how," agreed another. "Not in this lifetime, man."

"I am Berserker Class!" Carmen cried with such savagery, the men fell silent around her and stared. "The emperor reclassed me this morning," she said with a scowl. "He wanted me to have a gun in case I saw anything suspicious."

"He didn't tell me that," said the shiny-scalped general. He looked at Simone the way a cat looks at a bird with a broken wing.

"I don't think the emperor's compelled to tell you everything he does," Carmen replied, arching one perfectly shaped brow. "In fact, to even suggest such a thing could result in a Redemption Session for you." The general's expression tightened as he moved his gaze from Simone's cleavage to Carmen's face; she gave him an unpleasant smirk. "Or," she continued, "we could forget all about this little disagreement, and I'll make sure you get the first taste of the merchandise—once the emperor's done with her, of course." She gripped Simone by the arm and dangled her out like a prize.

"Deal," the general replied. He settled his icy stare on Simone again. "I'm looking forward to taming this one."

"Me too," another general growled. "I want a piece of Cunt Eastwood." The men all laughed, and Simone lowered her gaze to hide her fury.

"You'll have you turn, boys." Carmen clasped the doorknob. "But we can't keep the emperor waiting." She opened the door and motioned Simone through.

But before Simone could comply, the blond general had gripped her by the shoulders and was squeezing them hard. "I'll see you soon," he whispered in her ear. "Don't forget about me."

"I won't," Simone quietly replied. She looked into the general's eyes, and the man was taken aback by the burning hatred he saw in her gaze. Suddenly, he was struck by the feeling that something terrible was going to happen and he thought about drawing his revolver. But she looked down again, breaking the short staring contest, and the general chided himself for his foolishness. This was just another brothel bitch—he knew that. She was nothing to worry about. The emperor was the paranoid one, not him. He knew better than to waste his time worrying when the New Empire was as safe as could be.

Behind him, the women entered the house.

LOST AND FOUND

"I'm back," Cody said, entering the school library in an optimistic frame of mind. He couldn't stop smiling; his trick had worked. He had found the generals at the front of the school and told them the highway barricade was under attack. Always on the look-out for a fight, the drunken generals had ridden off in a hurry, leaving the school completely undefended. Cody had returned through the blackened corridors of the school with a bounce in his step, feeling like nothing in the world could stop them.

Then he saw Hazen's face, and all of that changed.

"What are we gonna do?" the tradesman was muttering to himself. Still seated in the middle of the library, he rocked in his chair and raked at his hair with his fingertips. "We're going to die here!" he cried, looking up and locking eyes with Cody; his gaze was that of a drowning man's.

"Don't talk like that," Zeff snapped from somewhere deep in the bookshelves. "We need to be thinking constructively."

But Lewis was already thinking constructively, his mind whirring and ticking along like a pocket watch. Just now he was thinking about the night Emperor Horus told him about the gun cache. It had been the second night of their acquaintance, and the two men had sat together on the green velvet sofa, smoking stale cigars and having a rousing discussion about politics and gun control in the New Empire.

"Hence it comes about that all armed prophets have been victorious, and all unarmed prophets have been destroyed," the emperor had remarked before drawing deeply on his cigar; Lewis remembered the way his pointed cheekbones looked as if they would burst through his pockmarked skin as he smoked. "Machiavelli," he said, looking at Lewis intently, "now follow his logic through: less arms, less armed prophets, which means fewer assassinations attempts on my life. And more stability for the people, of course."

"I have an interest in Machiavelli myself," Lewis had replied. "But, my good fellow, the man was not saying that only the prophet should be armed. He was saying the prophet should have an army at his command."

"The Berserker Class is armed!" the emperor shouted, making Lewis jump in his seat and drop ash on his pants. "I see no need to arm the rest. My generals have methods of keeping the peace that don't involve guns." Then he smiled at Lewis in a manner that was quite sinister, although the inventor had attributed it to indigestion at the time.

"What about an assassination attempt by an outside force?" Lewis challenged the emperor then, in full professor mode. "My dear man, how can you be certain what the future will bring? It could bring a marauding army to your door."

"I'm not certain," the emperor had replied, staring at Lewis with his strange black eyes. "I'm prepared." He got to his feet and looked out the window, although the night had been impenetrably dark. "I've got gun caches hidden throughout the New Empire, and they can be distributed whenever I want." He turned toward him again and smiled. "For security reasons, I am the only one who knows their location—and that wasn't easy to accomplish. It's almost impossible to hide anything in the New Empire. But I've been with my men for a long time. I understand how they think." Horus laughed. "Hide something; they'll search for it. Lock something; they'll break it open. Those halfwits will get into just about anything—except libraries and churches. I'm afraid they're rather uncivilized these days."

"Lewis? Lewis, what do you think?" Like a pointed hook, Grace's voice skewered his brain and drew him back to the conversation everyone else was having.

"I believe the emperor was telling the truth about the gun cache," Lewis replied. "I'm sure he wasn't deceiving me."

"What are you talking about?" Grace scowled. "I mean what do you think about the plan—the plan we were just discussing? I think we should give up the school and follow Simone to Horus's manor. We can focus our efforts on killing him at least. Lewis? Are you listening?"

Lewis was listening; he just wasn't hearing. Grace's voice became a birdsong in the background as he stared at the overstuffed bookshelves that lined the back wall. There was something strange there, something amiss; he just couldn't put his finger on it. In a trance, he moved closer and began pulling the books from the shelves, throwing them over his shoulder and onto the floor behind him. The pile of discarded books grew around him as he worked, his movements becoming rhythmic and methodical. But when the book pile surged around his waist, he stopped and leaned against the bookcase, wheezing slightly.

"What are you doing?" Zeff asked.

"Oh, nothing," Lewis replied, his tusked moustache framing a deep frown. "I just thought..." he trailed off. Moving a lantern closer to the bookshelf, he gave a hoot of laughter and pulled a thick, dog-eared hardcover from its place. "Look at this! *Horus the Great: Deities of Ancient Egypt.*" Something flashed from the depths of the bookshelf. Lewis pushed the surrounding books onto the floor, and a small metal doorknob came into view. He shouted with excitement and turned the knob. Books tumbled around his head as the hidden door opened outward, moving slowly under its heavy load.

"Lewis, you've found it!" Hazen cried. "You magnificent bastard! We've been delivered! Halleluiah! Amen!"

"Let's not count our chickens before they're hatched," Zeff cautioned. "We don't know what's what yet."

"There's only one way to find out, and we don't have much time." Grace stood at the doorway of the secret room; she held out her hand. "Lantern, please."

The hidden room was long but shallow as the group filed in, squinting in the weak lantern light. Immediately, their eyes lit upon rows and rows of guns mounted on every available wall in the place. Wordlessly, they took in the hulking cabinets and cupboards, the collection of barrels, and the hanging baskets filled with grenades. Everyone smiled at once; the cache was intact.

Feeling his way over to a metal gray filing cabinet, Zeff pulled open a cabinet drawer, and five handguns clinked together inside. Beside them, he felt a leather pouch, which contained a modest supply of cartridges. He opened three more drawers. There were guns and clips in all of them. He felt a Smith & Wesson under his touch. He picked it up and pressed it to his lips.

Running high on relief, Grace and Hazen began passionately embracing at the back of the room, pressing themselves against the barrel collection that stood stoutly against the wall. Nearby, Cody examined a rack of shotguns and rifles with shy pleasure. Lewis whistled a jaunty tune as he took off his hat and began filling it with shells and cartridges from a desk drawer. The room was dim in the flickering light, but everything shone like treasure.

A few shells fell from Lewis's hands, clattering to the ground and rolling to a stop against a small bin in the corner of the room. As he bent over to retrieve the shells, he noticed the bin was empty, save for a crumpled piece of paper that looked achingly familiar somehow. Intrigued, he pocketed the runaway shells and picked the paper out of the garbage, smoothing it with his fingers. With a growing horror, he realized he was staring at the blueprints of the flamethrower he had drawn for Horus. A large X had been scrawled through the middle of the design. Was this what the emperor thought of his work? Was this what the emperor thought of him?

Lewis examined the blueprints, shaking his head. His design was flawless, his calculations, impeccable. He was dumbfounded. Perhaps the emperor wasn't sophisticated enough to understand his vision; perhaps his goons were incapable of putting together such a complex piece of machinery. *Why didn't he come to me?* Lewis wondered. *This could have been one of the greatest innovations of the Empire.*

He sighed; it was a long-winded noise that sounded like a balloon deflating. *In what kind of world does a two-bit convict consider himself smarter than a tenured physics professor?* he wondered. *Tenured!* Lewis felt jittery with outrage just thinking about it. He took a few quick breaths and tried to think of all the nice things people had said to him over the years, fumbling through his trove of well-thumbed memories. But to his horror, Lewis found he had forgotten them all in an instant, stunned by the violation he had suffered at the hands of someone he had considered a friend.

For Lewis, the pieces of the puzzle snapped into place: something was wrong with the Emperor.

"Let's load up." He was barely able to choke out the words. "Cody, get the caravan." He pulled his safari hat down around his eyes to hide the wet disappointment he could feel shining there.

Sorting through the weapons and ammunition went swiftly with everyone pitching in to help. The group decided what to keep and what to send to the brothel in record time—and with only minor incidents of squabbling. Grace took a rifle and went up to the roof for first watch as Hazen and Lewis explored the rest of the school, looking for torches or anything else that could be prove to be of use. All the while, Zeff worked with Cody loading the caravan—until Cody disappeared.

At least, it seemed that way to Zeff. He had given Cody a load of revolvers to take to the wagon, and he hadn't returned for some time. Concerned, Zeff left the weapons room and found his way out of the library and down the long corridor that the Cody would have taken back to the wagon. He inwardly cursed when he realized he had left the lantern in the weapons room, but continued on in complete silence, careful in the placement of his feet along the sticky, debris-riddled floor.

When he heard a loud bang, he froze. Was it Cody? Lewis? Hazen?

There was the fleeting rush of silence before the darkness was filled with an unearthly shrieking sound that set his teeth on edge. The cry reached a desperate, high-pitched note before falling away again like a sob.

Zeff knew the noise had come from underneath him. Yet the scream had been so loud, so terrified, it hadn't sounded muffled in the slightest. Heart beating fast, he picked up his pace. He heard footsteps ahead; a dim glow came into view.

"Are you sure?" he heard Hazen ask, further down the hall. "I'm always sure!" Lewis cried. "I tell you, it came from downstairs!" There was the sound of a door being opened, and the dim glow disappeared. Zeff heard men's boots thumping down a flight of stairs, and he followed after them, trying not to be too reckless in his pursuit. The light seemed fainter, but he could still hear Hazen and Lewis ahead, their voices echoing in the shadows.

Reaching the bottom of the stairs, Zeff followed them down a long hallway and then into a room that stank of vomit and rotten meat. He walked cautiously inside, feeling a tile floor beneath his feet. He peered around the room, straining his eyes; in the dim light, he could see the wall was lined with objects he recognized as lockers. Many had been removed from the wall, most likely scavenged and dragged away for other purposes, but a good number were still intact, waiting proudly in the dark for the next period of gym class. Zeff sincerely hoped that would happen.

Turning to his left, he pulled open a locker door before reeling back immediately, covering his nose and mouth. The putrid smell of hot garbage assailed him and seemed to cover his face with its oiliness; he could almost feel it seeping through his eyes, through his ears, through the pores of his skin. He closed the door again and furrowed his brow. *Why are they storing garbage down here?*

Ahead, Zeff could hear the sound of Lewis and Hazen pushing through another door.

Swoosh!

"Oh, God!" That was Hazen's voice.

Swoosh!

The door closed behind them.

Zeff drew his newly acquired Smith & Wesson, and followed after his friends, moving as quickly as he could, fumbling for the doorway and locating it easily; he could see the lantern light coming from the other side. Squaring his shoulders, he pushed his way through.

There was a terrified shriek.

"Lower your gun!" Cody cried. "You're scaring them!"

Zeff immediately holstered his gun and squinted in the lantern light, but all he could see was a squat-looking room that looked like a small stable. He squinted harder. Was this an old shower room?

"Are they keeping goats down here?" he asked.

"I wish," Hazen replied. "Look harder, Zeff."

There was a slight pause.

"Help us," a man moaned; there was the sound of rattling chains.

Zeff moved toward the man and almost slipped on a foul-smelling slime that coated the floor under his feet. "What is this?" he cried. The smell had become almost unbearable.

"This?" Cody sounded like he was crying. "This is a slaughtering pen."

With terrible clarity, Zeff realized that what he thought were stalls were actually wooden restraining devices with high sides and slatted floors. Upon them, six men and women lay in a pile of their own excrement. They had been stripped naked and tied down to the floor so they couldn't move.

Zeff was horrified. His face paled and grew pinched. "You mean they keep people down here?" he asked quietly. "Like this?"

"Yes," a rasping voice said. "And they kill us down here too."

"Help us!" cried another voice. "Please!"

Zeff went forward to help; Lewis took a step back. The inventor was deeply disturbed by this room—and the terrified, abscess-covered people who had been confined here. Once they were freed from their human-veal crates, he tried not to stare at their nakedness, or at the vile looking sludge that covered their thighs, legs and feet. He raised his eyes to the creeping lantern light that scurried across the tile-lined room. There, he noticed six jagged-edged funnels hanging from hooks, covered in dried chunks of vomit.

They're force-feeding them, he realized, struggling to suppress a gasp. *Human foie gras.* Lewis was taken aback by the thought. And more than that, he couldn't help but wonder what kind of man would force feed his subjects, but wouldn't construct a flamethrower? Lewis continued to reflect upon this thought as Zeff, Cody, and Hazen got the freed captives into comfortable seated positions. They were all incredibly weak and dehydrated from their confinement, so Hazen went to find some water.

Up on the roof, accompanied by a rifle and lawn chair, Grace peered out over the field, blissfully unaware of the terrible discovery three stories below. Flexing her fingers around the stock, she held the weapon comfortably in her hand and smiled; she had come a long way, baby. But she still preferred knives.

On the ground below, Lewis and Cody emerged from the school. She had been watching them load the wagon. They appeared to be finished now and were readying themselves for the journey ahead. She waved to them as they set off for the brothel at a careful trot, wondering if she would ever see them again.

Above her head, the Big Dipper glittered like a diamond pendant. An unexpected draft of wind hurried by, and Grace stopped smiling and shivered. Uneasy, she rose from her chair and gazed ahead, but all she could see was the wagon in the distance, just visible in the darkness as it trundled south.

She could hear a door close on the ground below and watched Zeff and Hazen exit the school with armfuls of torches.

"Hello?" someone cried out to them; it was a new voice and yet incredibly familiar. "Hello there?"

For an instant, Grace felt like she couldn't breathe. "Don't shoot!" she cried to Zeff and Hazen, before flinging open the emergency exit and racing down the stairs. *Don't shoot; oh please don't shoot*, she thought as she made her frenzied descent. Bursting through the exit, wild and out of breath, she could see five men standing in the torchlight with Zeff and Hazen.

"Dad!" Grace cried, running to the tallest one and throwing her arms around him.

SHOWDOWN

The door to the emperor's manor banged shut; Simone had entered her quarry's lair. The first thing she noticed was the smell: fresh-cut flowers, sharply floral and sweet. The light from the torches outside shone through the windows, and in the ruddy darkness, she could see Horus's foyer was every bit as grand as the outside of the house had been, featuring a lavish chandelier, and slick marble flooring dappled with chic Persian rugs. Paintings in large, ornate frames hung from the walls. Vases, filled with attractive wildflower displays, were stacked in every corner. In the center of the room, a gently curving staircase held court, enticing guests up to the second floor.

"The emperor's room is upstairs," Carmen whispered, pointing ahead.

"Good. Now give me the shotgun," Simone replied, bumping her hip against a small side table. It wobbled alarmingly. Mouthing several colorful phrases, she grabbed the table to steady it, and when she pulled her hands away again, her calloused fingers snagged against a piece of fabric. Leaning closer, she peered at it in the low light. It was a rectangle of woven bunting, thickly trimmed by a dark stripe of color. The center bore the image of a bird, wings spread as if in flight, clutching a human skull in its talons. A long coil of rope lay off to the right. She realized then it was a flag, a symbol of what Horus had created here: a human wasteland devised to feed his every appetite.

Simone looked around for Carmen and was disturbed and not completely surprised to find the young woman had already left the room. Her heart sank, and her fingers itched for her shotgun. She moved haltingly toward the stairs.

"Carmen?" she whispered as loud as she dared. There was a light footfall above her.

Simone sprinted up the stairs, taking them two at a time. The stairs squealed and groaned under her heavy work boots, and by the time she'd reached the top, Carmen was already halfway down the hall. The young brothel madam had kicked off her prized heels and was running with a speed Simone had never imagined her capable of. Racing desperately after her, she felt Carmen and their entire plan escaping her.

A patch of light winked from an open door ahead, and Carmen raced toward it. She stopped there, silhouetted against the softly lit entrance.

"Carmen! Wait!" Simone whispered. The silhouette turned its head, looked at her for a moment, and then leaped through the open doorway.

"Freeze, or I'll blow your brains out!" she heard Carmen cry.

"Where'd you get that fucking gun?" It was Horus. Harvey. Him.

Outside the door, Simone faltered, gritting her teeth. The plan was in motion now; she would either kill him or go down trying. With quiet breath, she unsheathed the knife hidden in her boot and moved into the room.

There, she promptly found herself on the wrong end of a vicious looking tommy gun. Horus appeared smug as he wielded it, still seated in a leather office chair with her shotgun across his lap and obviously enjoying himself. Cleaned up and right at home, the man looked different from the one she'd encountered in the slaughterhouse. Tonight, dressed in a pair of dark pants and a button-down shirt, he looked like the man Simone had seen in court. Tonight, he looked like Harvey, not Horus. There was no war paint here, no executioner's mask, no theater—just the man's oddly angular face and his mad, glittering eyes.

"Well," he said, leaning back in his chair. " Here we are again. Thank you for returning your shotgun to me." Turning in his seat, he propped the weapon against the desk. "And I see you've brought a knife as well. That's very kind of you. Just drop it there." He motioned with the tommy gun. "Right where you're standing."

Simone dropped the knife, and it clattered to the floor.

"I had the feeling I would see you again," he said, almost tenderly. "I knew you'd come to me."

"I haven't come to you," Simone replied. "I've come *for* you, Harvey."

Rising to his feet, he glowered at her. "You're so predictable it bores me," he said. Brushing a piece of lint from his pants, he neatly tucked his tommy gun under one arm. Then, cocking his other fist, he walloped Simone across the face with it. Bright stars exploded behind her eyes as she fell to her knees.

Hauling herself back to her feet, Simone wiped the blood from her mouth. She looked at Carmen, who was standing beside Horus and staring at her scornfully. Simone spit a tooth at her. "You've made a deal with the devil," she said. "No one can help you now."

Carmen's smile was full of spite. "Help me! Oh, Simone, you're cute. Look at me, sweetheart." She gestured to the diamond earrings that sparkled in her ears, to her tailored business suit. "I'm clean. I'm healthy. I'm eating regular meals. Does it look like I'm suffering?"

"No, you're happy to leave the suffering to others," Simone replied. "We've already talked about that. Right, coward?"

The smile faded from the young madam's face.

"Oh, Simone." Horus shook his head at her. "Sad Sister Simone. You're always so sad. So spiteful. You just hate it when other people are happy." He smiled cruelly. "Because you can't relate to that feeling anymore."

Simone narrowed her eyes but didn't respond. Horus's smile grew wider as he continued. "And yes, perhaps some are happy here at the expense of others, but isn't that how society works?" He hooded his reptilian eyes. "Isn't that so-called civilization—to live together with the knowledge that some *unfortunates* in this world are born to be the instruments of others? Throughout history, haven't millions and millions of lives been sacrificed so that a precious few may taste life's bitter pleasures?" He leaned closer. "Well now me—my men—my civilization, we're the precious few."

Horus backed Simone up until she was standing against the desk. He ran his finger along her throbbing jawline, his touch lingering over the sorest spot. "I can see you don't believe that, do you?" he observed. "You'd rather believe you're saving people from—"

"A monster?" she said.

"Yes. That's the term people apply to things they don't understand. But I'm not a monster. I'm a father—to a new chapter in human civilization."

"That's bound to be a short chapter."

Horus pushed Simone against the desk, causing the lone candle behind her to shake and shudder, throwing the light in the room. "Let us speak frankly," he said, clenching his jaw. "You're no angel. You're no saint. You don't give a shit about other people's lives. Admit it—you came here for yourself. You wanted revenge for what I did to your brother, and that meant killing me as I sat peacefully in my own home. So who's the monster, Simone?"

"That's an easy one," Simone replied. She moved her face so close to his, their noses touched. "A monster is someone who tortures people for sport. A monster is someone who enslaves others for his own sexual gratification." Her voice was rising. "A monster is someone who breaks into houses and murders an entire family before stuffing and mounting their heads on the wall. And a real monster—an honest-to-God, bona fide monster—is someone who forces others to become monsters too, just to rid the world of its poison."

"Will you kill her soon?" Carmen interrupted, sounding bored. She had taken a seat on Horus's four-poster bed and was slouching there with a petulant expression on her face. "She brought others, you know. Who knows what they could be up to right now?"

A loud boom in the distance seemed to answer her question. The windows rattled in their frames.

Face twisted with rage, Horus threw open the bedroom window. Over his shoulder, Simone could see flames in the distance, lighting up the night sky.

"What the fuck are you doing?" he bellowed to the guards on the porch below. "Investigate that explosion! The empire is under attack!" The generals scattered like ants, shouting obscenities at one another as they ran off in separate directions.

This appeared to satisfy Horus momentarily. But by the time he had turned to face Carmen again, he looked furious. "If she came with other people, why didn't you bring them all to me?"

"Do I have to do *everything*?" Carmen flung back, her voice high and shrill. "I've already saved your life once tonight. And what thanks do I get for it?"

"What thanks do you want for it?" Horus asked in a low voice; his eyes seemed to bulge in their sockets.

Sensing peril, Carmen softened her demeanor, appearing smaller somehow, almost fragile as she looked at him beseechingly. "Please, Emperor, I need a gun," she said. "I don't care what kind.

I would even take that old shotgun over there." She pointed at Simone's discarded weapon. "You have so many already, you won't even miss it."

"You make a lot of demands," Horus remarked.

"I bring a lot to the table."

"Including the stink of treachery," he said. "If I give you a gun, you'll betray me, just as you betrayed your own family. Did you think I would forget how readily you served them up to me? You turned on them the first minute you could."

"That's ridiculous!" Carmen shouted. "I've been nothing but loyal to you! I had that gun in my hands, and I gave it to you! I brought Simone here to save you—to save the empire!"

"No, you brought Simone here for the reward I would give you." Horus grit his teeth. "Otherwise you would have fed her to the generals outside."

"That's a lie, and you know it!" Carmen cried, scrambling to her feet. "You ungrateful bastard! I should have let her kill you! Then I would have gotten what I deserve!" With a sudden leap forward, she dove for Simone's shotgun.

This was the moment Simone had been waiting for. With one swift motion, she blew out the lone candle that had been lighting the room, plunging everything into darkness. There was the staccato burst of the tommy gun and strange surges of light, followed by the metallic ring of casings hitting the floor. She could hear Carmen screaming in pain. Simone dropped to her knees, kicked her boots off, and crawled for the doorway. She could feel the bullets screaming by her head as Horus swung the machine gun in her direction. Once she reached the hallway, she rounded the corner and jumped to her feet, running madly through the dark. Behind her, Simone heard Carmen's shallow gasps and Horus cursing. There was the sound of the tommy gun again, and a loaded silence fell over the manor.

Suddenly, Horus laughed loudly, a raven's croak in the dark mausoleum of the hall. She could feel the chill of his presence behind her, and she threw herself to the ground again, rolling toward the nearest doorway as the tommy gun sent bullets pounding down the corridor. He was wasting his ammo, and he didn't seem to care. Horus was as greedy and reckless with death as he was with life.

The spray of bullets stopped, and Simone waited in her hiding spot by the door. She didn't move. The hallway was dark again and thick with smoke, but there was still some light to see. She could hear Horus fiddling with the gun somewhere, followed by stomping noises. There was a crash and the sound of the desk drawer opening, followed by a banging noise; he was muttering something. The banging got louder. Simone smiled to herself: if Horus didn't have more ammo for his tommy gun, he would grab her shotgun next, and it had two shells left. She had concealed two more shells in the work boots she had kicked off in her haste to escape; she hoped he wouldn't find them.

Simone crawled further into the room and stood up. The dark was as thick as stew, and she delicately felt her way around, careful not to knock anything over. She realized she was in a bathroom, with nothing much to offer as a means of defense. She fingered the throne-like chair that had replaced the toilet in the room. A hole had been cut through the seat, and a bucket sat patiently below it. The chair was bolted down, but the bucket smelled promising. Either Horus had recently used the facility, or his attendants were failing in their commode-emptying duties. Either way, it would serve her purposes well. Simone picked the bucket up by the handle and moved to the doorway; the contents sloshed around the receptacle, emitting a sulfuric barnyard smell.

Horus was coming down the hall again, more quietly this time, moving like a hunter. She heard him clench the weapon in his hands, and Simone knew it was her shotgun, just as she thought.

She loved that shotgun, but she knew its weakness: it was lousy at close range.

There was a muffled thud. Horus was in the room next door, tearing the place apart. She could feel the air vibrating with the violence of his search, until everything stopped.

There was silence again and then quiet, slinking footsteps.

Horus was almost upon her. Simone backed into the darkened bathroom and waited.

With a muscular speed, Horus lunged through the doorway. Before he had time to turn his head, Simone threw the toilet bucket over him, soaking him in fecal-smelling waste. The gun went off once, shooting a hole in the ceiling. Flailing blindly, Horus struggled to get the bucket off his head with his free hand, striking the air around him with the shotgun. But Simone was safely out of range by that time, squatting in the corner of the room as she watched him struggle.

With one savage jerk, Horus pulled the bucket off his head and stared at it angrily. His back was to her as he threw the bucket into the hallway and swore at it. Thoroughly enraged by this time, he used vicious, swiping motions to wipe his face with his shirt. It was apparent that he thought he was alone in the room—that she had fled in fear.

Crouched in the corner behind him, Simone smiled grimly. Nothing could be further from the truth.

Horus spat a gelatinous gob of something on the ground, before moving toward the door. With thousands of hours of loathing propelling her, Simone rose silently to her feet and charged him from behind, grabbing for the shotgun in his hands. Once she had a firm hold, she wrapped her fingers around the trigger and squeezed. The shotgun roared to life, knocking them both off balance with the kickback. She felt the shell fly harmlessly into the ceiling—the second shell. If Horus hadn't found the other shells hidden in her boots, his arsenal was depleted, and they were on fair ground.

Now let's see who hates each other more, she thought.

Simone drew her lips back from her teeth and kicked at the backs of his legs, knocking Horus to the floor. He clawed at her knees, trying to bring her down with him, but she kicked his hands away before stomping on his face, feeling something cave under the force of her foot. He shrieked.

Simone ran out into the hall.

Behind her, Horus brandished the shotgun and pulled the trigger. Click. Click. Click.

It was empty; he hadn't found the other shells. Sailing high on the winds of relief, Simone entered another room on her left. Using her hands, she fumbled her way across the floor until she located a bed. Hurriedly, she felt under the mattress, hoping to find a gun or even a knife stashed there, but there was nothing hidden, nothing that she could find. She knelt down on the floor and reached her arms under the bed skirt. There was the mouth-sick scent of decay before Simone's hands made contact with something furry and wet. She jerked her hands back and wiped them on her pants in disgust.

"Simone!" Horus taunted loudly from the hallway. "You think you can kill me with a bucket of shit? All you've succeeded in doing *is pissing me off!*" A metallic sound rang through the huddling darkness. "I've got a sword now, baby. And it's time to give you a little taste."

He was moving again and moving swiftly. Simone ducked behind the door and held her breath. He was entering the room next door; she didn't have much time. Slipping out of her hiding spot, she tiptoed further down the hall. The next room she entered was smaller than the last and smelled strongly of food. It was Horus's personal pantry, filled with shelves of canned fruit and baskets of salted meats and sugar. She found a hamper in the corner, loaded down with apples and potatoes. She could tell by the scent that they were beginning to rot; it smelled like the filthy trappings of greed.

She could hear Horus in the hall again. His footsteps had quickened, and they fell stridently; he no longer made any effort to conceal them. Simone could tell his anger had taken hold, which was exactly what she was hoping for. Because anger is a weakness, and every weakness can be exploited.

Simone took some salted meat from its package and rolled it thoughtfully between her fingers. She popped the lump into her mouth, working it between her teeth. An idea had taken seed in her mind, and it was beginning to sprout.

Horus charged through the darkness. The sword felt heavy in his hands, but it also felt powerful, sexy, exciting. The scavengers had brought it to him that afternoon, and when he saw it, he knew it was time for another Redemption Session. He longed to use its gleaming blade, to feel a body shudder under its beautiful length of steel. And who better than Simone, the impudent slut who'd actually laughed in his face? He would make her pay for that; he felt his cock stir ever so slightly at the thought.

Entering another room, he held his breath and listened. Thinking he'd heard something, he tiptoed over to the closet and wrenched the door open with his free hand. There were jackets and sweaters hanging inside but nothing else. No Simone. He slashed at the clothes with his sword.

There was a creak in the hallway, and Horus rushed to the door, willing the sound to come again. He lurked in the doorframe, waiting, but the manor was silent, and the stillness felt stiff and unyielding. Moving into the hall, he looked over the banister of the staircase, scanning the foyer below. Undulating torchlight filtered in through the front windows of the house and alighted on a curious object on the ground. It was Simone's hat, lying just a few feet away from the front door. He grit his teeth at the sight of it. Had she run away? It didn't matter if she had. He knew he would find her again; he would devote every waking hour to it.

He started down the staircase, smiling unpleasantly and still eyeing the hat. It was the perfect trophy to remember her by—especially because her body would be unrecognizable after he had finished with it; he had already decided that. And there was something so satisfying about killing a brother and sister—years apart; he didn't want to forget such a special occasion.

Still gazing at the abandoned hat, he descended the last three stairs with palpable impatience. He longed to hold it in his hands and run the brim through his fingers, breathing in the smell of her, of her fear. Then, of her death.

Reaching the bottom of the staircase, Horus was making his way toward the door when he had the distinct feeling he was being watched. Turning sharply, he glanced behind him. Seeing nothing but the manor's tasteful furnishings glowing softly in the torchlight, he continued on toward his prize. It was still warm when he picked it up—his favorite.

Then he noticed the figure on the stairs.

Her.

Simone.

The figure flicked her hands in his direction, making a throwing motion. As he turned to face her, only a half cry issued from his lips as the lasso caught hold, pulling his arms against his sides. His sword pitched forward and slipped from his grasp, slicing his leg badly at the knee. Falling to the ground, Horus wiggled after it, struggling to free his arms, but the rope held fast; he couldn't escape it.

There was a thump, followed by a snap in quick succession.

Pain raked at Horus's body with white-hot fingers as he realized Simone had jumped off the stairs and landed on his back. He was soaked in something. Was it blood? Face contorted in anguish, he turned his head and looked over his shoulder. She was still standing there, watching him, treating him like a bearskin rug.

"Damn you," he choked, gasping for air.

She stared down at him, and in that instant Horus realized her eyes were as dark and merciless as his own. A horrible idea crept through his mind: *what if he'd underestimated her? What if—*

Simone jumped off his back and kicked him in the face, hard. His head reeled and he could taste the dirty leather of her work boot as he struggled to focus. Where was that sword? He needed that sword; he would do anything to get that sword. Then he would wreak unholy havoc with that sword.

Sword.

"I'm the emperor," he said, enunciating each syllable as if she were hard of hearing. He drew his eyebrows together and soured his gaze. "Death needs my permission!" he shouted. "And it doesn't fucking have it!"

"Well I'm not death, *Harvey*," Simone replied. "I'm just a woman with a motto: live by the sword, die by the sword." She paused. "Incidentally, I'm also a woman with a sword."

His eyes widened as Simone lifted the weapon above her head.

"No!" Horus cried. "If you kill me, you'll never get out of the Empire alive!"

"That's interesting," Simone replied. "Because if I don't kill you, I won't get out of here alive, either. And I much prefer you dead."

"Wait! I can help you! I don't know anything about your brother!" Horus cried. "That wasn't me! That wasn't—"

The rest of his plea became a low gurgling sound as Simone ran him through with the sword, again, and again, and again. His body was unrecognizable by the time she had finished with it.

The emperor was dead; but this was only the beginning of her revenge.

Simone picked her brother's hat out of the pool of blood and wiped the rim before tapping it on her head. Then she walked out the front door into the smoky, screaming night.

HOT UNDER THE COLLAR

Libby sat in the wagon with the other women as it wheezed its way toward the generals' clubhouse. They were packed together like sardines, and the dark interior of the carrier was ripe with the smell of perspiration. Outside, the horses seemed to be moving slowly under the heavy load—or maybe it just seemed that way to Libby. She examined the gun she held in her hands: a Beretta M9. She had chosen it because it seemed manageable, compact, something that wouldn't blow her off her feet during the attack.

The attack.

The words rattled around her head as Libby felt the cold breath of fear on her back. She tried to get ahead of it by staying positive; that had always helped her on game days before. She had noticed that postapocalyptic warfare, although different from girls' high school basketball, did have its similarities.

Chewing on what remained of her fingernails, she considered the upsides of their current situation: Cody was in the driver's seat—that was good. He and Lewis had made it back from the school in one piece—that was really good. They had found the gun cache and brought guns for everyone—that was excellent. And while the others were gone, a notorious general had stopped by the brothel and was promptly kicked to death by everyone inside—that part hadn't been too shabby either.

She smiled, and her thoughts returned to Cody, the only general she liked. She remembered thinking he was kind when she first saw him. That had only been a few days ago, although it seemed much longer to her now. But the instant Libby had laid her eyes upon him, she knew he wasn't anything like the others. Cody was a man among beasts.

So what? Libby sighed and put her head in her hands. She had noticed Cody looking at the twins with interest, Raven in particular. *Her*, on the other hand—well, Libby wasn't sure what he thought of her, *if* he even thought of her at all. Most people didn't, so why should he? She had spent her life as Carmen's ugly little sister; she had gotten used to being overlooked.

The wagon hit a large pothole in the road, causing the carrier to lurch to the left. Libby slid on her seat, slamming into the woman next to her. There were indignant cries and curses.

"Sorry!" Cody called back to them.

Pulling herself upright again, Libby surveyed the crowded wagon. "Lewis, did you really have to bring those?" she asked, pointing at the two mysterious barrels that were crouched in the back, and taking up valuable space.

Across the small aisle, Lewis finished his thought in his notebook and closed it, tucking it neatly in the pocket of his blazer. Then he looked at Libby with a grave expression on his face. "My dear, if you are referring to the gunpowder kegs, let me assure you, it is indeed a *necessity*." Craning his head, he noticed the other women were watching; he decided to make the most of it. "Ladies, we are at war," he boomed, invoking his bravest seated position. "Lloyd and Claire are sending civilians to the school for refuge as we speak. It is up to you to keep the generals distracted—no matter what it takes. Like trained soldiers, you must put up with all sorts of uncomfortable situations." He took a deep inhale as if he was going to continue.

"Mr. Lewis, are you comfortable?" Raven asked in a quiet voice.

Lewis looked confused. "Well it's Professor Hutchinson, dear, but never mind that."

"The only reason I ask," Raven pushed on, "is that you must be nervous facing such danger. Being a man in the field—well, that's pretty dangerous, wouldn't you say? I mean, one of us could accidentally kill you."

"Yeah. Like, a friendly fire type situation," Ruby added.

Friendly fire? Lewis swallowed hard. Was *he* expected to fight? Suddenly, the back of the wagon felt stifling.

"I need to get some air," he said with as much dignity as he could muster. Then he hurried to the front of the wagon, away from Raven and Ruby's muffled laughter.

"Thanks for the company," Cody said with a friendly smile as Lewis climbed out of the wagon and settled on the seat beside him. "I haven't seen a soul this whole time. It's making me nervous."

But Lewis was preoccupied with his own thoughts. "Yes, well," he remarked in a faraway voice. "If this should be my last night on earth, I might as well enjoy the stars." He frowned before petting his moustache tenderly.

For the tenth time that night, Cody wished that Zeff were here. That man was always so reassuring, so capable. And Lewis was always so...Lewis. Determined to take shake off his worried thoughts, the former general tilted his head back and looked into the night sky. "Do you like looking at the stars?" he asked.

Lewis was quiet for a moment. "I do," he answered finally. "Do you know why? Because when I look at the stars, I see hope. A brighter existence. A new way of being." He repositioned his safari hat before continuing. "Some days I comfort myself with the thought that when we leave this earth, we will leave darkness and ignorance behind. Only then will we see the stars for what they really are."

Unexpectedly moved, Cody smiled at the inventor. "I guess when you think about death that way, it doesn't seem so bad," he said.

"Death? Who said anything about death?" Lewis cried. "Dear fellow, I was referring to space tourism! Humans are an ingenious species. We could still see it in our lifetime."

For the eleventh time that night, Cody wished Zeff were there.

The wagon swung down Poppy Drive. They were moving away from the residential area of town and toward the old park and baseball diamonds that formed the agricultural hub of the New Empire. They passed crops of zucchini, soybeans, carrots, and corn, followed by shaggy fields of rye and wheat. A large sign stood above the waving shafts of grain. *Welcome to Freedom Park*, it read. Lewis was about to comment on it when he noticed a large object protruding from the ground.

"What is that?" he asked, pointing at it.

Cody reined in the team and slowed the wagon. "I heard it used to be a church. Unitarian or something like that. It was built right into the ground. That's the walkway there. It swoops around to the left, and then there's another long walkway to the entrance. That bulge in the ground used to be a giant skylight, but the glass is broken, so a lot of houses empty their chamber pots down there now."

Lewis felt positively jump kicked by inspiration. "Are we close to the generals' clubhouse?" he asked with excitement, clamping his hand over Cody's knee. "Could we walk from here?"

"We sure could. It's right there." Cody pointed to a hulking building ahead with faintly lit windows.

"Perfect." Lewis rubbed his hands together and rolled up his shirtsleeves. "I have a plan for the gunpowder. Tell the women to draw the generals to the entrance of the church, and I'll take care of the rest. Then stay to the north and keep the horses away."

Cody stared at the inventor. "Are you going to—"

"Of course I am!" Lewis cried leaping to the ground the instant Cody stopped the wagon. The young general climbed down after him, and Lewis grabbed his hand and shook it hard. "Let the great experiment begin!" he said with a grin. "Good luck, my dear fellow! Oh—and do try to stop mentioning death so much. It's rather off putting."

For the twelfth time that night...

Once the women had unloaded the barrels from the back, Lewis scurried off with them into the darkness. Considerably lighter, the wagon continued its forward march to the clubhouse.

"You ready?" a voice asked, and Cody nearly jumped out of his skin. Startled, he turned to see Libby standing by the wagon flap behind him. He was amazed by how glad he was to see her.

"It looks like you are," he replied, ducking his head.

"I wish I could see the Empire at night," she said. "It's probably too dangerous for me to sit up here. Someone might see."

Cody looked thoughtful; then his face brightened. "We can hide you under this blanket," he said, pulling one out from under the bench. He unfolded it and handed it to her. With a nervous smile, Libby wrapped herself up in it and hid in front of the driver's bench, peeking out at the sights that they passed.

"Well," Cody said after a long pause, "what do you think of Lewis's plan?"

"I think the more generals we kill, the better," she replied. "Present company excluded, of course."

There was another long pause.

"I'm glad you said that." He smiled.

The wagon continued down the moonlit road, where tangles of crops gave way to a stump-pitted meadow. Hacked-up tree trunks shone like torsos in the gloom, bone pale and brutalized. *That will be us if we lose,* Cody thought as the wagon reached the generals' clubhouse. *Hacked up and rotting by the roadside.* He guided the horse team into the parking lot, where several other rigs sat at rest. The place was thick with the smell of horseshit, although no other horses could be seen. They must have been stabled for the night.

"Do the generals live here?" Libby asked from under the blanket. The wagon rolled to a stop.

"Most of them live in the houses they supervise," he answered. "The clubhouse is just a place for them to unwind. But most of the guys get drunk and end up sleeping here anyways." At least that's what Cody had been told. He had never spent much time in the clubhouse, even though he was a general with the same privileges afforded to him as everyone else. He had been there once and found it to be a noisy, stinking place to which he saw no reason to return. That, and the other generals had beat him up and thrown him out of the building.

Cody unhitched the horses and shooed them away, watching them disappear into the night. He turned back to look for the other women and spotted a dozen heads already bobbing through the thick patches of thistle and chickweed that surrounded the building. They were already making their advance.

"Remember, draw them toward the church," he whispered once he'd caught up with them. "Then stay clear of the entrance and keep north. You don't want to be there when the generals reach the park."

Once these instructions had been given, Libby whistled a single, unwavering note. In one smooth motion, everyone ducked down, disappearing into the shoulder-high weeds. She whistled again, two short notes this time, and Raven popped out from the undergrowth. With eager, catlike bounds, the twin made her way through the waist-high flora, moving toward the front of the clubhouse. Once she reached the path that led to the large gym doors, she collapsed onto the ground and let out an anguished howl.

"Help! I've been shot!" she cried.

The noise in the clubhouse ceased, and the light faded from the windows. The generals had put their candles out.

There was the squeaking sound of a window opening. "Who's there?" A male voice called.

"Help me, please!" Raven cried.

The front door of the clubhouse opened, and a man with a torch glared into the darkness. Observing Raven's body on the path ahead, he opened the door wider, and two generals came out, swaggering toward her with a distinct lack of suspicion. Once they reached her body, they stood over her, uncertain of what to do next. She lay on her chest, her face tilted to one side. There was no blood, no visible wounds on her body. One of them nudged her sharply with his boot; she didn't move. The generals looked at each other before they both crouched down.

"Maybe we should flip her over," one suggested.

Raven kept her eyes shut until the men had rolled her over onto her back. Then she shot them both in the face.

There was the sound of shattering glass and gunfire; the Berserker Class had started shooting from the windows. Raven scampered off the path, diving into the scrub around her as the bullets whizzed past, ripping up the brush ahead. From the ground, the women returned fire, and a general toppled out of one of the windows, thudding to the ground below. Raven could hear her sister crying her name in the midst of all the chaos. There was more gunfire, and suddenly Ruby was above her.

"Oh, God! I thought you'd been killed!" Ruby said, reaching for her.

"Get down!" Raven cried, but the warning came too late. There was more gunfire, and Ruby's body shook as multiple bullets ripped through her, killing her instantly. She fell to the ground.

"Ruby!" Raven screamed, leaning over her sister's body. The gunfire churned the air around them, but she didn't care. She simply sat by Ruby's side as the bullets pummeled the earth with life-stopping speed. She felt too sick to cry.

"Fall back! Get to the church!" Libby was shouting from the parking lot. The women around her were retreating to the road, but Raven didn't move. There was a panting sound; the undergrowth was rustling ahead. Someone was coming, but still Raven didn't stray from her sister's side. There seemed little point in doing that; there seemed little point in doing anything at all. She took Ruby's hand.

"Raven!" It was Cody, struggling through the weeds. He grabbed her by the arm. "Come on! They're coming out of the clubhouse. We gotta go!" But she didn't move. He tried pulling her up, but she fought against him, hitting him in the chest with her fists and bursting into tears.

"My sister!" she cried. "I can't leave her!"

Cody turned and saw Ruby's lifeless form lying on the ground. He swallowed hard and put his arms around Raven, pulling her to her feet. "You can't help her now," he said. "Ruby wouldn't want you to die. Not like this! We've gotta get out of here!" He started to run, pulling Raven along as the bullets tore after them. Suddenly he hollered out in pain and stumbled forward, losing his grip on her hand. There was the smell of blood; Raven felt something hot and sticky on her cheeks, and she realized Cody's arm was gone, shredded to pieces below the elbow. All that was left was jagged bits of flesh and bone; Cody was hyperventilating.

That's when Raven noticed the generals behind him. They were coming.

Three shots rang out, and one of the generals fell. "Run!" Libby screamed, bounding into view. "Get to the tree trunks!" Then she noticed Cody's arm. Without a word, she pulled off her bandana and made a tourniquet to stop the bleeding. Then she grabbed Cody's good arm. "Let's go!" she cried, pulling him along with her. "C'mon! Everyone else is ahead! Raven, help me with him!"

The women ran through the darkness, heaving Cody along after them as the generals chased them into the road. Bullets beat the air around them. Nearby, somebody was screaming, and Raven wondered if it might be her. They kept running until the ravaged forest came into view, and they threw themselves into its ghoulish shadows. Libby turned and fired a few shots at their pursuers, and they ran on with the swiftness of prey fleeing an imminent death.

"Get past the church," Cody whispered, as the sloping pathway came into view. "Go north." He was glistening white under the moon's tepid gaze. Libby could feel him growing colder, fainter. "We've got to move faster!" she cried.

The women dragged him past the church, past the derelict skylight that shone in the night, cracked and broken like a decomposing eggshell. They kept running until they reached the safety of the wheat field where the other women were hiding. There, they dropped to the ground, breathing hard as the obliging shafts of grain drew in and around them, concealing them from view.

The breeze kicked up and rolled through the field with a light-fingered tenderness, sweeping the hair back from Cody's stricken face. His eyes were open, watching Libby, but he didn't speak. He didn't have strength enough for that.

"Where are the generals?" Raven whispered to Libby. "They must be at the church by now."

Her prediction was remarkably correct.

From the shadows of the church, Lewis watched the generals approach as he crouched in the rancid and stinking doorway. The barrels of gunpowder sat open behind him, their lids stacked neatly to one side. He cast a nervous look at the cavernous entrance behind him, the actual doors, long since removed, allowing pungent fumes of sewage to climb their way out of that melancholy place and escape into the night. Lewis tried to breathe through his mouth, shuddering at the thought of going in there. He had tried to a moment ago and had gotten as far as the end of the front hall but was driven back by the stench. He had, however, been rewarded for his little misadventure; after all, fortune favors the brave. Grinning, he looked at the ancient beer bottle he'd retrieved from the human cesspool behind him. He had torn his collar from his shirt and soaked it in the last of his grain alcohol—pretty potent stuff. He poured a little more into the bottle and stopped the top with the fabric. It would work—he was sure it would work—and when it did, it would be magnificent.

Lewis grabbed his pistol and fired at the light of the coming torches. He could hear angry, bellowing voices. The torchlight seemed to stop and then turn in his direction. He fired again, and the swarm of generals was suddenly running down at him from the road. The sound of falling footsteps was like thunder in the dark; the ground trembled beneath his feet. He could see flashes of a mob rushing toward him. He caught glimpses of knives, clubs, and cruel faces, and he wondered, just for a moment, if he had bitten off more than he could chew.

Lewis moved past the barrels, seeking refuge once more in the stinking, fetid doorway. He buried his nose in his shirt and took a deep breath to calm himself. *This is not a time for panic*, he told himself. *This is a time for glory.* Though he may be facing a horde of marauding Vikings, the mightiest warrior of all was in *his* employ. And that warrior was science.

His fingers shook as he removed a match from the box in his pocket, the last of his souvenirs from the emperor's bunker. Lewis slid it along the strike strip, summoning a small flame. Carefully, he lit the fabric wick, waiting for the fire to get a solid grip before heaving the bottle toward the open barrels of gunpowder. As he plugged his nose and ran into the bastion of the church, Lewis heard a deafening roar behind him. An abrupt and fearsome heat flayed his back. The inventor was aware of his body leaving the ground and hurtling forward. Then he wasn't aware of anything more.

TEARS AND FEARS

There was a boom in the distance; Zeff felt the earth shake beneath his feet. A deep silence followed like a question mark, and for a moment, the activity inside the school ceased.

"Was that ours or theirs?" Hazen asked.

"I sure as shit hope it wasn't theirs." By rote, Zeff loaded another shotgun and leaned it against the wall.

On the rooftop, the stars were riding the very coattails of the night as it made its gradual and most welcome departure. It was early morning now; a fine mist blanketed the school, threatening to smother the torches below. The echoing roar in the distance worried Grace, but she felt steadied by the navy-blue dawn and the air that clung to her face like a wet sheet. In the distance, a red-winged black bird cried *chek-chek-chek*; a predator was near.

Standing next to her at the guard post, her father, Dr. Bruce Gateman, put his arm around her shoulders. "I thought I'd never see you again, Grace," he said hoarsely. "Now here you are, saving us all." His eyes gleamed with pride. "I should have expected as much."

She looked up into her father's face: thin, haggard, and sun-burned, and so much like her own. "Well, I wasn't going to leave you here," she said, grabbing his hand and giving it a squeeze. But when she caught sight of his fingertips, she gasped in horror; they were soft, pulpy, and covered in scabs, the fingernails, torn away. "What did he do to you?" she cried.

Bruce pulled his hands away and turned his head slightly, leaning over to grasp the rifle Zeff had given him. "Never mind, sweetheart," he said in a quiet voice. "Some things are better left unsaid." He winced a little as he lifted the gun, and the fleeting expression tugged at her heartstrings. Her father was still a tall, broad-shouldered man, but he was more stooped than before, and gray where he used to be blond. He had aged a great deal in a matter of months. Taking a deep breath, Grace decided to ask the question she'd been dreading to ask, but yearning to know: "Dad, where's Lora?"

Her father put the rifle down and stared at the ground. When he met her gaze again, his eyes were glassy and red rimmed. "Your sister's dead," he said in a wavering voice. "She was killed the day we were taken."

"Lora's dead?" she said, bursting into tears. It was what she had suspected all along, but now it was real; it was a fact. She felt like she had lost her sister for a second time, and it hurt twice as much. Sobs wracked her body and she ached and trembled with the violence of it all. She continued to cry as her father hugged her, holding her until she could catch her breath.

"Lora would be so proud of you." He released her and walked to the edge of the roof, where he gazed bleakly into the horizon.

"I'm really going to miss her," Grace said. "All over again."

He didn't say anything for a while as the dampness of the early dawn settled in around them, sprinkling their shoulders with a consoling dew. "I'm really going to miss her too," he said, finally.

By this time, Grace's grief was converging with her anger. "Those bastards will pay for this," she hissed. "We'll make them pay for this." She picked up her gun and pointed it at the forest, willing someone to come out of it so she could have her revenge. Her father did the same.

Yet both Gatemans were surprised when a few moments later, someone actually did come out. Wordlessly, they watched a tiny light emerge from the perimeter of the woods, a pinprick of white in the still, dark morning. Once the light reached the field, it began moving toward the school, advancing in hesitant darts and dashes, getting bigger as it drew closer.

"Looks like a mason-jar candle," her father whispered.

"What does that mean?" Grace asked, still staring through the night sights of her rifle.

"It means lower your gun, Grace. The good guys are here."

On the field below a second light emerged, then a third, appearing to make their way cautiously through the fog. Soon, it looked alive with fireflies as more and more people joined the migration across the soggy yard, and a vigilant few became a parade of many. There seemed to be a festive atmosphere below—or at least an optimistic one with several groups waving underwear hooked on branches. Others were running with their bedsheets flapping behind them like flags. The residents of the New Empire skipped, hopped, limped, and staggered their way toward the school. The air crackled with a desperate communal excitement.

Grace threw open the rooftop door, shouting to the others below. She watched as Hazen made his way out into the field, his trademark charisma seeming to draw the escapees in as he greeted everyone with a natural ease, shaking unsteady hands, patting thin shoulders, and directing the citizens toward the school behind him. His manner was reassuring and kind as he smiled to all in greeting.

"Do you love him?" her father asked, following her gaze to the tradesman. "It seems like there's some chemistry between you two."

Grace was unnerved; she had forgotten how perceptive her father could be. "Yeah, well." She blushed. "He's got his flaws."

"Don't we all," he replied. "I know this won't sound very fatherly of me to say, Grace, but if there's something that I've learned through all of this, it's don't hold back your love for somebody." She started to laugh with embarrassment, but her father pulled her close and kissed the top of her head. "I'm serious, sweetheart. If you really love someone, tell them. Otherwise you'll only live to regret it."

"Who said anything about love?" Grace rolled her eyes.

Her father laughed at her reaction. "You're stubborn, Grace. And that's just one of the things *I* love about *you*."

The breeze picked up and flitted across their faces, stirring up the fog below and carrying the sound of voices across its back. Grace squeezed her father's shoulder. For one slow heartbeat, she felt like they had a chance—*like they were winning.*

The feeling was short lived. A swelling of movement in the distance drew Grace's eye to the perimeter of the forest. There were more figures running across the field now, but these ones were coming in fast and low. And they had torches.

"Generals!" her father cried. "We have to get everyone inside!"

With anxious shouts, they yelled and waved at Hazen below, but he couldn't hear them over the noise of the crowd that was slowly filtering its way into the school. He moved further out into the field to aid a woman who had fallen. He couldn't see the generals coming.

"I've got to warn him!" Grace shouted, raising her gun to fire a shot into the air.

"Don't shoot!" The urgency in her father's voice froze her finger on the trigger. "If you shoot, the generals will shoot back. I bet some of those boys are packing." His voice seemed to trail off as he craned his neck forward. "And what in the Sam Hill is that?"

Below, a group of generals were pulling a giant wooden contraption onto the field. It shook and shuddered as it moved like a sorely used beast.

"It's a catapult!" Grace cried. "I've got to get down there!" She put her gun down. "Here, you keep this. You'll need all the ammo you can get."

"Grace, are you sure?"

"Dad!"

"Please be careful, honey," he said, and kissed her roughly on the cheek. "I love you."

"Love you too, Dad," she said, before throwing open the emergency exit door and rushing down the stairs.

"I'll cover you!" he called after her. And couldn't help but add, "I hope you're using that railing, Grace!"

In one final bound, Grace reached the bottom of the stairs and threw open the fire exit. She charged her way through it, running onto the field in one fluid motion. Racing for Hazen, she caught glimpses of haggard people on crutches and gaunt men and women ahead, dragging each other to safety. Some were walking with purpose; others appeared to be searching the crowd, calling out the names of their loved ones.

Please move quickly!" she ordered the throng of residents; she wanted them to hurry, but she didn't want to start a stampede. "Get inside as soon as you can!"

Nearby, two women tried to break into a run but were too weak to do so. They leaned on one another for support as they stumbled on doggedly.

"As quick as you can!" Grace called. She turned toward the field again, raking it with her eyes. Spotting Hazen in the distance, she began running in his direction as fast as she could. Once he noticed her coming, he turned and smiled. She waved her arms. "Get everyone inside!"

Hazen just tilted his head and looked at her. He couldn't hear what she was saying. He began jogging back in her direction.

"Hazen, the generals!" she shouted again. But her warning was silenced by a vicious cracking noise that tore the rest of it from her mouth.

The generals were here.

Hazen's face bore a look of surprise before crumpling in pain. He brought his hands to his chest before falling to his knees. Grace could hear the cries of fear as the New Empire evacuees rushed past, bumping and jostling against her in their desperate attempt to flee. There were more gunshots. Thirty feet away from her, Hazen toppled forward completely until he was on the ground and out of sight.

"Hazen!" A bullet whizzed past Grace's face. By now, she could hear her father's rifle on the roof. On her hands and knees, she crawled forward as the bullets screamed through the air around her. She could see Hazen ahead; he was unconscious. A general was standing over him, resting a foot on his leg. He cocked his gun and aimed downward.

Hate and loathing filled her senses. The world heaved and narrowed until all Grace could see was the general and his sneer. That sneer.

How desperately she wanted to wipe it from his face.

With a wild scream, Grace lunged at him, leaping on the general's back and grabbing him by the throat. Next, she squeezed with all her might, throttling him where he stood. The general's face grew red; his eyes bulged; veins stood out around his neck like extension cords under his skin. He crashed around the ruined field trying to pull her off him. When he finally dislodged her, he hurled her to the ground in a cursing, bloody-eyed fury. Still gulping for air, he raised the gun again.

Grace closed her eyes.

Bang!

She opened them again. The general was gone.

Or rather most of him was gone, having fallen dead into the corn. A rogue ear lay wetly at her feet. Grace kicked it away from her as armed New Empire residents began spilling out from the school. The boards covering the large classroom windows had been pulled away and filled with snipers, who were firing at the generals below. It was Zeff's handiwork, and it had saved her life.

Grace rolled onto her belly and crawled the rest of the way to Hazen's body. She knelt beside him, holding his hands in her own. His eyes were closed, his head thrown back. She could tell he was still breathing, but it was labored. He had been shot from behind, and the bullet had exited through his chest, leaving a serious wound in its place. She looked closer; they would have to cauterize it once they got to safety. Taking her jacket off, she pressed it against his brutalized flesh and started to cry.

"Hazen?" she whispered. "Hazen? Can you hear me?"

"I hear you," he said, slowly opening his eyes. He blinked at her twice and smiled weakly. "Hello, you beautiful angel."

Grace laughed through her tears. A slight measure of relief coursed through her body. "Even a bullet can't stop your charm," she said.

"A bullet can't stop the truth." Hazen's whisper was growing softer.

"Stop talking—not that I mind what you're saying." She pressed the wound harder. "We need to get back to the school."

"I'm dying, Grace."

"I told you to stop talking," she said. Her hair stirred slightly as an axe whizzed past her face. She gave Hazen a consoling smile and wiped at the trickle of blood that was flowing from his mouth. "You're going to make it, babe."

This time he closed his eyes and offered no reply.

THE FIRE BURNS OUT

Grace was still at Hazen's side when a low rumbling sound welled up from the ground, and the field began trembling around them. With a terrible sense of dread, she turned her gaze and confirmed the worst: the catapult had finally arrived.

A team of generals shoved the weapon into range. Now that she was closer to it, Grace could truly appreciate its massive size. It was enormous—even bigger than the catapult they'd had at Elwood's. And in a similar fashion, it had also been outfitted with wheels. But two of the wheels on this particular catapult seemed to jam every now and again, bringing the onerous contraption to a sudden and immediate halt and throwing the team of generals off kilter. Despite this, the men were moving the weapon steadily along, their bodies straining with effort as they struggled to get closer to the school.

"The catapult! Shoot the catapult!" someone cried. There was a rapid succession of gunshots as the snipers in the windows peppered the mighty behemoth that was laboring its way across the field. The team of generals dove for cover, but many were killed in the first hail of gunfire. Others went skittering back to the forest, and Grace didn't expect they would be back.

Hazen made a choking noise, and she looked at him anxiously; he seemed so cold in her arms. She felt again for a pulse, her fingers fumbling at his wrists. Her hands were shaking and it was hard to get a firm grip. Gritting her teeth, she pressed two fingers against his inner wrist and waited. And waited.

But there was nothing. No reassuring knock of life. No fluttering heartbeat under her fingers; only his cooling flesh and his familiar face that she couldn't bear to look at.

In a daze, Grace raised her anguished eyes back to the catapult. It was dangerously close to the school now, bucket at the ready. In the distance, she could see a fleet-footed general racing toward it in swerving, unpredictable patterns. He carried a lidded pot in his hands; his face was intensely focused. The snipers at the school were firing at him, but he was a difficult target to hit. Grace could smell grease and burned hay as he drew closer.

A bullet buzzed the general's shoulder, and he cried out but continued running, tucking his wounded arm for support as he charged toward the massive weapon. With a flying leap, he hurled himself toward it, opening the lid of the pot. He was still in the air when the snipers cut his body down, and he fell to the ground, twitching and shuddering. But the substance from the pot had landed in the bucket—for the most part. Patches of thatch still stuck out around the edges, and gobs of grease coated the sides.

Next, Grace watched the second phase of the plan materialize as four generals in body armor surrounded a fifth with a torch, and they rushed down the field, bunched tightly together. The snipers fired at the huddle, bringing down the two men at the front. In one seamless motion, the generals at the rear took up their position, protecting the torchbearer until they too fell, and the man was left running alone.

Grace fumbled for Hazen's boot. Moving his pant leg upward, her hands found the knife he kept sheathed there. Keeping her eye on the runner, she pulled the knife free, balancing it on the flat of her palm to feel its weight. The general had almost reached the catapult by the time she got to her feet and threw the knife.

The small dagger went sailing through the air, and looked at first as if it was going to miss the torchbearer entirely. But in the final moments of flight, the blade seemed to swing around and catch the man's torso, burying itself up to the hilt. With a surprised grunt, the general bent over at the waist but continued to stagger forward, still holding the torch out in front of him. There was more gunfire, but it came too late. He slumped forward, dumping the torch into the bucket. The grease caught fire with an unearthly roar.

At the base of the catapult, the torchbearer twitched, rolled onto his stomach, and pulled a knife from his jacket. Somehow, he was still alive. Grace turned toward the school; she could see the snipers were still in position. "Get away from the windows!" she screamed. "Everybody get down!" She threw herself back on the field, sheltering Hazen's body with her own.

The general slashed at the catapult's restraining rope, and the bucket swung high into the air, hurling the grease fire in the direction of the school. There were screams as the New Empire residents disappeared from the windows, diving for cover. With a low roar, the flaming liquid hit the building, grasping at the brick walls like a living creature, bubbling and dripping in a frenzied rage. Some of the greased thatch fell onto the grass below where it smoked menacingly, but the ground was too damp to permit a grass fire.

The sun was beginning to rise in the east, a thin sliver of red on the horizon. There was no more gunfire now. Instead, Grace heard only the sounds of the wounded: terrible moans, screams of pain, and hoarse, begging voices. She carefully laid Hazen on the ground and stood up to scan the field, wondering if she should try dragging him back to the school.

At her back, a blade swung through the air, pink with the butchered dawn. Grace felt it part the fog behind her and turned, just in time to see it cut down a general who had been about to attack her. With a ragged yelp, the man dropped his weapon; the bloodstained hammer fell heavily to the ground. He followed suit. Grace stepped over his body and squinted against the sun, looking into Simone's grit-lined and weary face.

"You're alive!" she cried, throwing her arms around Simone, her own body sagging with relief. "Thank God you're here."

Simone hugged her back, revived by the sight of a friendly face. "It's good to see you," she said in a hurried tone. "The others came with me." She gestured over her shoulder, and Grace could see a small, ragtag army of ex-brothel women picking their way furtively across the field toward the school. Among them, Grace could see Lewis's safari hat bobbing along and would have smiled, if she felt better. He was a fair distance away but she could still see he was filthy, although he was walking along cheerfully enough. She recognized Libby and Raven beside him, listening to his chatter as they dragged a semiconscious Cody between them.

"Get inside!" Simone called over to them. "Help wherever you can!"

Grace waved over at the small group and then wrinkled her nose once they got downwind. "What's that smell?" she asked.

"Lewis," Simone replied. "On my way here, I found him climbing out of a shithole. Literally—the man was in a hole filled with shit." She raised the brim of her hat and wiped at her forehead before lowering it again. "Still pretty proud of himself, though."

The inventor turned and waved at them. Grace could see his clothes were ripped and tattered and coated in sludge. People were giving him a wide berth as they passed, but he didn't seem to notice. He gave the women a thumbs up before turning back again and disappearing into the school.

"Listen." Simone grabbed Grace's shoulder. "There are more generals on the way—coming in from the south. We need to get inside."

"Wait." Grace's voice caught in her throat, and Simone looked at her with concern. "Hazen's dead."

FINAL WORDS

In the fog-choked and smoky field, Simone dropped to her knees by Hazen's body, feeling for a pulse. There was a long silence as Grace held her breath, before leaning over and kissing the tradesman on the cheek.

Simone suddenly gasped and grabbed her arm. "I felt something!" she cried. "He's still in there! Hazen's alive!"

Grace sobbed and pressed her forehead to his. "We need to bind the wound before we can move him," she said. "Otherwise he'll die for sure."

Simone rocked back on her heels as she considered this. Then inspiration struck her—or rather poked her in the ribs. "I've got an idea," she said, taking her jacket off and exposing the corset, panties, and ripped fishnets underneath. "Don't," she said to Grace's raised eyebrow, but when she took the corset off too and crouched bare breasted on the field of battle, the second blond eyebrow came up as well. "Here, help me with him," Simone said, lifting Hazen's torso and shoving the corset underneath. Grace supported his neck and head as they lowered him back to the ground. Together, they pulled the garment around him and fastened it to bind the wound. It was a tight squeeze, but it fit if they used the last set of hooks and loosened the ropes that wound their way silkily through the lace at the front. To be on the safe side, they pulled Hazen's pants off and wrapped those around his chest as well, tying the legs together to secure the binding.

There was more gunfire, great thunderous claps that echoed across the field. Another wave of generals had arrived.

Simone pulled her jacket back on and buttoned up the top three buttons. "Shall we?" she asked, grabbing Hazen's arms.

"Let's do it," Grace replied, seizing his legs.

They carried him carefully toward the school, moving in a hunched, zigzag manner under a hail of bullets. Twice, they were forced to hit the ground when the fighting got too hot, and each time, Grace covered Hazen's body with her own, cradling his head like a child.

"That's real nice," Simone called over to her. "Hazen's a lucky man!"

"I'd do the same thing for you—if you were ever dumb enough to get hurt," Grace replied. She tried to smile but couldn't.

Forty feet from the safety of the school, the women tried crawling the rest of the way, dragging Hazen between them. But his body was too heavy and too injured to be taken very far in this manner. They would have to try something else.

Ahead, the door to the school flew open, and a small group of residents amassed themselves outside before shutting it again.

"Hey—it's Claire and Lloyd," Grace said, peering through the fog. "What are they doing?"

Simone realized the small group was staring in their direction. While she recognized the Lawsons, she didn't recognize the other people they were with. Nonetheless, it was clear they were involved in a coordinated effort of some kind, and she watched them hopefully as they wrapped a blanket over two hockey sticks and began creeping onto the battlefield.

"They're coming to rescue us," she said. "They've made a stretcher."

This time, Grace actually did smile. "Thank God." She checked Hazen's wound. "We've got to get him inside right away."

"They'll be here soon," Simone assured her. "Let's get him ready to move." When she looked up again, their rescue party had almost reached them; she could see Claire's long red hair flying out behind her and the look on Lloyd's face—the look of horror on Lloyd's face.

He was staring at something behind them.

Both Grace and Simone turned to see what that something was and were shocked to see a general close behind them, wearing goggles and favoring them both with a dark scowl. On his narrow, humped back was a large fuel-bearing canister. The snout of a nozzle and hose protruded out of his clenched hands. It was Lewis's flamethrower, brought to life.

The women couldn't see the general's eyes behind his dark goggles, but he drew his lips up in a vicious snarl. His whole body trembled like a dog on point as he watched them, his thumb lightly caressing the trigger on the nozzle.

Simone turned toward their would-be rescuers. "Get back!" she cried. They staggered back, still holding the stretcher between them.

The general lowered the nozzle so it was aiming directly at them. With an eager look, he pulled the trigger.

"Wait!" a rasping voice called. "Didn't you hear about Hooper? He—"

The rest of the sentence was drowned out by the sizzling hiss of the flamethrower. Grace threw herself over Hazen's body and tucked her head as she felt an intense heat radiating against her arms, but it didn't hurt.

Why didn't it hurt?

She heard screams and lifted her head. A human fireball was racing across the field, howling in agony. The wet morning air smelled like burned meat and propane. "Simone?" she cried.

"Right here," Simone answered, still huddled beside her on the ground. She pointed to the whirling figure in flames. "That's the general."

"But...how?" Grace asked, astonished.

"Leaky hose, I guess," Simone replied. "He went up in flames the second he pulled the trigger."

There was an explosion as the fire met the rest of the accelerant in the general's canister. His screams finally stopped as his body was torn to pieces by the blast.

Nearby, a wounded general who was lying on his back grumbled to himself and shook his head. "Same thing happened to Hooper when he tried using it, you know," he rasped. "The emperor said it was off limits."

"Shut the fuck up!" Grace yelled at him.

By now the gunfire on the field had slowed to the occasional winging bullet, and the would-be rescue party had already disappeared back into the school. Grace and Simone looked at each other, and not a word was said. Simultaneously, they got to their feet and grabbed Hazen before hurrying on.

The entrance to the school was approaching; they had almost made it. Above their heads, the whorled sunrise was as magnificent as a victory banner, and they could hear the sounds of cheering and clapping echoing inside. There were still a few residents standing at the windows, looking filthy, roughed up, and painfully thin. They were smiling vague, hopeful smiles, looking out over the quiet battlefield as if they couldn't believe their luck. A woman with matted gray hair put her head in her hands and began to cry.

Reaching the entrance, Simone banged on the door with her foot until someone came to open it for them. "We need a stretcher here!" she shouted.

"Simone?" Zeff said, hearing her voice in the hall. With a tentative smile, he separated himself from the celebrating crowd and moved toward the doorway. He was suddenly sick with the need to see her. "Simone—is that you?"

"Zeff?" he heard her reply.

He pushed his way through the busy corridor. Then he heard Grace's voice: "Hazen's hurt! We need help!"

"We need a stretcher over here!" Zeff yelled gruffly. He made it over to them and helped lay Hazen on the ground. He could smell blood in the air; tension was radiating from Simone's body. He understood in an instant that the tradesman's situation was critical.

"How's the emperor?" he asked.

"Dead," Simone replied. "Carmen too." She watched Zeff as he felt for Hazen's pulse and suddenly noticed how handsome he was. And so calm. It provided her with a small measure of relief after a long night of fight and flight.

On the floor, Hazen emitted a low groan and began coughing up blood.

"Where's that stretcher?" Zeff yelled.

"What's taking so long?" Grace asked, her voice shrill. "Where are the Lawsons?"

"The Lawsons are tending to the wounded in the gym." Zeff said, placing a hand on her shoulder. "Hazen will pull through, Grace. Just wait and see." To his complete astonishment, Grace pressed her head against his chest and burst into tears. "There, there," he said, patting her head gingerly. He was openly relieved when the stretcher arrived and Hazen was loaded onto it.

"I'll go with him," Grace said in a tremulous voice. "Make sure he gets there all right."

"Good idea," Zeff replied. "He'd like that."

Grace turned to Simone and threw her arms around her, kissing her on the cheek. "I'm so glad I found you," she said, before rushing off after the stretcher.

"Actually, I found you," Simone called after her, with a little laugh.

Then Zeff and Simone were alone—alone in the surging crowd. They fell silent, although both had so much to say.

Goddamn it, Zeff loved her so much at that moment. The feeling was so strong, it vibrated in his body, his bones, in his teeth. He loved Simone. He'd only ever loved Simone, and that was all there was to it. He was beyond caring if she would ever feel the same way for him. She could take his love and have it all; he'd always have more to give her.

"I thought you might die," he said.

Simone was so close to him, so still, frozen by the sight of his face and the emotion she read there. Deep inside her chest, her numb and hidden heart was waking.

Zeff's hand moved under her chin, tipping her face toward his. She parted her lips as their bodies moved toward one another. The moment seemed so inevitable; so natural. Then Libby was there, pushing her way between them, forcing them apart again.

"We're out of water," she gasped, breathless from running. "The wounded are thirsty. And Cody's not doing well."

"Damn it," Zeff cursed. "We're going to have get some water from the river and boil it. Any more war parties on the way?"

"Looks clear from the roof," Libby reported. "Most people around here are already celebrating."

Zeff grabbed Simone's hands. "I'll get the water, if you get a fire going," he said, fighting off his frustration. "It's not far by horse." Then he kissed her palm, something he had never done before. "I'll find you when I get back. We need to talk."

Simone nodded, shoving her disappointment into the back of her throat, where it lingered like a ghost. She couldn't let go of his hands.

"You heard him. He'll find you when he gets back," Libby said, pushing Zeff toward the door. "The water jugs are outside."

Zeff cast a final, strained look in Simone's direction. "Bye now," he said, tipping his hat to her. His broad shoulders dipped through the doorway, and he disappeared outside.

"I'm sorry, but we really need water," Libby said to Simone. Her apology was so serious that Simone wanted to burst into laughter. Or was it tears? Both? One thing was certain: she needed some sleep. The night had been long, and she had a lot to process. But first, she needed to build a fire.

She drifted down the hall in a trance as the citizens of the New Empire rushed around her in dizzying bouts of excitement and frivolity. The chatter was deafening, the air felt muggy, and the smell of dirty, sweaty bodies overpowered her senses, and yet her mind was full of Zeff and Zeff alone.

"Mom? Mom!" A gangly teenage boy cried down the stifling corridor. Three women turned their heads, but only one burst into tears. The boy ran to her, and she gripped him like a bear.

Shuffling past, Simone wondered what would happen when Zeff got back from the river. What would they say to one another? She glowed with nervous excitement; it was an unfamiliar pleasure, and it felt exquisitely novel to her now. She decided she would bask in the feeling like warm ocean water; she'd finished fighting it.

Then, amid the cries and laughter, amid the rugged hygiene and embracing bodies, there came a sound that stopped her heart.

It was a gunshot.

Simone heard it above the din in the hallway and was filled with an overwhelming dread. She rushed to the door and caught sight of a horse, galloping riderless in the other direction. Zeff was nowhere to be seen.

Pushing her way outside, Simone saw his body lying face down on the field. Filled with a black despair, she looked frantically for the shooter. She noticed a wounded general on the ground nearby, choking and gurgling with laughter. A semiautomatic flashed in his hands as he rolled onto his stomach and began crawling away.

She grabbed a blood-smeared bat from the ground and went after him. With one hard swing, she smashed the gun out of his hands. Another swing, and she crushed his skull. Hastening to Zeff's side, she turned him over, wondering what she might find on the other side.

A gasp tore from her lips. There was so much blood.

She pressed her hands against his wound, though she knew it was too late for that. His eyes fluttered open, and she met his misty-gray gaze. It was quiet. Gentle.

"You're crying," he said.

"No, I'm not," she said, wiping her tears away.

"Yes, you are. Even I can see that, and I'm practically blind. Don't know if you knew that."

"I knew that," she replied. "I know everything when it comes to you."

Zeff looked surprised; he smiled slowly. "I wish I could see your face right now."

Simone took his hand and laid it across her cheek. "Stay with me, Zeff," she pleaded with him. "I need you."

"No, you don't, Mona. That's what I love about you," he answered. "That's what I've always loved about you. You're an independent woman. You can make it on your own."

"I can't," she cried.

"You can," he said. "You've been doing it for years now. I've just been along for the ride."

"I love you, Zeff," she said.

He gave her a dazzling smile before the hand on her cheek fell away. With a ragged sigh, Zeff slipped from one mystery to the next, leaving her alone on the battlefield.

Simone sat by his side for hours, looking into the face that used to be his, until Grace came along and brought her inside.

EPILOGUE

S imone approached the town by horseback. In the early morning light, it looked as lonesome as a cemetery, filled with run-
down houses instead of tombstones. A pale, waterlogged sun was
rising, casting shadows on the empty streets below. Soon the place
would be alive with the drone of human industry. Even now, there
were signs of the residents beginning to wake: a candle winked in
an open window, a rooster crowed "good morning," and the fresh,
wet air was sweetened with the scent of flowers and wood smoke
and chamber pots. They were living a raw, uncut version of humanity, but they were making it somehow.

The hills, the trees, the waving lawns of potato plants grew
thick together and shone like animal pelts in the sun, green and
tropical from all the rain they'd been having that summer. It had
been a year since Zeff had died—a year, in fact, to the very hour,
minute, and second, which winged past Simone without her even
realizing it. But she thought of him anyway, as she always did on
morning patrol. Dawn was the time she felt closest to him, when
the morning quiet was as refreshing as his long silences and as
pleasant as his shadow on the trail.

She passed Rose Briar Lane and Magnolia Avenue and then
went down to the river. She watched a family of geese break the
glassy surface of the water, sending ripples across the mirrored

morning sky. Dismounting, Simone led her horse to the river to drink, tenderly patting Alfred's flank as he slurped up water. Good old Alfred. Her faithful horse had showed up in town a few days after the Empire had fallen. The reunion, although a happy one, had been another painful reminder of Zeff, and she'd cried.

Saddled up again, Simone crossed the limestone traffic bridge and turned down River Avenue where the brothel still stood. The structure was too valuable to pull down, despite Cody and Libby's repeated requests that they do so. But people were getting used to it—now that Hazen and Grace had remodeled the space. Hazen had pulled through his injury to return to his mercantile roots, developing a market exchange on one side of the strip mall. On the other side, Grace ran a small hospital with her father, and she had blossomed under his tutelage. They'd repainted the building with cans of paint they found in Horus's private stash: pinks, yellows, and a few saucy purples. In Simone's opinion, the place looked like a damn Easter egg, but business was thriving, and Grace and Hazen were happy—with their business and with each other.

Simone admired what they had. That didn't mean she wanted it for herself.

She turned down Lilac Lane, easing Alfred into a leisurely amble, and rode beneath the great elms until she reached a familiar gray bungalow. The porch looked freshly swept, and the kitchen garden was well tended. The only item that seemed to be out of place was the soiled safari hat sitting on the rocking chair in the corner. Simone was about to continue on her way when the front door of the bungalow swung open with a jolly bang.

"Goodness! Simone? Is that you, my sweet?" Barbara called from the doorway. "We haven't seen you for days, darling! Won't you come in and have some fresh blueberry bannock?"

Simone's stomach grumbled at the proposition, but she knew the word "we" meant Barbara, Lewis, and Monty, and she wasn't interested in putting up with Monty's surliness this morning. She had once hoped the move from Elwood's Compound to New Sonoma Heights would have alleviated some of the self-entitlement that had made him so unbearable. Then Elwood had died on the way, and after Barbara reached the New Empire, she and Lewis got married. Somehow, this made Monty even more obnoxious.

"Sorry, Barbara, but I'm on patrol!" Simone called back. "I'll see you and Lewis at the town council tonight?"

"You certainly will!" Barbara replied. "I'm presenting the harvest report today! Good-bye, darling, and try not to be alone so much. I know you're the chief of police now, but it's an unhealthy habit, sweetheart."

Simone gave a vague wave to her old friend and turned to go. The sun was getting higher in the sky, and she had somewhere she needed to be.

She galloped Alfred down the road, toward the outskirts of town. They passed wet cornfields and sodden meadowland, speckled with drowsy sheep that huddled together for warmth against the dampness of the morning. She waved to the shepherd boy who was rubbing his hands by his fire. A little further on, the morning mist parted, and an overgrown willow came into view. Beside it stood a modest wooden cross.

Simone dismounted and let Alfred graze. Her heavy boots squeaked as she walked across the field, following the path her daily routine had stamped into the grass. Reaching the grave marker, she sat down before it, cross-legged in the morning dew. She took a deep breath in; this was the most important part of her day, and she'd learned to savor it.

Zeff Davis.

She read the name out loud as if she were calling him, calling him back to the warmth and the light of the earth that he'd loved so well.

But there was no coming back; that is the heavy price of existence. Like a shooting star, our lives glimmer only for an instant before everything goes black.

But to live! Oh, God, to *live!*

When Simone returned to the road, she was smiling.

THE END

ABOUT THE AUTHOR

Catherine Williams earned a BA in psychology from Queen's University and a master's degree in criminological research from the University of Cambridge. She currently lives in Edmonton, Alberta, with her husband and dog. This is her first novel.

www.ingramcontent.com/pod-product-compliance
Lightning Source LLC
Chambersburg PA
CBHW020519260626
47156CB00006B/2057